THE
WRONG
DAUGHTER

SARAH CLAYTON

THE WRONG DAUGHTER

SARAH CLAYTON

For Paul R Bear, my superhero, my ocean, my world.

PART ONE

Chapter 1

Eve

Perth, Scotland
12th September 2019

I am Eve Park; that may be a lie.

In the distance a muddy, purple sky hangs over Perth and the river Tay. Here, on the outskirts of the city, the sky is slick and black. The half-moon and a solitary star outline the surrounding forest that closets Tippermuir House. No one can see us. When we're silent we hear life, tiny feet scraping the forest floor, broken branches and breathing bark, the wings of a kestrel or a buzzard quivering the trees. It's bitter, the air is arresting. I tell Graham I'm going in now and reach up to pull my bedroom window closed. I tell him that after everything that's happened, everything that's changed in my life, it is a truth that, in fact, nothing has changed. Nothing at all.

'I've ended up the same way as the wolves that devoured each other,' I tell Graham; he won't understand yet.

In the musical, *Madness & Ecstasy*, Diana sings a song called 'Abandoned Children' and stops Dionysius from murdering the babies; Dionysius doesn't murder the babies, he changes them into wolves and the clever wolves devour each other so that the babies can return to the forest; I am a wolf.

I tell him, 'I have to devour myself to save the baby.'

Graham leans closer and forgets to whisper, 'You're talking in riddles, Eve, there are no wolves here. The baby isn't in danger.' He's kneeling on the woodshed roof reaching his hand up to me. 'Here, take it. See for yourself.'

He tries to put his phone in my hand so I can see the pictures on it. I don't take it, don't look. I can't. I inspect the patch of bald on his scalp, the thin strands of greying hair, tiny specs of dandruff that sparkle in the light from his phone.

'All right, Eve,' he says in that soft way I like him to talk to me. 'I'm sure it will come tomorrow. Maybe tomorrow. Let's wait and see, eh? Let's wait and see.'

Maybe tomorrow. I don't hang around to watch him slip off the woodshed roof and walk the short path back to the lodge and wait for him to wave to me from his front door. I'm freezing, I've been freezing for forever, but it's really only been since the other night.

It's as if I have tucked myself in my own bed and opened a book, and that's when I start to cry. That book is all about me, the writing on each page smudged with blood and mucus. But it isn't a book, it is my life.

I get into bed and think about the other night. I can see it in front of me, as if it's not me I'm watching but someone else; someone I don't recognise. I'd gone running to the lodge and in the bed that Graham shares with Blythe, I'd given birth to a baby boy. He must be a clever little boy because he'd hidden himself deep inside of me until that exact moment, the moment when he wanted to surprise me and Graham together. So clever he is because that day he knew the right time to choose to come into the world, when I wouldn't be alone, the only night of the week I spend with Graham. And there he came with no fuss and no pain, and he presented himself ungraciously onto Blythe's flowery, cotton sheet and he gave a fierce warrior cry, and when Graham held him up, his little hand reached for Graham's hand and his slippery fingers gripped on tight. Then Graham held the tiny bundle of flesh out to me, and I thought of Mother and drew back and buried myself under Blythe's duvet. I am a wolf.

Mother. Right now Mother is asleep in her bed because I've taken to putting a couple of Tramadol in the hot chocolate I have to make for her after dinner. Graham gives me the Tramadol; he has it for the pain in his leg. It's so Graham can come to the woodshed nightly, he's worried about me since the baby came. He can't understand why I can't accept our little boy.

I'm a wolf. I am Eve Park; that may be a lie.

***

Maybe tomorrow has taken four monstrous weeks. But this morning, I was sat up on the roof watching the sun rise and it was like something inside me shifted. The air smelt lively, and leaves hovered in the sky before settling at the root of a tree, waiting to be reborn. I stood tall on the roof and stretched my arms above me. It was as if, in that minute, I could clasp the clouds, as if I was part of them, all knowing and all seeing.

Moments before, Graham had given me the signal. I'd been watching the lodge from my bedroom window, waiting. He'd stood at his own bedroom window and blown a kiss from his tight lips. That was it, but I knew Blythe was at home because her car was parked, so I had to wait.

The hours have stretched to infinity.

I imagined being the one waiting to be reborn and that thought slithered about ominously inside me, and so I instead imagined what a child waiting to be born wonders at and I couldn't conjure up a single thought. And then, after birth, what the child feels like to be abandoned and that thought had me wondering; who matters most, the mother or the child? I cried then because I really didn't know the answer, but I knew what had to happen. All Graham wants is for me to be a mother, but he is trying to understand that I am a wolf.

If I am not Eve Park, if that is a lie, I have to find out who I, the thirty-eight-year-old child, am before finding out who future I, the mother, could be. I have to know, one way or the other, before I devour myself.

But at last it's now, and all the nerves in my body are crackling. I throw open my window, listen carefully for sounds inside the house, it's safe. Mother won't wake up. I climb out onto the roof of the woodshed. If I could figure out where she hides the keys to the front door I wouldn't have to make such a gawky descent. But Mother is smarter than me.

The ladder was Graham's idea, and he'd propped it up against the woodshed the day after the baby came. I didn't know a baby would come, I didn't know. Graham said I should have known, should've sensed it but I didn't. I remember asking Mother why I didn't bleed anymore, she told me it was that the menopause had come early because I'm so fat. She didn't say it was a baby in there with all the fat.

'I will take good care of you,' Graham said when he brought the ladder. No one has ever said that to me before. He'd thought about getting me a mobile phone but changed his mind. He said it was for my own good, in case Mother was to find it. We both know she snoops in my room. But it wasn't because of that, it was because he was scared Blythe would see my messages on his phone. I know this because it seemed obvious to me that he could get another phone for himself, one Blythe would know nothing about, but he didn't want to do that. Snoopy Blythe. Snoopy Mother.

Sneaking out of the front gate, I tiptoe down the dirt path to the line of fir trees that separate our house from the lodge, where Graham and Blythe live together.

I crouch behind the trees, hold my breath. Be patient. Blythe's car is still in the drive.

It's just as well I put my coat on. The pine-scented night air is whipping up fiercely. A wind that bites and sucks at the leaves. I press my lips tight so my teeth don't hurt.

Come on, what are you doing in there, Blythe? She should have left already. She works nights at a care home in Bridge of Earn. Why isn't Graham pushing her out of the door?

There she is, all bristly and plump.

I duck out of sight so she doesn't see me. Bite my tongue. Cover my ears with my hands. If I don't hear her then she can't hear my panting.

The slam of the car door echoes through the trees, the tread of tyres on gravel. I sneak a peek through the branches and spy the brake lights all the way until they disappear around the bend. Finally.

Skipping down the drive, I ring the bell and wait for Graham to let me in.

'It came in this morning's post,' he says, ushering me in.

We've been waiting for it, Graham and me, as if it were a gift from a mythical god. I imagine it is Osiris's falcon. It waits on the periphery of my life, with wings of violent green, and it hovers above us, and I know, I know, such a thing exists and that this is what is supposed to be happening.

'Come on.' Graham ushers me in. 'We can open it together.'

I head to the kitchen but, as usual, he steers me past and up the stairs to his and Blythe's bedroom. I sit on the bottom of the massive king-size bed where I'd given birth only weeks before and grip the fresh, scented duvet, while Graham begins to undress.

'No.' I get up and rest my hand on his shoulder. I haven't seen our baby since his tiny body slipped from inside me into Graham's waiting arms. Graham has hidden him away from what will amount to Blythe's wrath and Mother's revulsion. The infant is safe and looked after by Graham's sister Lynn who lives not so far away. Graham visits mostly every night when Blythe leaves for work, he draws the little body to rest against his heart, Graham has told me so. He's told me that soon, I will hold our child in my arms, that when we run away to Lynn's converted barn in the outskirts of La Rochelle, I will begin to love my son. 'No,' I repeat, and squeeze Graham's shoulder. 'Show me.'

The best thing to do is to face bad news head-on. When you've been forced into doing that you realise it really is the only way. Nothing can be solved by turning a blind eye. That's the expression Mother used when I confronted her about my birth certificate. 'Turn a blind eye, Eve. There are things in this world you're better off not knowing.' Mother likes her secrets, I've discovered.

'Take it,' Graham says, handing me the envelope.

I flap at the letter with my hands and it falls on the pale pink carpet, at Graham's feet.

'Bloody hell, Evie, is this just a game for you?' He pulls his jumper back over his head and stands in front of me with hands on his skinny hips.

'Don't be like that, Graham.' I pull him down beside me on the bed. 'You know I'm grateful for everything you're doing for me. For us.'

He always does this; acts as if he's permanently wounded. He is, of course, with his leg and back problems, but I don't mean physically wounded. He can get around fine, mostly. What I mean is he's sensitive, sometimes petulant. It's not just about the sex. Of course, that's how all this started. At the start, I'd been happy to give him my virginity, and even now, a year later, I don't expect to get anything in return. I don't want anything. That's not true, I do want something but Graham can't give me that. Or he could help me get it, but he only cares about France now, and he's only helping me so I go with him. He doesn't believe me when I tell him I'm not going.

He bends, picks up the envelope.

The thick, cream letter rests in my palms, as if I'm holding it for someone else. This letter is a part of me. It's all about me, so why don't I know? I should know.

Graham's waiting for me to open it. I hold the letter out to him. 'What do you think it will say?'

'Read it.'

'I can't.'

He takes the letter and throws it onto Blythe's dressing table, knocking over her little bottles of posh perfume. 'Come here.'

Graham wraps me in his arms and kisses the top of my head. 'I know a lot has happened,' he says, 'and we didn't bargain for this. But you have to keep hold of the bigger picture.'

Graham always talks about the bigger picture. I've gone along with everything because he's more experienced than I am. He knows how to do things.

At first, I didn't like the feeling of his lips on my lips. I didn't like the rough skin on the palms of his hands. I didn't like the way he bit my nose, my nipples, the way his tongue felt. But I wanted to experience something. And I wanted to experience it, whatever it might have been, more than I didn't like any of that.

'Do you feel better?' he asks me afterwards.

Numb, less than alive. In limbo. Graham wouldn't understand if I said any of this to him. He would remind me to look at the bigger picture. I get out of bed and pick up the envelope then I climb back beside him. The envelope is torn. Graham didn't wait for us to read it together. I pull out the letter.

'I'm sorry,' he says.

'It's not a mistake?' I ask.

'You know it's not, Evie. Remember we watched that video on YouTube.'

He pushes the hair back from my face. 'We'll find another way.'

I lie down and curl myself around the duvet. I am a wolf and I am alone. All Graham cares about is getting me a passport so I can go with him and the baby to live in France in his sister's old barn. Like a proper family, he says. How can we be a proper family if me being Eve Park is a lie?

'Eve?'

'I know. I'll go in a minute.'

'It's not that. What are you thinking?'

What's there to think? Graham has everything planned out. He even applied for my passport for me. But Eve Park can't get a passport, because Eve Park doesn't exist.

Chapter 2

DS Calmly

Dunkeld
Friday, 11th October 2019

I sign the book thrust at me by the policeman assigned to the tape at the scene. Ducking under the tape, I stand where I can get a decent view of the victim in situ.

'Morning, DS Lark Calmly. Or is it evening? Hard to tell.' Jack Bell shouts across to me from the other side of the blue-and-white tape. The sky is still black. It's nearly 4 a.m.

Jack's a good bloke, efficient, unsociable, often brusque, which is what you need to head up a SOCO unit. He always, always calls me by my full name. Years ago, I used to take umbrage, believing he was taking the mick. I once pulled him up for it and felt guilty when he explained he did it because he loved the way my name rolled off his tongue. Nowadays, I couldn't care less. If he stopped doing it, who knows? That might upset me more. I wave, and he disappears into an unmarked, police issue Transit parked in the middle of the road.

Detectives are concerned with whether a crime has transpired. They approach each unknown death scene with the idea that a crime has occurred, and they work backwards from that premise. Once they have established that a crime has not taken place, their mission has been fulfilled. In this case, there can be no doubt that a crime has taken place. Leaving the scene of a road accident is a crime. Leaving the scene of a fatal accident, in my book, is more than a crime, it's a barefaced tragedy. If indeed this was an accident. The copper first on the scene had no doubt, and he may turn out to be right but, and it may just be that I'm a pessimistic arse so I'm told, I like to keep an open mind. Especially in cases like this; cases of unfair advantage, where the odds were always going to be lower for the victim. Is this an accident or will it end up culpable homicide? That's the thing I aim to find out.

What I always do, when I attend a crime scene, is try to visualise how the event played out in those few minutes before the victim died. The victim is lying on the A923 Atholl Street in the small village of Dunkeld. His body is twisted half on and half off the road, his head and torso on the narrow pavement, the rest of him on the road. Did he just step off the pavement and get hit or had he seen the car and hadn't quite managed to get across the road before he got skelped? Or was this a deliberate hit? I'd say he's in the late sixty, early seventies age range. I bend closer to his head, and there's a distinct smell of alcohol. And fish, oddly enough.

'Can you smell that?' I ask one of the SOCOs attending to the body.

'Yep. A mangled trout, wrapped in foil, was taken in for evidence. It had been lying in the middle of the road, half eaten; most likely by a rat or a fox.'

'A fisherman?' I ask.

'Would you go fishing in that suit?'

I take her point. The victim is wearing a plain, russet tweed suit, frayed at the cuffs and hems, and it's difficult to tell from where I'm standing, but it looks at least one size too big for him. He has on a pale brown shirt, faintly checked, and an olive green tweed tie, tight around his collar. He hasn't yet been identified. With the smell of alcohol on him, it's my guess he was on his way home from the pub.

I leave the body and the SOCOs to get on with their job and go to stand outside the pub on the other side of the road, and then I take the walk back. Seven steps, not more than nine, depending on how steady the victim was on his feet. I'd guess he was heading home, in a northerly direction. At the seventh step, let's say, the victim was interrupted. In my head, I see him struck by a vehicle hurtling towards him, its headlights casting shadows across the road, front wheels mounting the pavement. For a flicker of a second, the victim imagines throwing himself out of the way, but the vehicle's bumper has other ideas and licks his left side, at the knee, before its wheels tread his torso. His head crashes to the ground. His blood stains the road. For a second or so, the victim notices his own body, perhaps feels no pain, so he mentally checks all his major muscles, tender joints and he's noticing these things while being aware that somewhere outside of himself there's a noise he can't quite grasp the like of. The rumble of the engine, as the merciless driver slams his foot down, the sound of tyres kicking back their tread and screeching off into the distance, dying away just as the victim takes his last breath.

'What you thinking?'

I turn swiftly at the voice that has sneaked up beside me. 'You're late, WPC Dunbar.'

'Sorry, sir,' she says, looking more shameful than I'd like.

'Kid trouble?' I raise my eyebrow deliberately to show her my understanding side. Instantly her shoulders relax. That's better.

'Aye. I'm thinking of putting the little shite into a home,' she says, her mouth twisty and angry. But her eyes are smiling, and I get the feeling she has everything at home under control.

'Take a good look,' I tell her. 'Tell me what you make of it.'

She does as requested. I give her a few minutes then bid her to follow me. We go back to stand outside the closed doors of the pub, the Old Bear Inn. It's about halfway down the main street on the left-hand side of the road heading towards Blairgowrie.

We stand shoulder to shoulder, her head with its wild, fiery red hair, a few inches higher than my own. 'Well?'

'I hate hit-and-runs,' she tells me.

Who doesn't hate this sort of thing? That's not what I asked her. I hold my patience, give her a chance. She's not without intelligence. I let her waste time attempting unsuccessfully to tuck her wanton hair under her police issue cap.

'I'd say he's from around here and he lives alone,' she says, eventually. 'Because, for one, there's a main street and nothing much else and, if he had a wife, why isn't she out here searching for him?'

I'm sure there are plenty of wives that wouldn't but I keep my mouth shut about that and say instead, 'That's if you're right and he lives around here.'

'Unless he's a drink driver, I'd say he spent the night in the pub here and was on his way home. He's a local. Once the village wakes up, we'll get a better sense of who he is and where he lives; someone around here will know him. There are no onlookers, nobody about we can stop and question. Nobody saw this, unless of course, someone saw it from a window or, unlikely as it sounds, someone has CCTV. What about the pub landlord? What did he see? Who called it in?'

That last question would've been my first but, no matter, we as humans are all different and assess things from unique angles. That's why it's good to have a partner to bounce ideas off. And since I happen to be partnerless at the moment, Dunbar may as well get some experience she can tuck under her bulging police constable's belt. And besides, I like her. We've worked a couple of cases together; she's almost too good to be a floater. I doubt it will be long before she gets her promotion, and it won't do any harm to nudge her in the right direction. The major investigation team need people like Paula; she's gutsy, not afraid to make mistakes and she's never minded putting up with my 'decrepit bullshit' as she calls it.

'A bloke called Fisherman Bob called it in. A slippery fish by all accounts. Uniform haven't been able to track him down so far.'

Paula groans. She's not a fan of my puns. 'Gone fishing?' she says, grinning.

'You're not funny.'

'Aye, it's early yet,' she says.

I turn and bang on the pub door. 'We'll have a word with the landlord. He may be able to enlighten us somewhat.'

'Aye, sir,' she says, fussing about with her buttons and straightening her uniform. 'By the way, one of the SOCOs is trying to get your attention.'

I turn and see the same SOCO I'd been speaking to earlier waving me over. 'Wait here. Don't go in there without me.'

'What is it?' I ask the lass. The smug look on her face gives me hope. Evidence equals progress, at least until I discover how useful or not it is. 'You've found something?'

'Too right,' she says. She hands me an evidence bag. Inside is a piece of crumpled paper.

'It's just a betting slip,' I say, not bothering to hide my restlessness.

'Look closer, on the bottom of the slip.'

Whatever's on it is difficult to decipher, so I step closer to the paladin light. Written on the bottom in red pen are the words, Tippermuir House.

'Any idea?' I ask.

She shrugs her shoulders and observes me expectantly.

I've never come across Tippermuir House; haven't a clue where it might be. Could be nothing to do with what's happened here but worth investigating, even if to just rule it out as evidence pertaining.

'Where was it?' I ask the SOCO, who's needlessly holding her breath, awaiting my reaction.

She gazes at me with wide eyes full of the vitality of youth. 'It was folded into the top pocket of his shirt, sir.'

I take a picture of the betting slip with my phone and hand her back the evidence bag.

'Nothing else?'

'Not so far,' she says.

'Excellent, well done you,' I say. I'm never all that sure what to say when I mean to praise someone younger than myself, without it sounding patronising. By the look of her scowl, I suspect I failed miserably. I head back across to where Dunbar is waiting for me. The pub door is half open, no sign of the landlord.

'He's inside,' Paula tells me.

I flash the picture of the betting slip on my phone and ask her if Tippermuir House rings a bell. She shakes her head and writes it in her notebook.

'I'll check it out,' she says.

Exactly my thinking.

Chapter 3

Eve

Perth, Scotland
10th October 2019

'Why bother eating if you're going to die anyway?' I say this out loud, but there's no one to hear me. She's through there, in the drawing room, haughty and impatient. I've waited all day to confront her about the letter I got yesterday.

No conversation. 'Breakfast,' she'd said this morning.

No conversation. 'I want my lunch.'

No conversation. 'Where's my dinner?'

I'm scared of not keeping to the script, as Graham puts it. For now, the most I can do is practise by confronting the potato in my hand.

'Are you waiting to be peeled, potato? Or are you waiting to find out if you will be peeled?'

I'm mostly certain that people don't wait around to see what's going to happen to them. What if I threw this potato at the window? Would there be a loud crack, shattered glass in the sink? Mother would smack me about the head for sure. Then what?

'Then what, potato?'

'Eve. Eve. Is that you? Are you shouting at yourself? You better have dinner on, I can't smell anything cooking. Why can't I smell cooking?'

If she got up and came through she'd see for herself, but she won't. Mother has never peeled a potato in her life.

The potato rolls from my hand into the basin. Mother has always said she'll die soon. It used to panic me when she said it. Now it's like a threat.

Bugger it. If I use boiling water from the kettle and we have boiled instead of mash, dinner might just be ready on time. Mother will only eat if dinner is on time. A late dinner gets thrown on the floor.

I bang the pot of potatoes on the hob, take the mince pie out of its box and sling it in the oven. I slam the door shut. The noise of the oven buzzes in my head, clashing with the musical score that nags at me all day long.

There's always music playing inside my head. It only happens inside this house and that means all of the time, if you think about it, because, until I got with Graham, I never left this house. It happens because this house is homage to Mother's past; a glittery, magnificent past in musical theatre. There is music in the ancient, beaten chesterfield sofa that was left over scenery from one of Mother's productions, music in the curtains that dominate the windows because the curtains are always closed, music in the wallpaper paste that glues the house together, with Mother content never to leave what she calls the comforting cloak of her memories.

Dinner is awkward. Mother is making a show of mashing her potatoes on her plate and chucking a load of butter on top. Apparently, not giving her mash was a deliberate act of malice on my part.

'Is this how things are going to be around here? Eve, since when do you disagree with me? Why start now?'

When will now stop being now? What will now be, after? The thought won't leave me alone and is getting mixed up with all the important things that Graham told me to say. Like, who is she? Who is Mother?

I ask this thought, demand it tell me, but the thought ignores me and carries on poking me, as if I haven't said anything inside my head when I have.

I can't bring myself to look at Mother across the dining table. So many bulbs in the chandelier are broken; the few remaining shed a faint light across half of Mother's face. The dark side of her face is disturbing.

It's just as well Mother likes silence at the dinner table, or at least, for me to be silent. It's ridiculously hard when you have to be silent and there are questions inside your head that need answers. The pie churns up acid in my stomach.

Dinner is finished. I slump on the sofa in the projection room, dishes all done. I could hear her tutting every few minutes from the drawing room. Mother's tuts travel and come with lots of baggage. They travel even as far as upstairs, to be heard wherever I escape to. Things are going wrong. Everything is upset and maybe Mother is right to ask if this is the way things are going to be now. Mother is difficult, but until now, she was my mother. She was my mother and I was Eve Park. Now, I am a wolf.

The cluttered projection room hugs what little warmth the day has brought. This is my favourite room in the house, because it contains numerous dusty replicas of Mother, in the oil paintings and framed promo posters on the walls, in the glitzy photographs fighting for space on the black marble fireplace. And perched on top of the oak dresser is a clay bust, a perfect image of her as she was before I was born, when she was celebrated for her magnificent voice and captivating performances. I stare at the bust, I imagine, and I can easily because I've done it so many times before, running my finger down the face of that bust. Who are you?

According to Mother, dinner wasn't worth the effort of swallowing, she tells me, coming to sit, hunching up in her armchair. Her hands twist together on her lap.

'Are you ready, at last?' she barks.

I nod. Mother's hand is poised on the remote, the projector all set up for her to press play. Tonight Mother has chosen her 1982 premier performance, *Madness & Ecstasy*. The most played of all the reels. Her final performance.

There is nothing that could make today feel any better. A whole day has passed, and I've failed in courage to broach the subject of her lie. Now I will have to wait a bit longer. In this instance, that's okay. At least, for the next couple of hours it will be like nothing has happened. The wolves will sing their song not mine.

The screen comes to life halfway through a final rehearsal. That's the best thing about Mother's collection, each of them has captured a bit of rehearsal, usually the final rehearsal before the dress rehearsal, like this one.

There is Father standing beside Mother. It's different from watching them together in the actual performance. There are little exchanges between them that make me feel extra special, like I was born from a love that was greater than any love imagined. Sometimes, I think about whether I will ever find love and this thought used to make me smile, because I never thought I needed love. Who else can say they were born from the greatest love there ever was? That's what I've always thought.

Occasionally, I imagine what life might have been like if Father hadn't died. But I've always tried to resist those imaginings, because they always lead me to feeling disloyal to Mother and then I feel guilty and feeling guilty makes me annoyed at Mother and being annoyed at Mother comes with a price.

In this performance, Father is Dionysus and Mother plays the role of Diana; two dazzling people, three if you include The Taxidermist. He is played by Father's best friend, Gilroy Flynn.

Father had guts, it's easy to see that in the way he presents himself to the stage and, from the little Mother has said about him, he was just like he is here, playing Dionysus. A heavenly man, Mother is fond of saying.

Nobody has ever sung as splendidly as Mother, her eyes glistening as if she means every word. In this clip, she's singing to The Taxidermist, not Dionysus. He must've loved her as much as Father; it's not difficult to imagine that every man would back then. In the clip, she turns her back on him and now she's singing, the way I like to think of it, straight to the audience, secretly announcing her joy of being with child, because, of course, I had already been conceived. That's why Mother watches this video more than all the others. It's not because, as she says, this was her best ever performance. On that stage, inside of her, is supposed to be me. But can that be true? Did she give birth to me? Graham reckons that's not possible, but what if it is? Is it best to say nothing? Maybe it's all best forgotten?

'Here we are,' Mother says, settling back in her armchair, a glass of straight gin in one hand and a fag in the other. 'You know this, Eve? Back then, I never believed I was sophisticated enough to do Diana justice.'

I've heard this before, countless times. On the sofa, I tuck up my knees and rest my head on one of the cushions, pretend to myself it is yesterday and, just for this second, I can close my eyes, inhale the bitter, woody smoke from her fag, feel the utter completeness of my life with Mother. I open my eyes so not to miss the glow on Mother's face as she sits watching, the twitch of a smile appearing.

'The composer believed in me. He said he knew it before I even opened my mouth. Gilroy believed in me, he never tired of telling me so. Murdo McAllister believed in me, and everyone in the theatre knows that musical directors are never satisfied with their leads and it's true, he was a man who knew what he was talking about and he hated everybody. But he believed in me. Do you know what he did? He bought me lavish new gowns, paid for from his very own pocket.'

'Father must have believed you were sophisticated enough.'

'Yes. Yes, I suppose he did.'

The rehearsal clip ends and the screen flicks to the title credits.

The overture begins, the relentless pulsing rhythm, it penetrates through every sinew. Every other second, I switch my gaze to Mother, watch the way her head sways, as if she is the one conducting the music, and the way her hands loosen to lay softly on her lap.

It's magical. Magical to know what's coming and to know, really know that this moment can be repeated over and over again and nobody can take that away.

Mother and Father created something together. A mystery I thought I'd spend my whole life pondering. And they created me, or so I'd thought. That is the real mystery.

'Time you went to bed,' Mother barks when it's finished.

I sit bolt upright, fold my arms, raise my chin. 'Who am I?'

My words sound weak and lifeless, but at least it's finally out there. At least I've asked the question.

'Oh, Eve. I can't be bothered tonight with your crazy wandering mind. Just get out of my sight. I'm tired.'

'You've told me many times that, during that performance, you were pregnant with me. But is that true?'

Mother eases out of her chair, bends, picks up a log, but instead of throwing it onto the fire, she stands before me, tapping the log in her hand.

She whispers, 'What have you been up to?'

'Is it true?'

She throws the log at my chest. It doesn't hurt. I was prepared;

saw the shine in her eyes. When I see that shine, I imagine I have a body made of stone.

'How do you dare to doubt what you've always known?' She bends over me, picks up the log that's fallen onto the cushion and wields it above her as if she's going to smash it down on my head.

'Who am I?' I scream at her. I've never done that before, never screamed at her, never questioned her. Never.

She turns her back to me, tosses the log onto the fire. 'You are Eve Park. That is the name I gave you.'

I get up and move to the back of her armchair. 'You gave me a name. But you didn't give me life.'

'Of course I gave life to you,' she says evenly. 'I am your life, and you are mine.'

I try to scrabble about in my head for the words Graham used, the way he phrased it, the things he told me to say, but nothing inside my head makes sense. Mother is all I have known. All I have needed. Yes, it's different now, yes, yes, yes. But different is difficult to stomach.

'I'm leaving soon,' I tell her because it will rile her.

Mother laughs. 'You could no more live without me than I could live without you.'

I look after her, every minute of every day, make sure she takes her medications, call the doctor, well I get Blythe to do that, bath her, feed her, cut her nails, style her hair, wash her clothes, read to her. I've spent every night of my life in front of that screen watching all her musical performances, over and over again. She's not even sick. And now, I'm not even Eve Park.

It plagues me to imagine a life without her, to imagine living like a family but without her. To imagine living anywhere else but in Tippermuir House, with her. I can't tell her about the baby. It would destroy her.

'You don't know everything,' I tell her. I wish I could tell her everything. I wish she could be different.

'I've never had an interest in knowing everything,' Mother says. 'Except, I'd like to know one thing, Eve.' She sits back in her armchair, crosses her legs and lights up a fag.

I move away from her chair and stand by the fire and wait for her to continue. I gaze at the portrait of Mother that hangs above the fireplace. She is young and vibrant in her golden Diana dress and her shiny-bronze, swept-up hair.

'What has happened to cause such silly doubts in your head, Eve?'

Of course, I can't tell her. Think about this carefully. I am in a body that doesn't belong to me, and I have no idea what that body wants to think. I stretch my fingers, straighten my back, roll my head, every movement is alien. She's waiting for me to say something, but I don't know what to say. It suddenly feels wrong to have confronted her, as if she's already conjuring up a lie; one lie, to cover up another.

'Nothing has happened,' I say at last. 'It's just that, when I asked you for my birth certificate, remember, before? You said I couldn't have it.'

'Just that? Is that what this is all about? You want something you can't have. Oh, Eve, I've taught you better than that.'

'But why? Why won't you give it to me?'

'What for? Look, Eve, we've been through this already. Nobody needs their birth certificate. What in goodness' name are you going to use it for?'

'I said, didn't I? I need it to get my passport. I'm leaving.'

'No you are not leaving. Who would look after me if you left? Who would take care of me? There is nobody but you, Eve. A mother must rely on her child to do the right thing. And where would you go? You've never been out of this house. You just don't know how dangerous the outside world is. I have kept you safe, and I will carry on keeping you safe. It is just the two of us, Eve. It's always been the two of us.'

'It's different now,' I tell her, wishing with all my heart it wasn't; a nasty, guilty wish.

'Different?' she bellows. 'Different how? I am still the same. You are the same. Nothing is different.'

She doesn't know it, but I am not the same. I mustn't forget that. 'You don't have my birth certificate, do you?'

'Yes I do. But you mustn't want it. Why do you want it, Eve? Why?'

She's not going to accept that I'm leaving. I knew she wouldn't, I should never have told her. I've just complicated everything.

'I won't leave if you give me my birth certificate.' I didn't know I was going to say this. I'm trying my best not to lie to her. It's all Graham's fault. He made me ask for the birth certificate so he could get my passport so we could go to France.

She isn't going to give it to me, because it doesn't exist.

'You haven't told me,' she says. She grasps for another cigarette but doesn't light it. 'What has happened to make you want your birth certificate? Has someone been telling you lies? Who have you been speaking to?'

'I met someone,' I shout at her. Then, a little quieter, 'Someone who knows things.'

'What things?' She springs up and slaps my arm. 'What are you talking about? Who did you meet?'

'A man.'

'And what did this man tell you? Rubbish, I expect. Lies.'

'Why would someone tell me lies, Mother?'

'Where is this man that will tell you such lies? You mustn't see him. He mustn't come here. He's dangerous, Eve. Dangerous.'

Mother comes to stand where I am, my back to her portrait. She stands so close I can examine the deep grooves in her face, the loose skin of her jowls and her sweet, mildewed breath settles, wet against my neck.

'Everyone lies. The only person, the *only* person you can trust is me. Never, Eve, never listen to anyone who tells you different. Do you hear me?' She takes my face in her hands. 'There is not a single person in this world who doesn't have a reason to lie. Now let's stop this silliness. If I show you your birth certificate, will you promise to stop?'

'Yes,' I say, just so she will release her fingers from my jaw.

'Fine. Good. Tomorrow. I will forget about my own plans and engage in this useless hunt for the certificate tomorrow. Now, you don't have to tell me the name of this man. He's nothing. He's a liar and he'll take you away from me. Just forget about him, all right? It's just the two of us, Eve. Always remember that. Forget about him, he won't be bothering you again.'

'Yes,' I say again. But, of course, it's a lie.

Chapter 4

Eve

Perth, Scotland
10th October 2019

I'm in my own room, in my pyjamas, in my own bed, in my same life with the light off. If I pretend there's not a new life to think about, I can almost feel the me I've always been, the me I've always thought I was.

Graham will be disappointed with me, because I'm not going to be able to get a passport and go to France with him and the baby unless I find out who I really am. Mother isn't going to tell me. Knowing her, she'll go to great lengths to make sure I never find out. I should never have told her I was leaving, that was stupid, I should've stuck to Graham's script and demand Mother tell me my real name. I don't want another name, although I can't tell Graham that. I am Eve Park. I want to keep on being Eve Park. I want to keep on being Eve Park and have that other life that's waiting for me. There must be another way. There will be another way. Eve Park must be devoured.

That's Mother's voice coming from downstairs. Who can she be talking to? I climb out of bed, ease open my bedroom door and stick my head out.

It's like she's talking to someone, but who? I don't hear another voice. It can't be that she's on the phone, because we don't have a phone. If we need to call the doctor, Blythe does it for us. Mother must be talking to herself. I can't hear what she's saying, her voice is muffled; it must be coming from the drawing room.

I whip off my socks, because there's a slight chance that socks are noisier than bare feet when a person is trying to go about in the invisibular. I press my back against the cold stone wall at the top of the stairs and take one step down. One or two more steps and I should be able to hear what Mother is saying. I move quickly, because Mother might decide at any second to stop talking. The steps are carpeted and, to be fair, I've not once, ever, heard a creak or anything like that.

Isn't this silly? And it's freezing. I should've slung my dressing gown on. What if someone is actually in the house? I should've thought of that before now, it would make perfect sense. Except it wouldn't, because it's after nine o'clock and nobody knocks on doors after nine o'clock. Not any respectable person. Actually, now that I think about it, no one ever knocks on the door, whatever time of day. Except Blythe, but when Blythe comes, Mother won't speak to her, it's me who has to do all the talking, and I hate talking to Blythe, even more so now. Hate it.

I sit on the fourth step down. This is a risky business. If Mother was to come out of the drawing room she would see me quite clearly. That would mean a hiding, no doubt about it. I wouldn't normally listen in to Mother's conversations but that's because Mother never has conversations with anyone except me. This is too peculiar to ignore. But everything about today has been implausingly peculiar. Implausingly, that can be the word for today. I must remember to write it down.

From here, Mother's words are coming across a bit strangled. I grab the railing with both hands and pull myself closer to the banister, closer to Mother's voice and where I can see through the slightly ajar drawing room door. At that point, Mother drops the phone to her lap.

Mystery solved, because I can't doubt my own eyes. Mother is sitting on the sofa – not her own armchair – both her hands clasping a mobile phone. Mother's head is down, she's staring at the phone. Is she waiting for it to ring again? Had I missed the phone ringing or did Mother make a call by herself? Where did the phone come from?

Mother turns her head, and I pull back and flatten myself against the wall. Stupid, because Mother's head can't turn around that far and, unless she was to actually stand up and turn, there's no way she can see me. I'm not going to find out who the mystery caller was if I dive back to my room like a jittery mouse. Wait a minute or two in case something happens.

Nothing is happening, Mother hasn't moved an inch. She's still grasping the phone, her head down, she's just staring at it.

Several minutes pass. A fit of yawning grips me. Making a silent yawn is, if you don't know already, actually impossible.

Take yourself to bed, I tell myself.

I hunker down under the duvet. Take yourself to bed. Words Mother would say, on an entirely uneventful night-time after an entirely uneventful day. My thoughts about today are wrapped up in fog. I decree that concluding the events of this day, there is not a single unthinkable thought that is worth thinking about.

In my drifting off, I remember that I've forgotten to write my word of the day in my book. I peel the duvet back and prop myself on my elbow with the book in my hand and the pencil poised.

Implausingly

Underneath I ready the pencil to write the meaning, stopping to think about it properly. Yes, that's it. Yes. I write:

Implausingly = the impossible truth

Chapter 5

Eve

Perth
11th October 2019

One minute late. The fried egg is congealing close to my left slipper, the yoke oozing onto the torn kitchen lino. Unfathomable. The alarm had gone off when it was supposed to, I'd got up straight away, all as per usual. The stupid egg dropped itself because a starling peeked its head out from under the eaves just as I'd been passing the window with the egg nicely balanced on the fish slice, making its journey from frying pan to plate.

Mother will berate the late minute. She notices everything. I carry the heavy tray with both hands gripping the handles, trying my best not to shoogle the teapot too much and spill the tea over the Lurpak-laden toast. Careful steps are taken through the hallway, past the stairs to the back bedroom. This is Mother's private space with the door kept an inch or two open to make sure I'm not getting up to something I shouldn't.

I bang my backside against the door, but this morning the door is decidedly closed. It won't budge. Another minute late.

It must be a mistake. An open window causing a draught perhaps? No, because all the windows are nailed shut. I take another minute to ponder the last time anything unexpected happened. Well, discounting all of yesterday to be fair, and if I'm being truthful, the most of the past year. I balance the tray on one arm and use my other hand to turn the handle, the door swings open.

Inside, Mother is still asleep. Everything is out of sorts again today. Everything.

Mother is supposed to be, should be, sitting up a full ninety degrees, the shiny rose coverlet carefully folded across her lap, her hands resting, her head slightly back, her chin poised, readying her mouth to assert her usual disgruntled morning sermon.

I place the tray on the bedside table and throw open the curtain, not something I'd ever normally do but if today is going to fight me, I am going to fight back.

I stand by the side of the bed, allowing my knees to rest against the mattress. Mother is lying on her side with her back facing me. All I can see of her is the tuft of burgundy hair from the top of her head.

The sparrows are chirping away outside, as if rooting for me, so I choose my words carefully.

'I know I am not Eve Park. I have a DNA test to prove it. Now, right now, you're going to tell me who I really am.'

Mother is silent. It's good that she's taking the time to think.

I sit on the edge of the bed and wait.

Mother doesn't like it when I ask questions. But I thought about it all last night, a person doesn't always know what they like and what they don't like. Mother doesn't like making phone calls, but she made one last night. Maybe I'll ask her about it? If I can convince Mother that things around here could be different, if I can convince her to see how things could be better for both of us, that there is really no reason for us to part, then wouldn't that be the better way for all of us? Well, maybe not for Blythe, but nobody likes Blythe.

Take for instance the fact that neither of us ever gets a letter (with the exception of Mother's little padded envelopes that always come the second Friday of the month). It would be nice, in truth, to get a letter from somebody, but Mother has always said she would hate to get a letter, whoever it's from (obviously Mother doesn't include the little envelopes within which there is no letter). She must've got at least one letter before I was born else how would she know she doesn't like letters? When I was little, I didn't like scrambled eggs, but now I eat scrambled eggs three times a week and sometimes even dream about eating them.

Mother is taking a long time to decide what she thinks about my question. I pat her shoulder.

'Maybe you would like to eat your toast and eggs, drink your tea, while you're thinking about it?'

The toast is looking a bit stiff and the tea in the teapot will be reaching the point of strength that Mother won't like. The sparrows seem to have stopped singing, which is a real shame, because even if it's a less than sunny morning, birdsong never fails to be uplifting. I generally tune into the birds while Mother goes over all her aches and pains and what needs to be done to make her more comfortable and her day more bearable.

'Mother?'

I give her shoulder a little shake.

'Mother?'

I get up and walk around to sit on the other side of the bed so I can see her face. Taking hold of her hand, I study the loose way her face is resting on the pillow, the way her eyes are open and staring out at nothing.

Oh.

I count backwards from one hundred. Ninety-nine, ninety-eight, ninety-seven, ninety-six...

I get up and pull the chair from the dressing table to her bedside and sit. Stroke the back of her freezing cold hand, from the wrist, down in between the bones, over the sharp knuckles and down the length of her middle finger. I didn't put Tramadol in her gin last night.

'Mother. Wake up. Wake up.'

I try to squeeze her hand but it's rigid.

'Now who am I?'

Chapter 6

Graham

Graham falls out of bed and blindly makes his way to the en suite. Half dry, he climbs into his freshly laundered – by himself – jeans and neatly ironed – by himself – T-shirt and makes his way to the kitchen. Like the rest of the lodge, the kitchen is spick and span, thanks to him. It makes a man feel good. It's important to help Blythey out. She's a worker, always has been; nothing like that witch, Maureen, Eve's mother, at Tippermuir. Now that woman's got a lot to answer for.

In the kitchen, he switches on the kettle and gets the bacon frying in the pan. That's Blythe's key in the lock, nice timing, she'll be desperate for a cuppa. He piles the rolls with bacon, warms the teapot, shoves in the teabags and fills it to the brim with hot water from the kettle, then sets everything on the table. Job done. Blythey will be knackered but this should set her up.

He sits, waiting for her to hang up her coat, kick off her shoes and put her slippers on. They've had the same routine for years and it suits him. He pours milk into the cups and tries to imagine his new life, away from all this, but then stops himself. This business with Eve's birth certificate is doing his head in. By now, they should all be in France together. It's all set up. Lynn and Stuart have spent the last few months doing up the barn. When he spoke to her on the phone yesterday she was in a panic, and he can't blame her, she was supposed to be in France by now, not left behind holding his baby. They own a house out there, a way for them to escape the Scottish winter. Lynn jumped at the chance to rent their newly renovated barn to him. Stuart's not too happy either, and that's no surprise having been left to get on with the finishing touches to the barn. Well, Stuart should be a better husband to Lynn and maybe she would listen to him more.

It will come together, he's sure it will. The worst part is that all this nonsense with the DNA, and not being able to get Eve a passport, is only prolonging the pain of letting Blythey down. That's the worst part.

'There she is,' he says when Blythe enters the kitchen. 'Come and sit down, hen, it's all ready for you.' He pours tea into her cup and looks up, seeing the large cardboard box she's carrying. 'What's that you've got there then?'

Blythe shuffles into her seat, placing the box at her feet. 'Ah, you've no idea how much I need this cuppa,' she says, sipping at her tea. She takes a bite of her bacon roll.

Graham waits for her to swallow. 'What have you been buying?'

He grins at her. She's always buying this or that. Never anything outrageously expensive, never anything they actually need.

'Now, don't you be angry at me,' she says, her eyes pleading with him.

She's nervous and it's making him nervous. He's never angry at her, why would she say that? Does she suspect? Has she found something out, spoken with Lynn? No, Lynn would never drop him in it. Stuart might though.

Blythe bends and opens the cardboard box. She puts a finger to her mouth and then points to what's inside.

'Come and look,' she whispers. 'But be quiet, he's sleeping.'

'He?'

Graham doesn't move. There's something crafty playing out behind her eyes. He doesn't like it. Not one bit. The last time Blythe did something out of the ordinary, in fact it was just the other day, when he'd caught her trying to work his laptop, he thought he'd been rumbled and his heart had sunk so far into his groin he thought he was going to die, have a stroke or a heart attack or something. Two oddities in one week, that's a warning. Nah, Blythe can't know about Eve and the baby because, if she did, they wouldn't be sitting here like this, having breakfast together. Over the past year, he's tried to work out how Blythe would react to his affair. But he's never had much of an imagination for these things. Best all round for him to leave with

Eve before Blythe finds out. Cut out the stress and anguish. Keep the bigger picture in mind.

'Go on then,' Blythe urges him. 'Meet the new member of the family.'

He chokes on his own saliva, tries to cough, but the cough gets stuck in his throat. He thrusts back in his chair, drops his head between his knees and tries to catch his breath.

Somewhere in the panic he hears Blythe sighing. Now, she's slapping him on the back. It helps. He straightens himself and lets Blythe wipe away the tears from his eyes with a tissue she'd found in the pocket of her apron.

'What's wrong with you?' she asks, laughing. 'I didn't expect it to be that much of a shock. It's only a wee puppy. Come on, take a look.' She takes his hand and leads him around the table.

He loosens his shoulders. Jesus.

Inside the box is a sleeping silky-brown lump. 'It's a chocolate Lab,' Blythe tells him proudly. 'I couldn't resist him. He was the runt of the litter and nobody wanted him.'

'Blythe,' he says, straightening up, 'the last thing we need is a puppy to have to take care of.'

'It might be the last thing you need,' she says. She sits and takes another bite of her bacon roll. 'But what about what I need?'

He crosses to the sink, not sure what to think. A dog, for Christ's sake? He gazes out of the window, up at Tippermuir House, standing looking eerily empty on top of the hill, and wonders if Eve is up and about. What is it about women? He's been with Blythe so long he's got used to her ways. But with Eve, it's like every day is different with her. One minute she's bouncing all over the place, can't stop talking about what their life in France will be like, the next she's hardly saying anything, worrying about leaving her mother. What about now she's a mother herself? Anyway, you'd think she'd be grateful to get away from that place; she's a prisoner in there. That woman is evil. What kind of mother locks their kid away from the outside world and forces her to do stuff she shouldn't have to do? Once Eve comes to her senses and realises this, it means she's free; everything will get back on track. She'll stop all this silly talk about being a wolf and start talking about being a family. A wolf, she's got some imagination. A wolf. He's heard that women can be funny after giving birth, that's all it'll be. He'll figure out how to get her a passport somehow. Maybe Lynn will have an idea. It's one problem after another and now Blythe with this puppy. Suddenly, the bigger picture feels blurry, out of focus, like, somehow, he's falling backwards.

'You have everything you need, that's what you always tell people,' he tells her without turning round. If he looks at her right this minute, she'll likely see everything he's thinking, it would be in his eyes like a flashing notification: I am a bastard the notification would read and he would have to tell her everything and beg her forgiveness. But then what?

'Absolutely,' Blythe says through a mouthful of roll. 'But needs change.'

Now he does turn around. This would all be easier if Blythe was the one to decide their marriage was over.

'What do you mean?'

'Well, life can be a bit lonely around here, you know.'

'You've got me,' he says then immediately hates himself. By rights, he would be in France by now and she wouldn't have him. She'd rue the day she ever met him. The very thought makes him want to sink to the ground.

'I know.' She motions for him to come and sit with her at the table.

He sits and she takes hold of his hands. 'You're just a man,' she says.

'Thanks.'

'You know what I mean. You can't be expected to meet all of a woman's needs. I just want something for me. You can understand that, can't you? And it will be good for both of us as well. We can go on walks together. It will bring us closer. Things are a bit stale around here these days, haven't you noticed?'

Nausea is bouncing around in his gut. 'I need you,' he says. It's true. He's always needed Blythe. That's why this is all so mixed up; it scares him to imagine how he will be without her. At the same time, this thing with the puppy, she's taking the mick. After all that's she's said over the years, the sacrifice he made for her. How can she do this to him now? And why now? It can't be a coincidence that she wants them to be closer. Does she know about Eve, does she know it all? If she does, she's keeping shtum. Either because she's going to do everything possible to keep hold of him, or she's going to use what she knows to destroy him.

'Yes, but it's not the same,' she grumbles. 'I hope you're not going to be difficult about this, Graham?'

'Difficult. Me?' He jumps from his chair and back to the sink where he doesn't have to look at her or the puppy. 'People have children to make them feel needed. Not dogs.'

'I knew it.' He hears her stir the teapot noisily, and then a teaspoon flies past him. It just misses his ear and comes to land with a clink in the sink.

He doesn't turn around. Maybe she should have a puppy; it will be good company for her when he's gone. But, why now? After all these years, why now? It's not because Bentley died, because she didn't give a monkey's about him.

'I knew you would bring that up. I told myself you would, all the way home I said to myself you won't just be happy for me, you'll kick up a fuss I said to myself. Absolutely.'

'Happy for you?' He swings around to face her, he can't help himself. 'What about when I was begging and pleading with you, eh? What about all those years of cajoling and what? You are too stubborn, Blythe. If we'd…' He throws his arms up. 'Forget it. Keep the puppy, but it better not get under my feet.' It's not just what he's given up for Blythe. There's not a dog on the planet that would make up for losing Bentley.

'Go on, Graham, say it. Get your rocks off.'

'I'm saying nothing.'

'Oh, that's typical of you.

'What does that even mean? Get your rocks off?'

'You're deflecting. I know you. You want me to feel bad because it was my decision to not have babies. I can tell you right now. I don't feel bad in the slightest. As I've always said, if you want children, you should've married someone else.'

'I might just do that,' he says, letting his temper get the better of him. He's almost on the verge of telling her everything. That wouldn't do either of them any good. And it would cause a whole lot of trouble for Eve. But this spat with Blythe is at least helping him to be a bit more sure of himself, see the bigger picture. The puppy is a good idea.

'I'm sorry, Blythey,' he tells her. It's best to keep on her good side. Still, he's surprised at how much the thing about kids still rattles him, even now, even with his new life in front of him and his son. If only he was a bit younger. 'You're right. The dog will be good for you.'

'Aha. I knew you'd come round.' She gets up and puts her arms around his waist, leans her head between his shoulder blades. 'You're a good man, Graham.'

He lets her sink into him. It'll be a wrench to give all this up.

'Now,' she says, releasing him, 'let me find a bowl and give the wee man some water.'

For the first time, Graham steels himself to have a proper look inside the box.

'Where's he gone?'

'Eh?' Blythe swivels around, sees the box is empty and runs about the house in search of the pup.

Five minutes later, the box is still empty and Graham and Blythe flop down at the kitchen table, neither quite knowing where to look next.

'Do you think he might've got out?' Graham asks.

'How? The front door is closed. This is your fault you know. If you hadn't shouted at me he never would've run away. Or we'd have seen him wake up and climb out of the box.'

Graham lowers his head. It is his fault. 'We'll find him.'

'Did you look in the sunroom?' Blythe asks.

'Had a quick glance around, he wasn't there.'

'Were the French doors closed?'

'I locked up last night before coming to bed like I always do.'

'Aye, but I opened those doors when I got in, to let the fresh air in. I was going to make up a wee bed for him in there and it was awfully stuffy.'

They spend ten minutes outside searching and calling. All they can call out is 'puppy' as he doesn't have a name yet. Like his own son doesn't have a name. Eve won't name him, she's adamant he can't have a name yet. At least Blythe had had the sense to close the fence gate across the drive after she'd parked the car. Both the lodge and Tippermuir House are surrounded by a stone wall so there's only one direction the pup could've taken. They decide to extend the search into the garden of Tippermuir House.

He warns Blythe not to go anywhere near the house itself. But no sooner has he said the words, Blythe marches up there regardless.

'There is a proper path, buried under all this,' she mutters.

What's she like, trying to step over the worst of the gorse and bracken that's clawing at the front of the house and half obscuring the downstairs windows?

A fissure of trepidation makes him call out. 'Blythe, don't go up there. You know what that woman's like. It wouldn't surprise me if she had a shotgun, and she'll use it if she catches us poking about.' Blythe ignores him.

He could grab her and force her back home. Bloody woman, always thinking she knows best. How is Eve going to react if Blythe goes banging at that door? He could just go home and leave them to it, but the very thought makes him shiver and he imagines the weeds around his ankles twisting up his legs, pulling him down a chasm in the dirty earth, to face his fate ill-equipped and inept.

With a growing sense of panic, he scans the area surrounding Tippermuir House. Finding the puppy would stop Blythe in her tracks. He's not prepared. Aye, he's thought about Blythe finding out, thinks about it all the time, but not like this. Not like this.

Blythe is shouting something, but he can't hear her. He could ignore her and go home, then whatever happens would be nothing to do with him. She's not going to listen to him, whatever he might say, she's determined to get in that house. It's always been her dream to own that house. It used to be all she talked about, but she hasn't mentioned it for a while and he hopes she's given up. Like he'd told her then, he's not spending his entire compensation payout on a wreck of a house that will take more than he could ever dream about to make it liveable. He hates that house, the way it stands stark and accusatory above the woods as if it's more important than the nature that encloses it. The way it glares down at him, like its warning him away, as if its chosen solitude has been disturbed and it's all his fault.

Blythe is motioning for him to come. He has one more glance around the overgrown garden, then back to the fir trees at the bottom of the hill, there's still no sign of the dog. He could try and make sure Blythe doesn't ring the bell, try to coax her away from the house, tell her the pup has probably found his way back to the lodge by now.

He tramps through the tall weeds that traces where the original path should be. Blythe's holding something up for him to see, and it's not until he gets a bit closer that he realises what it is – a key.

'I know where she keeps the spare key,' Blythe is saying, with that smug look on her face that makes her look just a wee bit ugly.

'I thought we were supposed to be looking for the pup,' he says. It's an ancient key, and the sort you might imagine would unlock a castle or the great wooden doors of an old keep.

'Can you see the pup? It's obvious, don't you think, we've been looking for ages. He must've somehow got in the house.' She points the key at Tippermuir House and, if he didn't know better, he'd swear she'd let the dog loose on purpose just so she could use that key. What worries him is the reason why. It can't be just her hankering to own this house; he's convinced he caught something sinister in the tone of her voice.

She could be playing him. Blythe's played dirty in the past, like that time when he was at his worst in hospital after the accident and she stole his password and transferred all his personal savings into her own account without telling him. She'd tried to say she was safeguarding his money so that it would all be there for him for when he got better. But if she'd left it alone, it would've all been there for him anyway. She'd thought he was going to die and didn't want to wait for the solicitors to sort everything out before she got her hands on the money. At the time, he'd felt sorry for her and, the truth is, what she did made him stronger in the end; made him want to get better. His savings were a pittance compared to what he got as compensation, but he didn't know that at the time and he didn't want to die, leaving Blythe destitute.

'Blythe, we can't just unlock the door and walk in uninvited.'

'Why not? We have a legitimate reason. That puppy is fragile, anything could happen to him. It's our duty to find him and make him safe. If that means we have to disturb Maureen fecking Park then that's what we're going to do. You're scared of her, aren't you? Well I'm not. I'm absolutely not at all scared of her.'

Eve and her mother have lived in Tippermuir House for more than thirty years. Before that, the house had lain empty. Graham remembers how Blythe had fought him for years. She wanted to buy this house, but they never could have afforded it. Blythe's dream was impossible and their constant arguments over it had almost finished him. He was on the verge of walking away, but he loved her, even if she loved Tippermuir House more than him, even if she sometimes made him feel worthless. He loved her. Why else had he sacrificed himself, and chosen Blythe over having the children he'd always taken for granted that he would have? In hindsight, Blythe's determination not to have children is to blame for his affair with Eve. He can see that now. Blythe got her wish. Now it's his time to achieve his dreams.

Blythe unlocks the door and calls out but gets no response.

'Maybe they're both out?'

Graham reluctantly follows in behind her.

'Let's just go home, love. It would be a nice surprise, eh? If the pup is back home, snuggled up in his box in the kitchen?'

'We'll just have a quick look around,' Blythe says, and she takes a few further steps inside. 'Anyone who stupidly leaves a key under a plant pot at their front door is asking for someone to walk in and steal their belongings.'

'You didn't find the key under a plant pot.'

'I know. I'm just saying. Actually, the key was on the lintel above the door.'

'How did you know where to find the key, anyway?'

'Maureen told me where it was. Years ago. Said she puts it out every night before bed.'

'Why would she do that?'

'Why are you asking me, I don't know. I do know that it was a secret and I wasn't to tell Eve about it, not even when Eve got older. She made me swear. If Eve had ever asked me I would've told her. I don't swear to anything, as you know. Eve never did ask though. Oh my word, Graham, what do you think that is? The smell in here is beyond words.'

Blythe is right, the smell is nasty. They're in the main entrance hall, which isn't as grand as it might be with all the clutter. But amongst the damp and the smell of something rotting there's another smell that seems to separate itself from the others, a smell that's physical, as if it had shape and form and you could reach out and touch it, taste it.

'Where first?' Blythe asks.

'Let's go home, we shouldn't be here.' Is she testing him? It's not like Blythe to hold back and now that she's here, why isn't she raking about, running through the rooms? He knows she wants to, can see the passion for it in her eyes.

'We'll check down here first,' she says and steps over the clutter to make her way along the corridor directly facing them.

He follows.

Blythe doesn't wait for him. She throws open the door at the end of the corridor but stops short. He catches up with her and reaches behind, as she grabs hold of his wrist. He peers over her shoulder.

Eve is sitting by the bedside holding her mother's hand. She nods in their direction, as if everything is normal. Everything is not normal.

'I know a dead body when I see one,' Blythe hisses.

Chapter 7

Graham

Tippermuir House
12th October 2019

'Graham,' Blythe says as if underlining her words. 'Maureen Park is dead. Absolutely.'

Eve must know her mother is dead and yet she's just sitting there holding the mother's hand, like she might be asleep or something.

Somewhere in the house, a clock chimes. Still gripping Graham's wrist, Blythe counts out loud, eight chimes.

'It's not every morning one finds a dead body,' Blythe says.

He's not quite sure what to do about anything.

'Enough,' Blythe says. 'Enough of this standing about. Eve.'

Eve raises her head, her chin in the air. Silently she stretches her neck, but she doesn't turn towards them. Instead, she lets her head fall downwards, and tilts it slightly to the left, before her gaze, once again, falls to the body in the bed; that dead hand, resting in Eve's living one.

Blythe takes the few steps to the bottom of the bed. Graham wants to stop her, but he doesn't want to go anywhere near that bed and there's nothing he can think of to say to Eve. Not now, not here. Not with Blythe fussing about and Maureen Park dead right in front of him, the putrid smell of her flesh snaking around him.

Blythe is saying something about the emergency services.

Eve shakes her head.

'When did it happen?' Blythe asks Eve.

Eve doesn't answer, but she does turn to Blythe. This is progress.

After a few excruciatingly awkward silent minutes, Eve says, 'She didn't answer my question. It might be that she was already dead by then.'

'What question?'

'It doesn't matter now.'

Blythe nudges Graham and points to the breakfast tray at the side of the bed. 'You mean you came in with her breakfast and you didn't notice she was dead? Look at her.' Blythe turns to Graham. 'She's probably in shock, but who sits by their dead mother's bedside and doesn't call the emergency services? The woman probably died peacefully in her sleep, what she needs is to be dealt with. It's no use putting it off.'

Graham jumps when Blythe claps her hands loudly several times. Maybe she's trying to rouse Eve, but it doesn't work, so she tries talking to her instead.

'She's not going to wake up, you know. No amount of staring at her is going to bring her round, Eve.'

'I'm not staring at her, she would hate that,' Eve blurts out. 'I'm keeping her company. That's what she likes me to do.'

Graham's legs almost go from under him. This is the woman he's going to make a future with but, in this second, all he feels for her is fatherly sorrow and that makes something twist inside of him. By the look of her, Eve is in one hell of a state. He tries to push away the fear that she's likely to blurt something out.

Blythe tuts loudly. 'I don't think your mother's noticing you sitting beside her.'

Blythe walks around to the other side of the bed and puts her hand on Eve's shoulder.

'I think you've kept her company long enough. Let's you and I go and call the doctor. I can do it for you, if you like.'

'No. I shouldn't leave her. She wouldn't want me to leave her.'

'Someone will come, eventually, and take her away,' Blythe warns. 'The doctor will want to know what happened, Eve. Can you tell me that, at least? What time did you come this morning, bringing her breakfast, do you remember?'

Graham forces himself to take a step into the room, another step. That's it, he can't go any further.

'Stop badgering her, Blythe. Can't you see she's in shock?'

'I always bring her breakfast at eight o'clock,' Eve says to Blythe.

Graham is beginning to wonder if she's even noticed he's here.

She hasn't looked his way once.

'I was one minute late,' Eve says, and he can hear the despair in her voice. 'If I hadn't been one minute late, would she still be alive?'

'You weren't late; you were early, because we were already standing right here at eight o'clock. We heard the clock chime.'

'I didn't make her breakfast this morning. That was yesterday. Today, I didn't want to leave her.'

He inadvertently takes a deep breath in, sucking in the air poisoned by death, and he wipes at his mouth with the sleeve of his jumper. He watches Blythe's hand drop from Eve's shoulder and the significance of Eve's words hit home. Eve's been sat here since eight o'clock yesterday morning and all the while he's been whittling away his time at home, when he should've been here to take care of her. Since she'd got the DNA test, she's stopped letting him come to her window at night. He should've been more assertive with her. What kind of hero is he going to be in front of his son?

He's so annoyed at himself he can no longer look at Eve. He notices the breakfast tray; a china cup, a matching teapot, a neatly constructed plate of toast and scrambled eggs, a solitary fly inspecting the grey eggs that must've once been yellow. He could be that fly, the way it's judging the pile of eggs as if they're a mountain that could potentially collapse.

'Did you bring your mobile?' Blythe asks him.

He shakes his head.

'Neither did I,' she says.

'You go,' he says. 'I'll wait here.'

'Eve doesn't want you hanging about her at a time like this. Get away with you, man, and phone the doctor.'

He's not budging. He's not leaving the two of them together, anything might be said between them and this is no time for all that to implode.

'You're better at that kind of thing than me; talking to doctors and the like. You know what to say. You go. And I'll just wait here, keep an eye on things.'

Blythe sucks in a huge gulp of air, loudly. 'You're a fecking lump of useless,' she says on her way past.

As soon as Blythe's out of sight, he crosses to Eve's side and drops on his knees. He tries to take a hold of her hand, but she won't let go of her mother, so he makes do with rubbing her back.

'Eve,' he says softly. 'Eve. You're finally free.'

Is she pretending he's not here or does she really not see him? She's not even acknowledging the stroke of his hand on her back. He whispers her name, over and over. Nothing. Not a glint of recognition.

He stands, suddenly the room is bitterly cold and it makes him shiver all the way from his neck down to his feet. He runs his finger down the side of Eve's face. Still, she won't look at him. It's no use, he's no use to her now, in this moment, when it seems as if he'd never existed in her life. He kisses the top of her head and turns to leave then changes his mind. With both his hands, he seizes Eve's wrist and tries to wrench it away from Maureen. All he succeeds in doing is to lift Maureen's arm off the bed and, for a second or two, he's transfixed by an image of the arm dislocating from the body, flesh dripping from the bones and slipping to the floor at his feet. He lets go, steps away from the bed. Blythe's right, he is a useless shite. Eve deserves more. She deserves someone strong and capable, a man of power and certainty. To be a man like that? He wouldn't even know where to start. Eve's had it tough; she's not a clue how tough. Eve's kind of normal isn't your average, run-of-the-mill upbringing. He thought he could give her normal. She said to him, late that first night, after they'd done it, she'd said, 'Show me what the world is like, Graham.' And he promised he would, and he can, he can, with all the plans he's made. Just that one hiccup with the birth certificate and that can be fixed, he can show her the world and he will.

He steps closer to Eve, tucks a strand of her hair behind her ear.

'That's not going to bring her round, let me,' Blythe says puffing into the room like a steam train. She marches up to where he's standing, raises her hand and slaps the back of Eve's head.

Eve releases Maureen's hand and lets out a long, guttural howl. She leaps from her chair and throws her arms around Graham's neck, leans her head on his shoulder.

This would be the time to tell Blythe everything. All this deceit, it's not doing any of them any good. Maybe once it's all out in the open, Eve will be able to see that at last she's free. Free to accept her son.

From the corner of his eye, he catches Blythe collapse on the edge of the bed, and she's sobbing.

'I know what she's going through,' Blythe says, between deep, involuntary breaths. She gazes up at Graham. 'When you had your accident, I sat by your hospital bed day after day, night after night. I felt like she does now, numb, helpless, utterly beside myself with grief. I thought I'd lost you. Thought my world was about to end. I know how Eve feels, I truly do. It's hellish.' Blythe rises from the bed and pulls Eve away from Graham and eases her back into the chair. She says to Eve, 'We share a bond, you and I.'

The air in here tastes sour and unnatural. He can't bring himself to tell Blythe he's leaving her, not now. Right now, it's as if he's in a room full of people he's never met but who despise him anyway. Let Blythe have her moment. It will be short-lived, but at least he'll have given her that, even if he's about to take it all away again. Nothing stays the same. Even if Blythe does have an inkling about him and Eve, she's smart enough to get through and carry on. That's all a person can ever do in this life.

'Did you phone?' he snaps at Blythe.

'Nope. I only got as far as the kitchen. This place gives me the heebie-jeebies. I'm not going any further unless you come with me.'

They go in search of a phone, leaving Eve in the same position she was when they arrived. Blythe never believed Maureen didn't have a phone; she said long ago that Maureen just got her to call the doctor for attention.

Maureen Park had once been a looker, if you can believe that. Everywhere you look there are countless prints, ornately framed oil paintings and theatre posters and in all of them is the face of that bloody woman.

They're in what Blythe says is the drawing room, but that's just a fancy name for a living room and it's not cosy like their own living room. It's chilly with a dark, miserable atmosphere and that smell that he sometimes gets a whiff of from Eve's skin, which makes him think of potato peel.

Blythe flings open the curtains to let some daylight in. The sun is up and it takes a few minutes before his eyes adjust to the light.

'Here, a mobile,' he says, finding it after raking through a drawer in the oak dresser by the window. 'It's not got any charge,' he says handing it to Blythe. Even with the curtains open, the room has a dull, unlived in feel about it. The muddy brown carpet, the sofa, dining table and chairs all match the dark oak of the dresser, and it all pales against the many faces of Maureen, in her colourful costumes, smiling in a hundred different ways of evil, from every wall.

Everywhere he looks, Maureen's eyes dissect him. There's a gilt-framed oil painting above the black marble fireplace with Maureen glistening, as if just out of shot there are fireworks being set off in her honour. He turns his back to the painting and scans the room. Maureen's stare lingers behind his eyes.

'Graham, you go home and get your phone, will you?'

'No.' He can't, he's not going to leave Blythe here alone with Eve, that's asking for bother. 'I mean, we could just plug that one in, it won't take long to charge.' There must be a charger around here somewhere.

'Och, who knows if it even works. Go on, it'll just take you a minute.'

An alarm sounds, and he dashes out of the room expecting there to be a fire raging in the hallway.

Chasing after him, Blythe slaps him across the shoulder.

'What you like?' she says. 'It's just the doorbell.' She pushes past him to go and open the front door.

'Don't open it,' he hisses. 'Apart from the fact we're not even supposed to be here. Blythe, for Christ's sake, there's a dead body back there.'

'Don't be ridiculous, man,' she says.

Too late, she's already opened the door.

Standing shoulder to shoulder is a grizzly looking man with a shiny bald head and square-cut shoulders. Alongside is a tight-lipped, steely eyed police woman with a head of wild, red hair escaping from her cap. Both of them present their ID cards at the same time.

Now what? The police? Life always has to be one bloody complication after another. Along with the breeze coming in from the open front door, a wave of unjustified guilt settles over him. He's sandwiched between a dead body and the police force. This is not going to be easy to wriggle out of, the police will want to ask questions, poke around into their lives, pull apart his carefully constructed plan that Blythe knows nothing about and Eve is in that much of a state she's liable to tell all.

'No, I'm not the owner of this house, that's Maureen Park,' Blythe is saying, in the usual curtly manner she adopts with people of authority.

'I'm Detective Sergeant Lark Calmly,' the bloke says, as Blythe shows them both in. 'And this is WPC Paula Dunbar.'

'Well I know that already, I've just read your identification,' Blythe says sharply.

Quickly he introduces himself and offers his hand to the officers, and he tries his best to shake each of their hands with conviction, so he shows himself as being capable; a man who can take charge, stand his ground, a tower of strength, and any other crap that alerts them to him to being an honest and upstanding member of the community.

An awkward silence has him scratching the back of his neck while he tries to come up with a way to put this. There's a dead wifey in the back isn't quite what he's after.

But Blythe beats him to it. 'Typically you've arrived too late. But what amazes me is that you officers have managed to find your way here, just as we were thinking of calling you. Are the police trained in the art of precognition these days?'

'*Chortle, chortle.* That's really funny, Blythey. Officers,' he gives Blythe what he hopes is a stern scowl then clears his throat, 'what my wife's trying to tell you is that it appears that Maureen Park, the owner of Tippermuir House, has died in her sleep. She's through there.' He points to the open door at the end of the corridor. 'Eve, that's her daughter, is sitting with her right now. It seems she's been sitting there since yesterday morning, poor thing.'

Blythe snorts and turns on him. 'Poor thing? Poor thing? Since when have you had any sympathy with the Parks?'

He's beginning to see why his marriage is slowly disintegrating. Shut up, shut up, shut up, Blythe. There's a lot he'd like to say to Blythe but, once again, now is not the time. He makes do with grunting at her and turns his attention back to the detective.

'We were just about to call the authorities,' he says. He whips the mobile from Blythe's hands and presents it as evidence. It's only then he realises they weren't going to call the police at all. It was the doctor they were attempting to call. 'What are you doing here?' he blurts out before he can stop himself.

Neither of the officers take much notice, especially since Blythe is already corralling them along the corridor. He hurries after.

Once they've all piled into Maureen Park's bedroom, the female officer, WPC Dunbar he seems to remember, goes to the opposite side of the bed from Eve and lifts Maureen's wrist.

'You won't find a pulse there,' Blythe informs her. 'It's my guess she's been gone a good while. And not a bit of sense out of that one, the daughter, not since we've been here.'

The detective turns to Graham. 'Do you and your wife reside here, in this house, with Maureen Park and her daughter?'

'Eh, no, Detective. We only got here about ten minutes ago, maybe a wee bit longer than that.'

'I have a key.' Blythe fishes the key from her cardigan pocket and holds it up in the air like an Olympic medal. 'For emergencies, you know. Maureen said I could use it in an emergency.'

PC Dunbar looks up from the body. 'Emergency?'

He watches, helpless, as Blythe plumes herself like a peacock. 'Isn't it enough for you to find a dead body, Constable? You need more?' she says, and he can tell she's almost on the verge of a squeal, that snobby, squeaky voice she uses when she wants to appear upper class. He needs to take control of the situation but all he can think about is Eve; Eve, sitting here in her own closed mind, still holding her mother's hand. He's been watching her eyes and they haven't moved. Not a single blink. Could he really, like he wants to, go to her and take her in his arms, steal her away from here? It feels impossible, no matter how much he longs to do it. In his head he is Tarzan, but the reality is that he's a lot less formidable and a little bit more of a chicken. He folds his arms tight to his chest, if only to make sure his heart is still pumping and it is, in fact, it's pumping in time with the pain that's throbbing in his temples. Just get over there man. There's no harm in comforting someone who's just lost their mother. Any decent man would. But then he thinks about all those romance movies Blythe watches on Netflix and how the cheating couple are found out just because someone sees how they react to each other when they're together and he remains rooted where he is.

He gets a fright when Detective Calmly fires a question at him that he hasn't quite heard. Something about his relationship with the Parks.

'We're neighbours,' Blythe fills in for him. 'We live in the lodge. You'll have passed it on the road to get here.' Then Blythe goes on to tell the story of the puppy and how they came to find the body, giving him time to recover and compose himself. The puppy's probably long gone by now. Poor Blythey.

When asked if they're close neighbours and if they spend a lot of time in each other's company, Graham finds his voice.

'No. No. Not close. No. As far as I know, Maureen Park doesn't leave the house and as for the daughter, lucky if I've said two words to her since they moved in here and that was nearly forty years ago, Detective Calmly.'

The detective's searching gaze lingers on him too long for his liking, creeping under his skin and making his arms itch. He doesn't risk sneaking a look at Eve, as that would definitely give the detective something to chew over. He doesn't even know if he can rely on Eve to keep her mouth shut. It's bad enough deceiving Blythe, but now they're going to have to lie to the police and Eve's going to be questioned. They'll have to question her, won't they? She was here when it happened, when Maureen died, even if she wasn't in the room when it happened, they'll still want to question her and she'll have to lie about everything and if they think she's lying, which they very possibly might, he doesn't know how good a liar she is, how well she'll hold up under questioning. It's been hard for her this past month, she's still not right in the head, and they have talked a few times recently about how life would be simpler without Maureen in it. Just talk. But it's not just talk now, is it? Maureen is dead and he's got himself trapped in this room with nowhere to hide his lies. Let's just hope the bloody woman died peacefully in her sleep, because if she didn't, if it wasn't natural causes, or even an accident, then what does that mean for Eve?

Chapter 8

Graham

Tippermuir House
12th October 2019

'It's not normal,' Blythe hisses at Graham.

'Come on,' he says and grabs her arm to pull her through to the kitchen where they've been told by Detective Calmly to wait.

'Maureen, God rest her soul, gone in the true sense of the word, but she's been gone for most of her life, truth be told. Absolutely.'

'Put the kettle on, Blythe.' She's best kept busy, take her mind off what she's just witnessed. But nothing will stop her talking.

'No longer the socialite she lusted after being and, who knows, she might once have been. After all, there's no denying she was a beauty, looking at the countless framed pictures and posters adorning the walls of every room in this house.'

It suits Blythe no end that Maureen's never shown an interest in being neighbourly, who needs all that? Neighbours coming around with nothing but gossip and jealousy and prying eyes. She's got a real evil streak in her where Maureen Park's concerned.

'Was it a stroke, a heart attack?' Blythe asks.

Eve isn't saying but, then again, she might not know.

'There's something broken inside the daughter.'

He sits at the kitchen table. Can't she just shut up about it?

'It's no surprise, thinking about it, she's had no life of her own.' Blythe says, placing a China teapot and a chipped cup in front of him. 'That's likely why she was holding on to that cold hand and not letting go. Eve can't, most probably, imagine what's ahead of her. She'll move house, won't she Graham? Won't she?'

Not that again. He tries to ignore the pleading in Blythe's voice, as she pours his tea and rattles on about what she calls 'future potential', her eyes glistening.

Tippermuir House was once a farmhouse, the lodge belonged to it until about one hundred years ago when the land was split in two and rented out to the farmworkers. Now there is no farm, the farmer having sold the land over to forestry and the house and lodge in two separate sales, made a fortune for himself. Blythe begged him to buy the lodge and he relented, back then he'd have given her anything she wanted. That was more than forty years ago. It just so happened that his accident coincided with Tippermuir House coming up for sale and she'd begged him once again. It had always been at the back of her mind to own Tippermuir House. The lodge wasn't good enough for her. She'd moan that the big house looked down on her, made her feel like she was poor or something, that the house was better than her or something stupid like that. He hadn't relented then and whatever Eve decides to do with Tippermuir House, the money from selling it will come in handy for them, but what if she didn't sell it? What if the pair of them moved in? That would hurry things along a bit, for sure. But then, they'd have Blythe at the bottom of the garden in the lodge. He'd have to tell her everything.

His thoughts, and Blythe's nattering, are interrupted by the entrance of DS Calmly and PC Dunbar.

'We were looking for our puppy,' Blythe says when they ask once again what brought them to visit this morning. She's shown no interest in finding the pup. Once they're through answering questions, he's going to find the wee thing. The hope has to be that no harm has come to it already.

'And besides,' Blythe chirps on. 'I was going to have words with Maureen Park. I don't like getting woken up in the middle of the night. Once I'm awake it's impossible for me to get back to sleep, and I bet you don't suffer from restless leg syndrome but I do, and you've no idea, drives a person crazy. I have to pace up and down on the kitchen linoleum for hours and then Graham wakes up and he's grumpy and, if it's not enough I have to put up with that, Graham goes back to sleep five minutes later and as soon as I try to settle back into bed, there's he, off with his snoring. And let me tell you, there's no sleeping when Graham gets going; ended up on the couch with a cup of tea and my book. Just as well I'm the resilient sort.'

'What was it that woke you up?'

'Well, you know, I just can't say I know exactly. I heard a noise, and that's not unusual, absolutely not, living so close to the forest. I listened, but no sooner had I woken, I heard it again. I ruled out it being an owl; pesky blighters. The sound was short, like a yell.'

'What time was that?'

'I don't pay much attention to what goes on at Tippermuir, Detective.'

'But you're certain there was a yelling sound? Did you look out of the window?'

'It was instinctual you see. I got out of bed and pulled back the curtain, but I didn't see anything. I didn't see anybody. Absolutely. Now it's high time Graham and I got back to looking for our newest member of the family. Goodness knows what's become of the wee soul.'

'Wait, I need you to do something for me.'

DS Calmly nudges his colleague who rises and exits the kitchen.

'I think you'll agree, Detective Calmly, that we two have given quite enough of our time already.'

Graham holds down Blythe's arm. 'Let's do what we can.'

The police officer returns with Eve in tow, she looks half alive and sits quietly beside Blythe at the table. He wants to reach across and touch her face, try to bring her round a bit more, but he daren't.

He shudders instead when DS Calmly places his hand on her shoulder. 'Eve?'

'I told you,' Blythe says, 'like she's in a trance or something.' Blythe nudges Eve with her elbow. 'Come on, Eve, it's time to let your mum's soul leave and go up to heaven.'

Eve speaks out, to no one in particular. 'What? Her soul can't go to heaven, it can't leave. She can't leave me.

'No. No, no, no,' Eve cries. She breaks free of the table and tries to pull Calmly with her. 'You have to save it. Please, you have to save Mother's soul. Come with me,' she says, running from the room.

'Well I'm backafronted,' Blythe says, not at all backafronted.

'Shall we?' Calmly says.

They find Eve in a small, dismal room next to the living room. Dunbar hasn't come with them, presumably she's tasked with guarding Maureen until someone comes to take her away. Then there will be trouble with Eve, Graham can see that, as if trouble is able to materialise in human form and it's standing in front of her now, a knowing finger pointing in Eve's direction.

Eve switches on the projector at the back of the room.

'I think we'll take our leave now and let you lot get on with it,' Graham mutters.

'Actually, Mrs Burrell, it would be helpful if you would stay. I think Eve could use a friend right now.'

Blythe's sudden willingness to be a friend in need makes him nervous. He tries to urge her to leave with him, but instead she parks herself in a low armchair, shuffling her bottom in an effort to sit up straight.

'This bit, see, this bit,' Eve says and points the remote control at the screen. The picture on the screen is frozen, capturing one sleekit eye belonging to a young woman.

'Mother had a saying,' Eve says. 'To live anywhere other than here meant that you were nowhere. That's what she always said.' Eve sitting on the sofa, her back turned to Blythe, she's talking to the detective standing at the window. 'Mother wouldn't ever want to leave here, she wouldn't ever not want to sit here with me and watch her musicals.'

'You have to watch this,' she says. 'This is how you're going to save Mother's soul.'

For the first time, Graham realises it's Maureen Park they're all watching on the screen. This must be a recording of one of Maureen's stage musicals.

'Isn't she beautiful?' Eve says.

Blythe does her best to be heard above the music.

'Shh, you have to watch and listen,' Eve growls.

'Eve, I don't have time for this rubbish, and do you think it's appropriate to be watching a musical when your mum...'

'Save her soul, that's what you said. Watch and you'll see. Lilian saves Bill's soul. Here, here, it's coming, listen to this song, Detective. The words will tell you what you have to do.'

'What's the song called, Eve?' the detective asks.

'It's called 'Surabaya Johnny', when Lilian sets out to save Bill's soul. That's what you have to do, DS Lark Calmly, you have to set out to save Mother's soul from going to heaven like Blythe says it will. Shh for now, widen your ears.'

Chapter 9
DS Calmly

Tippermuir House
12th October 2019

PC Dunbar has correctly evidenced the position of the pillow that lay by Maureen Park's head and also the very slight bruise on the left side of the dead woman's face. Like me, she was instantly alerted to the fact that something wasn't adding up here. It may well turn out to be that Maureen Park died of natural causes but, should that not be the case, I'm quite content to dismiss the others and sit here with the daughter and see if any crucial information materialises. It's not entirely unnatural for a daughter to sit with her dead mother, but for a whole day and night?

It's interesting, this notion that's filled Eve Park's head, of saving her mother's soul. There's something about the way she's transfixed, watching the projector screen. The curious thing is that the song Maureen Park is singing on screen – 'Surabaya Johnny' – doesn't appear to have anything to do with saving souls. Quite the opposite, if the lyrics are anything to go by. Does Eve think this is love?

I remain seated and quiet for a time. I don't want to be the one to tell Eve Park her mother isn't coming back, soul or no soul. Delivering that final news is normally something I can easily shrug off, but a mother and daughter? In such incidences, I prefer to leave it to someone else, usually my partner. Paula may think she's ready for that, but I have my doubts.

The worst was having to deliver the news to my own mum. If it had been the other way around and I'd had to tell Jenny that her mum was dead, our mum, that may have been easier. As it is, I make the decision these days, usually, not to invest myself in the delivery of that final blow to strangers.

'Do you have a mother, Detective Calmly?' Eve asks me out of the blue. She's staring at me intently. The musical has moved along without me noticing and she, at least for this moment, has turned her attention to me, I hadn't noticed that either. Was there something in my face that gave me away?

'I do.' I say this with false confidence.

'And yet you have a job. Does someone else look after your mother, Detective?'

'Do you want to talk, Eve? Should we turn the music off?' I go to reach for the projector, but she shakes her head furiously.

'Oh no. I wouldn't know what to talk about.'

I sit, I must say, somewhat uncomfortably, and once again wonder why I'm hesitant to leave. Something about the line of Eve's jaw. Or is it the way she keeps swiping at her fringe like that? It's odd that I was thinking about Jenny just now but, there it is, in fact, a kind of resemblance. Not anything anyone else would notice, she doesn't remind me of Jenny in any photographic sense. It's the tiny impulses, perhaps even Eve's quite obvious naivety too.

'I have a sister,' I find myself telling Eve.

'And she looks after your mother. That's nice,' Eve says.

I nod. I don't have the heart to draw her attention to another death.

She stands suddenly and switches the projector off. 'I don't believe souls can be found,' she says, her voice much firmer and self-assured than before. 'I made that up.'

Now we're getting somewhere. I had an inkling there wasn't any craziness to worry about with Eve.

'It's not Mother's soul I want you to discover, Detective Calmly,' she says. Eve points resolutely to the painting of Maureen Park that dominates the wall above the fireplace. 'It's her damned lies.'

Chapter 10
DS Calmly

Tippermuir House
12th October 2019

Until now, I've been able to close my eyes, take a deep breath, and the unwanted thoughts have gone away. But since my hour or two sitting with Eve this morning and watching her overexcited ways, her simple demeanour, I've not been able to think straight. Thoughts of Jenny keep getting in my way. I want to be amused by the notion that a glance or the tone of a voice is all it takes to blacken one's mood with floods of memories. But I've spent a great deal of energy believing I was over all that occurred around Jenny's death. A flick of Eve Park's eyelid and here I am, once again, glancing at my hands and haunted by my sister. This will not do. This will not do at all. Something isn't sitting right with me, the vague connection with Tippermuir House scrawled on the betting slip that may amount to nothing. Nevertheless, this case or these two cases deserve better from me. I know Paula thinks this thing with the mother is pretty damn obvious, with Eve centre stage as prime suspect, but I'm not convinced. The forensic investigation carried out on Maureen Park's bedroom revealed nothing of interest. If the cases are connected, Eve doesn't drive, so there's something amiss there. That said, rarely is anything what it seems.

I am, once again, at Tippermuir House. The evening air is damp and the silence is unnerving. Yes, nothing is what it seems. Tippermuir House is rather a grand name for this dilapidated stone monstrosity. I'm having to trudge through weeds and overgrown brush just to get to the front door. That looks like a tree growing through the roof. And the silence… well it's hardly that. Surrounded by woodland, I sense more isolation than silence. The way the moon and trees cast eerie shadows that follow my tracks. There's no one here, just the night-time song of the birds and the whistle of the wind. But since sitting with Eve this morning, I've not been able to shake off that feeling that I'm being taken to task. Standing a few feet away, the gritty dust from the stone walls somehow finds a way to sneak into my throat.

I rap on the front door.

Eve's face is both sleepy and curious, and inexplicably familiar. I'm beginning to wonder if I'll ever outrun Jenny. She welcomes me in without uttering a word, and we sit opposite each other at the kitchen table.

In my clearest investigative voice, I begin to tell her why I've come. I'm not altogether sure myself, but I have to say something so I settle for reaffirming her belief that Bruce Lawrence, the victim of the hit-and-run, has no connection to her.

'I know four people, Detective Calmly,' she says. She counts them off on her fingers. 'The doctor that never comes, her name is Dr Wood. She doesn't come any more because she knows there was nothing wrong with Mother. Mother never needed her and Mother doesn't like it when people suspect what she's really like.'

Eve holds up a second finger. 'Graham Burrell from next door.'

A third finger. 'Blythe Burrell from next door.'

She forgets about her fingers and wraps her arms around herself and lowers her head. 'Then there was Mother. So I suppose, Detective, you can say I only know three people.'

She lifts her head and her shimmery, wide eyes fix on me. 'I know you,' she says. She grins widely at me and that smile, the way it snags the corner or her mouth, a true and genuine smile; it's a Jenny smile and it tugs at my soul.

'That's right, Eve. Now you know me. And I've come tonight to help you.' I hadn't expected to say anything of the sort. I'm not here to help her, help her with what? There's a question over whether she murdered the mother, we won't know for sure until the post-mortem, but I thought I'd come to get a jump on that, and perhaps, just perhaps, to find something in her defence. Yes, now that, that is possibly something I may be able to help with. I'd like a chance to do that. If the post-mortem confirms Maureen Park's death was suspicious, what chance will Eve have without proof of mitigating circumstance? If indeed, there are any. With any luck, I'll also be able to rule out any connection with Bruce Lawrence. That betting slip could've belonged to someone else, or someone else wrote on it. There could be a simple rationalisation that has nothing to do with Eve and what's happened here.

'Oh I don't need any help, Detective Calmly,' Eve says. 'I've sorted everything by myself.'

Has she, indeed? That sounds rather ominous, although if the bright and breezy glint in her eyes is anything to go by, I don't believe her 'sorting' has any link to the death of her mother.

'I thought we, together, might have a look around the house,' I say, candidly. If she gives me permission to search, I might find evidence that will lead to an unexpected outcome, one that doesn't have Eve Park arrested for at least one murder. I struggle to believe she had a hand in anything untoward.

'Yes,' she says, and leaps eagerly from her chair. 'Let's find Mother's money. I need that money very much.'

Money? The first I've heard about this. 'What money?'

'Mother's little envelopes. She hides them away and I don't know where she hides them. Come on, let's look in her bedroom first.' Eve darts out of the kitchen.

Same height, same build, different hair colouring. Same interminable torrent of energy. Eve reminds me so much of my sister. There is a subtle difference that I clearly can't ignore and that is Eve's underdeveloped self-regard and pure naivety compared to Jenny's rather more self-absorbed, egotistical view of her own importance in the world. Jenny's' soul consisted of nature's twisted roots, complex and sophisticated. I follow Eve.

There are dresses strewn all over the bed, shoes scattered here and there on the floor, bags piled up on the green velvet chaise lounge. I make some comment about Eve already having searched in here, but she shakes her head.

'No. No. I've been trying on all Mother's clothes. I didn't think to search for the envelopes until right now. Where should we start?'

She's standing at the bottom of the king-size bed, both hands rubbing each side of her head. She gets on her knees with me and we pull out three suitcases, but they all turn out to be empty. Eve searches the dressing table drawers, and I take the occasional chair, that's sitting by the window, and position it in front of the wardrobe, sweep my hand across the top and come up with nothing.

'They're not here,' Eve says.

No.

Rational people tend to keep important documents together. I don't for one minute think that Maureen Park was anything close to rational.

'Eve, didn't you ask your mother for your birth certificate? Did she say where it was?'

Eve sinks onto the bed. 'I don't have a birth certificate. Mother lied to me. Ask Graham, he has a copy of my DNA letter that is proof. I'm not who I thought I was. I'm not Eve Park.'

Eve goes on to explain about her plans to run off to France with Graham but, without a birth certificate, she couldn't apply for a passport.

All the while she's talking, it strikes me that I've overlooked an important piece of evidence. If Maureen Park wasn't Eve's mum, who was? For her whole life, Eve has thought that the Park woman was her mother. What about her father? Is it the truth that the fellow Eve pointed out to me, the chap in that musical she had me watching, that he's the father? It shouldn't be too difficult to find out who he is. I'll have Paula dig a bit deeper into Eve's background.

'I'll need that DNA certificate,' I say to Eve.

'Graham has it. Oh, but don't ask him for it in front of Blythe. She doesn't know anything.'

Eve has already pulled everything out of the wardrobe, so we go to begin searching in the drawing room. The room is suffocating, cramped with all the varieties of Maureen Park memorabilia. Eve begins searching the bureau but some inkling takes me to the painting above the mantlepiece. It's heavy and clunky, but I manage to lift it and I position it on the settee.

I sense Eve watching me. 'Mother wouldn't like you touching that,' she says.

I imagine the dead woman watching me; another angry spirit seeking vengeance. I sense Maureen Park will be shaking her fist at me. I feel the wall with the flat of my palm. Eve asks me what I'm doing, an unmistakable hopeful tone to her voice that I'm loathe to disappoint.

Finding no secret hiding place, as I'd hoped, there's not really much I can say, so I shrug, shake my head and give her my best smile of encouragement.

'What now?' Eve asks.

'I don't rightly know. Yet.'

'We can keep looking,' she says and starts lifting things up around the fireplace, the log basket, the poker, the photos of Maureen Park along the mantlepiece. It's only then that it dawns on me, there are no photos of Eve in this room, or anywhere in the house I suppose.

'What's that?' I ask.

She won't know; she doesn't seem to know much of anything. The painting is laying with the face up against the back of the settee, the back of the frame facing me. Attached to the back is a small envelope.

'That's one of Mother's little envelopes,' Eve says and swipes it, ripping it from its tape. She opens the envelope and takes out a metal hook that fits in the palm of her hand. 'I wonder,' she says.

'What?'

'What it's for.'

I was wondering the same thing. Nobody hides a simple hook unless its use is for something valuable, or to hide a secret. But where?

I turn to ask Eve, she may know more than she realises, or than she's letting on? She's lifting an ashtray, and the doily underneath, from a table by her mother's chair. Except, it's not a table, as such.

'It's Mother's box,' Eve tells me.

Huh. Mother's box. Couldn't she have said something about a box before now?

'What box, Eve?'

'Mother is very protective of her box, Detective Calmly. I don't think you should move it.'

To hell with 'Mother'. Where would Mother keep her little envelopes of money? Right under her nose where she can keep an eye on them.

The keyhole isn't obvious, but I haul the box out of its place by the chair and into the middle of the room, feel around it until my fingers come across a tiny hole.

'Give me that,' I instruct Eve, and point to the hook she'd tossed on the mantlepiece.

Nothing simpler, the hook fits snugly and, with a deft turn, the lid springs open. Hallelujah.

It makes me wonder if Eve knew all along about what's in this box. She looks innocent enough, but nothing is ever what it seems.

'There you go,' Eve says. Happy that she's solved the problem, she goes back to her search. She needn't bother. I put my hand in the box and lift out a bundle of envelopes. I sneak a quick search inside. There's nothing else in there but more envelopes, dozens of them by all accounts. I perch on the edge of the settee, place the bundle on the table in front of me and lift the top envelope from the pile. Eve kneels at my feet, seemingly satisfied that we've found what we're looking for.

She looks at the envelopes curiously, says, 'Everything will be fine now.'

'Do that again.'

'Do what?' she asks me.

'That. The thing you do with your hair.'

'This?' she says. She tucks one side of her hair behind her ear.

'It was more than that,' I say.

She licks her fingers and pulls on her fringe.

Yes. That.

Mum used to say it was a nervous habit of Jenny's, but I, for the life of me, could never see an ounce of nervousness in Jenny, her whole life. By the time Jenny reached her teenage years, I'd already convinced myself that Mum didn't know her daughter half as well as she imagined she did.

I open the envelope in my hand and pull out a bunch of money.

'How much?' Eve asks.

I take a minute to count the notes. 'One thousand pounds. Where does this money come from?'

'I don't know,' Eve tells me. I wonder what historical data Paula has unearthed surrounding the Parks and Tippermuir House.

'There must be other documents your mum kept, Eve. We're just not finding them.' Something that points to where this money comes from. There's nothing in any of these envelopes other than the banknotes.

'I have a document from the solicitor, would that help?'

'Let me see it.'

Half an hour later, Eve insists on making me a cup of tea. I leave her to it and sit at the kitchen table studying, for the umpteenth time, the Tippermuir House title deeds that show ownership belongs to a Mr Gilroy Flynn. I'll need to run a proper check on this Gilroy Flynn, but a quick google search on my phone throws up something interesting. Flynn has connections with the theatre. Most recently productions in London and Edinburgh, and there's one or two articles announcing a new production taking place in Glasgow. I can't say I think this is anything to do with what's happened to Maureen Park, but there must be at least thirty thousand pounds in those envelopes from an unknown sender. If Flynn owns this house, it seems to me to be more than a tenuous link that will need investigating should the death of the Park woman turn out to be a result of anything other than natural causes.

Chapter 11
DS Calmly

Perth
13th October

I'm a Skye man. I say that as if it's some kind of birthright and perhaps it's right to think that way in a genealogical sense, but truthfully? I've spent most of my latter years here in Perth and here feels more like home than there. I'm sitting in my car thinking about Eve and feeling right now as if I don't know everything.

Something I like to do, if I remember, is to dig deep for the little surprises each day can bring. It's a habit I've been cultivating since turning fifty, because I've found that, as I get older, there's less and less that surprises me.

Everything about Tippermuir House and its recently bereaved occupant surprises me. If only I knew why.

I'm meeting Dunbar at Maureen Park's post-mortem. Paula has taken an instant dislike to the daughter, Eve. Sometimes it happens; PC Dunbar doesn't like to mess about. That's what I like about her, she's a doer, likes to get cracking, even if she does lack subtlety. That's okay; subtlety is not part of the job description. But I think, in this case, we're not going to get too far without employing a measure of sensitivity.

Starting the engine, I make my way towards Jeanfield Road and the mortuary.

***

Around the side of the mortuary, Dunbar is slouched against the wall, oblivious to the rain dripping down her neck. She's puffing furiously at an electronic cigarette. I nudge her elbow and we go inside.

The mortuary is a funny place; you can be in here for a few minutes and then emerge feeling as if you've lost a day or two. We make our way through the labyrinth of corridors and I try to desist from the urge to speak that always comes over me when I'm here. When you speak you end up coming off as if you're shouting, and anyway, Dunbar isn't one for jibber-jabber.

If you've never been in a morgue before, forget about what you're imagining. It's not about the fluorescent lights, the steel furniture or the retractable saw, keep that for your nightmares, it's about the life that has just come to an abrupt end. It's about the body that you can either choose to see in your mind or not see; it doesn't matter. It's about the manner in which that body exited life, and about what happens next, about the person who no longer exists in the flesh.

The person lying under the sheet in front of us now is Maureen Park. Maureen Park is interesting to me. By all accounts, this lady was disturbed perhaps, but in good health. Why is she dead? We don't know the answer to that, but I am hoping we are about to find out.

'You've missed the main event, I'm afraid, DS Calmly,' Mike Scott tells me.

'That's fine by me,' Dunbar says, following in behind me and letting the door swing behind her. The safety bar is broken, so it crashes shut causing a draughty echo and a shiver in my shoulder blades.

'Aye, Paula, but just since it's you, I'm going to make your day even brighter.'

Dunbar doesn't like dead bodies. Well, this is not strictly true, she has nothing against a dead body unless she has to stand for any length of time and breathe in the stench. I didn't mention the stench earlier because I didn't want any distractions and, as I say, if you've never been in a mortuary before…

I watch the pair of them, Dunbar and Mike; he with his hand on her elbow, she with a glint in her eye. You couldn't make this stuff up.

'Just get on with it, will you. Tell me it wasn't suicide, for Christ's sake.'

'Aye, wisnae suicide, you're right enough,' he says, patting Maureen Park's midriff. He removes his gloves and tosses them in the bin and stands at the feet of the body with his hands on his hips, as if he's waiting for me to say something.

Why in the world all pathologists irritate me, I have no idea. I've never met an unkind or bullish one. Contrary to what others may choose to think, I am not the kind of man to go in for conflict when it's unnecessary. For this reason, I wait patiently for Mike to go on, when what I really would like to do is poke his inflated ego with his own scalpel.

'So, what was it then?' Dunbar pipes up. She is born of little or no patience. A blessing, in this case, but it is not always so, I can assure you.

'Asphyxiation.' Scott tells us. 'Not in the standard manner, as one might expect. The method of extinction here was very close to that which my esteemed colleagues of centuries past would keenly have referred to as burking. A term generally used to indicate suffocation carried out in such a way so as to leave no or few traceable marks of violence on the body.'

Scott nods curtly toward the body. 'In this case, I suspect your murderer climbed onto the chest and covered the mouth with their hand. What the intentions were for the body are not for me to surmise.

'She actually sat on her mother's chest and... what? Held a hand to her face?'

'You're jumping ahead of yourself, Dunbar,' I say and wait for that look. There it is, her bitter look, I call it. She doesn't like that, doesn't like to think she's bitter but she is, although, I'm not certain I know why. She likes Eve as a suspect in her own mother's murder. Is it possible? Yes. Is it the only possible? I don't think so.

Scott says, 'There's post-mortem hypostasis on the back of the body suggesting a heavy weight on the chest. There are marks on her jawline that indicate a hand. I found copious secretions at mouth angles and nostrils, petechial haemorrhages on the sclera of the eyeballs, acral cyanosis, congested internal organs and the dilated right side of the head. I've sent the pictures through. No way of identifying prints, it's my guess a glove was used.'

'The weight of a person,' I ask, 'what would that have to be?'

'Och, you doubt me, man? Look, see for yourself.' He pulls back the sheeting. 'A 2 by 2 cm reddish abrasion on the outer aspect of her lower lip and a reddish abrasion of 2 by 2 cm below her chin.

The inner surface of both lips were contused. Internally, 2-6 left side ribs were fractured, with haematoma into surrounding intercostal muscles. All organs were congested. Right side heart was dilated and blood filled. Cause of death, combined smothering and traumatic asphyxia. That good enough for you?'

'How heavy is what I'm asking?'

'She wasn't young and robust, as well you are aware. Average weight would do it. No toxics in her system.'

'So about 60-62 kg?' Dunbar pipes up.

Scott puts his coat on. 'Wouldn't need to have been any heavier.'

'It's my guess that's about what Eve weighs,' Dunbar says, turning to me, her bitter eyes now a perky shade of smug.

'Right, you two need to get lost. I promised the dog a jaunt up Kinnoull, and if I don't go before we lose daylight he'll refuse to get out of the car and spend the rest of the night in a huff. Stupid mutt is scared of the dark.'

'Wait a minute.' I lean against the door so Mike has no alternative but to listen. 'Anything more you can tell me about the hit-and-run?'

'I've told you everything I know. You might want to speak to wee Mary at the lab. She has some forensics for you, so I was hearing.'

'And?'

'It's not really my job to…'

I keep my hand firmly on the door handle.

'They've collected fragments of paint from the suit of the old geezer that may materialise as a lead.'

***

Outside, the sun is making an appearance and you'd hardly know it had been raining, the pavement all but dry. I unlock the car for Dunbar to get in but I'm reluctant, it's a nice feeling to have the sun's rays on the back of my neck. It's been one day since we happened across the body of Maureen Park. Suspicion was there, lurking somewhere at the back of my mind but, until now, I'd had no good reason to treat the Park case as a murder enquiry.

I get in the car, pushing through a sudden weariness in my joints. I drive back to the station, for want of something better to do until I can declutter this mess. Dunbar rumbles on, giving me her full account of method and theory and setting her sword at the feet of Eve Park.

In all honesty, I'm not listening. My entire thought process is already overwhelmed by just one problem.

Is this two separate murder enquiries? Or one enquiry with two murders?

Either way, I have already fallen off the cart and the horses are galloping off into the distance, smothering us under the dust from their hooves.

Chapter 12

Eve

Tippermuir House
14th October

It's the morning after the second day Mother died. I don't know if I can get used to every day being yesterday. But someone, or something, is screaming inside my head that there are to be no more tomorrows. That today will soon be yesterday and that's all there is.

I'm sitting at Blythe's kitchen table, just inches from a blade of sunlight that's bouncing off the Formica and ricocheting between the silver teapot and silver sugar bowl. Blythe is standing at the sink watching me with her suspicious eyes. PC Dunbar is sitting to my left, her pencil poised to take notes. To my right sits Detective Calmly.

I've had to go over everything all over again. It's exhausting.

'Eve, are you sure you didn't move any of your mother's pillows?'

I nod my head.

'You didn't try to make her more comfortable?'

'She was dead,' I say clearly. 'I don't think you can make the dead more comfortable.'

The police woman looks past me at Detective Calmly. Now she's writing something in her notebook.

'What are you writing?' I ask. I wouldn't like it if she was writing something about me, using words to describe me. She can't use the word 'implausingly', because that word belongs to me, but does she have 'wolf' in there, in her notebook?

She doesn't answer me. Instead she asks, 'If you knew your mother was dead, why did you sit with her for twenty-four hours?'

She didn't answer me, so I'm not going to answer her question.

'Why didn't you call the emergency services?'

I don't answer. Detective Calmly touches my elbow.

'Eve, did anyone else come to the house while you were sitting with your mother?'

'Graham and Blythe came. They let themselves in with a key. Blythe's already told me about the key and where she found it. Another of Mother's lies to me.'

The police woman is writing down everything I say. That must mean that what I'm saying is important. It's nice to feel important. And it's strange, Blythe isn't saying anything. That means I'm more important than Blythe. This must be why Graham has chosen me as his family and not Blythe. He's said many times that we are precious. He's talking about me and the little boy we made. The first time he said we were precious was that night our baby was born; he said it just before he called his sister Lynn to come and help us. He'd said he would treasure us forever. I've heard that people searching for treasure never find it. Graham is lucky.

Detective Calmly is flattening out a piece of paper on the table with the side of his hand. He pushes the paper in front of me and asks me to read it.

The aroma of sausages and bacon from breakfast is making my stomach churn, and I don't know how many times Blythe has harped on about how I should eat something but what honest person can swallow something whole when all their thoughts are consumed by their dead mother?

Last night, I was forced to sleep in Blythe's spare room. Imagine. I was scared to close my eyes. What if Blythe came at me with a hatchet while I was sleeping, what if she can smell a wolf or… or what if the soft, tender flesh of a child born on her mattress incensed her, or what if Mother appeared at the bottom of the bed wielding her walking stick? I have to sleep here tonight too, because they won't let me back home until everywhere has been searched. They won't find Mother's box because Detective Calmly let me bring it with me. I like Detective Calmly.

I kept wondering if Graham would poke his head in, but he didn't, and I was mostly relieved. Since yesterday, if there's a spare second I'm alone, Graham is right beside me, telling me that now, at last, I am free.

I don't know what he means by 'free'. Free from what? That's it exactly. You have to mean something to somebody in a relatable way in order to be free of them. And I have no idea if I am related to another human somebody. I have no idea. I call her Mother because, for my whole life, I thought that's what she was, my mother. But, if she was ever a mother at all, she wasn't my mother.

Early this morning, on my way to the toilet, I bumped into Graham on the landing, and he did that whole trying to comfort me thing but it was like being in a silent movie. He kept telling me to shush, even though I wasn't saying a single thing. Except I did try to ask him if everything was okay at his sister's house, but all Graham kept whispering was, say nothing to Blythe, to anyone, and this is all for the best, and keep focussed on the bigger picture, Evie. And he squeezed my hand. I was about to tell him that I've already told Detective Calmly about us and about the baby, but I stop myself in time. Instead, I ask him if a child doesn't know its mother, can he miss her, but he'd already turned away to disappear into his bedroom and be with Blythe.

This is why this is all so wrong. How can I ever be a mother if I have no idea who my own mother is?

There is blue-and-white tape surrounding Tippermuir House. I've not been allowed inside since yesterday afternoon. All the people came, and it reminded me of the day Mother died, when we'd all left, one by one. Mother was the last to leave. Two stalky, grave-looking men with grey suits had come and put Mother in a black bag with a zip, carrying her past me as if she were a piece of furniture being repossessed. It seemed to me that I hadn't thought much of anything until that point. As Mother was floating out of the front door, nobody asked if I wanted to say anything, like goodbye or please don't go.

There were other people I hadn't noticed had come into the house until I watched them leave. It didn't matter who they were, in their white, hooded suits and masks. They were poking around in Mother's bedroom, dusting things, lifting things up and putting them in clear plastic bags.

Yesterday, I'd been forced to watch the comings and goings from outside, from behind the blue-and-white tape, as if it was someone else's life being picked apart.

Sometimes I don't trust what's in my head because quite often it doesn't make sense. And, today, sitting here trying to answer the questions for the detective, there's only one thought inside my head and that's: Who Am I? But the thing is, DS Calmly is a nice man and I don't want to let him down or show myself up, so I try to look at what's on the crumpled piece of paper that he's put on the table in front of me.

'Tell me about Bruce Lawrence,' Detective Calmly asks.

He wants me to tell him about a man I don't know. He's gazing at me with quiet eyes. His face is round and in two parts, the top half bald and the bottom taken up mostly with a beard of interesting wolflike greys. Yesterday, it was as if we were friends, but today he's acting as if he's just met me and I'm just someone that knows things he wants to know, only, I don't know anything.

I've been sitting here trying to decipher what's on this piece of paper that's been in front of me for the past ten minutes. It's words and boxes and Tippermuir House is written squint on the bottom in red ink.

I take a sip of water and clear my throat. 'I don't know anyone called Bruce Lawrence,' I say, truthfully.

Detective Calmly's face is close enough for me to count his teeth. I can see tiny skin particles forming at the edge of his beard, flakes of skin on the lapel of his navy blue suit.

'Are you sure you're not familiar with that name?' he asks me.

'Well, yes. Of course.'

'Did your mother know the name?' PC Dunbar snaps.

Mother would've disliked PC Dunbar, with her thick layer of wrinkled make-up and bushy eyebrows. Mother was partial to quiet voices that lift your spirits like a song.

I shake my head suitably so that they understand I mean no. Saying no doesn't feel appropriate, but what else can I say?

It strikes me as odd to be asked questions I don't know the answer to. 'That man's name isn't on this piece of paper,' I say for want of nothing better to say.

'Bruce Lawrence,' DS Calmly says, and he tells me that this man has just died in a road accident.

I nod and realise, for the first time, that even a dead man has a name.

'There's been a hit-and-run, Eve. Whereby, in the early hours of the 11th of October, a man, identified as Bruce Lawrence, was hit by a vehicle travelling at speed. I'm afraid his injuries were fatal. We found this in the pocket of his shirt. Naturally, as you can see for yourself,' he points to the name on the bottom of the note, 'Tippermuir House is a curious finding that links Mr Lawrence to you and your mother, and it's our job to investigate that curiosity so we can rule out any suspicious activity linking to the deceased that may, or may not, have occurred in the hours and days leading up to his unfortunate death.'

'That was three days ago, Detective.'

'Yes,' the police woman says, 'the day your mother was murdered.'

I glimpse PC Dunbar from the corner of my eye, watching me with her piggy eyes, her mouth is open and her tongue is caressing the roof of her mouth. She makes me squirm. She makes me think she isn't going to believe a single word I say. I turn my body ever so slightly away from her so I can't see her face even from my peripheral vision. That's better.

Detective Calmly has the kind of face that makes it hard not to smile at him. I try and remember what it was he said.

'Mother didn't have friends,' I say. 'So she couldn't have known this man.'

'He didn't come to Tippermuir House?' the detective asks me.

'Nobody comes.'

'He didn't phone, or write a letter?'

'We don't get letters.' This is better. These are questions I know the answer to.

Blythe uncrosses her arms and plants her hands on her hips. 'You must have family somewhere, Eve,' she says.

She's making it sound as if I'm lying, and I wish it was Graham here and not her. Graham would be able to tell them. I can't say it. I can't say it. I've spent my whole life with Mother-Not-Mother. I don't know the words to say out loud that I am an orphan, a mother and a wolf. I don't want to look at any of them, so I shrug and stare at my hands in my lap.

It's not like I'm trying to hide anything, but I've suddenly remembered the phone call. Is it too late to say now? Should I tell

Detective Calmly anyway? Maybe it won't make any difference? I don't want to complicate things. I don't know what to do now they've said that word; murdered.

I gaze up at Detective Calmly, but he's not looking at me, he's looking instead at the piece of paper on the table. He's not asking me questions. There isn't anything else he can ask me I suppose. He'll go away now and I haven't mentioned the phone call and, I don't know, but it could be important. I might have the only clue there is that will help him find out what he needs to do his job. Although, it wouldn't have been whomever Mother was speaking to on the phone because she didn't know Mr Lawrence, not really. Mother wouldn't want me talking about her business.

'Eve,' Detective Calmly says. He has a soft voice that Mother would have approved of. 'Can you think of any reason why Tippermuir House is written on this betting slip?'

I shake my head. 'I don't know anything about this,' I say, and I push the piece of paper away to where Detective Calmly's elbow is resting on the table. 'But I remember that Mother was talking to someone on the phone the night she died.'

DS Calmly looks at me, as if I'm a truly interesting person, with interesting things to talk about. 'Who do you think your mum was talking to on the phone, Eve?'

'Could you hear any of what she said?'

No is the answer, but if only there was something I could say instead. 'She promised to find my birth certificate. That was a lie, of course.'

'Eve, do you think the phone call had anything to do with the confrontation you had with your mum earlier that night? About your birth certificate?'

I've already told DS Calmly about the DNA test and Mother's flippant reaction to my saying I was leaving her. He can't expect me to tell him everything.

'Why would Mother being on the phone have anything to do with that?'

'Did you hear the phone ring? Could your mum have called this person?'

'It's true, I didn't hear the phone ring. I just heard Mother talking.

She could have made the call, it's possible, except, Mother doesn't have anyone to call.'

'Eve, I'm sorry, but she must have had someone to call. Otherwise she wouldn't have made the call.'

Blythe pats my shoulder. 'Don't worry, Eve. I will look after you. Maybe there's someone I could drive you to, a relative or someone you want to stay with for a few days. Is there a relative? Someone to take care of you?'

DS Calmly sits back, crosses his arms and studies Blythe Burrell. I decide to do the same, and shuffle my chair a touch to the left so I can get less of a side view of Blythe. I've never had a reason to think about Blythe. It's not as if Blythe has ever offered to help with anything before. Except that time Mother kept making me get Blythe to call the doctor. But after that stopped, I almost forgot about Blythe. She's a stranger, just like everyone else. It's fascinating to spend time with strangers, and this idea has just opened itself up to me and I wonder at what point a person ceases to become a stranger. And when that happens, what becomes of them?

'Mrs Burrell,' PC Dunbar signals for Blythe to pull up a seat at the table, 'did you hear a car on the night in question?'

'Well, no,' Blythe says. 'That night I couldn't sleep, I work night shifts and it was my night off and often I find it difficult to switch off, you know. I took to the sofa with a cup of tea and my book. Our lounge faces onto the lane, and I would have heard if a car had come along the lane. Absolutely.'

'Mrs Burrell,' I say, exactly the way PC Dunbar would say it. I'm starting to like PC Dunbar, she has quick eyes. I just caught those eyes darting between all three of us and when they landed for that split second on me, I instantly knew myself to be inside the police woman's thoughts and I wonder, if I was to whisper something in her ear, what that something would be.

'Mrs Burrell,' I repeat, this time I let a smile tickle the side of my cheek, the same way as happens with PC Dunbar.

I bang both my hands on the table. 'Yesterday morning,' I say, and surprise myself when I actually do sound a lot like PC Dunbar. 'When you found Mother dead, and me sitting by her side, you let yourself in with a key. Might I suggest you also let yourself in the night before, killed Mother then drove to Dunkeld with the sole purpose of running over an old man who none of us have ever met?'

This is so much fun. I sounded a lot like PC Dunbar then. Blythe tries to smile around the table but, when her gaze falls on me, I get a fierce glare, as if I'm out of my mind. But the face on Blythe! It resembles mashed potato, and if she tries any harder to smile her face may fall off in little splodges to splatter onto the table.

'Nobody is accusing anyone of anything,' DS Calmly says. He stands and says he has everything he needs for now. He talks about investigating every eventuality and ruling things out and it all sounds deliciously exciting suddenly.

I'm left to myself for the rest of the day. I go to bed early so I can think about things. I wish I didn't have to feel sad for the old man who died. It's hard to make yourself feel sad for two people at exactly the same time. I wonder if he'd known he was going to be run over and killed that night, what would he have done differently with his day?

DS Calmly said the dead man had no wife or children or any family that they have found, so far, that the man was tipsy and it may well have been an accident, but DS Calmly hadn't said this with any conviction and straight after he told me he was sorry about Mother, which he had said with real sorrow in his eyes. There's to be an investigation about how Mother died.

Newness.

The word sounds just as nice out loud. A word like that, an attractive word, something so appealing about it, but for the moment that something sits vaguely inside my skull.

Chapter 13
DS Calmly

Dunkeld
14th October

What I need now is evidence that there is a crime of intent here.
Before I return to Bruce Lawrence's cottage, I want to have a chat
with the two men who spoke to him last.

I've come alone. Mostly because I wanted a relaxed, informal
chinwag, the kind that's likely to get me what I want – the why and
the who of Bruce Lawrence's demise – and partly because Paula's
kid has been up to no good at school once again. I'm not going to be
responsible for getting in the way of that. It can't be easy raising a
kid alone.

The Old Bear Inn is what used to be referred to as a working
man's pub. Nowadays, you get bistro pubs or swanky boutique bars
that remind me of a canteen or a chain hotel dining room, crammed
with as many tables and chairs as can fit.

I walk through the door of the pub and there's not much room,
not many places where you can sit. Not many people either, although
it's early yet, fifteen after noon. There's a couple of tired-looking
men, leaning on the bar, their heads together, ignoring the stools
beside them.

The barman is at the other end of the bar, a newspaper spread out
before him. That's good. On his own, he may be more forthcoming
than the brief statement he'd provided on the morning of the hit-and-
run.

'You Grant?' I ask. I drag a stool and position myself with my
back to the rest of the bar.

'Aye, that's me,' he says, folding his paper. 'You'll be the police,
I expect. I've already given a statement. But I can get you a drink if

you're thirsty. Terrible business you're dealing with, I might add.'

He gives me the water I ask for, and I ask him how well he knew Bruce Lawrence.

'Like I said, I've already gone over what I know. I'd rather no think about it at all, never mind talk about it. I kinda feel responsible, ken.'

'How's that then?'

'Well, you'll ken that I was the one called the police. Bruce like. But if I'd had my wits about me, I'd have found it, found him, a damn sight sooner than I did. I didnae hear anything, like, before you ask.'

'You live upstairs, I understand.'

'That's right. Bruce was my last customer. I had to punt him out, like. Thought he was never going to leave. He was one of my best customers these past few months.'

'A heavy drinker, would you say?'

'Normally I would say that. But that night, he sat staring into his drink as if he was saving it for a rainy day, like. I think I'm right in what I said in my statement, two half Deuchars and two Grouse chasers. That was a bit light for Bruce, if I'm honest with you. He wasn't a bit unsteady on his feet when I sent him packing and locked up after him.'

'What did you do after you locked up?'

'Well, see, that's the thing. I'd normally hang around, do the glasses, cash up and the like, but my back was biting me something awful, so I just headed upstairs and went straight to my bed. My bedroom faces out back, not to the street. See, if I'd stayed and done what I was supposed to do, I might have heard the car and been able to go and help him. Do you think he'd still be alive if I had?'

The pathologist thinks it would have taken seconds rather than minutes for Bruce Lawrence to die. We now know, courtesy of the fatal collision investigation, that the acceleration marks on the road made by the vehicle that hit Lawrence make his death less likely to have occurred as an accident.

'I don't think it would have made any difference, no.'

'Aye, but still. It's no nice to think of the poor sod left out in the cold all night on the road. You should be speaking to Fisherman Bob. He's the gent that found Bruce and came belting on my door. That's what got me up. I'm no usually up so early, seeing as I don't get to bed till late.'

I look at the two men at the other end of the bar who still have their heads together. 'Is he here?'

'Nah. You won't get Bob until four. He's in every day, like.'

'Do you have an address for him?' This character, Fisherman Bob, had got Grant to call the emergency services then hopped it, so we've not been able to track down the one person that might've seen something.

'Nah.'

I don't believe him. Dunkeld is a wee place. Everyone knows everyone. This Bob is a local. I give him my quizzical raised eyebrow. He at least has the grace to blush. I'm still waiting to find out if this vanishing fisherman owns a car. I'm not ruling him out as a suspect. I don't like it when an individual related to a case does something out of the ordinary. Although people seem a lot less keen to speak to the authorities these days, and that bugs the hell out of me.

'You'll get him in here at four. You can get his address then. He's got nothing to hide, I promise you that. He was on his way to the fishing, that's all. He's out early most days, even in the worst of the weather.'

I know enough to know I'm wasting my time. Village landlords like to keep their reputation in check. I believe him when he tells me there's nothing to be suspicious about. But I'm not going to let him know I know this. I tut and sigh and do the usual posturing and that's enough to give me the upper hand.

'So, tell me about Bruce Lawrence.'

'Not much to tell, that's the truth. He moved in tae the village a few months back. That old farm cottage of his had sat empty for years. It's verging on being a ruin, and I don't think Bruce got around to doing much in the way of fixing it up, like. Not even sure he had the intention to do anything. He wasn't a talker, not like most of them that come in. He talked a lot that night, though. Mostly to himself, mind you, or his half pint.'

'What did he talk about, Grant?'

'Well, I did have this one conversation with him. You know, I was trying a bit of banter with him. He was looking a bit maudlin and all that. It's a bit of a responsibility to keep punters in a good mood. And it was a quiet night, Fridays aye are.'

'Tell me.'

'Right, well, he was talking about some girl. Now, I already knew he lived on his own, it was common knowledge, so his talking about this girl, kind of caught my interest, I suppose.'

'Did he give a name?'

'No. Not for the girl in question, but he did say, now wait, see if I can remember right. He said, even if it's too late, Pauline will be pleased with him. See, he told me he'd found his girl.'

'His girl?'

'That's it. Showed me a betting slip, but I didn't pay much attention. He said she had to be the one. Something about how he was going to bring her to justice. I tried to ask him about it, like, but he just kept on about finding her, about Pauline being pleased, that was his wife like, she's dead I think. He didn't say much else. Just kept saying that over and over. I got bored and left him to it in the end.'

'Nothing else? You don't remember anything other than that?'

'No. Well, aye in fact. And it's a damned shame.'

'What is?'

'The poor sod,' Grant says, shakes his head. 'He said to me, I've got reason to live now. That's what he said. Damned shame.'

There's no point in bothering the two men at the end of the bar. The door-to-door guys would've picked them up.

I leave the pub and make my way across the road towards Bruce Lawrence's cottage. The road, part of the A923, is now open, cars trundling past on their way to and from Blairgowrie or Rattray. To close the road for the day yesterday had been tough enough. It's a busy wee place, and the road was never built for the modern car.

The road may no longer be a crime scene, but the cottage has been taped up in order to be thorough. We don't yet know for certain what has occurred here. For all we know, whatever led to Bruce Lawrence's demise originated from this house. I show my card to the PC on guard and wait until he scribbles it on his clipboard. The outside of the cottage doesn't look promising. Weeds, ivy and an abundance of bracken attack the frontage. There are missing and broken slates on the roof, and one or two cracks in the two windows each side of the rotten door frame. When the PC is finished I nod, then duck under the tape.

'I've got reason to live now.' Not the words of a drunken man, it seems. Ironic as it sounds, it may be that the reason Lawrence had to live is the same reason that got him mown down. So, what reason could that be?

There is no hallway as such, just a bit of room to turn around in. Cold stone walls, same as the rest of the house, could use a lick of fresh paint. I go straight through the open door on the right; the only bedroom. I'm thinking if I did miss something when I was here yesterday, it's most likely going to be in here. Under the window is a single metal frame bed with a burst mattress and an old tartan car rug, a grey duffel coat thrown on top; the only concession to warmth. There is an unused coal fireplace matching the one in the other room, with a small electric fire placed in front. No books, no magazines, no TV. No bedside table with a photograph. I take my time, careful to scan every inch of the room. There are no drawers stuffed with clothes, no spare shoes kicking about. No mirror on the wall, no pictures hung. Bruce Lawrence died wearing the only wardrobe he had.

While I expected not to find anything, I can't help feeling like I'm on the wrong track. Turning to leave, hoping I will get lucky somewhere else in the house, I catch myself and stop to muse over thoughts that are rearranging themselves. Did anyone check the pockets of the duffel coat?

The first twenty-four/forty-eight hours of any major incident, known as the golden hours, are the ones where we have the best chance of gathering the best evidence to lead us to the perpetrator. It's not unheard of for things to be missed, especially when the first crime scene, the street outside, is threatened by factors such as keeping the road closed and protecting the scene from contamination and then, gathering as much evidence as we can before the rain drives everything away.

It's obvious, now, holding the duffel coat, that this isn't Lawrence's coat. It is at least two sizes too big for him and, in any case, it's clearly a woman's coat. He could've picked it up from the second-hand shop along the street, if he'd gone looking for a blanket and this was as good as it got. But something tells me that's not it. I check the pockets, find nothing. No name tag, not even a label.

I hate it when you think you're on to something and it comes to nowt. Bruce Lawrence might as well have not existed. I check the pockets again, just to make sure and to give my frustration something to work on. Both pockets have holes in them. Laying the coat flat on the bed, I feel my way along the bottom lining of the coat.

There's something flat and square and pliable. I rip open the pocket closest to what I'm sure is a photograph and pull it out. A Polaroid.

The photograph is of a young woman, in her early twenties, I suspect. Brown hair, blue eyes, one broken tooth. She is sitting in a hospital bed, looking pleased with herself, a newborn baby in her arms, wrapped in a hospital blanket. Might this be Bruce Lawrence's Pauline? Or she could be the person he seemingly found. Whoever she is she needs to be identified, then we will know for sure, one way or the other. And, with a bit of luck, that will lead us to the identity and whereabouts of this child. There is a date on the back of the photo, written in blue ink. March 1981.

Bruce Lawrence died for a reason, I am certain of it. This was no accident. Someone wanted him dead. Whoever you are, I'm coming for you.

***

The remainder of my search of the cottage yielded nothing. I'm sitting back at the end of the bar in the Old Bear Inn. It is 4.05 p.m. and I'm waiting for Fisherman Bob to make an appearance. He is late.

The door swings open. 'Lo and behold, it's you.'

'I've come to take you back to the station,' Paula tells me, squinting her mouth in an irritating, admonishing fashion. 'Bob Jack is being interviewed as we speak.'

'And who might that be?' I ask.

'Your fisherman. The guy who donated the foil-wrapped trout? Then later, the body?'

'Ha. Right. What?'

'I sent the bobbies out this morning to search the riverbanks.'

'Did you now.'

'Had an inclination that the reason we couldn't pin him down had something to do with illegal fishing.'

She's a clever one. I'm saying this to myself, and I'm not sure if I'm being sarcastic or if I'm impressed. She doesn't wait for me to figure it out.

She takes my arm and pulls me outside and we get into her car.

'The decision was taken by the DI to go lenient with him when Bob made it clear he had intel for us.

'You're having me on?'

'Wait, sir. Following the fisherman's interview, I made a call to Inspector Brian McManus.'

I'd liked to have had a word with Fisherman Bob myself. 'It didn't occur to you to call me, PC Dunbar? You'd rather do my job for me, is that it?'

Paula switches the ignition off and gives me her best aghast look. I wonder about the kid at home and what he makes of his mum when she's on the point of telling him off.

Paula is about to give me a mouthful, I expect, but shrewdly desists. She clears her throat.

'Inspector McManus is a police wildlife liaison officer. He's part of a nationwide operation against osprey egg thieves called operation 'Guan Ju'.'

'Guan Ju?'

'Och, it's a Chinese poem or something…'

'Dunbar, I've already wasted my own time and now you're wasting my time for me.'

She switches the ignition back on.

'Sir, there are nest robbers in Loch of Lowes. Operation Guan Ju is in place to crack down on the thieves. They tightened security at the nest locations but it wasn't enough. They wanted to track evidence of the vehicles coming and going. So they set up round-the-clock ANPR.'

Paula stops talking to overtake a caravan before the dual carriageway narrows to one lane.

'Can't you talk and drive at the same time, Dunbar? I hope you're about to tell me that the ANPR picked up our likely hit-and-run vehicle?'

'That's it, sir.'

The traffic slows as we reach Inveralmond.

'Registered to?'

She's making me work for this, wants me to show my appreciation for her ingenuity. She needs to get herself better versed in Nietzsche. Praise is more obtrusive than reproach.

'It's a Ford Galaxy registered to Mr Gilroy Flynn.'

Ah, our leading man of the boards. So, we have more evidence linking Lawrence with the Parks. Interesting.

I direct Paula to the North Inch. Paula turns left into Bute Drive. She is subdued all of a sudden, saying nothing until she parks up on Rose Terrace.

'By the way, the DI is looking for you. Something about community policing at the Gypsy encampment, I think. Nothing to do with this case, is it, sir?'

'Nope. Just a favour. It can wait till we're cleared up on this. The Gypsies aren't going anywhere. Is the DI up to date with this latest find, the Flynn link?'

'Not yet. Thought you'd want to fill him in yourself.'

'Good.' I hand Dunbar the photo. 'When you get back, I want you to see what you can dig up from this.'

'Lawrence's wife?'

'Could be. There's a date on the back. Start there. See if there's a link to Maureen or Eve Park.'

'There's something about Eve Park, and I don't know what it is, but I can't shake it off,' she says, finally.

'Go on.'

'I don't buy her apparent childlike innocence.'

'Come on,' I say. 'A good walk is what we need to think this through.'

Chapter 14

Eve

The Lodge, Perth
14th October

I'd never thought life could be any different, I was happy with my normal. There's nothing normal about staying in the room next to the room me and Graham have had sex in, the room I gave birth in. This room is smaller, with a single bed that isn't comfortable, and how can I sleep anyway, when I can hear Graham snoring next door and I know he has Blythe next to him instead of me.

I at least have the puppy to snuggle in to. He doesn't have a name yet, but I'm sure he's happy to not be dead. Graham kept saying he'd be dead by now. I found him. I found him alive. He was in Blythe's airing cupboard sleeping against the boiler. I woke him up and he was happy to see me. Since then, he's followed me all over the lodge. Blythe tried to take him away from me, but he kept yelping and so she had to let him loose so he could come and chew at my trainers. Blythe refused to name him after that and so Graham said it was my job. It's a big responsibility. I tell him it is okay, because I don't have a name and I'm still breathing.

It was Graham who'd stolen my normal. But I'd liked the newness of Graham and, for the first time, I really understood what all Mother's musicals were about. They were about love. Love with all its different, astonishing tentacles. For the first time, I wondered what real love was, the kind of love between a man and a woman. Oh, it's not like I hadn't tried to have the conversation with Mother, of course I had, but she was never interested in what she called 'That kind of talk'.

Once, maybe she'd had one gin too many, I don't know, but there was this one time, after we'd watched *Madness & Ecstasy* for the third time that week, and it being only Tuesday. I remember that night, afterwards, when I'd gone to bed, thinking Mother had been briefly struck down with guilt because, that morning, she'd fallen asleep after breakfast and had forgotten to dismiss me and believe me I tried really hard but in the end I wet myself and it went all over her bedroom carpet and she thrashed me with her redundant walking stick. Well, that night, as I said, after the musical, she told me that love wasn't worth having, she meant the kind of love Dionysus felt for Diana. Mother said that the only love worth anything was the kind between mother and daughter. I never had any reason to doubt she was telling the truth. Back then, Mother lying to me would be an idea so preposterous it would never have entered my head. Then I met Graham.

That had been a miserable week, weather-wise. The angry sky had brought a vicious storm that threatened to crash through our windows and, when the worst of it was over, we were left with rain that fell in thick, straight lines, which pounded the earth and was relentless.

The house was damp and cold, and Mother was especially grumpy because her pretend pain, she said, was at the mercy of barometric pressure. By the Wednesday, the air inside was suffocating, so I decided to sneak outside after Mother had gone to bed. I don't know why the idea to climb out of the window had suddenly come to me at that moment, and hadn't ever entered my mind previously. Graham says it was a sign. I don't know if there's any truth in that, Graham has funny ideas sometimes.

It must have been about ten months ago, now that I come to think about it, the first time I climbed out of the window and the first time I met Graham properly. I'd caught sight of him several times over the years. Sometimes he would wave to me, but I never waved back. I pretended not to exist; it was better that way, better that he didn't come to the house. Why that was I couldn't say, it was a feeling, that's all. Now I know.

Before Graham gave me the ladder, it wasn't easy climbing out of the window, but I managed it fine by easing myself onto the roof of the woodshed and dropping down from there. It hurt my feet, but all I had to do was breathe in the air and I forgot about the tingling pain.

The fresh air was magical. It was like I'd walked through a gate into the gentle arms of an invisible protector who willingly embraced me without judging me. The rain was a caress that soaked through my pyjamas and brought my skin alive, and it was like I'd taken my first breath. I walked around and around the outside of the house and then worked up the courage to venture a bit further, closer to the forest. I touched everything; plump tussocks of damp grass, spongy moss, wet tree trunks, flowers sparkling with vitality, the shadows and colours sneaking between the trees. I lay down on the needle-strewn path and let the rain pummel my body and buried my face in the rich, sweet-smelling earth. How sure I was of myself in that moment, of who I was and where I'd come from.

Making my way back to the house, I noticed the door to the woodshed was slightly ajar. There's no lock, but I always make sure the door is tight shut to keep the rain out. I was about to close the door when the thought sprang to mind that I didn't want to go back to bed, not just yet. But the rain was thrashing down harder and I was, at once, so very cold, so I dived into the woodshed as a kind of compromise. I was right to do so because the shed smelt as lively as the forest and, although when I looked up I couldn't see the sky, I could hear the rain and it did still feel as if I were in a magical natural world, miles away from the confines of my stuffy life.

It was in the woodshed, that night, where I found the dog dying. There was no electricity, but it's my job to bring in the wood so I knew my way around and, in any case, it's a tiny shed and the wood had not long been delivered that month so there was really nothing much to do but feel about to find the least damp place to sit, which is what I was doing when my hand encountered the wet, heaving chest of the dog from the lodge. He was lying on his side and, when I placed my hand on his chest, I could tell right away that there was a problem with his breathing. I didn't know his name, but I knew where he came from, because I'd seen him often enough when Graham would take him in the little back garden of the lodge and throw a ball for him. The dog was square-jawed and muscular and he was so playful and mischievous, and I found I liked watching him. Once, I'd taken one of my old childhood encyclopaedias down from the top of my bookshelf and looked up the type of dog and discovered he was a boxer. It said that boxers are renowned for their great loyalty to their families.

I kept my hand fast to the dog's chest. His breathing was faint, his heart missing beats, and every now and then his legs would spasm and give me a fright. I've never owned a dog, but some inexplicable instinct warned me that he was dying. I knew, I knew desperately, that I should run to the lodge and get Graham or Blythe to come. But I'd lived in this house all my life, the Burrells had lived in the lodge all that time, and yet, I'd barely ever spoken with them. As if each house, and its occupants, existed in an invisible but impenetrable bubble. I wouldn't have known what to say, or how to say it. How do you tell bad news to someone you've never uttered a word to?

It didn't feel right to remain in the shed, to be witness to the death. After all, I was a stranger to the dog. We are all animals of one sort or another and, at the time of our deaths, we ought to be, in my opinion, in the company of those who love us or better be alone. I felt sad for the dog, who had to die alone, because I didn't have the courage to seek out his family.

I tiptoed out of the woodshed, closing the door tightly behind me. Pins were prickling my skin all over my body, and I looked up because I was certain, at that moment, that rocks were about to fall from the sky to crush me. But, as I walked around the shed and began the awkward climb back up onto its roof, I imagined I heard the dog whimper, and it felt as if I were the one whose breathing was about to stop. I just couldn't do it, couldn't let him die alone.

Before I could convince myself otherwise, I ran away from the shed. I bolted through the tall, tangled weeds, following the path I remembered from my childhood, slipping and sliding in the mud, tripping over rocks, and I kept running until I reached the line of fir trees, pushing my way through, through the garden fence, up the well-manicured path, banging, banging, banging the door with my fists and spitting the words from somewhere deep in my throat. When at last the door was opened, I tried my hardest not to balk at the startled look on Graham's face when eventually he began to make sense of what I was saying.

Back in the woodshed I stood, flat against the cold stone wall, holding up Graham's lighted torch, as he howled and bawled, and clutched the dying animal close to his chest, buried his face in the dog's neck and, in Graham's arms, the dog must've felt safe enough to let go.

Eventually, once Graham's sobs subsided, I knelt down beside him and he told me the boxer's name was Bentley and that he had been sick for a short while, with a tumour inside his brain. I took the shovel from the wall and Graham gently carried the dog to the edge of the woods, and we buried him. I tied two twigs together with a long blade of grass, a makeshift cross, and Graham planted it, to mark the grave.

The rain had finally ceased. Under the light of the torch, Graham's eyes were red raw and horrifying, his thinning hair flat and lifeless, his face appeared to sink in on itself and his shoulders heaved with every other breath. As he knelt at the grave, I patted him on the back, and he scared me by grasping my hand to his face. I didn't know whether I could or should pull away, so I stood like that for what seemed like hours although it couldn't have been because the night sky remained stubbornly black.

Without a single word passing between us, I walked with Graham back to the woodshed, he still grasping my hand and me still unclear about what I was supposed to do. We sat side by side on the dusty, stone floor while Graham told me the story of the dog, Bentley. I can't remember most of what he said but the gist of it was, he'd lost his 'One true friend'. Often since, I've tried to imagine what it would be like to have a one true friend, but I've come to the conclusion that friendship must only be real in the world of fiction and that Graham must have a soft heart.

The light changed and revealed more of Graham to me. The pale, thick hairs in his nostrils that were a different shade from the thin strands of hair on his head, the broken tooth, the bitten fingernails, his eyes drowning in misery, and I realised how much the warmth of his hand made me feel comfortable, useful, important.

A little bit later, Graham turned to me and looked directly into my eyes. Our faces were so close together I could smell the soap on his skin, a different kind of soap from the sugary-scented one I'm used to, and to me it felt like the perfume of a warrior. He kissed me and I didn't flinch, not once. I cried, I cried with such joy as I'd never experienced before.

On that night, in the woodshed where the dog had died, Graham and I made love for the first time. It wasn't the last time, but it was the only time that mattered.

Chapter 15
DS Calmly

Perth
14th October

It's a muted early evening, the clouds are hanging low and there's the odd spot of rain that doesn't appear to want to come to anything. We leave behind us the busy traffic on Atholl Street and walk along towards the war memorial, left of the Auld Brig.

I admire the kilted soldier that always gives me pause for thought when I'm in the middle of a murder case and wonder why it sometimes feels as if the value of a life decreases as each decade passes.

'He's a handsome chappie, don't you think, Paula?'

She takes her time to walk around the 51st Highland Division Memorial. She reaches up and runs her finger along the bronze shoe of the little Dutch girl presenting the soldier with a posy of flowers in thanks for her liberation.

'There'll be none of that after Brexit,' she says. 'Maybe if Boris was a handsome chappie, as you call it, he'd be more inclined to see himself as European?'

We sit on a bench and watch the quiet flow of the river. A couple of ducks cruise by. It's relatively peaceful, my shoulders loosen and my head feels lighter. The water brings to mind the hues of old silver. I have no intentions of discussing Brexit with Paula; I'm already on the brink of hopelessness with this convoluted case without being reminded of how little control any of us have over anything other than how we choose to live our own lives.

'Let us focus on what we've got,' I say.

'Right,' she says. She takes a deep breath. 'Bruce Lawrence, mown down on 11th October. On the same day, two or three hours or so earlier, Maureen Park is murdered.' Paula stops to reflect on this.

95

'It's possible we have one perpetrator.'

'Possible,' I say.

'You don't sound convinced.'

'That's because I'm not.'

I sometimes worry that I'm giving Paula too much freedom. She hasn't said anything I haven't thought myself, but the line of least resistance can easily lead one off the edge of a cliff.

What it comes down to is Eve's story. I put it to Paula.

'It would be possible for someone to break into Tippermuir, murder Maureen Park then hop it up the road and bump Lawrence off. But if we're to believe Eve, that Lawrence has never been to Tippermuir or met either mother or daughter, or even if we don't believe her, we still don't know what the motive for either death is, let alone for both murders to have been committed by one and the same person.'

'Are you forgetting Gilroy Flynn? He owns Tippermuir House. Maybe he wanted to sell; it's his pot of gold at the end of the rainbow. What if Eve and Flynn conspired to get rid of Maureen Park?'

'We don't know Eve and Flynn are aware of each other, much less whether they would commit murder together. And why?'

'If he wanted rid of Maureen Park, maybe she was refusing to exit the property.' Paula refers to her pocketbook. 'Flynn is currently producing a musical in a theatre in Glasgow. Once you've had your chinwag with the DI, he'll have us getting on to the local bobbies…'

'Let's not get ahead of ourselves.' I pause, and give Paula a chance to remember I'm her senior officer. 'We know very little. Nothing worth going to the DI with, if you see what I mean. We have two victims, without any clear direction in the way of suspects.'

Paula bristles at that, but I let it pass and carry on.

'Flynn owns the property that was listed on Lawrence's betting slip, connection number one. Connection number two, Flynn reportedly was once a friend of Maureen Park, some thirty or so years ago. A good friend, by all accounts, given that she and her daughter have lived in the house since that time. The owner of the betting slip and the occupier of the house are our two victims. We have yet to discover a direct link between Flynn and Lawrence.'

'Eve Park.'

Paula sits forward and drops her head.

'Eve doesn't drive,' I remind her. 'The vehicle that killed Lawrence was registered to Flynn.'

'Eve wanted her mother dead.'

'There is no evidence to suggest that.'

'Wouldn't you? I mean, I'd be bloody raging if I was Eve. Her overbearing and abusive mother, or who she thought was her mother, lied to her for her whole life.'

'For argument's sake, let's say that Eve killed her mother. What does that leave us with?'

'Two murderers.'

'Bit of a coincidence maybe?'

Paula shrugs.

Someone sat on Maureen's chest, as she lay prostrate in bed, and held their hands tight across her airways. If it wasn't Eve, then who? And how did this person gain entry to the house?

'We need to return to Tippermuir House.'

'The DI's waiting for you to report back, sir.'

'Let's have him wait a bit longer, eh.'

I don't know why this hasn't struck me before. The key to Tippermuir was put out upon the lintel above the front door, nightly. Either someone knew the key was there, or it was a lucky find. I at least have to rule this out as a possibility before putting Eve firmly in my sights as her mother's murderer. Who was sending the envelopes of money? There may well be a person of interest as yet unknown to us.

I take a shot of the photograph I found at the Lawrence place and send it to the team along with instructions to identify the woman and child.

'Let's go,' I say to Paula. 'We shall return to Tippermuir House, but first I want to dig a bit deeper into both Lawrence's and Flynn's background.'

As we're driving off, I note the look of satisfaction on Paula's face. That irks me. Eve has spent her whole life at the hands of an overbearing mother. Immediately thoughts of Jenny surface. My brain is struggling to untangle Eve's experience with Jenny's. Our mum may be overbearing, but she wasn't unkind. Jenny never understood that Mum was doing what she thought was best for Jenny. Maureen Park was cruel to Eve, only for Eve to discover that she'd been lied to throughout that treatment of her. Eve has no protector. Jenny had me. So she believed, at any rate.

'It is my belief that Eve is the victim here,' I say, ensuring PC Dunbar catches the finality of my words. Smugness in a woman is a less than redeeming quality.

Chapter 16

Eve

Tippermuir House
15th October

I am wearing one of her dresses, and she wouldn't be happy knowing how much better I look in it than she did. It is a perfect fit; tight across my waist with a string bodice and a skirt that falls to my ankles and sways soft, shimmery pink.

It feels different to be me. In a good way, I think. It is very odd, but being at Blythe's the past couple of days, away from this big, cave of a house, has started me thinking. The first thought I had was why I don't think. Well, of course, I do think, all the time. I think about making breakfast, about the dusting, about what Mother would prefer for lunch and could I get away with giving her a quick flannel wash or will she want me to sit in the bathroom with her and read to her while she's in the bath? I think about extraordinary words in the dictionary like, monotonous, self-entitlement, flimflam, obdurate, omnishambles and limerence.

I think I would like to think new thoughts, proper thoughts that mean something. Words in the dictionary are meaningful, but what happens when I put them in a sentence? Take the word, beautiful, for example. I am beautiful in this dress. The dictionary tells me I look very attractive. But that doesn't really mean anything. The word beautiful needs more thinking about than a simple dictionary definition. In the way life needs more thinking about. Because, when I look here in the mirror, I seem transformed into a whole other version of me. I like this version. I like it very much. This version could be capable. This me could actually be someone that matters. I want to be the person that wears this dress. I'm not sure, yet, how to go about that, how to know what sort of person that is, but there has to be a way. I want to choose what matters so that I can matter; so that I can matter to someone else – to my son. Graham calls him my son but, until I know who *I* am, I can't know what *mine* is. I want to have a name.

In the drawing room, I'm sitting in Mother's armchair. This is nice. Across the room, I beg the mobile phone to ring. When Mother was younger and used to wear this dress she had friends, went to parties, like Blythe said. Blythe thinks it must've been someone from the theatre that called her before she died, because Mother didn't know anyone else. Blythe is right.

Mother's chair is positioned so that the sitter can view the painting above the fireplace without distraction. I've always wished it had been my father up there in that portrait. I'd like to have known him, to see if I was like him in some way, learnt about what his dreams were, what he'd dreamt of for me. Now I have no parents, leaving me dreamless.

At least I know that Mother-Not-Mother was a star. To be a star seems to be a fine dream to have. It stands to reason that I must have the makings of being a star too, for even if the DNA is telling the truth, I am still Mother's daughter.

A memory flits into sight then escapes before I can fully grasp it. It was from long ago, not long after I'd had to give up school to care for Mother. Days when my heart used to dance every time I thought about the theatre, listening to Mother's stories, lying in bed at night with my eyes closed, watching her make-believe world where she took centre stage and every time she sang, the faces of the audience would shine back at her with expressions of gratitude and wonder; a make-believe world full of meaning and kindness and joy. Must it be make-believe? Is this the dream I was always meant to discover? Is this what will make me human, a good person, not a murderous wolf, the kind of person capable of loving another human being and of being loved?

There must be someone from the theatre who knows who I am.

***

'Do you recognise me, Blythe? Do you? You don't. I know you don't by that twisted look on your face.'

I throw open the door to let her in and swirl my skirts around the entrance hall. My glittery heels clippety-clopping on the tile floor. Blythe's jowly chin is set firmly. I've lit pretty candles all over the house and, under the glistening light and shadow, even she is changing from her orderly self to something less ordinary.

'It's okay. I didn't want you to recognise me.'

I link my arm in hers and dance her into Mother's bedroom.

'Now that you know it's me, I want you to help with my make-up. See, I've found Mother's stage make-up.'

'Oh, I don't think you should use this stuff. It's old and crumbly. Look.'

I grab the compact from her. She's messing it up. Mother would be livid.

'It will make your face sore,' she says. 'And anyway, I came to talk to you about something; two things, actually. Come and sit down here, on the bed with me.'

'Oh, Blythe, I'm too excited to sit down.' Wearing this dress makes me want to dance forever. I'm so very alive. 'I've decided. In this dress don't you think I look like Mother? I could be her, you know. Be just like her, on the stage, singing and dancing. Be Mother.'

I whirl around the bedroom making sure not to dig my heels in the carpet, because they might stick and trip me up. The faster I turn the higher my dress rises, and it's as if I am floating. Life is so magical. The candles flicker as if dancing alongside me to the tune inside my head. I don't even recognise the tune which, you would think, would discombobulate me but, instead, I am surprised and surprise is glorious.

'It's nice to see you're making plans for your future, Eve. Now, when the funeral is over and done with it makes sense that you wouldn't want to hang around here.'

Blythe only ever talks. She doesn't do anything all day but talk. I don't want her at Mother's funeral. Mother wouldn't want her there. Mother should just come home and we can bury her in the woods, close to where Bentley is buried so she has company. Nobody has told me when she's coming home. Somebody has her. She won't like that. That's okay. It doesn't matter any more.

'You'll be wanting to sell this place, now. That's a sensible idea. A fresh start will be good for you. Absolutely.'

'Yes. I'm going to be a musical theatre superstar, just like Mother, and then everyone will know who I am.' I flop down beside her on the bed, exhausted. 'My life is going to be meaningful.' The wind from my skirts flares the candles by the bed, blowing them into each other. Two of the candles die out.

'Well, I imagine that will take a lot of money,' Blythe says, patting my hand. 'Singing lessons are expensive.'

'Oh, I won't need lessons. I have natural ability. Would you like me to sing to you?'

'Not just now, Eve, we have something important to discuss. Now listen, I've spoken with Graham and, let me tell you, it was no easy job to convince him, but I want to help you out, Eve. It's the least I can do after all you've been through.'

'That's very kind of you. But you don't know anything about the theatre, so I don't see how you can help me.'

'I will buy this house. It's a lot of money, Eve, money you will need if you want to succeed in the theatre.'

It's not Blythe's fault. She doesn't understand anything about succeeding. I'm sure you don't need money if you have talent. It would be nice to not worry about money, but I can't sell this house. I say no to Blythe.

'I should think you'd thank me for the offer, Eve. It's not going to be easy to sell this old house. And you won't get a better offer than the one I'm giving you. Take your time and think it over. And, you can keep the puppy. I think he misses you.'

'No, I can't keep the puppy because I'm leaving to be a star.' I sit for a minute to think about everything. The puppy is part of everything, I know that now. Until I know who I am, I can't be a part of anything.

She stands, getting ready to leave. I'm glad, all of a sudden, I feel just like that candle when its light went out.

She kneels down in front of me and takes my hands. 'Think it over.'

She pulls me up off the bed and takes me into the drawing room.

Daylight is fading. The candles are sprightlier than before, enervating the air.

'Oh Eve,' she says, turning me to face her, 'I've found the very person to help you become a star of the musicals.'

'Who?'

'Now will you listen to me? His name is Gilroy Flynn. I know where he is. He must be dying to meet you, absolutely.'

Gilroy Flynn?

'I know him. He was a friend of Father's. Do you think he would help me?' I ask. I think I should be kind to Blythe.

'I know he needs money,' she says. 'I read on the internet that he wants to rebuild his theatre. Think about it, Eve. With the money you get from selling me this house, you could make a deal with Mr Flynn. You have the money he needs and he has the ability to make you a superstar. And I can make that happen for you. I have cash, Eve. You could sell me this house and be on your way to stardom in no time. Now will you think about selling me your house?'

I nod.

The front door bangs shut. It's nothing to do with me who owns this house.

Chapter 17

Graham

The Lodge
16th October

It wasn't as if last night's storm amounted to much. Graham slept right through it but then was woken at 5 a.m. by Blythe bellowing his name as if he'd managed to get something wrong in his sleep. He didn't waste any time getting up and found her in her craft room at the far end of the landing. He barely ever comes into this room, but it's the best room in the house because Blythe can spend hours at a time crafting whatever takes her fancy and he gets to relish that time to himself, a chance to swallow a few beers and fall asleep in front of the telly without her nagging him about wasted hours and squandered potential.

He's forgotten she's taken a week's holiday from work, because his mind is so twisted around the Eve situation that nothing at home feels worth bothering about. Blythe taking a holiday out of the blue like that is a worry, though. Blythe is a planner, she plans everything to the nth degree and, anyway, she usually saves up her holidays so she doesn't have to work over Christmas and Hogmanay, because that's her favourite time of year. His too, since for most of it she's in this topsy-turvy craft room, making decorations or whatever, to give out at the Hogmanay party in the Tibbermore village hall, so all the villagers can fawn over her and worship her outstanding contribution to the community. She'll not be making anything anytime soon. He pushes her out of the way and positions the pail he'd snaffled from the shed under the steady stream of water pouring in from the ceiling.

'You'll have to get up there right now and fix that,' Blythe mutters.

'I can't do it now. Have you seen how heavy it's raining out there?'

There's a bad smell around here. Something's not right. Blythe isn't her usual self. Yes, she can be demanding, but it's not like her to be unreasonable.

But now she's looking at him like she doesn't recognise him. She's standing with her arms tight around her chest. She's not really looking at him, but looking straight past him. He turns, but there's nothing of note behind him. He pulls his T-shirt down, wishing that he'd slung on his jeans.

Now, she's pointing at him. 'And have you looked at how quickly that pail is filling up. See.'

She stupidly grabs the pail and thrusts it at him. He takes it and bungs it back under the leak. She's not wrong. Give it ten minutes and that pail will overflow.

'Are you forgetting this?' He slaps his useless left leg. 'I won't even manage up the ladder, never mind scrambling across the roof to replace tiles.'

'Doesn't stop you running about after her up at that house.'

'Who?' He turns away from her, grabs the first thing that comes to hand, and stoops painfully to mop up the massive puddle on the floor.

'Don't give me that. You know exactly who I'm talking about. Eve Park.'

The rag isn't much use. He eases himself up from the floor and wrings it out in the pail, which isn't much use either, all it's done is to raise the level in the pail.

'This will need emptying,' he says.

She grabs the rag from him. 'Are you listening to me?'

'Do I have a choice? I've not got a clue what you're saying. What about Eve Park?'

She glares at him, her face flushed and furious. This is a hellish nightmare.

'You're always running about after her.'

'That's a lie.' Is she jealous? Is she suspicious? Does she know about Eve? Nah, how can she know anything? Since when did life become so complicated? He looks around the room, at all of Blythe's handmade knick-knacks. He tries to tuck his T-shirt between his legs, all at once he feels exposed. This is Blythe. His Blythe. The woman who was there to hold his hand when he nearly died after the accident. She's taken a week off to spy on him. What's happened to them? It's his fault. He should never have started this thing with Eve. It's as if he's slipping into a horrible, muddy hellhole of his own making. And there's no going back. The bigger picture has been thrown off track and somehow he's going to have to fix everything that he's broken. Somehow.

'It's no lie,' Blythe says, crisply. 'Don't think I didn't notice the way you were gag-eyed at Eve when she was here.'

Now she really is being unreasonable. 'Her mother had just died. How was I supposed to look at her? Eh? And as for running about after her, when exactly? What's wrong with you, woman?' Had he given himself away without realising it?

Blythe begins busying herself moving things out of the way of the leak. She's humming a tune he doesn't recognise.

'It's fine,' she says, breezily. 'I'll call a man who can fix the roof.'

'Blythe?'

Quick as a flash, she turns on him. 'Do you think I care if you've got a fancy for that lass? Make a fool of yourself if that's what you want. But I'll tell you this. I want that house. You're going nowhere until you get me that house.'

'What are you talking about, Blythe? Eve's house isn't for sale.'

'Eve's house. Eve's house. Hark at you. You think you're going to move in there? Cosy up with your little paramour? Ain't gonna happen. You make her sell that house to me. Then you can run off, if that's what you're planning. To France, is it? I'm not stupid, Graham.'

She knows everything. Well, maybe not, hopefully not everything.

'I'm not listening to this.'

***

In the kitchen, Graham grabs a bottle of Stella from the fridge. He plonks himself at the kitchen table and tries to get his head around what's just happened. Maybe, this is what's meant to happen. Maybe so. Blythe was bound to find out sooner or later. He was hoping it would be later, once he and Eve were settled in France as a family. His plan was to leave without Blythe knowing; thought he couldn't bear the look on her face when she discovered his betrayal. Because that's what all this is, he's betrayed his wife, like a callous man. That's what he is, a callous man. Worse than that, he's a coward. But after what Blythe's just said, she cares more about bloody Tippermuir House than she does for him. Blythe knows full well she needs his signature to release the money they've been holding on to. It's his money; compensation from his accident. His accident. A little nest egg. Well nests are for families. A man and wife does not a family make.

He hears Blythe on the phone. She'll be calling someone to fix the roof. There was a time when he'd been the man who can; wouldn't have thought twice about getting up on that roof. Not now, not any more. What kind of man does that make him?

Blythe bursts into the kitchen. 'I'm making stovies for lunch.'

He tries to say something nice, but she butts in before he gets the chance.

'I'm talking,' she thunders.

He sighs. 'Why don't you talk and I just sit here and listen then,' he says, but she ignores his sarcasm and he decides not to push it. He doesn't want to have the conversation. Not until he can plan the best way forward first.

'I'll make extra for Eve. She'll not eat when she's on her own. The way she was yesterday, looked as if she wanted to die herself.'

The words stick in his throat. He takes a slug from the bottle and shakes his head. Blythe bangs the pot on the cooker and begins slicing potatoes. She's talking without drawing breath. About the changes she's planning on making to Tippermuir House. It's just words bouncing off his head, because she's talking nonsense. She's talking as if she already owns Tippermuir.

Tippermuir is Eve's house now. Why has it taken him so long to figure this out? All the hassle over a passport. Could he really move in there, to Tippermuir House, with Eve? Could he stay here, in Scotland, and still have his family? Now that Blythe suspects about him and Eve, it's actually not a bad idea. He'd never wanted to move to France. For one, he hates Stuart. And, after all this, he's stretched his relationship with Lynn so tight, the thought of living only a few feet away in their refurbished barn was beginning to make him sweat.

He'll get it in the neck from Lynn, changing his plans and all, but it's something to think about at least.

But first, he'll have to rein in Blythe's obsession with Tippermuir. Well, actually, there might be something in that. Eve's not fussed about getting married; she's already told him that. What if... what if... nah, now he's dreaming. Blythe would never... Would she? She's only taking food up there to convince Eve to sell up. But what if Blythe was understanding about the baby? What if they could all stay in Tippermuir together? Like one big happy family?

Chapter 18

Eve

Tippermuir
16th October

Too bad you can live only so long. It's a line from a song. I wonder if this is what Mother was singing when she died? Richard Versalle had a heart attack after singing this line. He fell from a ladder on the stage of the Metropolitan Opera's premiere performance of *The Makropulos Case*. Mother used to tell me all sorts of stories like that. Every time I asked her about her life. Every time I begged her to take me to the theatre. Every time I asked about my father.

My father didn't abandon the theatre like she did. She said she wanted to make a grand exit, in the prime of her superstardom. I never understood. If something is so super, why would you want to desert it?

What must it be like to be applauded? To stand on stage and take a bow and have the entire audience up and stamping their feet, clapping, crying, laughing. What must it be like inside? The feeling of it? A feeling that matters. To do something that makes your life count for something. To stare back at the audience from the pages of a glossy programme? What must it be like to have someone paint your portrait? To be adored.

I found an undergarment of Mother's. It is very fine, made of purple silk and white lace with bone to shape the bust and buttocks. I've spent the last hour trying to slip it on and was pleased it almost fitted, but I couldn't wear it properly because someone needs to tie the laces at the back and there is no one here. It is most certainly the strangest of feelings to be alone in this house.

I can sing out loud now and not just inside my head.

I don't feel like singing.

I listen carefully. There are many noises in this house. The birds in the roof. The sleet on the window. Dust falling. Insects in the walls.

The phone never rings. DS Calmly says he can find out who Mother called, or who called her. Maybe the person will call back. I would like this person to call back, because the detective asked about Edinburgh, so maybe he thinks this person is from the theatre there; the King's Theatre. I would like to speak to someone from the King's Theatre. I would tell them that I am the daughter of Maureen Park and they will want to see me. Want to put me in a show. I could be on the stage, singing musicals just like she did. Nobody from the theatre would come here and kill Mother. And I don't have to mention the DNA test to anyone there.

Everybody.

All and sundry.

One and all.

Every Tom, Dick…

Everybody in the theatre adored Mother. She told me so.

***

I am sitting in Mother's armchair. It's not as comfortable as my seat on the couch. *Madness & Ecstasy* is on, but I have the sound off. It's painful to hear her voice. This was her very last performance. She plays a Greek goddess called Diana and wears a golden dress that shimmers brighter than the stage lighting and is slim and elegant. Her hand is at her chest, her neck stretched, her mouth awful exaggerated.

I am on the stage too. She told me this once and then would never speak of it again. You're not showing yet, but you are there, inside my tummy, she said. I've never forgotten. It's easier to forget that it was a lie. For now. Graham is giving me time to come to terms with things, even though now we don't need time because Mother is gone. But she hasn't really gone, because I can look at her now, on the screen, and can almost wish myself curled up inside her tummy.

It is thrilling to imagine I have already been on stage; been a part of something so majestic. I wonder what I could've been thinking about. I'm sure I would've been thinking, because I've always thought about things. When I think about this particular thing, I get this knot in my chest and it's hard to breathe, as if a hand has reached inside my throat and is squeezing it tight. Breathless. And then I remember; it's all a lie.

It's worse now that she's gone, because I never asked her. I should've asked her. I always meant to, and I hate myself for not having the courage in the end. I will never know now if she really did give up superstardom because of me. I've always believed this to be true, because she said it was true. But I've never understood why. I don't want to believe it is true any more. It doesn't feel true. It feels like another lie, and I want there to be another reason. Graham says it was a lie. But to me, it only feels like one.

I want her to be me. Me on that stage singing, in the golden dress, so that my son can look back in awe at me. I place my hand on my chest and sing the song. I sing from my very own soul and my mouth does not feel exaggerated to me. I stand and move around the projection room, practise the carefully choreographed steps. I am Diana. I am a Greek goddess. I am magnificent. I am Eve Park, the superstar of musical theatre. Stop.

Rewind the reel, start from the beginning. Keep the sound off. I know every move, every word of every song. I know all my lines. In my head, I have rehearsed this role a million times. I do it now for real. Do it. Again.

Do it again. Again. Again.

***

Daylight is sneaking under the curtains. In here, there is only the glimmer from the screen. For the past six hours, I've rehearsed. The audience has applauded. Over and over. Applause is like drinking from a goblet of magic. With every applause, the magic overflows. It is agony.

There are no breaths left inside me. I switch the projector off. Turn Mother off. She is ugly. Grotesque. She is despicable. To love is to know who you are. Mother knew who she was, and I loved her. But she chose lies over love. I have to put those lies right. I have to turn her lies into truths so that I can love and be loved, so that I can know who I am.

I hate her. I hate her for her lies, for stealing my love. Her soul has probably withered and died by now. DS Calmly may as well not bother looking for who killed her.

I can't bear to as much as imagine her.

DS Calmly thinks I killed her. What if I had? What if I'd reached inside her throat and squeezed?

Chapter 19
DS Calmly

We pull up outside Tippermuir House. Paula is out of the car before I have a chance to gather my thoughts. We don't know enough yet to point the finger at Eve, regardless of Paula's intuition.

'I'll check round the back,' Paula tells me when I join her at the front door.

'No one answering?'

'Nope.'

I give the bell another push and wait. By all accounts, Eve rarely leaves the house. Everything is delivered, food, household supplies, medication, and what can't get delivered they don't want. I say they, but now there is only Eve. Could be she's decided she doesn't care for the hermit life now that her mum has gone.

Paula returns, shrugging her shoulders and shaking her head. 'Bet she's done a runner.'

'Or, she's out enjoying her freedom?'

'Are you sure you're in the right job, Lark?'

I think about the envelopes of money that, by rights, I should've gathered as evidence. Well, hindsight is a wondrous thing. I had no reason, no proof, no clout to gather evidence at Tippermuir when I came across that money. It worries me. Has she used it to run off, escape prosecution? Och, I doubt it. I can't take Eve as a suspect seriously.

'Let's go and have a chat with the neighbours.'

We make our way down the slope to the Burrell's house at the bottom of the hill.

'What do you mean, am I in the right job?'

Paula stops walking. What is it about people who can't walk and talk at the same time? Not wishing to appear rude, I stand and wait patiently for her to continue.

'I've never met a colleague who consistently gives suspects the benefit of doubt as much as you do. What I mean is, you aren't the usual type, your view of the world isn't clouded with scepticism in the way it is for the rest of us.'

'You're talking about our job as if it's some kind of secret club.'

'Aye,' she says, 'and you're no a member.'

She saunters on, leaving me wondering if she was joking or not.

'We've just got a couple of questions, Mrs Burrell,' Paula says when Eve's neighbour opens the door.

'I don't know where she is,' Blythe says flatly. 'I heard the door slam shut in the early hours this morning. Woke us both up. Of course, Graham was back asleep in seconds but not me; once I'm awake that's it. I was thinking of going for a nap just as you knocked, as a matter of fact, so you won't mind if I don't let you in.'

'No, that's fine, Blythe,' I blurt out before Paula gets all haughty. 'Any idea where she was going?'

'None at all. She never said anything to me.'

'When did you last speak to her?'

Blythe is interrupted by both our mobiles. I let Paula take the call and repeat my question to Blythe.

'It was last night, about eight o'clock. She wanted me to sit and watch one of those musicals of hers. I've seen enough of them to last me a lifetime.'

'How did she seem? I ask.

'What do you mean? I'm not her mother, you know. She's not my responsibility. If you're expecting me to mollycoddle her then you can think again, I've enough on my plate with Graham.'

Without meaning to, I seem to have put the woman on the defensive. It could prove fruitful, mind you.

'I mean, has she been acting differently? Anything strange you've come across?'

'Strange. That girl is strange all right. Don't tell me you haven't noticed as much yourself. She's most likely out gallivanting, getting up to all sorts, I imagine. She'll get herself in trouble, mark my words. Maybe you should get the social work involved. She's not worldly wise, if you get my meaning. And by that I am not saying she's vulnerable; far from it.'

Paula hangs up and remains silent. I can tell she has some good news and is itching to tell me just by the way she's folded her arms tight around herself and is looking at her feet.

'That's certainly something I will think about, Blythe.' I'm happy to wait to hear what Paula learned from the phone call. There's a fissure of something from Blythe's penchant for gossip that makes me want to take the time and coax it out of her. 'What makes you think Eve isn't vulnerable?'

Blythe opens the door a bit wider so she can lean closer to me, as if she's about to tell me a secret.

'Yesterday, Eve was dressing up in her mum's costumes. She did her hair up like her mum wore it in that painting above their fireplace. If her mum was there, it would be hell to pay. Eve told me her mum used to smack her about the head with that old kettle they have on the stove. I wouldn't put it past the daughter to have done away with the mum. That's my thinking on it, take it or leave it, that's up to you.'

I give her a few minutes to see if she has anything more to add.

'I hope you're going to do something about it, because I'm not too happy to be living next door to a murderer.'

'It's like what you hear on the telly, Mrs Burrell,' Paula pipes up, 'everyone is a suspect until proven otherwise.'

Blythe sniffs at that. 'I hope you're not including me in your list of suspects, missy.'

Paula is about to respond, but I give her my tongue-in-teeth look. I trap the tip of my tongue between my teeth and smile. This is a look I've perfected over the years and it never lets me down.

I fill the silence wisely. 'Is there anything you and Eve talked about yesterday that could point us in the direction of where she may be right now?'

'All she bloody talks about is musical theatre.'

'You think that's where she might have gone? A theatre?'

'I might as well tell you, it's no skin off my nose. I wanted to buy Tippermuir House. I tried to buy it years ago but was priced out of the market by Maureen Park. So I went to Eve and asked if she would sell the house to me. I thought she was thinking it over, but I asked her again last night and she showed me the title deeds to the house. Took the wind right out of my sails, I don't mind telling you.'

'Come on then, what are you telling us?' Paula's impatience causes Blythe's shoulders to stiffen and her hips to shoogle.

There's a slight growl in Blythe's response. 'That house isn't owned by Eve, wasn't even Maureen that owned it. The name on the title deeds is Gilroy Flynn, and I know he is a musical theatre producer. What do you make of that? Eh?'

***

Back in the car, I ask Paula to hang fire before she starts the engine.

'I want to talk this through and see if I've got it straight.'

Paula rattles off through my thoughts. 'We know Gilroy Flynn owns the house that Maureen and Eve Park live in. Maybe he even pays all the bills, that's worth finding out. But the interesting fact is the update I just got from the team.'

'Yes. Tell me we have something to go on.'

'It's still to be fully corroborated, but they've have come up trumps on that photo you found. An old headline in the *Edinburgh Evening News*, and a story about a stolen child. Parents are named as Bruce and Pauline Lawrence.'

'Ah. And was the child ever recovered?'

'The team are working on that, sir. But this was front-page news at the time, and they've been able to unearth bits and pieces relating to the lives of the Lawrences prior to the abduction, including snippets from friends and neighbours. One of those neighbours was a Mr Gilroy Flynn, whose wife had been in Simpsons Maternity hospital, in the next hospital bed to Mrs Lawrence.'

'Do we know the name of the wife?'

'She was just recorded as Mrs Flynn. I bet you she was Maureen Park.'

I shake my head. 'Makes no sense,' I say. 'Maureen was married to the other bloke. He was in the production of that musical I sat and watched with Eve. But he died.'

'I'll check that out before we hand this over.'

What is likely to happen now is that the case will be handed over to the team in Edinburgh, especially since there is now a clear link between the hit-and-run and the death of Maureen Park. That link is Gilroy Flynn. And now there's a lost child in the mix. And Eve, with a DNA test that leaves us with yet another mystery.

'What if,' I say to Paula, 'we were already on our way to Edinburgh when you took that call?'

'Why would we go to Edinburgh?'

'We are chasing our suspect. Eve has deliberately absconded. Remember?'

'Nice. You're coming around to my way of thinking.'

'No, I'm not. I'm swerving us around bureaucracy.'

Paula starts the car, but we don't move. 'I'm not convinced,' she says.

'I'm okay with that. It's not you I need to convince.'

It's not until we're heading for the M90 and we stop for fuel before Paula speaks again.

'They're in it together.'

'You like your conspiracy theories, Paula.'

'What if, Flynn took out Bruce Lawrence but stopped at Tippermuir House, on the way, so as to murder Maureen Park so that him and Eve could be together?'

'So why didn't Eve go off with Flynn when she had the chance?'

'You wouldn't, would you? You'd want to say around and be the grieving daughter for at least long enough to get us off your back. They've planned it together. Now Eve has gone to be with Flynn and, for all we know, they have tickets to anywhere we won't find them.'

I give this some thought; slightly uneasy about my deliberate ignorance of the money envelopes.

'I can tell, by your silence, you think I'm way off the mark.'

'Sounds like a bad Channel 5 movie to me.'

'Didn't the Burrell woman say Eve had started dressing up in her mum's clothes? Why would she do that? It must be for a man, it must be.'

But this is Eve. In the brief time I've spent with her, it seems absurd to imagine Eve could be so brutal. Don't think me naive, or arrogant. It wouldn't be the first time I've been proved wrong. I'm as happy to be wrong as to be right, as long as we get a result. Do understand when I tell you, if Eve is involved in her mother's death, I want to be the cop that can prove it. Indubitably.

Paula pulls into Tesco's for fuel and supplies. I let her loose and answer the call that's vibrating in my pocket.

The last person I expect to speak to is Fletcher Cunningham.

PART TWO

Chapter 20

Gilroy

Glasgow
9th October

'God on high, hear my prayer. Get out, you emaciated cretin. This is a theatre, not a jester's playground.' He throws the shoe back at the useless wretch. It had slipped off at the precise moment she was supposed to be gracefully exiting stage right. 'What does she know about performance? About passion? Musical tone? Did you hear, did you hear?'

'Gilroy. Please. Be patient,' Murdo says, standing by his side at the edge of the stage.

'You interrupted me. Patient? Is that your irrepressible sense of humour?'

He'd timed this just right, the crew are raising the flats and enough of the cast are hanging around the wings. The cleaner, Annie, she's a good bet, smack bang in the middle of the auditorium with her duster and all-seeing eye, she has nothing better to bring joy to her life than theatre gossip.

When all said and done, this is a life-or-death situation, is it not. The Glasgow Heritage Court Theatre is about to take the world by storm.

He allows himself a visible bristle. 'It's my reputation at stake, not yours. And most certainly not hers.' He throws his book at the girl and instantly regrets doing so when she bends to pick it up.

'Leave it. Leave it. Keep your dirty mitts off my book.'

Sprinting across the stage, he gathers the book to his chest. Cold sweat trickles down his back. 'I have to get out of here, get fresh air, whatever; away from this agony. Must I bear witness to my very life disintegrating before me?'

'Are you alright?' Murdo asks. 'Are you deliberately sounding like your father for my benefit?'

'Start over,' he barks and departs the stage to get a better view from the stalls. Murdo's comment unsettles him, out of the blue the way it came like that, as if he suspects something.

He lays his book on his knees, keeping it closed, runs his fingers down the black, leather-embossed cover. Everything he's learnt, everything, the shape of his soul, it's all in this, his mother's notebook. Each and every word speaks to him of greatness, his mother's legacy. He doesn't need reminding of the fate of his father.

His mother is here, somewhere within the walls of this ancient theatre. Particles of her dancing in the dust, observing. Relentless.

'Gilroy Flynn,' he whispers to himself, 'do you beg for divine intervention, or shrink back in utter shame?'

***

Back in his office, he lays it on thick, his devious plan, having dismissed from his mind anything Murdo may think he knows. 'I want rid of her.'

'But,' Murdo whispers, taking a chair by the scarcely burning fire where both wolfhounds are curled up sleeping. 'Gilroy, she can sing. Still you are blind to all but the memories inside your mind.'

Murdo is feeding the dogs again. Is he deliberately being spiteful? His memories, eh? First his father, now Ariadne. Well, he and Murdo share a lifetime together; some memories slice deeper than others. No doubt Murdo thinks, as usual, he can get his way by throwing knives at him. One knife in particular is his habit. The one with Ariadne's name carved into the handle. Ah, but he cottoned on to that a trick a long time ago.

'We're talking about the girl, not me.' Gilroy slaps the treats from Murdo's hand before slumping at his desk. 'You are to blame for this. You, of all people, must've known Polly Burke wouldn't be good enough. But no, you don't care if you ruin me. Go on, get out of my office. Go have your play date, you old pervert. Get it over with. Then find me a Diana that can actually sing the part.'

Murdo will forgive him for this.

'You are being unkind, my friend.' Murdo clicks his tongue against his teeth; the sucking sound sends Gilroy's exasperation soaring without any effort on his own part.

Gilroy examines the man sitting across the desk, hunched back in his fading orange silk overcoat, the black woollen cap with wispy hairs escaping, his yellowish beard that hasn't seen a trim for decades. Decades, they've succeeded together, always together.

'I am everything you made me,' he sneers. If Murdo is going to be stubborn about this, the problem is solved.

Murdo throws his arms out in a gesture that reminds Gilroy of what it felt like to be a boy watching his hero. When he was young, it wasn't hard to picture Murdo as his god of all things, even after his father was taken away. 'We have big hearts, little Gil,' his mother told him. 'We can forgive.'

'Look around you. See how far you've come,' Murdo snipes at him.

Gilroy rises from the desk and moves to the window. The bright October sun has encouraged the droves out, to mill about, as if there is nothing wrong with the world. Numerous times over the past months, he's stood here and tried to guess who of the passers-by will make up his audience on opening night. If only he could interrogate everyone that buys a ticket. The thought plays ragged in his mind, keeps him awake at night. But it must come down to trust. And he trusts the population of Glasgow. It had to happen here, back in Glasgow. The people here know how to love.

'It's out there that matters,' he tells Murdo. 'Not in here.'

'You will never find an Ariadne, Gilroy.'

Ariadne. Back at his desk, he picks up his pen and points it at his director. He should say something glib, something caustic. But nothing comes to mind.

'You are risking your own victory,' Murdo says. 'The media coverage and editorials are far beyond our expectations. You're already a hit. People remember, Gilroy. The people want you to shine so they can applaud you. They want to be a part of you, just as they were before.'

'Before, before! Today's audiences are not equal, and you know it.'

Everything changes. He's long accepted that. His mother taught him that greatness never comes without pain. Murdo is trying to cover up the fact that this time, the audience doesn't just want a part of him; they want his soul. To produce something of this magnitude, this musical production, his production, that's been five years in the making, is nothing less than a miracle. That's what his audience wants from him now. Before, it was his voice they were in love with. And then it was his love for, Ariadne. She was nothing without him. For a long time, he'd thought he was nothing without her, but her gift, this that he has become, this is what he traded, this is what it was all for. The pain of the true Ariadne, the pain of losing her, the sacrifice he made, the debt he owes his mother, everything, everything is resting on his success, his delivery of a miracle. There is no other option.

'Don't pretend to me. Not me, Murdo. You disappoint me, if you think I'm not aware it could all blow up in my face.'

'Trust me, my friend. You've never doubted me before.'

Gilroy turns away and pretends to examine documents that have been flung on top of the filing cabinet behind his desk. It's not easy deceiving the old man. 'You can't see what's before your very eyes. Where is the joy in her voice, the yearning in her eyes,' he thumps his chest, 'the ache that gets you right here?'

Murdo bows his head. His shoulders sag.

Gilroy swallows his guilt and softens his tone. 'In the end, it always comes down to a feeling. Polly Burke makes for a poor lead,' he says, decidedly. He watches Murdo closely. 'She had promise, but somewhere along the line she has lost it. That is your responsibility, your doing.'

Murdo doesn't respond. He rises from his chair, paces the room.

It is surprising the way the shine has been stripped from the splendour of this room, an omen, perhaps.

'Gilroy, we are almost upon opening night. Go home. You've not been home for weeks. You need a break. I will fix this.'

'You have to. You have no choice. At the end of the day, you get nothing for nothing.'

***

Gilroy doesn't go home. He positions himself at the edge of a masking curtain. From here, he is invisible from the stage. The girl and Murdo, close together, centre stage. Murdo steps back and the girl readies herself. From her position, she is about to begin her opening solo, without the rest of the cast on stage to cushion her.

Gilroy closes his eyes so he can listen without distraction. There is no doubt she has a clear, sharp musical voice. The resonance is there, the tone is on point. Murdo, the old fool, is hoping she will adore him and together they'll find their way out of the labyrinth. It's an unsettling thought, and perhaps is at the root of his own dislike of Polly Burke.

Murdo wouldn't leave him. It's a thought not worth having. His first major production with the promise of greatness for the future, even if it all collapses around them in absolute failure, Murdo will remain by his side; to encourage him to start over. That's what Murdo would say, but he has no intentions, never has had, of starting over. That would be like falling backwards. Every step he has taken has been a step up to this very point. Murdo only speaks of Ariadne to wound him, a way of keeping him in his place, to remind him of why all this means something. Everything.

Was that a fissure of nerves in Polly's voice? Excellent.

'Stop. Stop.' He reveals himself from behind the curtain, whipping it aside with the flourish of a celebrated magician. 'I won't have it. Get out of here and don't come back.' He scurries her off the stage and into the wings and stands watching Polly Burke run along the corridor, until she turns the corner. 'The understudy. Get the understudy,' he yells at Murdo.

Murdo hesitates; he knows better, he won't quarrel now. The smell of paint and dust and shame is catching his throat, creating the stirrings of nausea. It is time he went home.

He beckons the old man and puts his arms around him, holds him close, and rests his chin on Murdo's threadbare woollen hat. It's as if their roles have reversed and he now is the adult. If that's how it should be, it's not fair. For all their lives together, they have resisted change. It should be no different now.

'Go after her, Murdo. It's okay. Take the rest of the day. Just don't bring her back to my stage. There are some things worth murdering for.'

Chapter 21

Gilroy

Glasgow & Edinburgh
10th October

The understudy sings like a bird; a fusion of crow and pigeon. The cast are a fractious mob of rats; the unbearable, incessant repetitions. The principal male has taken himself off in a strop and Murdo is pacing the stage in his bare feet, as if hoping he might conduct some form of musical vibration from the boards.

Gilroy hadn't gone home last night, instead he'd slept on the daybed in his office. He'd got up several times, thrown open the window and breathed in the raw night air. There's something about the Glasgow air that soothes him; something human. A shared experience, even if half of him is missing. Glasgow was Ariadne's favourite place, and this theatre, the stage for their debut, the beginning of their life together until it was cut short by circumstance.

This morning, the Greek chorus performed their best yet and Gilroy's palpitations mostly settled. Diana (his understudy version) is at least enthusiastic, and he can't fault her tenacity. He is pleased with himself and his decision to replace Polly Burke. *Madness & Ecstasy* is, once again, a thing of beauty. There is definitely much work to be done, and there is something comforting about that; the knowledge that there is the possibility of yet greater courage in his creative endeavours.

***

For the third time, his mobile vibrates in his pocket. What is it with all these interruptions? Who has the patience? The vibrations stop, only to begin again almost instantly. Caller ID shows Jeremy Collins. He listens to what his private chef has to say then hangs up. He thinks for a moment. Ah yes, of course.

'What a palaver. What an absolute treat,' he thunders, throwing his phone to skid across the stage and come to a halt somewhere in the wings. Everyone stops what they're doing. Just so.

Murdo emerges, Gilroy's phone in his hand. 'What is the problem, my friend?'

Gilroy signals for Murdo to follow him to his office.

When they're both inside, Gilroy slams the door. 'We are in the process of being robbed and plundered.' He step marches around the desk.

'We are?'

'What to do about it, that's the article. What does one do in such cases, man?'

'I'm not quite understanding you, Gil.'

Gilroy stops marching and takes Murdo by the shoulders. 'Someone is in our home.'

'We're being burgled?'

He shakes Murdo then pushes him away. 'Negative. A burglar with an iota of intelligence would not refuse to leave.'

***

It's already late and Gilroy is weary. The M8 traffic between Glasgow and Edinburgh was a nightmare and now, to be confronted by a maniac lout, to spoil what had been a good day had been outermost from his mind. Gilroy doesn't recognise the burly man occupying his favourite Fritz Hansen chair. The man's boots are resting on the Bond cocktail table and his fingers are fiddling with the Faberge *Swan Lake* music box, given to him by his mother, something she hoped would replace the absence of his father. This man, this wolf, is a breath away from hell.

'Who the damn blazes are you?' he shouts, rather enjoying his role. He kicks the man's feet off his table and snatches back the music box.

'You took your time,' the man says, his voice measured, undertones of that undeniable Glasgow twang.

Gilroy turns to check Jeremy is paying attention, and finds him hesitating at the door of the sitting room. The chef shrugs his shoulders and walks away. He's about to call after him but stops himself, he doesn't want to appear weak and afraid. He should have brought the dogs with him, why didn't he think of that? This fellow, sprawled out on his chair, is twice his size by the look of him. He places the music box delicately on the top of the bookcase. At least he can try and keep that from getting broken. Had he given it some thought, he'd have orchestrated this one-act play from the barn outside.

It strikes him that he's facing a beating. He has a strong desire to hide in the basement until this reprobate gets bored and scarpers. But what? What kind of man is he? Sometimes he has to remind himself of his own capabilities and this is one of those times. Courage must pay dividends. This brute isn't going to make him cower in his own basement. Briefly, he senses pride somewhere deep within himself. He's never had a spat before. Fisticuffs and the like are generally the indulgences enjoyed by thugs, the like of which is sitting directly in front of him now. Is this how it felt for Murdo on that ill-fated day so long ago?

Jeremy certainly didn't hang around. Who can blame him?

'What kind of burglar are you?' Gilroy asks, out of pure curiosity. Is he now to be part of his own personal ancient Greek comedy? Who can tell what one may learn when one confronts the bulbosity of the human psyche?

Gilroy rubs his jaw contemplating the brute's stubborn silence. Fascinating.

Like the tempting voice of chaos, one's misdeeds never seem to forget us. Eventually our mistakes will become rampant hunters, seeking us out to haunt our living hours. Until we make a choice, a stand. Confront our demons and squash them. If he'd had time to prepare, possibly he might have come up with something charming to stop this envoy in his tracks. But as it stands...

The first blow is to the abdomen. Gilroy bends into the blow, gripping the flesh under his shirt, just above his belt. Luckily, the blow missed his ribcage. He'd like not to have a rib broken. So many performers suffer months of agony when a rib snaps. Of course, he must fight back. What on earth is he thinking?

Before he is able to straighten himself, there's another blow. This time, to the face, more precisely, the right temple. Not a well-directed effort but painful nonetheless. Even with his new-found impetus, this second blow sends him reeling backwards. His shoulder bangs against the open sitting room door before he lands painfully on his derrière.

'This is preposterous,' he blusters somewhere in the direction of his heavy-handed assailant.

'I can't be doing with bastards like you,' the thug says, towering above him, one boot pining Gilroy's wrist to the oak floor, the other positioned dangerously between Gilroy's legs. This farce is carrying on a tad longer then he'd expected, and with no witnesses!

'I know who you are,' Gilroy tells him. There is a way he can fix this. Just needs a minute or two. Think it through. Chances are he could make the situation worse for himself. A beating he can stomach. 'I think you've made your point,' he blusters.

The thug grabs him by the shirt, pulls him so they are facing each other.

Polly deliberately, he surmises, did not mention the girth of her beloved. Gilroy holds his one free hand up in surrender.

Spit lands in his left eye, blinding him. The crunch of forehead on forehead. The thud of his skull on the wooden floor.

The sound of sirens in the street below. The slam of a door. Exit stage left.

Chapter 22

Nora

Skye
11th October

The front door is wide open and, in an instant, I know something is wrong. Dad isn't here. It takes only minutes to have a first glance around the cottage, the living room, kitchen, upstairs in my bedroom, Dad's. Nothing has moved, nothing stolen. Dad's rocker by the wood burner is still, his glasses…

I check the upstairs bathroom, the downstairs toilet. I go outside, around the side of the cottage, climb down the wooden ladder that leads to the lower section of our land, where we have a stone barn, the donkeys, Dad's pig and a couple of uninvited geese. Most days, sheep or cows or the bull will wander down from the hill, but there's no sign of them. Bear, our ancient Great Dane who likes to sleep in the pigsty, hauls himself out of the barn and comes to greet me, nudging his weary head under my arm. There is barley straw all over the paddock, both donkeys munching, their bellies bulging, and an empty bucket of pellets lying on its side in amongst it all. Not entirely inconceivable, Dad occasionally forgets to bring the bucket in. He likes to climb the hill next to the paddock and sit for a while gazing out at the sea, and if he takes a different route down the hill, one that brings him to the front rather than the side of the cottage, he'd forget he left the pellet bucket out. Once or twice he's done this. But the straw is supposed to be in the trough, not strewn all over the paddock. The donkeys are neat creatures, having a frenzy with the straw isn't in their nature. Dad must've been interrupted halfway through feeding, he'd never have gone and left the paddock in this state.

Is that William Ghilista walking up on the hill? He's coming towards me, no, he's running towards me.

***

I'm on my knees; they won't let me near him. I can't see his eyes. I have to see his eyes. People just don't die.

The last thing I said to Dad this morning wasn't what I would've said if I'd known that, hours later, I'd be standing a few feet away from his dead body. He is face down, cushioned by the giant algae that fringe the island. The tide is roaring in, so the police are doing what they have to do, while murmuring that Dad stepped off the cliff at the bottom of our garden. I've heard mention of suicide at least three times. They have no idea of the kind of man Dad is.

The policeman is digging his fingers into my shoulders, keeping me restrained, as if I'm some kind of criminal. I wave my arms about and try to get up, but nothing I do has any impact; he's broader than me, taller, doing his job the way he thinks he's supposed to.

I ram my elbow into his groin. Bent over, his hands between his legs, I scramble away. The other police officer has his back to me, guiding the mortuary car that has just arrived, and is attempting a bumpy route onto the grassy verge at the opening to the cove.

Dropping to Dad's side, I lift his hand in mine and turn his head to face me. His eyes are open, but he's not there, he's not Dad. This is his body, but Dad has left me. I let his hand go. Let the policeman drag me away.

The police officer I belted walks me home. I sit in Dad's rocking chair, the chair Dad should be sitting in. He should be answering these questions, not me. He should be here.

'You know, it's a criminal offense to assault a police officer.'

'What if I'd been the one holding you back?'

He doesn't say anything, crosses to the window, stands with his shoulders square, tapping his notebook against his thigh.

'My dad didn't do what you said he did.'

'How has he been recently?'

'He isn't the kind to get depressed.'

'What did you talk about this morning? Before you went off to watch whales?'

He says that last bit with a sneer.

'We ate cornflakes at the kitchen table. What do you talk about in the morning? Neither of us had much to say. I told him what time I'd be back and then I left.'

My last words to my dad were unremarkable.

'Jackob wasn't very talkative then, was that unusual for him?'

This guy has a gift of taking my words and turning them against me.

'No,' I tell him firmly, 'not unusual at all. We have a routine, him and me. That's how we like it. We're close, always know how the other feels, and he was just the same as always, he loved his life.'

I get up and join the officer at the window, so we're both gazing out towards the bottom of the meadow. This is our plot of land, my dad and I have worked hard to turn what was once just rocks and seagrass into a meadow, one that attracts the sunlight and reflects the moonlight. The meadow ends at the edge of the cliff. In my head, I see the cliff roped off with police tape, a couple of forensics on their knees, picking away at the spot Dad fell from, searching for evidence. In reality, there's nothing and nobody there. According to my police escort here, there doesn't seem much point conducting an in-depth inquiry, as he puts it.

'You're saying there's no point to my dad's death?'

'Sometimes people just die. For their own reasons,' he says. 'Unless there's something you're not telling me, it's likely we'll never know why he did it.'

I throw open the front door and march outside, unable to bear his presence a minute longer. He follows me out. On the single-track road, a police car waits with its engine ticking over, another officer inside. I recognise him as the one from earlier, who had spoken to the driver of the mortuary car.

'There will be an inquiry in due course,' he says. 'We'll likely know more after the post-mortem. I'll keep you updated.' He climbs into the police car and it drives off.

There's going to be a post-mortem. At least that's something. I go back inside and start searching. I didn't say anything to the police officer, he's already written me off as irrelevant, but there's something wrong. I feel it. I just can't see it.

Chapter 23

Nora

Skye
16th October

Kneeling in front of his rocker, it hits me that I hadn't much noticed how Dad sat in this chair. Now I see him, as if he is actually sitting here in front of me, the way he holds his back straight, rests his hands on the arms of the chair. I can trace the mould of his fingers, his fingerprints. I brush my finger lightly over, but without touching, in case his fingerprints disappear. He should be sitting here now, with me at his feet, the way I used to do as a child, and he'd read the newspaper to me.

I pick a log from the basket; I probably should get the fire going, it's freezing in here. Dad's alarm clock breaks the silence, a piercing *bleat, bleat, bleat*. I hurl the log across the room, hitting a picture off the wall and it smashes against the stone floor. Picking up the shattered frame, realising what I've done, a wave of nausea rushes through me. The picture, now torn at the edge, is of my dad, his younger self, in his Navy uniform. He'd been stationed at Rosyth for most of his nineteen years' service. All those stories he's told me, hundreds of them. I want to hear a hundred more.

This is not how my dad's story is going to end. Something happened to him. One thing that keeps niggling me is something William Ghilista said. When I was searching for Dad and William came to tell me what he saw. He told me where I should be. I didn't think anything of it at the time, William spends his entire life searching, but he was right, wasn't he. He knew where Dad was lying, dead. How did he know? He said he'd come from The Point, where his view of my dad would've been blocked by the rocky hillside. But what if he'd got there much earlier, and was only pretending to casually walk past? He could've been lying in wait, in readiness to push my dad off the edge of the cliff. And that thing he said, that crazy thing about animals not escaping judgement.

I know of no vendetta William could have had against my dad, but what if Dad kept something from me? I've always refused to believe what they all say about William killing his wife and child. What if I'm wrong and Dad found out something that would prove William's guilt? It all makes sense.

***

The hush of the wind and quell of the waves down below take me by surprise. I'd expected the waves to be crashing, the trees to be thrashing about in a frenzy. Inside had felt so cold. I wriggle out of the padded jacket I'd thrown on and toss it on the back seat of the car. The early morning mist hangs low, as I make my way along the Aird of Sleat.

I'm heading to Broadford. Everyone knows William's routine, he walks the exact same route from one end of the island to the other, then repeats the journey over and over. He always has breakfast at Café Sound. Even if his journey had been briefly interrupted by... by...

I should still catch him. Briefly interrupted – the shame of it catches me in the throat, and my foot presses harder on the accelerator.

I arrive and park up, but there's no sign of William and the café staff tell me I've missed him by minutes. Back outside, I search as far as I can see, up and down the main road. If William has already taken off, I'm unlikely to catch up with him until he emerges at Portree. He doesn't take the straight roads. His pilgrimage takes him on a punishing trek through the rocky terrain that is Skye. Nobody really knows which way he goes at this point, and I suspect that's just how William likes it.

Matt, the café owner, shouts me over. 'Heard you're wanting the Watcher. You might check down at the boats. It's looking to be a fine morning, so he got takeout; said he wanted to enjoy his breakfast down there.'

***

It's a five-minute walk to the mooring down at the sound. Every step of the way, I'm figuring out what to say to William, if I find him. I consider whether I come right out and ask him if he knows what happened to Dad.

There he is. He is actually here. I just need to walk up to him. He's sitting on the edge of the pier. Because it's so early, no one is about. The Co-op isn't even open yet. As soon as William knows I'm after him to tell me what he knows, he could decide to shut me up as well. He's fit and strong; it wouldn't take much for him to seize me, get me in the water and hold my head under.

I need to stop hesitating, I can't hold back any longer. No one else cares what happened to Dad.

William is sitting with his legs hanging off the pier, eating something from a paper napkin, as if everything is normal. Inside, parts of me I've never thought about before have turned to jagged shards.

I steal up behind him and, before he notices me, slap him across the side of his head. No time to stop and think about what made me do that because he's choking.

The choking isn't stopping.

He's making some effort to get up, but his body is wracked with coughing, in between moments of breathlessness. Tucking my arm under him, I help him on to his knees and he's able to cough up the blockage and clear his throat, enough for him to look up, his eyes teary, face blotchy. Eventually he manages to get to his feet. He spits out my name.

'I'm sorry,' I tell him.

His eyes are questioning me, but he's not saying anything.

'I am sorry,' I say.

Taking a step closer, I can almost taste the odour of him, sweat mingled with peat and heather. I swallow, so I can speak crisply, confident.

'It's just… I need to… if you know anything. Anything? Did you have anything to do with what happened to my dad?'

'I know what people think about me. What they say. The more I keep myself to myself, the worse it gets.'

'Answer me.'

Something crashes behind me and a jolt of fear has me wavering on the edge of turning away or running at William, pushing him off the edge of the pier.

I look back. It's only someone from the Co-op running a delivery cage along the pavement, nothing to be scared of and yet my legs won't stop shivering.

That senseless, blank stare William is giving me. He's not going to tell me the truth, why should he?

'You know it wasn't me,' he says.

'What do you want me to do? What do you want me to do?' I hear myself screeching. Unable to stop; who knows what I'm screaming any more. Someone killed my dad. Someone did this. Someone.

William takes my hand, and I follow him along the shoreline. We reach a rocky inlet, and sit, gazing out across the sound, to the island of Pabay.

'I don't have a problem with you accusing me,' William says. 'I don't blame you. Tragedy always comes as a surprise.'

Guilt can make you say anything. I doubt I ever truly believed the rumours about him; rumours that swept the whole island from Ardvasar to Duntulm. My dad refused to listen to a word of it. In the end, that means nothing. People do all sorts of unexpected things for inexplicable reasons.

We're tucked in, away from the harbour and the main street. We've come to a place that, unless someone happens to be taking a stroll along the main ridge of the bay, no one can see us. If I really thought William was guilty of anything, would I hide away with him?

This landscape, it's supposed to be familiar but it's as if I've been dropped onto the other side of the world.

'I could never hurt your dad. He was a good man. Better than most. You're not going to believe me, Nora.'

It's true. I don't believe him. I could pick up a rock and smash it against the side of his head. He wouldn't see it coming. I could do that, if I knew for certain William had killed my dad. Murder, it can't always be black-and-white, but how would anyone know about murder unless it happened to them, it must be different for everyone.

The only common factor must be that someone has died at the hands of someone else.

'I do know something you will believe. Raymond Styles is back on the island.'

Of course, he's going to deflect the truth from himself. He's looking at me intently, and I can't tell if he's lying. Raymond Styles. That's too much of a coincidence and William knows it.

'Have you seen him? Where? Have you spoken with him?'

If William is telling me the truth, the police will have to investigate now.

'Yes. I saw him yesterday. At the Old School House.'

Eight months ago, I'd have struggled to believe Raymond Styles could ever have harmed my dad. Now, if it's true and he's back, he has only one reason to return to the island. He'll be wanting his revenge.

William picks up a couple of pebbles and juggles them. 'You know where to find me. I've nowhere to run to.'

I get up, shaking the stiffness out of my legs. He's right. William can wait, there's no chance he will flee the island and leave the memory of his dead wife and child. Raymond Styles may have already gone. He's done what he came here to do, he won't hang around.

'You can't do this on your own,' William says.

'The police aren't listening to me.'

'You are Jackob Winter's daughter, Nora. Make them listen.'

Chapter 24
DS Calmly

Fletcher Cunningham is a man I've barely spoken to over the last few years. Not since he bailed out of the urban landscape in favour of what he referred to as island life. I tend to view the island as bearing no reality to life in the slightest. In one respect, in my estimation, he swapped pollution and the bad element of society for healthy lungs and bullish behaviour. Not necessarily from the bulls, I fear. But he and I go a lot further back than eight years. We were chums at Tulliallan. Fresh-faced upstarts that the police college soon moulded into something more authoritatively upstanding and spat us both out with a lot less boyish expectation. Mind you, nothing could rid Fletch of his charm, even now, I expect he gets by quite well on it.

Apart from all of that, I owe Fletcher Cunningham a favour, which is why I've put the Edinburgh trip on hold for a day or two. Hang the reprimand, should the DI have a gripe about it.

I'm just about to alight from the ferry that's taking me to Armadale and the island of my childhood. It occurs to me now, that if I'd had a mind to, I might have given Fletch a good talking to about his island policing dreams. I chose not to do so, because a man's dreams are his own and who else has a right to thwart another man's ambition? Personally, it felt to me like a lack of ambition, but that's by the by. Fletcher is a city boy, or at least, he was then. I doubt much has changed in that respect. You have to be born to an island for it to be properly in your blood, that's what the locals will tell you on Skye. Whether there's any truth in the matter, that's not for me to decide. My mum was forever touting the fact that she raised her son with the toil of her hands alone and received help when she needed it from the island soul. I occasionally muse that perhaps this was not so much the island soul but one that belonged to the kraken. On a good day, my powers in sinking criminals and destroying their nefarious activities are what keep my policeman's verve alive.

I ease the car off the ferry at Armadale and make the long drive to Portree police station. I wouldn't do this for just anybody; drop a case at a moment's notice. As I said, I owe Fletcher a favour. He's calling it in. I knew he would, one day. It was never going to be a day that was convenient; turns out life isn't made for convenience. He's keeping an eye out for Mum. Not the kind of favour that is a one-off, done and never to be called upon again. Fletcher knows I'm more than willing to come to his aid, however often. I know he wouldn't have asked me to make the drive if it wasn't important.

Day is finally dawning, the clouds inching apart, the fog, while not yet dissipating, is less cumbersome, like taking a sweater off, and allowing Mother Earth to get under your skin. The car drives smooth and snug along the tarmac. It'll take me just over an hour to get to Portree. So far on this journey, all I've thought about is Eve and the feeling in my gut that there is a connection between the deaths of Bruce Lawrence and Maureen Park. I suspect Eve is involved at some level, but I don't buy Paula's theory that this is about an affair of the heart. Once we establish the link between Eve and Gilroy Flynn, we might get some traction on the case. Perhaps I need this distraction that Fletch has dealt me. Clear my head. I may even work up the courage to visit Mum at some point during the course of the day. I deliberately push thoughts of Jenny aside. I feel pretty sure, if she's willing to speak to me, we'll both steer well clear of that conversation.

Fletch said something about a suicide, some disagreement over cause of death. The daughter of the deceased is refusing to accept the simple explanation. Understandable. Not much I can offer in cases like this. Time is the answer. I wonder if Fletcher feels out of his depth. Can't imagine what he thinks I can do that he can't do himself.

The car drives smoothly into Portree. It's no less touristy at this time of year. I never thought I'd hear myself say it, but there's something nourishing about being back, something soulful, I might even say, healing. Who doesn't want some of that?

I slide into a diagonal space in the public car park directly opposite the station and climb out of the car, stretching my legs, cautiously, because my calves have a tendency to cramp after long drives. It's no small ask, having me make the four-and-a-half-hour drive and Fletcher knows this, so I hope he's got something more than hopeless for me. Fletcher is well aware of what happened to Jenny two years ago, and he knows it's not the drive that stops me from making home visits. He didn't have much call to really know Jenny, but since he's made his home on the island, he's got pretty close to Mum, by all accounts. At first, only at my bequest, but his infrequent emails tell me he's forged a bond there. He's had her side of the story rammed down his throat, no doubt, so I'm a tad nervous pushing my way through the station doors.

I'm sitting opposite Fletcher, my head in hands, elbows on the table, in the tiny interview room and I can hardly believe it. I'm certain, by now, that Fletcher Cunningham has called me here on a fool's errand and that just won't do. Fletch is wriggling about, stumbling over his words and generally more unlike the Fletch of old than I'd ever expected.

'Come on, matey, spit it out.'

'Lookie here, Lark. There is a real problem across there at Sleat. The woman just won't give it up. I feel heart sorry for her, know what I mean?'

'Get away with you, man. What do you expect from me? I know when I'm being had.'

The suicide occurred on the other side of the island, Aird of Sleat, where the bulls roam free and the tourists take their lives in their hands. I have a vague recollection of the dead man, but only because Mum makes local gossip her business and Sleat isn't all that far from Broadford, close enough for the gossip birds to fly. I doubt I ever met the man, or the daughter. She's the one giving Fletch the bellyache.

'I don't want to get involved in this, Fletch. Now, tell me why you really dragged me back?'

Fletch takes the time to clear his throat, lean back in his chair, scratch his armpit…

I kick the table leg, give him a start.

'Your mum's frightened.'

Nothing could make my mum as much as flinch. This is a ruse.

I don't blame Fletch, he's just a convenient conduit to me. I get up to leave.

Fletch springs up and blocks my way to the door.

'I expected better from you, Fletcher, than to take sides.'

He winces, shakes his head, looks at his shoes; arms across his chest. He taps his foot on the vinyl floor as if expecting I will change my mind sometime soon.

I wait, patient and silent, and eventually he looks me directly in the eyes.

'The longer you leave it, the harder it will be,' he says.

Somehow, since deserting city policing, he's adopted a grandfather-like tone, with the addition of that sing-song lilt I've never yet, myself, been able to shake off. He's more entrenched in this island than I ever believed was possible.

Seeing that I'm not willing to budge, Fletcher reasserts himself.

'Will you speak to the daughter?'

'I'm not inclined to do so.'

'As a favour to me?'

There it is. What can I say? I step back, perch on the back of the chair. 'What good will it do?

'You're from the big city. She'll more likely listen to you. I want you to convince her that she's got it all twisted in her head. Preliminary results haven't thrown light on anything suspicious, and I doubt the post-mortem will reveal anything other than the man stepped off the cliff under his own volition. He was a quiet man. He didn't have many neighbours but most held the belief there was something haunted about bloke. The daughter has started haranguing the locals, accusing this one and that. I've spoken to her, but she's threatened to take matters into her own hand and that's not going to end well around here.'

I study his face; an interesting juxtaposition of smugness and benevolence. He's taking care of business at home for me. I force myself to admit that it can't do any harm to have a word with the victim. I am but a man, affected by grief same as us all.

'I'm here now and that other business isn't part of the deal?'

''Course. 'Course,' he says. I don't think he realises he's shaking his head in the negative. Matters to me not a jot, as long as he's of the understanding that I've no intentions of appeasing my mum. As I said, that conversation is null and void. A quick visit, perhaps, that will take courage enough.

'Where can I find the daughter?'

'She'll be along soon enough.'

Chapter 25

Gilroy

'Who might this be, do you think, Gilroy?' Murdo nudges him, as he's preparing the set to bring out the dogs.

There's a chap striding down the centre isle of the stalls. Excellent, everything is working out as planned. His face looks worse than it is and will do nicely, and the bruises to his ribcage are healing.

'I don't know but get him out of here,' he bellows to the auditorium. There's no one there, but that notable panic rising up in the way Murdo is twitching across the stage is satisfying indeed. 'I need no distractions today,' says Gilroy deliberately dismissively. 'Who left the door open, anyway? Where are the dogs? Get them onto this stage.'

It had taken a while, but five months ago he'd finally managed to track down two Irish wolfhounds to take the roles of Artemis and Argos. The dogs are brothers, and they are malleable. Even Murdo is impressed with them. In fact, Murdo had liked them enough to agree to keeping the dogs at home. As a young boy learning the ropes, he'd helped Murdo with the dogs brought in for his mother's debut performance, the first premier of *Madness & Ecstasy*. Even then, he'd known Murdo would be a guiding light in his future career.

'Mr Flynn. Mr Flynn. Just a quick word.'

Gilroy turns to assess Murdo's reaction. 'This stranger has the gall to climb up onto my stage,' he blusters, pleased that Murdo, approaching the reporter, now with his blanket calm demeanour, appears unsuspecting of the trickery afoot.

'Get him out of here,' Gilroy shouts across to the stagehand closest to the blighter who is now almost upon him.

'I think you'll want to speak to me, Mr Flynn. My name is John Day, stage reporter from the *Glasgow Theatre Guide*.'

Murdo pushes past him, 'Leave it to me, Gil.'

Excellent.

'Aye, no, Mr Flynn, would you like to say something to our readers in response to the allegations made against you from your leading lady, sorry, that's ex-leading lady, Polly Burke?'

'Get out of my theatre. I've nothing to say to you. What happens with my production is my business. Not yours.' Gilroy growls, the imbecile continues to stand motionless, watching for him to crack.

Excellent.

'That's a nice black eye you've got there, Mr Flynn. If someone had done that to me, I'd have reported them to the police. Makes me wonder why you haven't already 'cause, if you had, I'm sure I'd have heard about it.'

Yes, the fake burglar may have enjoyed his role a little too enthusiastically for Gilroy's liking, but one can't help but be impressed by the outcome; a split lip and belter of a black eye may just be enough to make front-page news if he handles this properly. Murdo must take the lead; he can't be seen to be courting attention himself. The dogs bound onto the stage, scratching claws and piercing yelps, they leap and spring up and down between him and the reporter.

'Someone put those dogs on a lead and calm them down,' Murdo orders, pulling the dogs roughly by their leather collars.

'You, Mr-I-don't-need-to-know-your-name,' Gilroy points at the reporter, 'you've been listening to gossip. Trust me, whatsoever you want to print about this production, you'll do better to listen to me, if your career means anything to you.'

'Now, Gil, let's be sensible about this,' Murdo intervenes. 'The chap is just doing his job. Tell me, Mr Day, what's all this about?'

'I hear you've sacked your leading lady, Mr Flynn. You might want to tell me your side of the story.'

Gilroy waves at the air. 'What story? There's nothing to tell.'

'Gil?'

Murdo is worried about bad press. He is generally an intelligent creature, but his ancient approach to marketing will not do for today's more sophisticated audience.

'The *GTR* hasn't sent him; he's a freelancer, looking for dirt. What do you say, Murdo?' Gilroy's almost tempted to take a bop at the chap, but the angst on Murdo's face warns him otherwise. One can overact in these types of situations; there is a line he oughtn't cross. He winks at Murdo as if offering thanks for the old man's wise influence.

The reporter bumbles on. 'I get you. I really do. Can't be easy dealing with a diva like Polly Burke. Let me tell you, her name is dirt in the circles I mix in.'

Gilroy might even feel a bit sorry for poor Polly, he knows more about her than this moron. If anyone's a diva it's this reporter fellow.

'I dare say the circles you mix in, Mr Day, could hardly be expected to understand the complexities of musical theatre.'

'I hear she has a lot to say about you, Mr Flynn. None of it very flattering. Last I heard, she was threatening to go to the police. What are you hiding, eh?'

Ah, Polly has excelled herself.

Murdo, panics, asks the reporter why this should be, but it's obvious the guy is scratching for dirt.

Excellent. Of course, he won't find anything too caustic to Gilroy's career. His spat with Polly's boyfriend should be enough to get the people of Glasgow roused enough to keep the box office busy. What happened afterward is none of this fellow's business.

'Maybe you've got something to say about that, Mr Flynn?'

'I've nothing to say to you. Print a word of a lie and I'll sue.' Something nice and juicy for the reporter to wrangle over.

Murdo nudges him aside and takes the reporter's elbow. Excellent. 'Take a seat with me here in the wings. Perhaps make a feature of the dogs? I'm quite happy to sit with you. I may even give you a bit of insight into the production. That's really what you came here for, is it not?'

'Nah, not this time. Mr Flynn, I don't think you can rely on the 'all publicity is good publicity' shite. Criminal proceedings against you won't help your ticket sales.'

How naive, and when his feature hits the front page with just the threat of criminal misdeeds, of course he's playing the game. It's all a game in musical theatre. 'Do you know what you're talking about?

Who's threatening who here?' Gilroy awards himself with a smirk. 'First you want me to speak to the police then you tell me I'm being reported to the police. Can't you make up your mind?'

Murdo glowers at him. Excellent.

'Listen, Mr Day,' says Murdo, 'you really seem to have no legitimate reason for being here, and if our production holds no interest for you, I think it's time you left.'

Gilroy flashes his sharpest smile. 'That's it. You toddle off now.' He's about to turn his back on the chap when something suddenly strikes him as peculiar and rather disturbing. 'Wait. What did you mean when you asked what am I hiding?'

Smugness glows in the chap's face. 'I heard a whisper see, about your old man. A whisper that will have the law digging for dirt, and I don't mean in the metaphorical sense.'

Gilroy laughs a full belly laugh. It's only the startled look on Murdo's face and the curious tilt of the reporter's head that brings him round. Laughing probably wasn't the soundest choice of reactions given the circumstances. It was a momentary lapse, relief most probably. For a second, it looked as if his publicity stunt was about to backfire in the most heinous way. His outburst has made the reporter hungry for more. Let them scrape about in the dirt of his father's untimely demise. He's not afraid to stand shoulder to shoulder with poor old Murdo on that front. His father's unfortunate accident is the least of his worries; golly it happened so long ago, who'd be interested in it now, who would want to prosecute an old man who's kept on the right side of the law his entire life, apart from that one incident? Now, if that rat of a reporter were to find out what *he's* done, that's a whole other matter.

'Artemis. Argos,' Gilroy shouts at the dogs, 'fetch.' The dogs each get up, stretch their legs, stroll over to the reporter and sit. Bare their teeth. Some things are simple to achieve. He and Murdo have done well, teaching the dogs their part.

'Okay, okay, I'm going,' the reporter backs away. 'One last thing,' he pulls out his phone and makes to take a photo of Gilroy's face.

Gilroy pretends to be hampered from turning away or swiping at the phone by the dogs, he quickly flashes the most beaten side of his face toward the camera then pushes the dogs aside and whispers, 'Now, get out of here.' The dogs omit a long, drawn-out growl until the auditorium door slams behind the hack and Gilroy relaxes, content that he has achieved his purpose. Soon, his battered face will be on front covers everywhere that matters and the people will come in their droves.

***

Later that day in Gilroy's office, Murdo tackles him for encouraging bad publicity. Demands he reinstate Polly Burke, put the matter to rest and stop any further threats of any kind of police investigation.

'What threats?' he asks, cautious of Murdo's prickly tone. He picks up a pen and taps it on the desk, *tap*, *tap*, *tap*.

'It'll do you no good to have the police sniffing around, you know it, as well as I. Is that what you were doing when you disappeared in the early hours the other day? You were supposed to be here to meet the investors, to reassure them, put their minds to rest. Instead what? You disappeared for the entire day, conjuring up this nonsensical stunt of yours were you?

Murdo leans across the desk and grabs the pen from him. Gilroy settles himself in his chair, crosses his arms and beams at the old man.

'You can handle the finances, you always have. Am I not entitled to a day off, was it not you urging me to stay at home, get some rest and recuperation after my beating? Right then, so I took your advice as I am want to do. I stayed home. You charmed the investors I have no doubt?'

Murdo drags a chair closer to the dying embers of the fire and perches on the edge of it.

'Yes, yes, of course,' he mutters eventually. 'I entertained them and kept them onside.'

'Of course,' Gilroy says. Then, eager to change the subject, 'We shall keep our little understudy, I like her, she has grit. Polly Burke has shown her true motivation, as I see it; she hasn't an ounce of loyalty. The girl is a caricature motivated by the instant gratification the money I offered promised, utterly unable to see the treasure that the future holds. Her creative life purpose forsaken for a measly few gold coins. And you want to bring her back?'

Murdo leans closer to the fire, rubs his hands furiously. 'Why did you do it, Gil? What was the point of it? That underhand attraction of the press is dangerous. The priority should have been our investors. Where were you? I took it for granted you'd be here to greet them.'

'There's no jeopardy using the media to get one over on our competitors, Murdo.' Gilroy gets up from his desk and crosses the room so he can face the old man who is all hunched up and refusing to look at him. 'It's not like you to be timid.' What does Murdo know, eh? If anything. He can't possibly know what he did the other day. He was nicely out of the way, kept occupied with the investors. There is nothing to worry about. There is no threat to him here. He's sure. Still, there's something Murdo isn't saying; something that's twisting at the old man's insides.

He stands rigid with his back to the fire, and glares at Murdo. 'All this talk about danger. What danger?' There was at least a small segment of him that believed Murdo would shower him with pride, would clap him on the back and laugh with him. Nothing had prepared him for this. Murdo's abject disapproval is disturbing.

'Have you no faith in this, your, production?' Murdo blurts out, giving him a start. 'Have you no faith in yourself?'

Murdo is disappointed in him. This feels a tad more palatable than the other. He quickly turns away to face the fire, breathes in the thin, smoky air. Murdo suspects nothing.

The foolish man's anxiety over his apparent loss of faith, well of course, it is baloney. Of all people, he knows himself to be of sound capability, more than that, he possesses a kind of genius, solely for the stage, for the music, for the divine ecstasy that he can bring to audiences worldwide, he has no doubt.

'It is you who must doubt me,' he argues gravely. 'You talk to me about danger, man. As if I am capable of destroying what we have built together. You are the one afraid, not me.'

It suddenly strikes him that Murdo is projecting his own anxiety toward him. Once again, he reminds himself that Murdo suspects nothing. The old man's concern over the threat of police investigation can mean only one thing. He swings back to face Murdo.

'You are afraid I will divulge your secret. Let us be honest. It is you. You. You are the danger. Don't talk to me of causing danger and destruction. You did that when you murdered my father.'

Murdo rises from the chair and raises his hand as if about to strike him. He doesn't balk, instead he waits until Murdo thinks better of it, drops his arm to his side and turns away.

Murdo whispers something Gilroy doesn't quite catch. He grasps Murdo by the shoulder and turns so they face each other. Gilroy lowers his head and fixes his gaze on the old man's.

'To my face,' he says.

'Guilt can kill a man,' Murdo barks.

He hadn't been expecting that. He'd expected Murdo to condemn him for the accusation of murder. He knows well enough that Murdo's attack on his father had been defensive, was warranted and that the result was an unfathomable accident. Unfathomable because his father was a huge, lumping lout with a skull several times beaten by aggrieved husbands and law-abiding truncheons. Murdo had pushed and his drunken father had tripped on something that wasn't there. His head bumped a little on the pavement. His skull already weakened through his own doing. Gilroy barely remembers, he was just three years old. But his mother talked of that night in her bedtime stories to him. She talked of walking away and leaving his father to be found by a local man who knew what the lout was about. She talked of Murdo's courage in defending them both. She talked to him of how easy it is to forgive.

Chapter 26

Gilroy

Glasgow
14th October

They hadn't discussed it again but, since that reporter turned up, Gilroy has noticed a shift in Murdo. Throughout the day, he observes Murdo's confidence with the cast appearing lacklustre, his creative ideas ludicrous and inappropriate and his avoidance of as much as a quick glance in a direction that's anywhere close to where he knows Gilroy to be.

One must walk tall in the face of suspicion. Knowing Murdo, if, indeed Murdo knows anything about the secret Gilroy is keeping, he would come right out and say so. Why not, that is what makes the old man dependable, trustworthy? Has he to suspect some unaccountable change has befallen his old mentor, some transformation of personality? That is exceedingly unlikely.

What police investigation is Murdo so worked up about, if it's not the ridiculous idea that any police authority would have an interest in digging up the past? His father's death was recorded as an accident, case closed. What else? What unspeakable thing is Murdo suspecting him of? It's not like Murdo to be jittery in this way, is he ill?

Gilroy locks his office and tucks himself in at his desk, his mother's book laid out in front of him. He turns to the back page where he'd written down the phone number. He knows it by memory by now, but what if Murdo had taken the book, found the number and called it himself? He closes the book. He's going around in circles; Murdo most definitely would've confronted him by now. So what if he did? He slumps a little in the chair, tries to push away any thoughts of what might happen should Murdo turn on him.

But no! It's inconceivable that Murdo, his lifetime mentor, his replacement father, would see his actions as anything other than restitution. What else could he do but reinstate himself, it causes no threat to his production, his future, to his fame?

What threat has he caused Murdo, that's what he must fathom? The old man spoke of guilt, as if guilt would be the death of... Ah, the death of a man were the words he'd used. He'd known it; he'd known all along that Murdo understood.

Something unbearably hot rushed through him itching to strangle itself around his throat. An image of Dionysius crashes through his thoughts. Dionysius collapsing in front of the murdered children, his hand around his own throat, dying a miserable death, not from guilt but love, a twisted and diabolical love.

He shakes the image away and reaches across the desk for his carafe, pours himself a liberal measure of Merlot and swallows the lot. Murdo has issued him with a warning. He pours a second measure. Ariadne is the threat. This time he sips the wine. Ariadne has always been the threat. She loved him as Dionysius loved Diana. Love. Murdo is mistaken. It is love that kills a man. Somewhere, among that twisted eruption inside him is the love he's been burdened with all his life. Murdo's love, an enduring, diabolical love that Dionysius would fail to understand but... but isn't so dissimilar, why is he only seeing this now?

His thoughts are interrupted by a knock at the door. 'It's locked,' he bellows. 'Doesn't that tell you what you need to know?' He gets up and tiptoes across the carpet, puts his ear to the door and sneers as he listens to the sound of footsteps fading away.

About to return to his desk, he pauses, swivels around glancing at the walls. Why does he have all of these paintings of Ariadne hung up in here? Is this really how he wants to portray himself, as something that belongs to the past? No, no, no. No. This ancient theatre hasn't seen a performance for decades. It will be thanks to him for bringing the brick mausoleum back to life. Not back to the past. He must think of the future now. He will have them taken down, something else for Murdo to throw in the basement at home or hang in the barn. No. He will do the task himself. Why not? He is capable is he not?

He marches to the framed poster closest to the door. Begins by poking his finger on the glass, around the area of Ariadne's fake smile, Ariadne's long neck, draws his finger down her bare arm, stopping to caress the tip of her elbow. He bangs his fist against the cool, dusty glass. Ah, that felt good. Again, harder this time. Like Ariadne herself, the glass is tough. Harder this time, bang. He sucks in the satisfying sound of cracking glass. He lifts the frame from the wall and throws it across the room. He doesn't wait to see where it lands but quickly steps to the next frame, this time an oil painting, smaller, nastier, this he throws on the fire and scuttles across to watch it crack, frizzle, twist into itself.

Which one next then? Aha! That one by the window. He's never favoured it. A head-and-shoulders portrait in blue ink; the eyes disconcerting, the mouth squint, the jaw too proud. He drops it to the ground and stomps on it with the heel of his shoe. How satisfying. How revelatory. Murdo will be pleased. Why is this his first thought? Why must he think of Murdo at all?

Murdo's odd behaviour can't be left to take hold, it already has meant he's forgotten to assess the outcome of the investors meeting and figure out whether the old man was able to quench their fears about the extravagant additional costs, not to mention that bundle he'll have to find some way of explaining. His scheme with Polly Burke will pay off and that bundle will be nothing compared to what the box office will collect over the long run of *Madness & Ecstasy*.

He returns to his desk, closes his mother's book and places it gently, locking it away in his desk drawer. It wouldn't do for Murdo to know where he was the other day, most especially, who he met.

He takes a turn around his office instantly amazed at how much bigger it seems, and brighter. He can't help but feel that for the first time he is in charge of his own destiny. He will let no one stop him now.

With a quip he throws open the door and shoots along the corridor. 'Annie. Annie are you there? Annie.'

For so long, he's had the noise of Ariadne in his head. Most of his life has been directed by Murdo. He halts at the end of the corridor. Already he feels himself lighter of foot.

'Annie, there you are. Go to my office and bundle up all the artwork that's kicking about the floor. Take it to Murdo, tell him he can throw it in the basement at home, burn it, do whatever with it. Just get rid of it, will you.'

He leaves Annie to it, feels himself bursting with energy and skips up the steps to the wings.

Chapter 27

Gilroy

Glasgow
15th October

Gilroy raises his arm and brings his fist down hard to the side of Murdo's head. Murdo lands awkwardly on the rug. Gilroy grabs hold of the scarf around Murdo's neck, wraps the ends tight around his hands, crosses his arms and pulls hard, lifting Murdo up to face him. The scarf strains and constricts Murdo's breathing. Would it be so bad to squeeze the life out of his old friend? It's a fleeting thought that takes him by surprise, but he suppresses it and waits for the shame that has risen to his face to subside. There is some satisfaction to be had, even though his knuckles are tender, in the already impressive bruise forming on Murdo's cheekbone.

Gilroy tugs the scarf, drawing Murdo closer. Murdo's arms flail, bubbles of spit foam at his mouth.

'Why, why? Why lie to me? Do you know what you've done? Tell it to me. Don't think you can play games with me,' he spits. He releases the scarf. Murdo stumbles backwards but manages to grip the desk and right himself.

Gilroy straightens his back, tightens his shoulders in preparation for retaliation, but all Murdo does is to circle the desk and slump in the chair.

Murdo had walked into the office just as he'd finished reading the letter from the investors. The office door is closed. No one is lurking within earshot. Good.

'Alright. Alright, Gil.' Murdo puts his hand up. His head is down. 'I'm not willing to fight you on this.'

Gilroy takes the moment to relax, and tries to absorb the shock of what's just happened. To be at odds with his mentor feels like one day closer to dying. But perhaps it was always to be inevitable. He's outgrown the old man. The truth of the matter is that what he needs is to be free of the past. How can he have a future if the past is always threatening to pull down everything he's worked hard to achieve?

'What of it?' he shrugs his shoulders. 'You apparently are not willing to fight *with* me,' he says. He stretches across the desk and bangs his hand down hard against the blotter.

Murdo sighs, his head in his hands. 'It was unfortunate.'

He throws the letter up in the air. 'Unfortunate?'

Murdo laughs under his breath.

'What?'

'Yes, Gilroy.' Murdo uncoils the scarf from his neck, but he says no more.

He wrestles himself out of his jacket and unbuttons the top button of his shirt. Everybody lets you down in the end. Even his most trusted envoy. He's not come this far, sacrificed everything, to stand back and let someone, anyone, crush him.

He paces the room, tries to think this through, both dogs traipsing after him, doing their best to trip him up.

He yanks open the door and screams down the corridor, 'You. Annie, come and get these dogs and take them out of my sight.'

He grabs the dogs by their collars and almost throws them at the cleaner, slams the door, catching Artemis's hip and making him yelp.

'This is what I'm talking about,' Murdo says from the desk. 'You're not being rational, you're letting the pressure of this production get to you, and you're making mistakes, Gil. When ever before have you raised your hands to me?'

'You almost lost us our funding. Or should I say, you risked MY funding for MY production. And you call that unfortunate.' He's spent the last three quarters of an hour on the phone to the accountant. By some miracle, the accountant had the foresight to leap into action with guaranteed reassurances that Gilroy will meet with them tomorrow. 'You lied to me. You told me you met with the investors. Did it not occur to you that having them turn up here with neither of us to greet them would cause concern? Have you any idea how much money is involved here? How many times have you told me yourself, over and over, that without investment, *Madness & Ecstasy* will flop?'

'I don't take kindly to being beaten up,' Murdo replies, rubbing the side of his face, where Gilroy landed the punch.

Murdo leans forward on the desk, clasps his hands to his face. 'I cannot deny that I have steered you in certain ways. That by nurturing your talent I have, by necessity, overlooked certain aspects of your personality that, I see now, required closer attention. For that reason, I expect no apology from you.'

He places his scarf neatly on the desk.

'We must be vigilant for those who may wish to interfere, those who have the power to ruin us.'

Gilroy is incredulous. He leaps from his chair, his arms across his chest, and he's about to once more demand Murdo explain his absence at the investors' meeting when Murdo stops him short.

'You feel threatened.' Murdo scorns. 'Good. That is how you are supposed to feel. That is what will propel you to greatness.'

Greatness. 'You talk about greatness as if you know a thing about it. I can be great without you.'

'I imagine you can.'

Gilroy turns on him. 'It's shocking enough that you let me down with the investors but then to lie to me. Tell me you'd met them, been generous with them. To lie to me. To me?' He's never known the old man to be shallow. He returns to his chair, determined not to be defeated, but his body is weak, as if lifeless, his mind a blank. He worries his heart will stop beating, that the air he's breathing is about to strangle him.

'I was acting in your own best interests,' Murdo says decisively.

'Get out of my theatre,' he roars. 'I refuse to have you near me. Not now. Not ever.'

Murdo hesitates.

'Get out.' He springs up and points his finger towards the door.

'I will return when you've had time.'

'No. Leave and don't come back. You're not welcome here any more.'

Still, Murdo hesitates.

In the silence, Gilroy tries to reconcile himself with the knowledge that Murdo has it in his power to destroy him. If there is another way, he can't think of it. That their friendship could ever be broken is not something he could have foreseen.

'Get out,' he yells at Murdo, who remains silent and steadfast.

He marches around the desk to face the blank stare of his mentor, digs his fingers into Murdo's upper arms and shakes.

'Get out. Get out. Get out.'

Chapter 28

Nora

Skye
17th October

Portree is hooching with tourists as per normal. I resist the urge to scream in the face of each passer-by. Don't they know today is not a normal day? How can laughter, holding hands, banal chat, sightseeing and salty sunshine still be a part of living? All that's left for me is to keep on breathing. I keep imagining myself at the bottom of that cliff, what it felt like to hit the rocks. How long did he keep on breathing before the breath was stolen from him?

The copper at the desk leads me into a narrow room with a two-seater sofa and a hard-backed chair. I don't have to wait long. DS Fletcher Cunningham, the officer that took me home from the scene of Dad's death, ambles in with another man in tow. Fletcher sits by me on the sofa and the other guy stands facing me, hands behind his back.

'Nora, this is Detective Sergeant Lark Calmly. He's come from the mainland, from Perth, and wants to speak to you.'

Fletcher is refusing to look me in the eye; this doesn't feel promising at all. The other guy looks irritated at me before I've opened my mouth.

I ignore him and turn to Fletcher. 'Do you know Raymond Styles is back on the island?'

Fletcher escapes my gaze and fixes on the guy watching me. 'Now, Nora. I want you to listen to DS Calmly here. He's going to put your mind at rest about all of this unhappiness.'

'Unhappiness,' I yell at him. 'Are you for real?'

'Nora?' The other guy's tone is gruff and cursory.

I know how this is going to go. They're still not taking me

seriously, not even now that Raymond has returned.

'Unless you're going to tell me that you're at least going to interview Raymond Styles, I don't want to hear what you've got to say.'

This detective leans himself against the wall, hands in the pockets of his trousers and smiles at me. 'Nora, I'm sure they've already given you the guff on acceptance and time to heal and directed you to the nearest bloody bereavement counselling service which is probably in Kyle or even Inverness.'

I stay put and watch him intently. He has a local accent. That surprises me, gives me a tiny bit of hope that he might want to listen to me. Fletcher wouldn't have brought him here to talk to me if he didn't think there was something in what I've said about Raymond Styles.

'I would feel the same for someone I loved,' DS Calmly is saying, 'the disbelief, the betrayal, the loss of reality. I want you to know that the police, Detective Cunningham here in particular, is taking your grief very seriously, Nora. No one wants to believe they've been abandoned,' he says. 'I've looked at the report, and there's nothing in it that indicates suspicious activity. Whoever you think pushed your dad off that cliff, whoever this Raymond Styles fellow is, it's unlikely, in all probability, that anybody was involved in your dad's death.'

I'm about to stop him there, but he puts his hand up to stop me.

'It's my experience that the suicidal person isn't thinking about those they leave behind. You shouldn't take it personally, I'm sure your dad didn't mean to cause you pain.'

I've listened and now, I'm leaving. Dad isn't the only one who's abandoned me. It feels like the whole world has done that.

Chapter 29

DS Calmly

Skye
17th October

On Skye, nobody locks their doors. It crosses my mind that she'd sensed my homecoming and that's why the door is locked, but I shake the thought away and fish out the old skeleton key that's hung on my key ring since I was a boy.

The ancient front door scrapes along the tiled floor when I nudge it open, drawing me right back to the days of short trousers and sticky fingers. What would I have thought of myself back then if I'd known I'd turn out to be a copper? Knuckles rapped every time I got caught thieving. Mrs Rennie aye at Mum for recompense over a handful of Bazooka Joes or, if I was brave enough, I'd nick a *Beano* right from under Rennie's nose. My mum never paid up. I'll say that for her. Back then, she was always on my side, back before Jenny was born.

Her sharp dulcet tones reach the child inside me, reminding me of the arrogance of my youth.

A voice bellows from inside. 'Who's that?' Instinctively, I place a hand on my chest.

When I was little, I'd never had a sense of the distrust in her voice, but it had been there. For people like my mum, it's an innate quality. They say the same about pit bulls.

The narrow passage into the main part of the cottage is as dismal as ever. I hesitate for a moment. When I emerge into the sunlit kitchen, the familiar sense of home will not be coming my way. Those days melted along with the snow the morning Jenny died.

She's standing at the sink, her back to me, her compressed, burly frame in shadow form, with the light streaming in from the window.

I take a decisive step forward. A breeze from the open window welcomes me further, but I'm okay where I am.

'You've come back,' she murmurs, without turning around.

I'd hoped... Och... I don't know what I'd hoped for.

Steadily, she turns to face me. 'You might have let me know you were coming.'

'Why?' I take a seat at the table. I can pretend that somewhere deep within her and me, I still belong here. 'Would you have left the door unlocked?' I say. The pointed remark goes right over her head.

She busies herself with the beaten-up tin kettle on the stove. 'Times change, Lark Calmly, you of all people should know that.'

Giving up trying to prise the lid off the kettle, she slams it down hard on the stove, her hand gripping the handle as if it had been burnt on. I stiffen. She's going to belt me with it.

Instead, she releases the handle, drags a chair and sits opposite me.

'Say what you've come to say,' she says, her eyes fixed on me, her hands flat on the Formica table.

'I've been up to Portree,' I tell her. 'You'll have heard...'

'Aye.' She examines her hands, her nails. 'So, I'm just an afterthought, I suppose,' she says.

I watch her reach across, grab a tea cloth and wipe her hands with it.

'Two years is no time at all,' she says.

As hard as I try, I can't think of how to respond to this. And now I don't know why I'm here.

A rap at the front door hurtles through the silence.

Mum eases herself from her chair and goes to answer it. The smell of her as she passes me catches my breath, Badedas bubble bath. For the life of me, in this second, I almost leap up and wrap my arms around her. I hear a voice from somewhere deep within me. Don't answer the door. Listen to me instead. Hear me.

I almost want to tell her the truth. Almost.

It's the men from BT come to fit a telephone line. After what feels like hours of them explaining, her questioning, she lets them loose to get on with business.

The living room is where she wants the new phone installed. So, to keep out of their way, we resume our seats at the kitchen table. I ask her why, after all these years of resisting the very idea of being easily contactable, she's suddenly relented.

'Same reason you're here,' she says. 'I'm a woman on my own and there's someone loose on this island that has no right being here.'

This will be why she'd locked the front door, nothing to do with me turning up. I think of Jackob Winter and the phone connected in his cottage only a few miles along the road from here. What good did the phone do for him? Has anyone checked the phone records? That's something they could be getting on with up in Portree, if they haven't already.

'You shouldn't be concerned,' I tell her. 'The boys are convinced that what happened was Jackob's own doing.'

'Aye, and what do they know?' She pushes her chair back. 'You'll be wanting some tea, and a sandwich, I suppose.' She opens the fridge, 'I don't have much in these days.'

Minutes pass. I don't want a sandwich, but I know her. If I refuse it will only get her goat. She's always prided herself on taking care of her family duties. I want to ask her if this means she still considers me family, but I miss my chance.

She breezes past me and shouts through to the BT lads, 'You fellows want a cuppa and a bit of sandwich?' I have my answer.

They respond in the negative. She turns to face me and sighs, 'Just the two of us then.'

We eat and sup in silence. I check my phone. Nothing from Paula, so I still have time to at least begin the peacemaking process. It was never going to be easy. I begin by pulling my chair to the corner of the table, closer to her. She starts to lift the plates she'd served the sandwiches on, but I put my hand on her arm.

'We're at a crossroads,' I say, hoping she's willing.

'You might be, son,' she says quietly. Like a shot, she pulls her arm away from me. 'You were always in a rush when you were wee,' she snaps at me. 'Always after things being done before they were meant. There wisnae any telling you then. I suppose,' she growls, 'there isnae any telling you now, neither.'

I seize my moment. 'I want to talk about now. Today. Not then. Not the past, Mum.'

'Is it right for a person to always get what he wants?' she asks me, that stubborn jaw pointing in my direction.

'Don't you want it too?'

I squirm at my beseeching voice. I think of Eve and the life she's been exposed to and the pleading I'd heard in her voice. The difference between us, Eve and me, is that she hasn't a clue who she really is. I know who I am.

I look directly at my mum's face.

She knows it too.

Mum heaves up and puts the plates in the sink. 'Throw some wood on will you.'

The fire is already blazing, the heat in here claustrophobic. But I do as she bids, a block of wood in my hand, and stare at the gilt-edged urn, pride of place and incongruous on the ancient fire surround with its green, chipped tiles and broken mantle.

I'd like to know, if inside this urn, somewhere among the ashes, contains an essence of Jenny, still. If it ever did. Another conversation left unvented. I drop the wood block back into its basket and lift the urn, hug it to my chest for a second, then return it to its place.

She shouts something, as I beat my path to the door, brace myself against the sideways rain and the wailing wind. I don't hear her words. Don't listen. Perhaps if I'd be prepared to listen she'd hear me then? I'm stopped in my tracks by that sudden thought, my hand on the car door.

Chapter 30

Nora

Skye
18th October

The Old School House has been boarded up since Raymond Styles was taken by the police, first to a cell at the Kyle of Lochalsh and then to see out his twelve-month sentence at HMP Inverness. He must have got an early release, that's if William's telling me the truth and he's here on the island. There's only one way to find out.

The Old School House reminds me of stories my dad told me about his grandfather and the friendships he made there. One of those friendships was with the grandfather of Raymond Styles. Although the school closed and Dad and Raymond went to school on the mainland, they formed a close bond throughout their childhood years that continued into adulthood and led to them forming a partnership taxi firm that catered for the whole island for most of the last fifty years. Until one day, nearly two years ago, my dad discovered that Raymond was not the man he'd always thought him to be.

The dirt path leading down to the house is tricky to manoeuvre in a car and impossible at anything above one mile per hour. It's worse because Raymond will hear me coming and, unless he's waiting for me, he has plenty of opportunity to escape. If he did murder Dad, that won't be enough for him. He'll want rid of me too. He's had months to plot his revenge. It should have been me he came after. Or was this what he wanted all along, for me to suffer the loss of Dad for the rest of my life. What better revenge?

Finally, swinging the car into the gravel drive, straight away it's clear Raymond isn't here. At least, there's no car. There is a grey cat asleep on the front window and a row of starlings on the roof. It feels as if no one is here, as if there hasn't been anyone here for a while.

William may have tricked me.

I search around the side of the house, the front garden. This hasn't been a school since 1952. For as long as I've been alive, this has been Raymond's home. The tree house perched in the huge oak tree at the bottom of the garden, Raymond built that for me when I was a child, so that I could see along the coastline to home, when I needed to be here without Dad, and later, so that I could watch the whales.

He isn't here. I knock at both the back and the front door, but I know it's pointless. You can always tell when there's no one at home. A house seems to be just that little bit darker, as if when no one's home, it takes it's chance to close its eyes and rest.

On the ledge of the hill to the right of the house is a camper van. It's not unusual to see camper vans parked in passing places or on the edge of a cliff to get the best view. My father used to make up stories about an angry wind that would muster up a puff strong enough to ease any camper vans off the ledge, desperate to laugh at the sound of metal against rock. In my father's stories, there was always a she-whale called Nora that would soften the van's landing and rescue its occupants, which never failed to infuriate the wind.

This particular camper van looks brand new; rented, most probably. I can't ignore the feeling in my gut that's urging me to make sure it's not Raymond inside spying on me down here below. He knows he won't be welcome back to Sleat. He'd need transport, and a place to sleep where no one comes knocking at the door to make sure he leaves the island. He will leave, but not before he's seen me suffer.

I can't drive up and chance him seeing me coming. Instead, I make for a scramble up the hill that, when I reach the top, I will be close enough to surprise Raymond before he can do anything. There is just enough leverage for my feet and I hoist myself up, pulling at the tough sea grass as I go. I'm close enough now to see that there's definitely someone in the van, a shadow at the back window, the door at the front is wide open. I edge along a bit and emerge at the side of the van. I sneak around it, bend under the window, and I'm at the front door.

Raymond jumps down onto the grass, startling me. I straighten myself, and curiously, he looks dumbfounded. It doesn't matter that

I've lost the element of surprise. Just seeing his face insights that old rage I've held onto for the past year and a half, and I know he killed Dad.

'They won't give me the keys back to the house. Tell your dad to drop the compensation claim. He knows he has no rights to my property.'

'You took his,' I spit out, resentment spilling over before I can gather my thoughts. I lash out with my fist, catching the edge of his chin.

The smugness that had been there evaporates and is replaced with a flash of anger. He pushes me, full force, and I land painfully, flat out on my back, on the gravel.

Raymond is on his knees before I can catch my breath. His face pressed hard against mine. He grunts in my ear, 'Tell your dad I'm coming for him.'

He's leaning on my chest, my arm trapped under his legs. I struggle to get away from him, but he's pinning my other arm to the ground. He's using his other hand to call the police.

His nose is bleeding. I must've hit him harder than I thought.

Chapter 31

Eve

Perth
17th October

How does a person get to Glasgow? I've discovered that Gilroy Flynn's theatre is there and not in Edinburgh after all, Blythe told me. I have money. In my bag here are lots of notes, as many as I can carry, that I've stolen from Mother's little envelopes. Technically, I haven't done anything wrong, because I've not truly stolen anything. The money belongs to me now. That's what Detective Calmly told me. The money is tucked neatly in Mother's over-the-shoulder handbag. It's quite annoying the way the leather bag bumps against my hip. I'm walking along the grass verge on my way into Tibbermore.

I would like to get to Glasgow without speaking to anyone. Nobody must be able to find me. Graham just doesn't understand that I can't be with him the way he wants me to be. I can't be with his son. I can't call him my son because that would be a lie. I am a wolf; I am devouring Eve Park and finding the true mother so she can take her place.

First, I have to find out where I came from so that all my days aren't fake yesterdays. I would like real tomorrows. Mother wasn't a real mother, but she was very much a real superstar.

This is Tibbermore. I could go and ask for directions in the village shop. When I become a superstar like Mother, I will be real. Just like she was. I keep on walking, through the village, and I follow the sign to Huntingtower and Crieff Road, because that is the road that will take me to the city centre.

I drew a map for myself, copied from one of Graham's books. If Graham comes here looking for me, he might find out about me asking for directions. It's really okay, because I don't want to have to speak to anyone anyway. If Mother was alive, she'd never believe for a minute that I could make my own way to Glasgow. I'm going to choose to decide that I can. I will find my way to Glasgow. Mother doesn't know everything. At least she didn't know everything; except, she knew how to lie perfectly well.

Walking is really rather good. My muscles in my legs and arms are stiff, but it feels good to move them, good in a buzzy, electric kind of way. Walking makes me feel alive, like drinking a long, cold glass of water.

I've found a magic wand. It's the branch of a tree and it was stuck in a hawthorn hedge. It's the same length as my arm from my elbow to my wrist. I'm waving it in front of me and it's making me walk faster, helped along by the bleached sky and winter sunbeams lighting my path.

It's taken an hour and a half, and I've made it to the Crieff Road and B&Q. It started raining about twenty minutes ago and hasn't stopped; soft, windy rain. My head is wet with rain and sweat, and I'm incredibly thirsty. My feet are burning inside my trainers. It's like my body is singing with different kinds of pulsing. A fast pulse in my feet, a slow pulse in my knees, a lazy pulse in my calves and, if I wasn't so tired, I'd sing along with the pulse because it reminds me of the children's chorus in *Madness & Ecstasy*. I'd like to close my eyes and when I open them again I will be in Glasgow, on the stage, meeting my true self.

I take out a twenty-pound note from my bag and imagine I have the courage of Diana when she confronts Dionysus to rescue the wolves and the children. There's a burger van parked in the B&Q car park. I show the lady my note and point to a can of orange Fanta. She gives me my change, and I walk away quite satisfied. I had not had to speak a single word. But I must and I can. I make my way to the city centre and the railway station.

I've lived in Perth all my life but don't know the town centre or where anything is. I know there's a railway station, because Graham's sister came by train and took the baby away by train to where she lives for half the year when she's not in France.

It's taken me nearly two hours to get to the railway station. It would've taken me less time, but I took a wrong turning and found myself at the river. I stood there for a bit, because I didn't know which bridge I had to cross. Luckily, I spotted a signpost that said *Railway Station* with an arrow pointing in the opposite direction. It was a relief to know I didn't have to choose between three bridges; turned out I didn't need to cross a bridge at all.

***

I'm in Queen Street station. This is Glasgow, so the man at the ticket office said when I bought my ticket. All I had to say was Glasgow, and he said the train to Queen Street is in eight minutes. It came in twelve minutes and it took a further ninety minutes to bring me to this station, and I'm getting a really sore head, because I don't like all these people and pigeons and the squawky noise that they make. All that talk vibrates off the fan-shaped glass roof and pierces my skull.

Outside is horrific. It's hard to breathe with traffic and people coming and going, this way and that. There are hordes of people coming towards me. When I turn around, they're still there, still coming towards me. I cross the street at the traffic lights and walk fast and faster. I need to find a quiet place. Everywhere there are shops. Walking, walking, rain, sunshine, rain. I follow the street around, and the wind snarls at me and wraps around me as if it wants to drag me onto the busy road in front of one of those buses or perhaps that massive bin lorry.

The rain is getting heavier. There are no quiet places in Glasgow. Up ahead is a tunnel that looks like it will be a good shelter. Above the tunnel in gold lettering is *CENTRAL STATION*. I expect a big theatre will be somewhere central, and I already feel my spirits being lifted by the whole reason I am here. It's very dark inside the tunnel. For the first time since I got here, I see that people can be alone here. There's someone sleeping on the pavement, kept warm by a sleeping bag. The traffic continues all the way through the middle of the tunnel, I'm not sure how a person could get any sleep. Still, my legs hurt, my feet are sore and if I'd gone into every shop I passed, I think I could sleep here quiet easily. I sit on the damp pavement, quite close to the sleeping person and rest my back and shoulders against the stone wall. It feels good to stop. Whenever I look up into the faces of passers-by, they look happy. People smile here. So much talking to each other, I wonder what they talk about. What's it like to have someone to talk to who is willing to listen to what you have to say?

'You got a fag?'

The sleeping person is awake.

I shake my head and hold my bag close.

'What you got in the bag, then?'

The man is quite young, I think. He has sad eyes. 'They might sell cigarettes in there.' I point to a red and yellow shop across the street. On the door of the shop there's an advert with a pack of Benson & Hedges on it, the kind Mother smoked.

'You think?'

I nod, but the sleeping man has already turned his back to me.

I get up and walk across to the shop. I'm good at buying things now; I've already bought a train ticket and a can of juice.

I touch the sleeping man on his shoulder. He opens his eyes, and I hold up the two packs of Benson & Hedges I've bought. He sits up and glares at me. I throw the cigarettes on his lap and go back to my spot on the pavement.

Outside the tunnel the rain is lashing down, bouncing off the pavement. The sound of it almost drowns out the footsteps of passers-by.

The sleeping man lights up a cigarette.

I slide a bit closer to him. 'Do you know how to get to the theatre from here?'

'Nah,' he says. 'You got any scran in that bag?'

I shake my head, because I don't know what it is he wants and I only have the money in my bag anyway.

'If you get me more cigarettes, I'll tell you where the theatre is.'

I reach in my bag and pull out three twenty-pound notes, give them to the sleeping man. I can't be bothered going back to the shop and asking again.

'Aye. Braw. Ta,' he says and takes the money, slides it into his sleeping bag.

I wait, but he doesn't say anything more.

'Are you going to tell me?'

'Aye.'

He chucks his cigarette into the middle of the street in front of a passing bus. He points to the cigarette shop. 'Ask in there.'

'But I want you to tell me.'

'Have you got more money in that bag?'

I push my bag under his face and open it so he can see inside.

He folds up his sleeping bag. 'Come on,' he says. He nudges me with his elbow. 'You shouldn't be wandering about on your lonesome with a fancy bag full of money.'

I follow the sleeping man out of the tunnel.

'What's your name, missus?'

We turn right up an alleyway. He walks fast, and I have to hurry to keep up with him. I tell him my name.

'Right, Eve. I'll get you to the theatre on time. There's a braw baked tattie shop further up this street. You hungry? It's on the way.'

I nod. I am hungry. 'How long will it take to get to the theatre?'

'Ah, now Eve, that's a tricky question.' He stops and appears to think for a moment. 'What's the name of this theatre, anyway?'

'I don't know.'

'There's more than one theatre in Glasgow, I ken that much.'

There's nothing I can say about that.

'Nae bother. But if we're gonna walk aw roond Glasgow, you better eat something first, get your energy up. Ye ken, there's plenty pubs tae that we can stop in for a wee drink if we get thirsty, hen. We can make a night of it, thegether.'

I decide it's good to have company in a big city like this. I'm glad I know the sleeping man and he's being kind.

'What's your name?' I ask him just before we go into where we're going to eat. It smells glorious, oniony and, looking in the window, I see my favourite thing, cucumber. There are no seats, only a counter displaying boxes of cheese, salad and things.

'Tam,' the sleeping man says. 'My name is Tam.'

***

We're sheltering up against a metal shutter under the Mercedes Benz garage on Tyndrum Street. Tam says this is the 'by a long shot best place to sleep' in this part of the town. The rain has stopped and the air is dusty fresh and dawn is half a sleep. I don't think we've walked far. It took a long time to find the theatre, because there were a lot of bars on the way. Tam got very drunk, more drunk than Mother, and once he tripped over a kerb and smacked his face off the pavement. That was after we found the theatre. It's called the Glasgow Heritage Court Theatre. It was the second theatre we looked for; the Pavilion on Renfield Street was the wrong theatre, but the man at the box office pointed us in the right direction. He even knew Mr Gilroy Flynn, the producer, he said, quiet well. Said Mr Flynn was a big cheese and a numero uno in the theatre circuit. Only, by the time we got to the Glasgow Heritage Court Theatre, it was all closed up. So we've come to Tam's place to get a good night's sleep, and I'm going to go back in the morning. I close my eyes and let the cold wind hum me softly to sleep.

***

The sound of the shutter rolling up has woken me. It is almost light, the sky is turquoise and orange and intoxicating. That's a good word to describe Glasgow, I think.

My muscles are very stiff. I unzip the sleeping bag that Tam let me borrow last night. He is all curled up against the wall. I open up the sleeping bag and lay it over him. He is snoring gently. I don't want to wake him up. I don't need to, I know where I'm going now.

From my bag, I withdraw the mobile phone that Blythe gave me with her number on it and drop it in the pocket of my trousers. I wrap up the bag with the rest of the money, lift back the sleeping bag and tuck my bag under Tam's limp arm. We spent a bit of the money last night, but there's plenty left for Tam. He needs it more than I do, because he told me last night that he has nowhere to go. I won't need money now, because I do have somewhere to go. I have arrived. And it's good to be here.

Chapter 32

Nora

Skye
17th October

The custody officer is someone I vaguely remember going to school with. That's probably why he's lingering at the cell door, determined to feed me, water me, keep me company or something. I wish he'd go away. His prickly chin is quivering with guilt as if it's his fault he's locking me in this cell.

'Go away, Jimmy. That's your name isn't it? I'm fine.'

'You'll be in for the night. You know that, right?'

'They said so at the desk.'

'Okey-doke. Well, I'll check on you later, then, lass.' He turns to leave.

'Wait. I need someone to feed the animals.'

'I can maybe call someone?'

There isn't anyone to call. No one I can rely on. There's no one I'm willing to trust, not any more. I've played right into Raymond's hands. Now he's got me locked up here. I bet he's gone into the cottage, seeing what he can take for himself. I've made it easy for him. Worse, he'll find the door open, so he won't even have to break in. I didn't think, we're so used to not locking the door, my father rarely went far. Raymond won't find anything of value, but that's not going to stop him. He'll be scouring my father's paperwork, seeing if there's anything that will get him back what he thinks he's owed. I wouldn't put it past him to do something to the animals. He is a man with no soul.

I tell Jimmy to find William.

'William Ghilista? How am I meant to find him?'

Where was William the last time I saw him? Broadford. I try to calculate as best I can.

'He could be in Portree by now,' I tell Jimmy, but I'm not sure I've got that right. I'm not sure William will interrupt his wanderings for me. I do know that William wouldn't see harm come to an animal. That's all I've got to rely on.

'I'll give the station a call; see if they'll look out for him. But I'm not promising nothing.'

'Thanks, Jimmy.'

***

Raymond has plenty of motive to want my father dead. He's having me charged with assault to injure and, when it comes to it, I've no doubt he will be there, in court, to see me sentenced. They've told me I'll most likely get a fine, or even a suspended sentence, but the charge carries a six-month prison term. Imagine the joy that will give Raymond.

The mattress is comfortable enough, the cell is spotless and is neither warm nor cold, and the light coming in from the small window is dimming, a pale shade of sunset. I try to close my eyes and think of something else, but all I see is the look on Dad's face when he was falling from the cliff. It's different every time I imagine it, but the fear in his eyes is always the same. I don't remember a time in my life when I've seen fear in Dad's eyes. There is some comfort in that.

I wonder if the whale will notice my absence. Most sunsets I sit on the edge of The Point, the lighthouse behind me. It is my own island, not even the stray tourist that's scrambled their way to the furthest edge of Sleat can bother me. Just a mile or so out at sea, I will catch the swift, smooth surfacing movement of the minke whale. Nowadays, since we've formed our bond, she will swim closer and I can see her magnificence more clearly. She has a torpedo-shaped head and a pointed snout, a sickle-shaped fin about two thirds of the way along her back. She rolls along the waves, arching her back as if showing herself off to me. She is dark grey with a white lower jaw and underbelly and sometimes, if the light is good, I can see a white stripe on her fin. She plays with the gulls and the kittiwakes, and I imagine stories of dance, and joy and kinship. Often, it's just the two of us, as if we are a part of each other. Will she look for me? Will she mourn me? If I'm not there, will she leave, never to return? I've read that the whale spirit animal is the earth's record keeper for all time. That the whale can help us bridge gaps that are keeping us from connecting deeper with our loved ones. I like to think this is true.

Neither she nor I have missed a single sunset together in the last fifteen years, until Dad died. That day, when I couldn't find Dad, I waited and waited for her to show herself, to guide me. I waited until William found me and pointed me in the direction, along the coastline, to where my dad lay lifeless. Had the whale been there, further up the coast, watching my dad fall? Might she be the only witness to his death?

Chapter 33

Nora

Skye
19th October

They released me this morning. Raymond Styles wasn't at the police station, somehow he'd found out before me that I was getting a caution and nothing more. I try to be grateful for the simple repercussion of my accusation, but it's hard to believe a man like Raymond Styles will be happy to let things lie as they are.

Still, I'm home now, helping William lay out the feed for the donkeys. He'd spent the last couple of nights in the barn. When I asked him why he hadn't taken a bed in the cottage, he shrugged and got on with forking the hay.

When we're finished feeding the animals, I invite him in for a bite to eat and a well-earned cup of tea.

William isn't a talker. I sit across from him at the kitchen table and watch him take massive bites out of his cheese sandwich, then wipe his mouth with the back of his wrist.

'Thanks,' I say. I can't think of anything I can give him to repay his kindness. It's not just that he made sure the animals were fed and watered. The past two nights, lying in that police cell, I worried that Raymond would come here and all sorts of horrible thoughts kept me awake. I wouldn't put it past Raymond to have come and set fire to the barn, or let the animals loose.

'I should've come with you, stopped you from getting yourself in trouble. I had no business telling you that eejit was back.'

'No, William. No, I'm glad you did. It's better to know what I'm up against.'

'You're not wrong in that. But there's ways of going about things. Right ways. You're no match for the bloke, Styles. I thought you were going to go to the police.' He downs the rest of his coffee and stands. 'The more information you can give the police, the more likely they are to take an interest in what happened to your dad.'

'What did you see, William? You must've seen something. Someone? Are you sure there was no one there?' I get up and stand in the doorway, blocking his exit. There may be right ways to go about things but what are they?

My dad is dead and now it's just me. It's just me. Me. And I don't know. I can't think. I can't do this. My dad is dead.

'My dad is dead. Dead.'

William sits back at the table. 'I've already said. If someone pushed Jackob off the cliff, I didn't see who it was.'

'Now you're doubting me too.' I open the door wide. 'Just leave.'

He remains seated. I turn my back on him and gaze out at the sparkles as they tiptoe across the sea.

'He might've said something to his lady friend. Like, if he was worried about someone threatening him. He might've had an inkling, if you get my gist.'

I close the door. 'What lady friend?'

'You ken. That woman from Pabay.'

What woman from Pabay? I grab a notepad from the bookcase and search for a pen, finally finding one in the kitchen drawer.

Back at the table, pen poised, 'What's her name?'

'I dinnae ken.'

'Come on, William. Who is she and what's she got to do with my dad?'

'I don't know any of that.'

Dad never mentioned having a new friend, let alone a 'lady friend.'

'What do you mean by 'lady friend'? You mean like a girlfriend?'

My dad has never had a relationship. This has only just occurred to me. It's always just been the two of us. He never showed any interest in women. I guess I've always thought that together, we were enough for each other.

'It's not me you should be asking,' William says.

'Then who?'

'Have you got your phone there?'

I get up and take my phone out my coat pocket then hand it to him. A minute or two later, he hands it back. The screen headline reads 'The Time is Now'. Underneath is some smaller text and the Broadford Climate Change Group.

'What's this?'

'That's where he met her.'

'Met who, William?'

He grabs the phone back but then leans across the table so I can see him searching for the list of members. He scrolls down, then stops. 'Mhona Lindsay.'

'This is the name of the woman my dad was friendly with?'

William nods.

I had no idea Dad had joined a climate change group, let alone made friends with this Mhona person.

'Do you know anything about her?'

'Nope.'

'You know, it says here she lives on Pabay.'

'She's the one that bought the island then, bought it from that English bloke that wanted to build a hotel.'

I remember the uproar that had caused. 'I didn't know anybody was living on there.'

'This woman, I hear. Got friendly with your dad, she did.'

William's face is serious.

'You've been listening to the gossips, William.'

He lets the phone drop on the table. 'I'm just saying. She might know something you don't. You might want to ask Bert about her, he'll know more about her than me.'

'If any of this is true, she knows a whole lot more than I do. I should've known, at least, that she existed.'

If Dad did have a thing with this woman, why didn't he tell me? Why keep it secret?

'You said she was friendly with Bert?'

'Aye. It might be he was the one introduced them.'

Bert is one of those men, like my dad, that sits at the bar nursing his pint, gazing out of the window, saying not much of anything. Fixtures; as much a part of the pub's interior as the cosy fire and the stag above the door. The pair of them are likely to be lurking in the background of hundreds of tourist photos.

'I'm off,' William says. 'Don't you be getting into any more bother.' He closes the door quietly behind him.

I grab the notepad and write down the name; Mhona Lindsay, then chuck the pen across the table. It topples on the edge and, for a beat, I think it's not going to drop. It does, and lands on the floor.

Secrets; my dad kept secrets. William said he didn't know anything but, all along, he knew about this woman. Are William's secrets tied up with my dad's death?

***

Bert is exactly where I expected to find him, perched on his stool inside the Ardvasar Hotel, drumming his fingers on the bar. I hadn't expected there to be live entertainment. A small group of, presumably, hotel residents are attempting to rouse the one or two locals into an all-night session by the sounds of it. They've not travelled far, one of them has a strong Aberdeen lilt and the other two are Glaswegians or thereabouts.

I'd hoped to get Bert by himself. His glass is almost empty, and I'm not sure if I should offer to buy him another pint. This, I'm trying to decide while hanging around outside the hotel, staring through the window. It might be best to wait until he comes out but, if he orders another pint, it could be a long wait. It's just that, I'm not used to going into a bar on my own. In fact, I've only ever been in there three or four times in my whole life. My dad wasn't what you'd call a heavy drinker. He liked a pint in here at the end of the day and on the weekend. Those three or four times more recently, when I got a call from the landlord hinting that Dad might need a lift home, that was just my dad's way of dealing with Raymond's betrayal. The Ardvasar Hotel is the only pub between here and Broadford.

The music from the residents is decent; rowdy and uplifting. One has a guitar, the other a banjo. The pub door is open, and the notes ripple across the sound, bringing the night to life. The third resident isn't playing anything. He gets up and buys Bert a pint. Now I'm going to have to go in, because I'm not hanging around here all night on the unlikely off-chance that Bert has a mind to refuse free beer. It's a long walk home.

They're playing 'The Two Sisters'. It reminds me of my dad, and I wish I'd chosen a better moment to walk through the door.

'Ah, there's the very lass,' Bert says, throwing his arms up. 'I was jist saying aboot you, wasn't ah, Joe.' Bert leans into the man who bought him the pint. 'Saw you standing at the window, girlie. They're playing your da's song. I made a special request. Thought it might lift yer spirits, lass.' He signals the barman to pour me a dram and nudges Joe to pull out a stool for me. The barman puts a glass of something – whisky or brandy, I'm not sure – in front of me, and I sit on the stool by Bert. Bert puts his hand on my knee. 'Now you tell me, how are you bearing up, my girl? I'm no quite sure it's sunk in fer me yet.'

I'm not talking about my dad with Bert, not in that way. I'm only here to find out about this Mhona woman. This isn't how I wanted to do this, though, with the music playing the song Dad whistled around the house and the nauseous, cramping ache that Bert, a man that's as much a part of my dad as his animals were, might not be any better a man than Raymond Styles turned out to be.

'Tell me, lass. Are you coping?'

I want to fall into him. Let him wrap his arms around me. Let him soothe me with the songs of our lifetimes. I can't do that.

I could run out of here, keep running the whole five miles home.

'I want you to come outside,' I tell him.

He gets up straight away, a bit unsteady on his feet but he stands to attention, his hands on his hips.

'It's okay, Nora,' he says. 'It's okay.'

Outside, there's a chance to breathe in the cold, damp air and raise my head to the clouds in the hope that I can see this through. Bert crosses the road and sits on the low stone wall of the boatyard.

'There's something bothering you, and I'm no wellied enough yet to no realise it's something tae do with me, now.' He crosses his bony legs and leans his elbows on his knees, cupping his chin in his hand. He keeps his gaze fixed on me and waits for me to speak.

If I had to describe Bert in one word, I'd call him gentle. And if there were one man I could depend on, now Dad is dead, it would be Bert. He's so often round the cottage fixing things for my dad. I'm no longer certain I'm doing the right thing. Or even what I am doing. I've already spent two nights in a police cell after listening to William. Gossip, that's what I told William. But even if there's a fragment of truth in it, if this secret woman, or whatever it is I've come here to find out, got my dad killed, then Bert will know something about that.

Bert gets up and stretches his legs. 'It's a bonny sunset the night.'

Struggling to find a way to broach the subject, I take a deep breath and stand with Bert watching the pale grey light behind thin clouds that are fading from view over a shadowy Eigg on the horizon.

If I knew what Bert's involvement is with the Mhona woman, I'd have a better idea of where to start. I can't be sure, but was William hinting of a rivalry between Bert and Dad? If Bert wanted this woman all to himself, if he sees it as his last bit of happiness, even if it wasn't premeditated, if somehow the opportunity had presented itself and Bert had pushed my dad, out of frustration, maybe, or jealousy or desperation.

'I need to know about my dad and Mhona.'

He sighs, heavily, and sits back on the wall. I sit beside him. This way, he can't be sceptical of my motives; I'm simply trying to find out what happened to Dad. Leaving him out of it and making it feel as if we are colluding together. If he acts defensive or suspicious in any way, then I'll know he's not telling me everything.

'Aye, she's a fine woman, I'll tell you that.'

'Was it a thing, between her and Dad?'

He raises an eyebrow. 'Truth be told, I'm as much in the dark aboot that as you are, Nora.'

He sounds sincere but, with those words, I could sense a growl in his throat, his shoulders have stiffened and he isn't looking at me.

I want to move away from him. Part of me wishes I'd never come, that I'd been content enough to let the police do their job.

'You'll have to ask the woman yourself,' he says. 'Aye, and my pint is getting cold, mind.'

'Did you fall out with my dad before he died?' The question is out. If I don't ask it now he'll go back into the pub, and I don't think I could put myself through this again.

He gets up, steps over the wall and weaves his way through the boats tied up on the sand outside the boatyard. I'm not sure what to do. What to think. Is this an admission of guilt?

I catch up with him at the water's edge. Out of the shelter of the trees, the wind whips up the sound and catches at my throat. He picks up a handful of black sand and lets it seep through is thin fingers, all the while staring out across the water.

'We had words,' he says softly. 'But I didn't kill him, Nora.'

Those words, coming from his mouth, make me want to shake him.

'The two of you argued over a woman?'

He doesn't make a sound but drops his head and kicks at the shingle. 'It's no business of yours. It's nothing to do with anything. Your Jackob's lass, I ken that. But what two men wrestle over is for them to come to terms with. You need nae bother yerself wi a' that.'

'I'll bother myself with whatever I need to, until I find out who killed my dad.'

'I'm no gonna take offence with you, lass. Jackob was a grand old friend tae me. But if yer thinking what I think yer thinking, I'll tell ye this: I widnae put it past yer da tae have jumped himsel' off that cliff just tae help me oot. He kent she widav'e chosen me in the end.'

He picks up a heavy rock and throws it into the water. The sudden movement and the hefty splash startles me, and I stumble backwards.

'Nae mair words,' he barks and marches off in the direction of the pub, but then turns back to face me after one or two steps. 'Now away ye go and piss off.'

Chapter 34

Nora

I am awkward on a boat, clumsy. It used to make my dad laugh. I am back in Broadford, and it feels as if I've come full circle and yet got nowhere. This boat I've borrowed from Matt, the café owner, who either couldn't or wouldn't tell me anything about the woman on Pabay; Mhona.

I untie the boat, step in and begin the short crossing, just two and a half miles from Broadford pier. I love nothing more than to look out across the sound, but I'm not so likely to get in a boat. The sea no more frightens me than the next person, I just feel more comfortable with the rocky ground under my feet; more solid. I did think about bringing William with me, I've not been on Pabay before and don't know the terrain, although it's relatively low-lying. That's not what I'm worried about so much, it's meeting Mhona. If I'm honest, it's that I can't imagine my dad having a relationship with someone, that he didn't say anything, didn't tell me about her. I find it hard to believe there was anything my dad didn't tell me about himself.

The wee motorboat is easy to handle and, anyway, it's a calm morning and the sun has barely risen. It doesn't matter that I've lived my whole life on this island, it still manages to surprise me. Like the way the water laps against the boat, as if urging me forward, telling me I'm on the right path, allowing me to relax a wee bit. There is a soft, salty breeze with just a hint of the winter chill muting the sunrise.

I reach the island in under twenty minutes, and tie up the boat firmly to the stone pier. I know that feeling of being watched. After the severing of Dad's partnership, Raymond Styles began spying on us, every now and then. My guess is that he couldn't really be bothered, he just wanted to unnerve us, but only when the weather was fine. We knew when he was lurking, could feel his gaze following us as we went about our day tending the animals. So I know that feeling of being watched, and I sense it right now. I take the rocky path that leads to the only house standing on the island.

William had made some passing reference to Mhona going to the trouble of knocking down the previous owner's modern concrete house to build one of her own design, made of wood and glass. I stop to take a breath and can see the slanted roof of the house. It appears to jut out of the ground and the roof is planted, resembling an island meadow. I continue walking and the house comes into full view. The majority of the frontage is made of glass, and it's no wonder I had the feeling of being watched. It's my guess that Mhona has a view across the island and beyond from every aspect of her house. She probably could see me getting into the boat and setting off. She has the advantage on me in more ways than one then.

Well, I'm here now. The oak front door boasts an ornate brass knocker, but I don't get as far as knocking before the door opens and a bulky, woollen-clad woman steps outside.

She's all hips and bosom, her neck shrinks under the weight of her head, forcing her chin to rest on her chest and her eyes are disproportionally small, lost in the excess of flesh and weightiness of her eyelids. Her flyaway silver hair is tied back from her face in a haphazard fashion. She wraps her moss-green cardigan tightly around her and asks why I've come.

'My name is Nora Winter.'

'I know it is. I'm sorry about what happened to your dad, but you shouldn't have come here. I can't help you. I'll walk you back to your boat.'

Leaving her door wide, Mhona begins heading to the pier. I shout to her to wait, but she isn't listening. I could go into the house and refuse to leave until she talks to me, but I haven't handled things so well up to now. Dad would be disappointed with me if I got myself arrested again. Mhona doesn't strike me as the friendly sort, what was my dad thinking? She took advantage of his kindness, messing about with Dad and Bert. She looks a similar age to my dad; you'd think she'd know better.

I chase after her, but she's swift, reaches the boat before me and is standing with the rope in her hands. She can't wait to get me off her island.

'I'll hold it until you get in,' she says.

I grab the rope from her. 'I can manage, when I'm ready, but I'm not leaving until you tell me what was going on between you and my dad.'

'That's my private business.'

'Not if it's what got my dad killed.'

She walks past me and begins to head back to her house. What are my options? I could go after her, force her to talk to me. Or get in the boat and let the sea carry me away.

I pull the boat up and climb in, and I'm about to push off the pier when I see Mhona striding towards me. She reaches me, out of breath and teary-eyed.

'He wouldn't want you chasing around upsetting everyone, getting yourself into trouble,' she says.

Aye, she might be isolated on this island, but she's keeping up with the local gossip. She's probably right in any case.

'Neither would he want me to give up on him.'

'Oh, Nora, he gave up on himself.'

I close my eyes and feel as if my head might explode. She believes what everyone is saying. She couldn't have got to know Dad all that well if she thinks he could take his own life. Leave me without as much as a goodbye.

'You didn't know him.'

'Did you?' she asks.

She turns on her heels and walks off, and I don't try to stop her. I don't like the way she's suggesting that she knew my dad better than me. I absorb the sway of the boat rocking on the water for a bit before turning the motor on.

Dad was a proud man, not secretive exactly but he liked to keep himself to himself. I knew him better than anybody and Mhona, whatever she thinks, can't say any different. We were happy, just the two of us. I can't think of a single minute of time when that changed. But something must have changed. Something under the surface where I couldn't see it until it was too late. Was it Mhona that changed him?

I switch on the motor and head towards Broadford. Somehow or other, Mhona is going to speak to me. And when she does, it will be to tell me whatever it is she's not telling me. If there's something about my dad she knows that I don't, I'm going to find out what it is.

Chapter 35

Eve

Glasgow
18th October

The theatre doors are open. I walk in. There is nobody at the box office. A cleaner is hoovering the foyer. I switch the hoover off at the wall.

'I am Eve Park.' Would a cleaner know who I am? Why not? Cleaners are as much entitled to the magic of the theatre as anyone else.

She has steely grey eyes, this cleaner. She looks from the plug in the wall to me.

'Maybes you want to do the hoovering for me?' she says. She kicks the industrial-sized hoover over to me and hands me the hose. 'Be my bloody guest.'

Before I can think what to say next, she's gone. I drop the hose to the floor. Maybe I should follow her, make her listen to me. Or there will be someone else through those doors. Gilroy Flynn might actually be here right now, in this very building. Of course I'm going to go inside.

Just as I'm about to, one of the glass-framed posters on the wall catches my eye. It's her. It's Mother. This poster is of her playing the role of Diana in *Madness & Ecstasy* in the season of 1981.

Across the top of the poster, where it says *FEATURING*, there are three faces with names underneath: Gilroy Flynn, Ariadne Fairchild, Mathew Brent. Mathew Brent, my father. He had a very captivating face. I've always thought that. This isn't one of the posters that Mother put up around the house. It's a shame too, because her gold dress is breathtakingly resplendent. Grand, just as she must have been. Breathtakingly resplendent; two of the most delicious words.

How must it be, to be described so?

In this poster, Mother looks different to me. The posters at home have no writing on them. It's a puzzle. It really is a puzzle to see my mother's young face above the name Ariadne Fairchild. Young as she is in this picture, I recognise her. Mother. Maureen Park. Ariadne Fairchild. There's been a mistake.

'You still here then?'

The cleaner has returned.

'This poster has the wrong name on it,' I tell her.

'Those are from the auld days,' she says, as if that explains everything. She picks up her hoover, switches it back on and starts hoovering the carpet by the box office. 'Time you were going,' she shouts above the din and suck of the hoover. 'You're getting in my way.'

There are several doors, several ways to enter. Two sets of stairs. I may as well choose. I make my way to the door marked *STALLS*.

'You can't go in there,' the cleaner tells me. She throws her hose down, switches the hoover off and comes to stand in front of me, blocking my way. 'The theatre is closed. You shouldn't even be in here. I only opened the front doors so I could sweep the steps. I've done that already so now I have to lock up.'

'It must be hugely exciting to work in the theatre.'

'Aye right, if you say so. Come on now, I have to lock up.'

'But I have to speak to Mr Gilroy Flynn. You must know him. He is a friend of my mother and father.' I take her arm and position her in front of the picture poster. 'See, there is my mother, there is my father and that,' I point to the man on the left of Mother, 'that is Mr Gilroy Flynn.'

'You're Ariadne's bairn?'

'No.'

'Aye, whatever. Get oot now, you're holding me up.'

'I can help you with the cleaning. Until Mr Flynn comes. Unless he is already here. Is he here?'

'No he's not and, if he were, he'd have sacked me by now for you being here. Come on, out you go.'

She pushes me out of the front door and bolts it behind me. I didn't get a chance to make her listen to me. I can still feel her fingers poking my spine. I plonk down on the top step. The cold stone numbs my buttocks. At least it's enclosed here, under an elaborate canopy, out of the wind and away from the clamour of the street.

Maybe, right now, I don't look like a superstar. Nobody would turn away a superstar. I stand up and throw open my arms. I practise curtseying, pretend to lift the skirt of my glittering gown, keep my head perfectly straight, face the audience. With grace and poise, I smile. What I don't already know, Gilroy Flynn will teach me. I sit down and wait for him to arrive.

'I usually pop across the road for a spot of brekkie before my next job.'

The cleaner.

She's wearing a black, shiny jacket over her pinny and jeans.

'Are you coming then? I've not got long.'

The café she's pointing to is directly opposite. If I sit at the window, I can watch for Gilroy Flynn arriving. Maybe if I eat something I will feel better. It's a long time since I ate the baked potato with Tam. And if it's not going to take too long, it's not as if I have to talk to her.

From this table at the window, I have a good view of the theatre entrance. There is a fried egg roll and a cup of tea in front of me. Before we sat down, the cleaner whispered her name to me, as if we are part of a conspiracy; Annie Bingly from Easterhouse. She has to get two buses to the city centre and two buses home every day.

'I'm a grafter,' she says. 'Work seven days cleaning.'

I'm waiting for her to stop speaking so I can eat my egg roll.

'You're a quiet one,' Annie says.

'I don't like talking.'

Annie doesn't say anything more. I pick up the roll, but the yoke has burst and is oozing out onto the plate. It looks slimy and the roll smells of grease. Annie is watching me, in between mouthfuls of her own massive plate of bacon and eggs and sausages. I ate the baked potato in the street, walking behind Tam. I've never eaten in front of anyone other than Mother before. I place the roll back onto the yellow slime on the plate and cover it with my napkin so I don't have to look at it. No one has entered or left the theatre since I've been sitting here.

'Theatre folk are all up their own arse, if you ask me,' Annie says.

'You don't want to be mixing with the likes of them. Take that bloke over there, for instance.' She points her egg-smeared knife at a small birdlike man sitting at a corner table, drinking tea and reading a book. 'He thinks he's aristocracy just because he gets to have his name on the programme. And her,' Annie says, meaning the girl who just left after collecting a takeaway drink and something in a grease-soaked paper bag. 'That trumpet needs brought down a peg or two. Having a nice singing voice doesn't entitle nobody to be rude to somebody else.'

Mother used to say that critics of the theatre were all as thick as mince and couldn't tell the difference between musical theatre and vaudeville.

'Do you think it would be okay if I went across and spoke to that man you pointed out?'

'What do you want to do that for?'

I can't be bothered explaining anything to Annie. She wouldn't understand. I wonder. All of a sudden, here I am, in the midst of them all. There's hardly anyone in this café, and yet I feel surrounded by greatness. Annie is not going to be of any help whatsoever, but this man, this man, if he is named on programmes, he must be somebody. When I tell him who I am, he will be delighted to introduce me to Gilroy Flynn.

I sit myself at his table with my best superstar smile. Soon, very soon, I will think of something to say to him.

'What do you want?'

Of course, I have to tell him who I am. That will be a good place to start. He stands and shuffles himself into his coat.

I should tell him who I am. 'I am Eve.' The rest of my words come out as tiny, silent dust particles.

He shakes his head and flounces out, the glass door banging behind him.

I have a tingling sensation in my nose that is making my eyes water. The whole world is glaring at me.

A hand on my shoulder makes me jump.

'I have to go, see,' Annie says. 'I'm not allowed to be late. Them at my next job will dock my pay, like.' She pats me on the arm. 'You'll be alright now, will you?'

Whether or not I will be all right doesn't mean anything. If it did, I would never be alright.

'I'm alright.'

But Annie has already left.

I pace up and down the theatre steps until my body tells me it wants to lie down. I can't lie down, so I wander around the side of the theatre where there are some pretty plants and flowers in pots, lined up against a fence.

A bit further down I find a door; a side entrance to the theatre. Maybe this is how those theatre people that were in the café got in? I try the handle, but the door is locked. There is an entry keypad, and I press all the buttons but nothing happens. I try banging the door. Nobody comes. Kick the door, once, twice, three times. Nobody comes.

Chapter 36

Nora

Skye
21st October

There are no curtains at my bedroom window because, from my bed, all I can see looking out is the sea and that's the way I like it. It's the thing that gets me up in the morning. This morning the sky is a pale shade of pink with flashes of blue, reflections from the sea. If my dad hadn't been found, the sea would've gladly taken him into its depths, tossing him about until there was nothing left of him.

I get up and try to shake that thought off, think about breakfast. I've hardly slept, and my stomach feels as if it's twisted around itself. If I don't have to eat, the animals do. I can keep myself busy for the next hour or two until I think of what I can do next.

William called round last night and told me that tonight there is a meeting of the climate change group. It's to be held in Broadford Village Hall. He told me Mhona will be there, because she's the group secretary and so will be taking the minutes. He offered to go with me, but I don't want him there. William seems to always be around these days, visible in a way I've never known him to be before. And he's stopped walking. I know it's to do with me and my crazy accusation. He wants to prove his innocence, but there is no need. I told him as much and said he should get on his way. I didn't tell him I've already seen Mhona, he would've just asked lots of questions and I wanted him to go. It wasn't late when he called round; I just need to be on my own. I need to get used to that, except I haven't, because I keep starting to say something before I realise there's no one there to say anything to.

My feet are heavy in my boots, as I trudge down the slope to the pig barn. It's a fresh, biting wind, and it must've rained during the night because the stepping stones my dad laid are slippy with mud. I'm almost at the bottom before it registers that the donkeys are already happily munching their feed. The pigs are quiet, not squealing for their breakfast the way they always do.

I pull the barn door and the reason becomes clear. William is holding the pig pail, his legs surrounded by all four overly eager pigs. There's a makeshift bed of hay in the corner.

'Did you sleep here again?'

William nods, smiles. 'Thought you could do with me lending you a hand, just until after the funeral,' he says. He stumbles over his feet to make room enough to put the pail down and let the pigs fight over it by themselves.

Inside the warmth of the kitchen, I make a pot of tea and we sit letting it warm our hands. A part of me is relieved, to have the company, and maybe it would be better to take William along to the meeting tonight. It might make it harder for Mhona to shake me off like she did yesterday. Another thought has just occurred to me. With William happy to hang around for a bit, there's less chance Raymond Styles will come causing trouble I don't need. I'm not ruling him out as having something to do with Dad's death, it's too much of a coincidence, him arriving on the same day Dad died, but after the way Mhona reacted yesterday I'm convinced there's something she's not telling me. Once I know what that is, I'll have a better idea of who was involved and who wasn't. She had two men chasing after her, maybe there was a third?

'Does Mhona know Raymond Styles?'

'I couldn't tell you,' William says. 'He wasn't at the last climate change meeting.'

'When was that?'

'A month ago.'

'Well, he wasn't on the island then, was he? But none of that means he doesn't know Mhona.'

'I don't get it?'

'It doesn't matter.' The less William knows about what I'm thinking the better. Looking at him across the table, I can't help but imagine him as 'Cain the Giant' or the 'Lawless One' as the locals phrase it. Dad used to say that nothing the locals had to say about

William held water, and he would laugh and recall some scripture or other he'd read: 'The way of Cain was that of all human nature, making oneself the measure of all things'.

I've never had reason to give William much thought before now and hadn't bothered to ask Dad what he meant. William had always been a part of the landscape, sometimes visible and at other times forgotten.

As well as keeping Raymond Styles off my back, keeping William close means that when I do finally discover what happened to Dad, if William is in any way involved, I'll at least know where he can be found.

The silence is excruciating. Why is that? I'd sit here for hours with Dad, neither of us speaking, and it would feel normal, comforting, easy. William isn't used to speaking to anyone, and I don't want to speak to him right now.

'I'm going to nip down to Moira's,' I tell him and slip into my jacket. 'If you're going to be here, I better get us something for our tea.'

Moira owns a Portakabin, stocked with groceries, down by the boatshed. It's the only shop in Sleat. I make my way up the slope and begin my descent along the windy, gravelly path that will take me over hillocks and around the edge of the island. I'm about halfway when the sound of a motor travels up and over the hill behind me. I tuck myself into the rock side of the path. The path is narrow here and there's no point trying to walk on, forcing the car closer to the edge of the steep decline unnecessarily.

It's not a car but a tractor, and I recognise it immediately. It's Dad's old tractor that's been parked in front of the Old School House for the past two years. I can't see who's driving, because the sun is reflecting off the windscreen, but I have no doubt that it's Raymond Styles behind the wheel. I lean closer into the banking, keeping my eyes fixed on the tractor, hoping he won't stop when he sees me. I'm in no mood for him, and he won't be happy that, after me bursting his nose, all I got was a caution.

A sigh of relief escapes me and I relax a little when the tractor is close and shows no signs of stopping or even slowing down. Now I can clearly see Raymond behind the wheel. And instead of paying attention to the road, he's glaring at me.

The tractor's engine roars, steam belching from its ill-fitting bonnet. It's almost passed and he's not going to stop. I grip on to a grassy knoll and hold my breath. Once he's passed it will be okay.

The tractor swerves and, at first, it seems like an awkward way to manoeuvre the bend but, like a bull contemplating a tourist, the huge, muddy tyres skit the gravel to confront me. My stomach is turning in on itself. There's nowhere for me to change position, to edge further away from the tractor's bumper that's aiming for my shins.

Chapter 37

Eve

Glasgow
18th October

I am actually on a real live stage. It is 7.45 a.m. on the first day of me becoming a superstar. At least, that's what I intend telling everyone I meet here. Becoming a superstar would be wonderful, but it's a dream, I know. What might be true is that I find out who I am. I need to keep focussed on that.

I had to tell a little bit of a lie to the man who let me in the side door. He wasn't going to, said it was more than his job's worth, but I told him he'd been very rude in the café earlier and I was here on the behest of the great Gilroy Flynn. He sniggered a bit, but I think he was embarrassed and, with a shrug of his shoulders, he let me pass on his way out. He is in programmes, so Annie had said, but he can't have a very big role in musicals, his face isn't pretty to look at and he had a sharp voice that nobody would want to listen to. In his hand, he had a broken strip light that I thought he was going to hit me with, but he didn't. I didn't wait to see where he went, I nipped in and here I am now, centre stage, and it's terrifying.

'There are several ways to solve a problem and no certainty for success.'

The voice from the darkness frightens the life out of me, and I swivel around, but there's nobody there. With only the emergency lighting, it's hard to know if there's someone lurking in the wings. That's where the voice seems to have come from, but I'm not sure which side, left or right? It didn't sound as if he was talking to me, so maybe he hasn't seen me. I hide myself behind one of the urns on stage with my back to the auditorium.

'You've spent your entire life hiding,' the voice says. 'Now you are here, I would like to meet you.'

Is he talking to me? I can't hear another voice. I listen harder, but nobody answers him.

'Come out of your hiding place, Eve.'

He knows my name.

'I'm not a bad person.'

He has a tender voice, a comforting voice. I like it. I feel silly crouching down like this, I shouldn't be scared, I chose to come here and find out who I am. I need to be brave.

I stand up, and there is a man standing on centre stage, exactly where I was standing before.

'Hello,' he says. He holds out his hand. He is smiling.

Shaking his hand is thrilling. I imagine myself in a gold dress clutching a bouquet of flowers, turning to the audience and taking a bow.

I smile too, and think about saying hello, but the word is invisible.

'I am Dionysus.'

Still I can't think of anything to say. He already knows my name. There's a little giggle in my throat. I didn't know Dionysus was a real person. I can't say that to him, it would make me sound foolish. But he's known me all this time.

'I hadn't imagined you would come here,' he says. 'I didn't want you to, but I have to trust that we were destined to meet. I blame her of course. When she telephoned me and warned me that you'd been in contact with him. You see, Eve, you are meeting me for the first time, but, I, well; it was my duty to keep informed of your well-being, young lady. Ariadne and I were keen to ensure no harm would befall you. It wouldn't do, you must understand, for your existence to become common knowledge. We must consider the greater good, of course.'

'I didn't come to meet you,' I tell him. 'I came to see Mr Gilroy Flynn, because he was a friend of my father.'

'Your father?' he says sharply, and his voice travels all the way to the back of the theatre. 'I see. So when you met Lawrence, he didn't give the game up? How fortuitous of the man.'

Maybe this man is not as friendly as he seems, because people who choose to mock other people are not friendly.

'I don't know Lawrence and I didn't meet him, and it doesn't matter if you don't want to meet me because Gilroy Flynn will want to meet me. So you can go away, and I will just wait here until he comes.' I walk off the stage and take a seat in the first row of the auditorium. Lawrence is a popular name, I suppose.

'Wouldn't it be nice if we could swipe the past out of the way for good?' he shouts down to me. He's standing at the edge of the stage, his arms crossed over his chest as if he is a gladiator, but I don't see him as a hero. The way he's standing there, scrutinising me, I see him more as a priest, casting judgement on me.

I'm not altogether sure I want to be in his company. But that doesn't matter, because now he's sitting in the next seat to mine and I'm not going to leave until Gilroy Flynn turns up. If he wants to sit here I can't stop him, but I don't have to be friends with him.

'You want to meet Gilroy, do you?'

I don't even have to talk to him.

'I think I can help you with that since you are, as you say, the daughter of a dead friend.'

'Did you know my father?' I ask. Finally he understands.

'I did.'

I hadn't thought much that I might learn about my father from these people. I've only thought about being a superstar. About myself. About who I am and who I can be.

Self-centred.

Self-seeking.

Self-interested.

When Mother was annoyed with me, she used to tell me to stop nurturing my ego. Long ago, I looked up the word ego in my dictionary and underneath the vague description was the word, egocentric: thinking only of one's own interests and feelings. I wondered then if that's what all people did and, if that was so, I decided that I couldn't be like all people because for most of my life I've thought about Mother and her symptoms. Anyway, to know if all people are egocentric, I would have to know at least some people and I don't. But now, I will meet some people and be able to judge.

'What am I going to do with you?' he says, and I'm not sure if I'm supposed to answer. I think about DS Calmly who likes to ask a lot of questions but doesn't listen to the answers. I can choose not to listen to the question and ask for answers myself.

'I would like to know what my father was like,' I tell Dionysus. 'But first, I have to speak with Gilroy Flynn. I'm going to stay with him and be a star in his musical.'

'I know where Gilroy is. I can take you there, if that pleases you?'

Someone that knew my father can't be classed as a stranger. And even though Dionysus is a gruff sort, his words are kind.

'So, will you come with me?'

'Yes,' I tell him.

Chapter 38

Nora

Skye
21st October

'You're going to be okay.'

There's a faint lavender aroma hiding something underneath, is it antiseptic? I feel a warm hand on my arm. Opening my eyes, there's a sharp pain in my side, and my legs feel twice their normal size, plus there's a buzz from the monitors surrounding my hospital bed. Mhona is perched by my side, with a gentle smile and smiling eyes.

'You're in Portree Community Hospital.'

'Raymond Styles tried to kill me.'

'If it makes you feel any better,' she says, 'Mr Styles hasn't escaped from the accident quite as luckily as you.'

'Accident?'

'He lost control of his tractor,' she says, helping me to sit up a bit more.

'He tried to kill me.'

Mhona sits in the chair by my bed. 'Let's just get you better, there's nothing for you to worry about.'

'It wasn't an accident. Where is he? He needs arresting, locked up. He tried to kill me.'

I can see it now as if it's just happened, even with my eyes open, the savage look on his face, before I turned away to escape the wheels of the tractor coming towards me. But there was nowhere to escape to.

'Nora, you've had a shock. Now you have to get yourself better and worrying about what happened won't do you any good.'

'I'm not worrying about it. I know exactly what happened. And why. Raymond wants everything my dad owned. He wants rid of me.

He probably pushed my dad off the cliff. The police have to believe me now.'

Mhona doesn't say anything.

'Why are you here?'

Mhona isn't likely to believe me, she's the one at the crux of all this. She doesn't look the type to have to fend off men but, then again, what do I know?

'I've spoken with William,' she says. 'He was in a panic. Embarrassed, I think.'

'Why?'

'He was here earlier. He's gone to yours, he said. Said he's better with sick animals.'

My legs feel like concrete and it's hard to breathe. I can move my fingers and toes, just about turn my head to the side.

'You're a bit battered and bruised, but you will be back to normal in no time.'

'He tried to kill me.'

Mhona straightens the blanket covering my legs, pulls the sheet tight and tucks it in around me. 'You're not alone,' she says.

Again, I ask her why she's here.

'What happened to you was all the talk in the café, and Matt told me they'd brought you here.' She hesitates, then, 'I promised your dad I would look out for you,' she says. 'It's as simple as that.'

'When did you promise?'

'Plenty time to talk about that later. Now you're awake, you can think about what's best for you. I think you should come and stay with me for a bit, but it's your choice, I don't want you to think I'm taking over.'

The last thing I want to do is stay with her. 'I'll be alright on my own.'

'You'll have difficulty getting around, I'd say for a while at least.'

'Yeah, but you're not a doctor.'

'This is true, my lovely. That's why I asked the doctor myself. I'm only telling you what he said.'

'You've spoken to a doctor?'

'Aye.'

'About me?'

'I might be getting on a bit, but I'm as fit as a fiddle. I don't think the doctor would have much to say about me, now, do you?'

'He should've spoken to me. I'm entitled to my privacy. Are there not rules about confidentiality around here?'

'I maybe led him to believe I was your guardian.'

'Guardian? What do I need a guardian for?'

'Look, this isn't getting us anywhere. You'll get a chance to speak to the doctor yourself soon enough. For now, you need lots of rest, nothing to stress you out. See here, I brought you a book, to take your mind off things.'

She hands me a book, but I push it away. 'I don't want to take my mind off things. Get me the doctor, and where's my phone? I want the police here and that bastard arrested.'

'This is what I'm talking about. You need to give that twitchy mind of yours time to recover. You're in shock. Who knows what long-term damage you'll do to yourself, getting yourself all worked up. Listen to me, with your dad gone, I'm all you've got, but I'm a safe bet.'

'I've got William. He'll help around the place. I'll be alright.'

'Ach, he's a long drip of nothing. If it's because I was rude to you the other day, I apologise. I like to do things on my own terms, if you know what I mean. Sometimes it makes me a monster. But in truth, I'm a friendly beast, once you get to know me. Your father would be pleased, if we were friends.'

***

Mhona is still here. I have a fracture in my left foot and a dislocated right knee, a dent in my skull, plus a random assortment of cuts, grazes and bruises. The doctor sailed in a moment ago for no more than a second to tell me I can't go home. He at least gave me something to quell the nausea.

***

Mhona isn't fussing, something to be grateful for I suppose. She's sitting reading a tatty novel that she must've brought with her which, unless she always carries a book with her, means she'd planned beforehand to stay here by my bed and keep her beady eyes on me. I've given up telling her to get lost without actually being rude about it. I'm not sure what feelings my dad had for her, but he wouldn't want me to be anything less than courteous to anyone.

***

There's a needle in my arm with some kind of pain relief, morphine I think, but it's not doing a great job and each time I open my eyes, even though Mhona has pulled the blinds, my head throbs loudly and the nerves in my teeth make my eyes water.

***

It's dark, and all I can hear are the pages of Mhona's book turning.

'You didn't go home then?'

'Ah, Nora. How are you feeling?'

'Have you heard anything?'

The police were here earlier. Raymond Styles had had to be cut from the tractor and helicoptered off the island. He's in Aberdeen Royal Infirmary. Bits of him are broken, the police told me but I can't remember. I just kept thinking that bits of Raymond Styles have been broken for a long time.

'I've told you to forget about him now. He's not going to come near you again. Silly old fool.'

She hands me a glass of water. I can't read her face; she's avoiding looking at me.

'You were playing them off against each other, weren't you?'

'You'll be wanting an explanation, I know,' she says, tucking the book into her rucksack.

Now that I've confronted her, she's going to leave. Well, let her, I know this, even if she didn't push my dad off the cliff, she's at the root of all this.

'We can talk when you're feeling a wee bit better. Give yourself a few days to recover from the shock. You don't want to be storing up problems for the future by overthinking right now. Genuinely, my lass, come back to Pabay with me and we'll have all the time you need to talk it through. You'll be more comfortable with me than you are in here. But mind; don't think I'll be treating you like a princess.'

'You're not listening to me. I'm not your friend. Just because my dad… just because… My dad is dead. Dead. My dad is dead.'

'I know, I know and I'm sorry. I'm so sorry, lass.'

She perches on the side of my bed and messes about with my hair, strokes my cheek. She plants a kiss on my forehead and squeezes my shoulder. It's like I'm watching her doing all this, as if she's doing it to someone else, it's like I've flown away, and all that's left is my body.

'Let's get you out of here. Get you settled in my home. And then you will know everything.'

Chapter 39

Eve

Glasgow & Edinburgh
18th October

We leave the theatre in Dionysus's Ford Galaxy. I wish he would keep his eyes on the road, as there is an incredible amount of traffic on the Glasgow streets. But he keeps turning to look at me, with his wide eyes that remind me of the wrathful black cat that Blythe used to have until it sauntered into the woods one day and never returned.

As the car takes us out of the busy city onto quieter roads, I ask Dionysus about my father. I want to know everything. That way, I will find out if the man I've never met, who is dead, the man Mother told me was my father, was my father. Or if that was a lie too.

'The choices people make are not always easy to understand, Eve.'

'Was his death a horrible one?' I ask. I don't want to tell him that Mother would never speak of my father in case he thinks he shouldn't answer my questions.

'Do we ever know our fathers?'

I was going to say that he shouldn't talk about dead people as if they are still alive, but if people's souls exist after they are dead, as Dionysus seems to be suggesting, then it's right and proper to talk about them as if they are still with us.

After a while, the car slows down. We are driving along a quiet farm road, stone walls and overbearing conifers, oak and rowan trees, shaded by the late morning sun.

Dionysus swerves along an old muddy path and stops at a grand-looking farmhouse. The house is not as grand as Tippermuir, it's about half the size and rather than standing proud it appears to crouch in on itself.

There's a lot of barking coming from inside, and Dionysus hesitates, key in hand, at the door.

'Don't be afraid,' he says. 'The dogs will only do as I say.'

Dionysus enters the house first and I follow in behind.

'Wolfhounds,' he says. He makes a sound like a quiet breeze and both the dogs sit with their heads bowed. 'This grey one with the white face is Artemis. And this is Argos, he is an albino. Say hello to Eve, my loyal friends.'

Both dogs bark once.

The dogs are very big and spindly but their eyes are kind. Dionysus says I can trust them and I believe him.

'Let's have a talk, you and I,' he says, and he shows me into a spacious lounge and sits with me on a curved, grey leather corner sofa. I can see the dogs through the open door, they haven't moved from where Dionysus ordered them to stay.

'You don't really believe this will come to anything, do you, Eve? I mean, you've been provided for well enough, haven't you? I myself made sure of that, you and your mother wanted for nothing financially; a roof over your head, money in your pocket. Why did you come here? Is it greed that drives you, as it did your mother? I should have prepared for this. Your mother was greedy for adulation, is that what you're after, Eve?'

I don't know what he's asking me, so I don't have to answer. 'Is this where I'm going to be staying?' I ask instead. There are so many tiny ornaments in here and nothing is dusty. I turn away from Dionysus and pick up a little round ornament that's sitting on the glass table beside me. 'I like this, is it a jewellery box?' It is painted blazing blue with a gold lid and around it are graceful swans swimming, I've never seen anything as delicate as this. I open the lid. 'It's a music box.' I'm so excited I turn to Dionysus, but he swipes the box from me before I can listen to the tune.

'You shouldn't touch anything. You can't stay here. You can't be here.'

He leaps up and stands in front of me. I don't like his face.

'What was I thinking?'

'Why did you bring me here then?'

It's very quiet in this house. The only sound is the soft brushing coming from the dogs' tails swishing the parquet floor.

'Where will I be staying?' I ask when Dionysus doesn't reply.

'Perhaps, if you went home and didn't return, didn't come here ever again. But you would have to make a promise. And the question is can I trust you, Eve?'

'But I don't want to go home.' Bringing me here just to tell me to go home is a strange thing to do. 'You said you would introduce me to Gilroy Flynn. It's you who needs to keep your promise. You said.'

'She has brought you up to be stubborn, just as she was; always too stubborn to see her own self-entitlement.'

'A promise is a promise.' I stand up and so too do the dogs. 'Who are you to talk about me as if you know me? I don't know anything about you. I don't know you.'

That's right. I don't know Dionysus, it didn't matter before when I thought he was being kind to me. But now he's just confusing me and I want to leave.

In the hallway, the dogs are preventing me from passing, their eyes fixing on mine, as if waiting to see what I will do.

'You are correct, Eve,' Dionysus says coming up behind me. 'I made a promise and I must keep to it.' He puts a hand on my shoulder. 'You mustn't be annoyed with me, your arrival from the blue has dealt me somewhat of a blow, and I didn't mean to appear rude. Perhaps a spot of lunch? What do you say? Are you hungry?'

The dogs scramble off along the hallway, their claws clipping the floor, their shoulders rubbing side by side as if they're unused to being apart.

'You see how smart they are?' Dionysus asks. 'Everything is forgotten at the mere mention of a titbit. Come,' he says, motioning for me to follow. 'We shall eat and satisfy ourselves.'

In the kitchen, Dionysus pulls a chair out for me, and I sit at the table. He removes a half carved chicken from the fridge and a knife from a drawer and places both in front of me. Next, a bowl of beetroot and a larger bowl of mixed salad.

'Help yourself,' he says, handing me a small plate.

The dogs sit patiently in the corner. I nibble a piece of watercress and watch Dionysus rip off a piece of chicken and throw it to the floor, a few inches from the dogs. Neither dog moves, each watching

Dionysus intently. Another piece of chicken is thrown. Dionysus makes a clicking sound with his tongue and the chicken on the floor is gone, both dogs returning to their seated position, a look of hope in their eyes.

'You say you want a part in our musical production?'

'Oh yes,' I tell him. 'I want to be a superstar like my mother.'

'Like Artemis and Argos here, in their roles as Diana's loyal children.'

I'd like to say something that sounds important, but I can't think of anything. I can't tell from the way his eyes have narrowed whether he's waiting for me to speak or not. Musical stars have opinions. That's what Mother said once when we were watching an old TV interview she gave when that very first production of *Madness & Ecstasy* won the seven Tony awards and she wanted me to be impressed with her.

Dionysus is distracted by the piece of chicken in his hand. His hand is shaky, and he's passing the chicken through his fingers. With the other hand, he's tapping the side of his head. Apart from a sigh or a grunt here and there, he hasn't said anything for a long time. I'm too excited to eat anything. I'm eager to get back to the theatre, I want to meet everyone; I want to sing, and dance and be a part of it all. I want to be me, to know who I am and who I can be. I wish I hadn't come here, I can sleep in the theatre. I don't need anywhere special. That way I can speak to all the people who knew Mother, and maybe one of them will know where she got me from.

Dionysus gets up and leaves the room, just to return straight away, then leaves again. The dogs lie down in a corner of the kitchen.

It's warm. The sunshine is filtering in through the net curtains, the dogs are snoring, and the quietness is loud. Dionysus is taking a long time to come back into the kitchen. He needs to take me back to the theatre now.

There is no sign of him in the living room, so I walk back along the narrow hallway, past the kitchen, to the back of the house. There are two doors and I open the first onto a bedroom, neat and tidy but unoccupied. The second door, opposite, opens onto a set of stairs leading down. Somewhere down there is Dionysus, I can hear that click of the tongue sound he makes. I quietly close the door. It would be simpler if I just took myself back to the theatre, I don't want to wait any longer. I thought coming here was the right thing to do, but I was wrong. Dionysus isn't Gilroy Flynn and so he can't help me be a superstar.

The front door won't open. I try again but it's no use, I will have to look now for the keys for the front door, unless there's a back door?

I retrace my steps to the back of the house, past the kitchen and then, on my tiptoes, past the door that leads down to where Dionysus is. The hallway turns left and ahead of me is another door. This door opens easily but it doesn't lead to the outside, instead, this room must be an office. It's dark and there's no window. It's set up with a desk and bookshelves and filing cabinets. There is a door behind the desk with a lock the same as the front door. I try to open it but it's locked.

I turn to see Dionysus standing in the hallway secretly watching me. One dog either side of him.

Chapter 40

Eve

Edinburgh
18th October

Dionysus is inspecting me closely. The dogs look up at his face adoringly. I read somewhere that dogs are smart and won't go with bad people. I don't know why I felt uncomfortable just now, I'm silly.

'You possess an extremely interesting face,' Dionysus says. He smiles at me encouragingly.

He moves closer to me. The dogs remain where they are, following him with their eyes. He touches my face with his warm hand.

'I think you would make a compelling, Diana,' he says.

It's as if he knows exactly what I'm thinking. But this man isn't Gilroy Flynn. Isn't it Mr Flynn who decides who plays Diana? I can't help the tingling that's zinging through me all the way to my fingertips and toes.

'I'd like to show you something. Will you come with me, Eve?'

I nod, and he beckons me to follow him into the office room. He unlocks the door behind the desk. We are outside, at the back of the property. The wind whips at me almost knocking me off my feet, it brings with it the smell of the earth and I breathe it in, it feels rich and nurturing. In front of me is a big old barn and beside that a beaten-up caravan. Dionysus strides to the barn and slides the bolt and, with some effort, wrenches open the double doors. The door is covered over by a heavy navy curtain. He disappears into the dark. Seconds later, Dionysus pulls back the curtain, bright lights flicker on and I gasp.

Inside the barn is a glittering cave of treasures.

I take a step onto a wooden floor. In front of me are wooden benches on each side of an aisle that ends at a full-sized stage complete with red velvet curtain. It's just like a proper theatre. Above my head is a sparkling chandelier that sends light waltzing around the room. It smells different, smells of wet wood, and of rhubarb and manure.

'What of it?' Dionysus asks. 'Do you think you would like to be Diana?'

I can hardly breathe. I can hardly see, my eyes have filled with tears. He is Dionysus and I am to be Diana.

'Come,' he says. 'Sit with me.'

We sit together on the edge of the stage looking out at the empty benches.

'Will people come here? To see me as Diana?' The very thought is frightening. But to be who I am meant to be, that must be courageous. I can't let my fear bubble over and drown me. I am Diana. I am unaffected by chaos.

'Shall I tell you the story of Diana and Dionysus?'

'I know it. I know it already,' I whisper. I look at him for the first time properly. His lips are quivering and his small eyes sink into his face. He smells musty and unclean.

'I am afraid, Eve, that you do not.'

***

I am sitting eating cornflakes at the kitchen table. The sunlight from the window hops around the room, lighting Dionysus's face up one second, then leaving him in shade the next. He is sitting opposite me sipping at his tea. When his face is in the shade, he appears as rock, when in the light, his face is ghostly. He hasn't spoken for long minutes. I've asked him when Mr Flynn will come.

Last night, I slept in the caravan next to the barn. The door was locked. This didn't bother me; Mother often locked my bedroom door, to keep out the monsters. Dionysus unlocked the door this morning and popped his head in. He had a great smile on his face and welcomed me to the breakfast table.

I ask again when Mr Flynn will come.

'Not since *Evita*,' Dionysus says forcefully, 'had there been such flavours of flesh offered to the audience as was offered by *Madness*

& Ecstasy in its '81 premier performance. We didn't just follow the pattern of *Jesus Christ Superstar*, we gave birth to the greatest megamusical ever born; a triumph of stagecraft and wizardry. The audience adored Diana and Dionysus. She a beguiling and raunchy goddess of the hunt and mother of fertility. He, Dionysus, her perfect god, bringer of wine, cultivator of fruitfulness, hero and obsessed of ritual madness. There were seven Tony awards, including best musical. Did you know that, Eve?' he says, raising his China cup to me.

'Is the barn where we will all be rehearsing?'

He lowers his arms and glares at me. 'Oh no, Eve. The stage is yours and yours alone. No one will come to bother you there. You can rehearse until you exhaust yourself. Until I decide what to do with you.'

I haven't ever been to a rehearsal. But I have watched over and over again Mother's rehearsals and she was never alone.

'But you will be there,' I nod and smile at him. 'And Gilroy Flynn, The Taxidermist.'

'Ah, The Taxidermist, The Taxidermist. Of course.' He stands up and takes my arm and pulls me from the table. The dogs jump up excitedly and rub against my legs. 'He the whore, ruthless and ambitious. Perhaps. Perhaps,' Dionysus says.

***

He's left me on the stage in the barn. I heard the bolt slide and, when I tried the doors, they wouldn't open. I believe I am to rehearse and that this is the usual way of things. I must practise being Diana until lunch.

***

I remember it, as if I were sitting with Mother watching events unfold before me on the screen. I imagine myself on screen then berate myself. Why imagine it? I am here. I am on stage. I am Diana. The Taxidermist narrates offstage. He is intrigued by Diana. She lives in a beautiful old country house surrounded by woodland and animals of the forest. She, Diana, is alone in the forest, Dionysus having departed long since. He, the last remaining god, demands her hand in marriage. She, the protector of children is adamant. Diana will not marry Dionysus and be beholden to him. I know all the words to the first song 'All of my love'.

Don't take it away from me
You don't know what it means to me
Love of my children
Light of my life
Mother, child, life and love
Your mother, how do I try to help you, please help me.
All of my love

It's a huge empty space. The lights are dulled, the air empty of sound, the curtain limp. Empty sound is deafening. I sit cross-legged centre stage. I can't do it. I can't do it.

***

Yesterday, Dionysus didn't come at lunchtime. He came and brought me from the barn when the sky was dark and it rumbled with thunder. I stood between the barn and the farmhouse and sucked in the freshness of the wind, a thin strip of lightning far off in the distant sky, a rolling roar above us.

We ate tuna sandwiches. Dionysus locked me in the caravan after that. I was too fraught to stay awake and slept all through the long night.

This morning, Dionysus said things will be different now. He didn't ask me how rehearsal went and didn't give me a script. This I'm sure is because he knows I already know all the words. I don't know how he knows, but he is Dionysus, he must have a way of knowing everything. I ask him how things are to be different.

'Patience, my dear Diana, you must practise patience. Doesn't, in the end, Dionysus supply Diana with all the ecstasy she could possibly want? Doesn't Diana enjoy all the spoils of the land?'

I nod. A fissure of excitement grows in me. It's hard to remember that I am Diana. I have been Eve all my life. But I know now that Eve was not my name, that my life was a lie. I must work hard at not being Eve.

I ask Dionysus about Mr Gilroy Flynn.

He throws his spoon in his empty bowl, and the clatter makes me jump. I want to cry, but I squeeze my eyes tight. Diana is unaffected by chaos, no matter what.

'Mr Flynn is the greatest impresario there ever was and ever will be. Do you think he has time to pander to your desires? You are nothing to him, nothing.'

He makes to leave the kitchen but turns swiftly and moves towards me so quickly I back away and almost fall out of my chair.

He points a finger at my face. 'No. No. No. You are a danger to him, that is what you are; a piece of diseased flesh. No, Eve, you are not to as much as hint of your existence to Mr Gilroy Flynn.' He stands rigid, the dogs, by his feet, glowering at me. 'You are the cause of all my anxieties. You must be snuffed out. Extinguished.'

***

Dionysus has locked me in the barn. He called me Eve. He forgets I am Diana. I must practise and practise some more if I am to be believed to be the I of me.

***

The Taxidermist is summoned by Dionysus and commanded to turn the children of the forest into wolves. Diana is not dissuaded by this and continues to refuse Dionysus's hand in marriage. She loves the wolves as her own children; 'My child, my soul'.

> *Can I grow to love you?*
> *I'm treating you all wrong*
> *I haven't given you a name*
> *Will you love me?*
> *Will you wait?*
> *I am here*

I am here
I am found
Wait for me. Tell me your name.
My child, my soul

I don't know where I'm supposed to stand, this stage feels horribly unfamiliar. I want to wriggle out of Diana, shed her from my skin. Eve is a word. Like the word beautiful, it is vague and unknowable. Not like the word child. Child is a real word. It means something, something to somebody. I think about switching on Blythe's phone but change my mind. I have to be somebody first.

***

It is night, blackness and full of the noise of tiny animals, mice, spiders and weasels. Dionysus hasn't come. Dionysus hasn't come.

Chapter 41

DS Calmly

Edinburgh
22nd October

Paula parks up outside the farmhouse listed as Gilroy Flynn's home address. It's taken less than an hour to get to Edinburgh and then almost an hour to get here, somewhere on the outskirts of nowhere. There is a burgundy Ford Galaxy parked outside. We glance at each other; finally we appear to be getting somewhere. Paula rings the doorbell.

On the way here, I googled Gilroy Flynn and so I know that this man, who has opened the door to us, is not the man in question.

We flash our warrant cards, and I ask if we can have a word.

The man shakes his head at us and waves his hand in my face. 'Apologies,' he says gruffly, 'I was just on my way out.' He tugs the door behind him and locks it.

'We're looking for Gilroy Flynn,' Paula says.

I don't want her to make mention of the hit-and-run and give its owner the chance to hide it.

The man flusters about in front of us making a show of trying to get past. 'He's not here. I don't know where he is.'

'And what's your name? Do you live here?' Paula asks.

She takes a step back raising a hopeful look on the bloke's face until, evidently, he refrains from actual bodily pushing now that she's stuck out her elbow to make passing nigh on impossible. She hasn't lost the habit of doubling up her questions; it's an infuriating flaw.

'No,' the man says.

Exactly as I thought. If Paula had been disciplined and asked only the man's name, he would've had to answer, but now he's able to avoid that question.

'I come to walk the dogs when they're not required at the theatre,' the man says. 'Mr Flynn will not be best pleased if I'm late back, so if you'll both excuse me.' He points to the Ford Galaxy and holds up his car keys.

The man pulls back his sleeve and checks his watch. There is a droplet of sweat running from under his woollen hat, down the bones of his cheek, to land on his shoulder.

'Actually, it's Mr Flynn we've come to speak to,' I venture.

This riles the man enough to take a step to the side and circumvent Paula's elbow with the merest of brushes between them.

'You'll have to come back at a more convenient time,' the man says, and he hurries to his car.

'Wait,' Paula says. She manoeuvres herself between him and the car, preventing him from gaining access. 'If you just give us your name, for our records, like, and a time that would be convenient for Mr Flynn.'

There, she's at it again with her escapable questioning. Not that there's much we can do to stop this fellow from leaving, or to make him give us his name. We have no authority here.

'There is one thing you may be able to help us with,' I say. The man stops bristling and turns his frustration on me.

'I'm just a stagehand,' he says. 'I doubt very much that I can help you with anything, Detective.'

I ignore him and forge ahead. 'Do you know of a woman called Eve Park?'

He instantly looks at his feet, as if I've caught him in a lie before he's uttered a single word. Very curious indeed.

'Well?' Paula says, impatient as always.

The man lifts his head and takes his time to glare at both of us. 'It's not a name I've come across,' he says. 'No. I can't say I know anyone by that name. Now, if you don't mind, Detective. You'll lose me my job, you know, if you prevent me from leaving.'

Paula steps away, and we stand together watching the Ford Galaxy drive off.

'Who was that, I wonder?' Paula says.

'Run his number plate.'

'I don't have to,' she says. 'Look.' She shoves her phone at me so

I can see the picture of the man we've just been speaking to that she's captured from an old musical review. 'Clearly he's no stagehand.'

'Interesting. I like interesting very much.'

***

I rarely have much call to visit Glasgow. For the most part, I've generally thought of it as a grand old city. We're heading for the Glasgow Heritage Court Theatre to interview Gilroy Flynn. I expect that's also where we will find Eve Park.

I get a text:

RE: BRUCE LAWRENCE
Records found relating to a report filed Portobello 1982/3.
A child born to B Lawrence & P Lawrence, abducted
from Simpson Memorial Maternity Hospital.
Case closed. Child not recovered.

Paula weaves through the busy traffic with ease, and I get to thinking to what extent I can achieve anything by being here. Now there's another unsolved mystery; a cold case that in some way has to be significant. Unless I'm fabricating, in my own mind, a link between the death of Lawrence and that of Maureen Park. I should've let the local boys take over. I'd like to avoid communicating with them if possible and can only hope I can turn this case back around so it doesn't look like I'm stepping on anyone's toes. After all, both murders occurred on my patch. Maybe the local chaps will be grateful for not landing them with the grunt work.

'It could be that the van was stolen,' I say to Paula, mostly to distract her from her gripping the steering wheel and banging the horn.

'Then it wasn't reported.'

'It's just, it doesn't sit right with me.'

'Why?' Paula pulls off the M8 and soon we find ourselves driving through the leafy suburbs of Kelvinside. I remember coming here as a kid. My dad liked the railways. He was friends with a group of rail enthusiasts, some of whom later went on to form the Caledonian Railway Association. Not my dad though, he didn't go in for the formal aspects of social commitment.

I ponder the question of why this case isn't sitting right. I suspect that finding Eve will lead us to some answers but, for now, all I can do is guess in the dark. We drive past what used to be Kelvinside railway station. Now, it seems, it's been transformed into a swanky restaurant. The thing I liked best, back in those old days with my dad, was that his fascination for disused railway stations was not what it seemed on the surface. I realised, as I got a bit older, that those brief trips away from home were as much about what my mother wanted as it was about any passion my dad had for the railways. I'm sure he'd have preferred to go alone on those trips. But my mother ruled the roost, and I've not met anyone who didn't bow to her demands. That was until Jenny came along. Perhaps if Dad hadn't died soon after things would've turned out differently?

That thought takes me back to Eve and Maureen Park; a dead mother and a daughter who doesn't seem to be who she is. Plus a dead man not too far away from the Parks, who has a photo of his dead wife holding a child that was later stolen from them. Could the child be Eve? The link bringing these people together is Gilroy Flynn. I don't know what that link is. Yet.

'Maybe I should move to Glasgow,' Paula says.

'For why?' She may have her faults, but I'd miss her if she wasn't around, as would the rest of the team, no doubt.

'Not that I could afford for us to stay around here. Don't think me and Rory would fit in anyway.'

We're sitting at traffic lights.

'How do you get to be able to afford a house like that?' she asks, pointing to a four-storey, Victorian house set back from the street with a long driveway and an imposing gold-lacquered gate. 'Guess that's the kind of house a chief inspector's salary gets you.'

'Next you'll be after Cressida Dick's job.'

'And why now? You think I wouldn't make a good commissioner?'

'Keep your eyes on the road,' I tell her. She makes me laugh. I tend to believe Paula could achieve anything she put her mind to, given half a chance. She's had to work hard to get to where she is. And now, all her energies go into raising her teenage son, alone. Short on chances as it is, if this all goes belly-up, I will have cost her her career.

'This trip better pay off,' she says, as if reading my mind.

I don't fancy our chances of explaining ourselves if we go back to the team with nothing to show for ourselves.

'Finding Eve, that has to be our priority,' I say.

***

A young girl, dressed in a less than modest costume of silk pansies, shows us into Gilroy Flynn's office and leaves us, promising to hunt Flynn down. It's an extravagantly furnished room with a roaring fire and a faint whiff of lavender. Paula and I make ourselves comfortable on the plush leather sofa, and wait.

'Did you see?' Paula nudges me. 'Those framed prints we passed in the foyer; all of them of Maureen Park's performances. Don't you think that's odd? She hasn't performed for more than thirty years.'

'Not Maureen Park,' I remind her, after her pointing this out to me a few minutes ago in the foyer, 'Ariadne Fairchild.'

'Must be one and the same,' she says.

'A stage name most likely. Let's keep an open mind.'

The pansy girl returns to tell us Flynn can't be found. 'He hardly ever leaves, sleeps in here, but he must've popped out for a bit,' she giggles as if we're involved in an elaborate game of hide-and-seek. 'You're welcome to wait. Or would you like to leave a message that I can pass on to him when he gets back?'

'We'll wait,' Paula says firmly.

I've no argument with that. As Paula quite rightly pointed out, I'm loathed to return to Perth with nothing to gloat about.

On the pansy girl's departure, Paula gets up. 'May as well have a poke around,' she says.

Chapter 42

Nora

Pabay
22nd October

She's lain me on a plastic garden lounger which, to my surprise, is comfy. I'm outside, a few feet from Mhona's house, watching the sunset and listening to the stillness. Silence is something that grounds me, wherever I am on Skye. Silence that envelopes me, keeps me safe. It's hard to explain. A sound difficult to describe, you have to hear it for yourself, make it your own; own it. And if you do, you will never be alone. It is this thought that turns over in my mind, that there are different definitions of aloneness. My dad is dead and I am all that is left, alone without him. On the other hand, I am not truly alone, because he is still here, he exists in this silence.

The silence is, from time to time, interrupted by Mhona's sheep. I can't see them. She says they are on the other side of the island. The fact that I can hear them probably accounts for the lack of trees here. This is Mhona's obsession. Her magic carpet she calls it, to plant the island with trees. People have tried in the past, and a few trees have survived, dotted about here and there. There's even a small forest, you can see it from Broadford, and it stands proud and stubborn.

Mhona is not my friend. I am not her companion. As soon as I am able to walk unaided I will leave, and it's unlikely I'll return. But I am grateful.

Yesterday, after the nauseating, bumpy crossing, I was relieved to sink into the king-size bed in the pretty, sunlit room that she says she doesn't keep for visitors. Says she was brought up to be welcoming and accommodating and, while she prefers her own company most of the time, she likes to leave her options open.

She's avoiding me. I've seen her for all of five minutes today, long enough for her to help me out of bed, plonk me out here and bring me some tea and toast. Last night, she hardly said two words to me and every time I asked about Dad she either changed the subject or left the room, pretending not to hear me. Must be at least two hours since she skittered away, without saying what time she'd be back.

I rest my head and look up to the sky, the clouds are a murky charcoal, I don't think rain is far off. Broadford Bay is flat and still, looks almost black under the grey sky.

Before I left the hospital, I was given a pair of crutches but strict instructions not to use them for the first week or so. Mhona's parked the wheelchair beside me in case I need to go to the loo. I don't, but I wouldn't mind having a bit of a rummage around inside. There's definitely something she's not telling me, and there might be a clue to whatever secret she's keeping.

I drag the wheelchair closer to me and manoeuvre myself slowly and painfully to the edge of the lounger. Catching my breath, I hoist my backside into the chair, wait a minute or two, then I drag my right leg and position it carefully onto the footrest. The pain in my knee is crushing, shoots right up into my head. I grit my teeth and take hold of my left leg, the plaster weighing it down. It's awkward and impossible to do while keeping my right knee still, causing sharp, fiery stabs of pain to spike up and down my right leg. Is it even worth it, all this? I'll probably not find anything. I mean, what could there be to find? Really, all I have to do is wait until Mhona comes back and demand she tell me what she knows. But I'm in the chair now, and doing something, anything, is better than all this waiting.

I kick the front door open with my plaster. Thankfully, it's a big house, with wide corridors and spacious rooms. Having said that, the living room is cluttered, bookshelves from floor to ceiling with books piled on top of each other every which way, wool, knitting needles, half-finished projects on every chair. Does she go from one chair to the next, always between projects? An image of a group of ghostly women coming together to knit forms in my mind, and it makes me wonder who she's knitting for and whether, underneath all her protestations of preferring her own company, if, in the end, it was loneliness that drove her to my dad. He was up against Bert, his childhood friend, and perhaps even Raymond Styles, his unintentional enemy. Even so, even if he felt he didn't stand a chance with Mhona, he never would have killed himself. Never.

He wouldn't have left me alone like this, without any explanation, without a plan. My dad made plans; he had a plan for everything. He was planning to expand, to bring Highland cows to Sleat. He had it all written down. We'd gone over his plans together, night after night, ticking every box, making sure everything was tight, leaving no chance of the likes of Raymond Styles ruining everything we'd built. He made notes, my dad. Maybe that's what I'll find here, notes that he made, plans he was making with Mhona. Stuff he kept from me.

I push myself up to the dresser under the window. Scattered on top are holiday magazines. Had they been planning a holiday together? The thought makes me squirm. Or is she planning a holiday with Bert, or Raymond? Picking one off against the other must be easier now there's one less to contend with.

The dresser is comprised of two drawers and a cupboard. I open the cupboard first. It's crammed with boxes of Mhona's home-made fudge. She told me she makes it in batches and, once a month, goes to Portree, there's a shop that takes it from her. If this is her only income, maybe she's desperate, maybe she's realised she has to forgo her desire to be a hermit just to keep a roof over her head. It would take a lot more than a few batches of fudge to afford to build a house like this. She's probably up to her neck in debt. Me and my dad managed to keep things ticking over, that's about it. She wouldn't get any money out of him, what else could she have been after? Hardly romance at their age.

I open the left drawer; a stack of knitting patterns, nothing more. In the right drawer are cassette tapes, six of them, neatly stacked side by side. It's the neatest thing in this room, apart from the fact that one tape is missing; there's an empty space where it must've been. I pull a tape out. It's blank, nothing written on either the plastic casing or the tape itself. Who keeps cassette tapes these days? I look around the room for a tape recorder, but there doesn't seem to be one. You wouldn't have tapes and nothing to play them on. There has to be a tape recorder somewhere.

I wheel myself into the kitchen, but there's nothing plugged into any of the sockets. In the utility room, there's nothing there that I can see. I can't get the wheelchair past the door but, unless it's under the washing piled up on every surface, and that's unlikely, then it's not here. It's not going to be in the downstairs loo, but I check all the same. There aren't any plugs in here anyway. I open the cupboard in the hallway; mop, brush, cleaning products, nothing out of the ordinary.

Apart from the bedroom I slept in last night, all that's left is upstairs. I'm not going to be able to get up those stairs. I still have the tape I picked up on my lap. It probably is what it looks like, a blank tape. Maybe Mhona bought them for something then didn't use them. But I'm not going to know unless I can find a tape recorder, unless Mhona simply hasn't got around to buying one yet. Can you still get tape recorders? Why bother when it's so easy to record things on your phone? In fact, can you still buy cassettes? Maybe she's had these cassettes for years, shoved in a drawer and forgotten about.

I return to the kitchen and put the kettle on. From the window, I gaze across the empty expanse of water and wonder if the minke has returned to Sleat and if she is searching for me, missing me. I'd like to tell her how everything has changed. Would she even recognise me any more?

The kettle clicks off, but I can't be bothered now. I close my eyes and wish, as if wishing myself back home, back a couple of weeks. One week, one day, one hour, a second is all it takes, a second for life to lose its meaning.

There was an empty space in the drawer, a space for one missing tape. That tape must be somewhere, and the most obvious place would be inside a tape recorder. If the tapes are music recordings, wouldn't there be something written on them, to say what's recorded? If there's anything on the tapes, the only reason to leave them blank would be to hide what's on them. Maybe I'm just bored. Still, there has to be something in this house that is about Dad, he couldn't come here and leave nothing of himself.

I wheel back to the bottom of the stairs. There is a wooden banister and then there's the wall. Maybe it is possible, if I haul myself up on my bottom?

I try to think of the pain as just something getting in the way and I push it aside, grit my teeth, and ease myself out of the wheelchair and onto the second step which is the closet. From there, I push myself up using my hands, and try as much as possible to keep my legs out of each awkward manoeuvre. About halfway up, I stop for a rest. My wrists and neck muscles are aching already, but I can make it to the top, I know I can.

Sprawled out on the top step, I can see there are three rooms. The doors of all of them are open. The room to my left is a bathroom, no point going in there. The room opposite appears to be empty; dirty floorboards, no furniture, no clutter. The room at the far end of the landing must be Mhona's bedroom. I saw her this morning, standing, looking out of the window in that room, staring down at me.

I crawl along the landing, my legs dragging. All my muscles are resisting now, the effort to get up the stairs has exhausted them. My body isn't used to the lack of activity and my limbs have seized up, and now they're fighting me every inch as I drag myself along on my elbows. Thankfully, I'm helped along a little by the wooden floor.

I push the door open wider. Unlike the living room, this room is neat and tidy, the bed made, nothing lying around, no clothes left scattered, nothing you wouldn't find in any bedroom, except that old, battered tape recorder on the bedside table.

I haul myself closer, lean up against the skirting board, and pull down the recorder. Just as I thought, the missing tape is inside. I press play. Nothing happens.

The play button is down but the tape isn't moving. I pull the lead from under the bed and find the plug; it's not plugged in. I lie down on the floor and wait for my breath to return to normal. This is going to be a complete disappointment, some random music that Mhona likes to listen to in bed.

The socket is on the wall behind the bedside table, I have to reach under and stretch my arm. I bang the plug in hard with the palm of my hand.

A door slams downstairs. Damn it. Maybe it was just the wind. I press play again.

The tape is playing but there's nothing on it.

There are footsteps coming up the stairs.

'Nora? Are you up here?'

Mhona. She'll have seen the wheelchair at the bottom of the stairs.

The tape crackles, Dad's voice. That's my dad's voice.

Nora, I want to start off by saying I'm sorry. And whatever you think after you've listened to this... I want you to know that I love you. To know that, whatever you may think, I've always considered you to be my daughter.

'Stop that. Switch it off.'

Mhona yanks the plug from the socket.

'Did your father never teach you not to meddle? That if you do, you may not like what you find.'

Chapter 43

Eve

Edinburgh
22nd October

Let me out, let me out.

I wipe the blood off my knuckles on my jeans and try not to cry. My head doesn't seem to be bleeding but, since the moment I woke up, I've been feeling nauseous, and I have to keep closing my eyes to stop from being dizzy.

I've been banging on the door for so long my hands are raw; no one is going to come. I'm going to be stuck down here for the rest of my life.

Dionysus came this morning and brought me to the kitchen for breakfast. We had just sat down to eat when the doorbell rang. Before I had a chance to think, Dionysus grabbed me by the arm, dragged me to the basement door and pushed me down the stairs. He has locked me in.

I'm going to die here, without ever finding out who I am.

I can't get a signal on Blythe's phone no matter how I position it, and I've tried texting and phoning Blythe but nothing happens. Blythe's number is the only number I have since it's her phone. I wished I'd thought to put Graham's mobile number in the phone.

At least the glow from the phone lets me see where I am, and lets me see I only have forty per cent battery left. I switch it off and let the darkness swallow me whole. There's no light coming from anywhere, just a line of daylight peeking non-courageously under the door. Courage. Fearlessness. Bravery. I'm not a very courageous person. To be courageous is to be heroic, and I've never been a hero. If I were a hero, I would have a story to tell, a story to pass on. I could be someone, be a good influence. I don't know how you can be a hero if you don't know where you came from. How to be a mother.

I hear breathing. When I turn my head away from the door to face the darkness, I hear breathing. I position my phone in that direction and tap the torch.

Both dogs are standing at the bottom of the steps watching me.

'Why won't you bark? Bark. Make a noise, make someone come and let me out of here.'

The grey dog, Artemis, is tilting his head at me, his long tongue hanging loose, looking as hopeless as I am. The white one, Argos, isn't paying me any attention; he's nibbling the other's ear. Dionysius has sent them here to eat me.

I shuffle down the stone steps on my bottom, one step at a time. I stop about halfway down. The dogs are panting. They're getting ready to attack me, sink their sharp teeth into my flesh and rip it from my bones. I could already be dead. I touch my face; it feels real. My hands feel real. My torn knuckles sting raw and painful. You don't feel pain when you're dead. Or what if you do? What if, pain is the only thing you're left with when you die? What if, dying isn't the worst part? How can it be, when I've not had a chance to live my best life yet?

What if I die, right here in this basement, without ever finding out who I am? What if I die, without ever having mattered? Will my tiny baby know how much I love him?

Diana wasn't afraid of the dogs; she cared for them as if they were her children. Mother-Not-Mother wasn't really a good Diana. On stage, she was a superstar and played the role of Diana as if it really mattered. But in real life, she wanted me to care for her, and she forgot she was meant to care about me. I can't imagine why, now. I can't imagine it.

If I was Diana, I would be a hero and, like her, I wouldn't let Dionysus kill me. Who would be left to care for the children and the wolves? Dionysus has locked the dogs in here with me. Is it to make sure I don't scream?

Dionysus, enraged, intent on slaughter,
Takes his sword to the children to slay.

I shuffle down further, all the way to the bottom step. The dogs are thumping their tails on the dusty, concrete basement floor. There's a tiny whine, a clash of teeth. In *Madness & Ecstasy* the wolves don't attack Diana, because they know she is good and kind and their saviour. I tuck my phone away to save the battery.

To be brave is to be bold. I shove my hand out and wait. The dogs can't see me, but they will smell me, my sweat, my blood.

It's so silent my ears are ringing with the closeness of the stone walls and the weight of the ceiling bearing the house above. The air is thick with dust and tastes of cardboard and something else. Is it stale perfume?

Something nudges me, and I catch my breath. Hot panting, saliva; a dog baring teeth. I reach for my phone but, before I can switch it on, it's knocked out of my hand and clatters to the floor. I freeze. My breathing is deafening and I am invisible.

It's too hard to think with my head pulsing the way it is. I wasn't invisible when Dionysus chucked me down here, and I could've broken my neck falling down these steps.

There was someone at the front door, I remember. Had he meant to lock me up? Pushed me down so no one could find me? I don't know why anyone would want to do that. But he hasn't come back to let me out. I don't know how long I've been here, but it feels like a very long time.

I'm sure it was DS Calmly's voice I heard. I'm convinced of it. But it makes no sense, unless the police are looking for me. That PC Paula Dunbar, she thinks I murdered Mother-Not-Mother, and she wants to arrest me. She'll come looking for me, but I didn't hear her voice, I heard Detective Calmly's, or at least, someone that sounded very like him.

Nobody knows where to find me, because I didn't tell anyone I was coming to Glasgow. Not even Graham. Blythe swore she wouldn't tell. And there was no one at the theatre to tell about me coming here to Dionysus's house.

I feel about around my feet, hoping the phone is within reach and that it's not broken. Something dry and hot touches my hand, and I pull away. Stop. Listen. A dog's breath against my face. The tip of a cold nose brushes my hand.

With just a whisper I say, 'Hello.'

A dog is sniffing my head. Stay still. Stay still.

There is a dog rubbing his head against my hair.

'Which one are you then?' His short hair is rough and wiry. He pushes his face into my neck. I feel, with my hand shaking, all the way down the hard bone of his back.

He isn't ripping my skin off.

He sits on my foot, licks the side of my face. It gives me a jolt. I shuffle away and hear scrabbling claws, their feet padding on the stone floor, scraping up the dust. I cover my mouth to stop from choking. In the commotion, my foot finds the phone and kicks it into something. I scramble about on my hands and knees. I have it. I switch it on. The dogs are bouncing, weaving in and out of each other's space. There isn't much space for such giant-size dogs.

Argos licks the side of my face. If I am Diana, these dogs are my children. I sit down between them, and they seem happy for me to wrap my arms around them. They don't want to eat my bones or chew my flesh.

They must be thirsty. There isn't much air in here. I get up and, using the torch on my phone, look around, all there is are a lot of boxes piled in haphazard ways and along the walls are two clothes rails with what look like old, worn costumes. It must be these clothes accounting for the stale perfumy smell. There is no window, just a tiny vent up high on the back wall.

From what I can make out in the glow from my phone, the boxes, at least the ones I can see, have the same name written on each one: *Ariadne*.

I remember that name. It's the name on the poster of Mother-Not-Mother. I meant to ask Dionysus about that. No, I did ask him. Did he answer me?

Mother-Not-Mother's name was Maureen and she didn't say she had another name. When I first saw that poster in the theatre lobby, I thought it had been a mistake but that was stupid. Who would hang a poster with the wrong name on it, and if Mother-Not-Mother had seen it she would've ripped it off the wall. She has to have been Ariadne Fairchild. But why am I only finding this out now? No, actually, why should I be surprised? I am not who she told me I am. She is not who she told me she was. That's like lying. Like telling me my name is Eve Park when Eve Park doesn't exist.

I sit by the box closest to me. My hands are stiff and unwieldy, but the tape is old and wrinkly and easy to rip off. I open the box. I want to see inside before my phone dies. Ariadne was someone. There are all these boxes with her name on, all these costumes that might be hers and her name on posters in the theatre foyer. So, if this is Ariadne, then who was Mother-Not-Mother?

Inside the box there's just a lot of files, none of them look very interesting. Each of the files has something written on the front, boring stuff like utilities, income tax and insurance.

I rip the tape from another box, inside a whole bunch of scripts. None of the titles are familiar except one: *Happy End*. An original script for *Happy End*, Mother-Not-Mother's second most favourite performance.

I think about all those nights spent watching *Happy End* with her, and all her other performances, nights inside listening to her marvel about herself, nights spent alone. I was alone, because really, she barely noticed me. I was there for one purpose, so she could boast to me about her brilliance. But not tell me her name.

It's only now that this thought has shown itself to me. Countless nights spent with her, watching her, not once had I not believed. I believed, deep down in my soul, that she was magnificent.

I switch the phone off and let the dark crash in on me. I don't want the dogs to see me cry. Forgetting my hands are dusty, I wipe the gritty tears from my face.

I get up, feel my way around the boxes to one of the rails of costumes. I switch the phone back on and pull out first one, then another costume. It's obvious these dresses are Ariadne's.

The battery is now showing twenty-three per cent. It's not worth wasting the battery to rummage through stuff.

Wait. I climb over the boxes so that I can get to the far corner. Something shiny is peeking out from under a garment bag. Pulling down the zip, I see not the gold Diana dress but something as striking. No, this is exquisite, a gold sequin dress, strapless, the kind of dress that transforms an ordinary person into a goddess. I pull it off its satin hanger and hold it against myself. There are no mirrors in here.

It doesn't matter, just the feel of it against my body causes a surge inside of me, as if Eve Park has finally been devoured and the real me is charging through my bloodstream, preparing to leap out and announce itself to the world. The real me needs a name. A name I can pass on to my son.

I've never seen this dress before; not on Mother-Not-Mother, not on any of the cast in any of the musicals we watched. Has this dress ever been worn? I smell no perfume from it. Instead it smells of spring; juniper berries and cherry blossom, newly mown grass, that earthy smell you get after the rain, snowdrops and tulips and daffodil roots. Well, not really, but somewhere like that is where this dress should be worn. I hug the dress tight to me.

I check the phone – twenty per cent. Back at the door, I bang both my fists over and over and over; scream out for Dionysus. What would Diana do, locked in here? She would stand mighty in her gold dress. She wouldn't wait around to be rescued.

I don't know what she would do. Even wearing a gold dress as magnificent as this isn't enough to make me a hero. Heroes are not nameless. I toss the dress aside.

I return to the bottom step and sit.

Chapter 44

Graham

Perth
22nd October

'You're up to something,' Blythe says. 'I can feel it.'

Graham keeps his mouth shut. He's not happy about what they're doing, but nothing he could say or do will stop Blythe in her tracks.

'I've never known you to be on the phone to your sister so frequently as you have been these past few months. I know a red flag when I see one.'

She shakes the key furiously in his face.

'I have a secret of my own. Because I'm like, well you could say, and I did say this to the agent from NEXT HOME who will be here any minute now, I said I'm Eve's carer. Well I am, in a way. I mean, who else is there? I gave her my old pay-as-you-go phone, didn't I? So she can call me if she needs someone. You could say I'm her next of kin.'

Blythe has arranged for an estate agent to meet them. She wants a valuation done. Wherever she has buggered off to, Eve doesn't know about this. Still, this is the least of his worries. He's getting it in the neck from Lynn. That's understandable. He's not happy about his future being so unpredictable, his plans disintegrating before his eyes, his dreams of being a family with Eve in the gutter. He'll have to go it alone. Somehow appease Lynn. Maybe, when he reunites with his future, it will all come together, with or without Eve. But he can't go until he knows where Eve is. She may not want to share his family dreams, but that doesn't stop him confronting her with her responsibilities. And that means the first thing he has to do is find her. Blythe refuses to give him the number to call Eve on.

Blythe uses the key to let them into Tippermuir House.

'This house is screaming out for someone who truly loves it, to restore it, kit it out with stunning interiors, a brand new state-of-the art kitchen, posh bathrooms and, who knows, I might be able to fit in an indoor pool, or at least a Jacuzzi, if there's enough money left over. There will be, there has to be, this place is in ruins. It will sell for pennies and, with the spare equity, well, the potential is limitless. Absolutely.'

Graham checks every room, just in case Eve has returned without anyone noticing.

'See, you wouldn't listen to me about the title deeds. Once I know how much this house is worth, the exact figure, I can figure out the best way to approach Mr Flynn with my proposal. That article I read about him said he's aiming to restore his theatre, so the money from the sale of Tippermuir House will be a blessing to him. I bet he's hasn't thought about selling.'

Blythe prattles on as they open every door then return to the lounge and wait.

'I wonder if Mr Flynn is aware that Maureen Park is dead? Surely his solicitor will have informed him. But if not, he won't even have thought about selling.

'Oh, that's a car coming up the drive,' Blythe whispers.

She runs out so she can greet the estate agent.

They shake hands and usher the petite, middle-aged agent inside. Graham was hoping for a man; men are much easier to deal with in these situations, they ask fewer questions.

She introduces herself. 'I understand you are the broker for this sale?' she asks him. He nods enthusiastically, keeping the surprise to himself. Blythe might've warned him she'd put him down as a broker. The woman hands him some documents. 'These really should have been signed by the owner-occupier prior to my visit, but as long as you get Mr Flynn to sign them in the next day or two and hand them into the office, I can proceed for now with an initial inspection that will at least give you a figure to be getting on with.'

He nods again, smiles at her and leads her into the kitchen. While she's measuring up, Blythe asks her if she'd like a cuppa, but she declines with a dismissive look as if Blythe is nothing more than a paid cleaner.

Blythe takes Graham aside, out of earshot. 'Won't she be surprised when she has to hand the keys to this place over to me; me, as the new owner of Tippermuir House. That will wipe that superior look off her face.'

'Just to let you know, I won't be taking any photos today,' she says to Graham. 'I recommend that you give the place a decent clean and the walls could use a fresh coat of paint. In fact,' she says, while she's prancing around the room with her fancy digital tape measure, 'if all the rooms are like this one, the whole place will need a concerted effort to declutter.'

'I'm bloody offended on Eve's behalf,' he mumbles to Blythe. The woman buggers off to the drawing room.

Blythe has that sly look about her. 'I've always said that Maureen kept too much junk around here. It's not as if it's me that doesn't know how to keep a good house. Still, no point in upsetting her feathers, she may take it upon herself to lower the valuation just because she thinks she can get the better of me.'

He warns Blythe to shut up and they catch up with the woman.

'Oh my,' she says and sighs deeply.

Blythe takes Graham by the arm. 'I have to admit, I can see her point.'

'As I suspected,' the agent says, 'the whole house is going to need a massive declutter. Otherwise, this will be a property that's difficult to sell.'

'Will that affect the valuation?' Blythe asks.

'Not necessarily,' she says. 'I will note my recommendations for you to pass on to Mr Flynn. If he carries these out to the T, then I'm sure we can get a good price for him.'

'To the T,' Blythe says. 'Of course.'

Tired of seeing their faces, Graham lets the two women traipse off on their own and waits outside. Exhausted all of a sudden, he draws in some cool, fresh air and wishes Eve would come home.

When they're done, he gladly waves the agent away and heads back to the lodge with Blythe.

He shuffles about the tiny kitchen and makes a pot of tea. It's fine out. They can have the tea in the garden.

When the pot is ready, he places it and the mugs on the tray, takes it out to the garden and shouts to Blythe, 'Tea's up.'

They sit together at the table and Graham pours the tea.

'Do you think the police have found Eve by now?' Graham asks.

'They would have brought her home, I'm sure, or maybe even locked her up, if they'd found her.'

'I hope she's all right.'

Blythe clinks her cup down on its saucer. 'Do you?'

'It's just, it's not like her to go off without saying, know what I mean?'

'You don't know what she's likely to do any more than I do,' Blythe mutters. 'We hardly know her.'

'You're right,' he says. 'She was a prisoner in her own home.'

'No she wasn't. Don't be so melodramatic, Graham.'

'If you knew her, like I do, you'd know she's not the type to go gallivanting. She's vulnerable, you said so yourself to the detectives.'

'Vulnerable my arse. What do you know? I know more about it than you think.'

'Blythe?' Graham glares at his wife. What has she done?

'I helped her is all.'

'What do you mean? Do you know where she is?'

'Don't get your knickers in a twist, Graham. I've told the police. Eve's gone off to find that bloke that was friends with Maureen.'

'What's his name? Gilroy Flynn. It's him that owns Tippermuir House, isn't it?'

'That's it. That's what I told the police.'

'Why didn't she say where she was going? She just goes off, without saying anything. It's a worry so it is.'

'What have you got to worry about Eve for?'

'Not me. Just, well, the police, you know. The police must be worried. Her mother murdered and all that. Blythe, what if the murderer is after Eve too?'

'What's got into you these days? Why all the interest, all of a sudden, in the Parks? It's nothing to do with you. Was Eve that done for her mother, mark my words.'

'Ach, you know nothing.'

There's an edge to his voice that Blythe has cottoned on to, and she's now going to make his life more miserable which is not what he needs right now, as if he's not got enough on his plate. He's sipping his tea, avoiding looking at her. What's he hiding? He's betting that's what she's thinking.

'Luckily, it's my night off. I think I need to be keeping a better eye on you, Graham.'

Graham sits upright, tries not to squirm. Maybe this is what he needs, to get it all out in the open.

'It's to do with your sister. And, Eve. Something to do with Eve. Have you been borrowing money to give to her? I bet that's it. You've surpassed the allowance I've set and begged and borrowed more. It better not be a lot. If it is, if it means we can't buy Tippermuir, I will kill you.'

'Woman,' he says, resigned now to whatever comes his way. 'Now who's being melodramatic? I haven't touched the money. That's not the reason you won't be buying that old house. You won't be buying Tippermuir because there's a family that needs to be moving in there.'

Chapter 45

Eve

Edinburgh
22nd October

Only sixteen per cent battery. I sit for a few minutes listening for sounds from above, footsteps on floorboards, a door opening or closing. Nothing. The dogs are cuddled up together by my feet.

My stomach is aching and nauseous. Dionysus is probably up above. What's he thinking, what's he doing, why? I run up the stairs and scream till my ears ring, louder than I've ever screamed. I don't care what words come out. I don't listen to myself. It hurts my head to shout, but I can't stop.

Bang, bang, bang at the door with my fist. Nothing.

Bang, bang, bang.

Artemis is worrying at my legs. He barks, but it's a hollow, lifeless sound, a sound that brings me back into myself.

I slump on the top step, lean my back to the door and Artemis rests against my thigh. Argos, still lying in the corner, lifts his head and stares at me, the pale light from the phone casts a shadow across his face, distorting his eyes so they look like watery tunnels.

This is happening to me and I can do nothing about it. There's no way out.

There has to be something in these boxes, something that gives a clue to why I'm being held prisoner. Or something to help me unpick the lock? Yes. Why didn't I think about that before?

Switching the phone to low power mode to save the battery, I begin tearing off the tape from the boxes. They're full of odds and ends, bits and pieces, and the more boxes I open, the more I come to realise that this was Ariadne's life. Ornaments, candlesticks, china tea sets, a box of wigs, three boxes of shoes, a flat box that turns out to be a mouldy fur coat, a box of photographs.

I sit by this box and thumb through the photographs. Most of them are people I don't know. I spot Ariadne in many of them, one or two with my father in them and Gilroy Flynn, and a few of the cast members I recognise from watching all those performances. These photos are lying loose but, underneath them, I pull out an album covered in soft black velvet. There's no writing on the front but down the spine reads *Ariadne Fairchild* in faded gold lettering.

The album holds six photographs per page, the pages made up of stiff, cream card. The first few pages are of Ariadne alone, and I wonder if it's Father behind the camera. Next is a wedding, Ariadne the bride, and standing next to her is Gilroy Flynn. They look happy. In most of these photos they're standing side by side, holding hands, or leaning into each other or kissing. But this can't be. Mother didn't marry Mr Flynn. She married Father, didn't she?

What does it matter now? She wasn't my mother. Father probably wasn't my father; he's just a face on a projector screen.

I throw the album back in the box and begin tearing the tape from another until I spot something hidden away.

Sitting where I am, I see a box underneath a clothes rail and heave it out. Separate from the rest of the boxes, it's smaller and it doesn't have Ariadne's name on it. I rip the box open and inside there's another tiny box, a wooden box.

I take this tiny box and go and sit on the bottom step and, under the pale glow of the torch on my phone, I open the lid.

Inside is a little, brown leather book. I lift it out. There are no markings on it, but it has a small, gold padlock attached. I can't see inside, it won't open. I try pulling at the padlock but it's no use, it won't come off.

I want to see inside. This has to be Mother's book. A diary? What if it's a diary and she's written in it about me? She might have written about where she found me. She must've known who I belong to, where I came from, who I am. She *must* have.

I bang the padlock against the stone steps, over and over and over. It won't come loose. I toss it on the floor and stand on it but my trainers aren't much for it to defend itself against.

The padlock isn't made of solid gold; already I can see that I've managed to bend it out of shape. I just need... what?

Who keeps a diary in a wooden box? She was trying to hide it from me, she didn't want me to know who I really am; she wanted me to be Eve Park, to belong to her. Well I'm not and I don't belong to her. I told her that, before. I told her she shouldn't have done this to me.

I lay the diary on the step and pick up the wooden box and, holding firmly to the leather, I bang the box down. Bang, bang, bang, bang, bang, bang.

The padlock springs open.

Flicking through the diary, there's nothing written in it. Nothing.

I start again, peeling each page carefully, one by one. It's on the inside of the second page, in black ink. The words:

But if I connect with so many things,
I must stand for something, apparently,
Have some value?
And if I stand for nothing,
Why then,
do I suffer and weep?

It's nothing. It means nothing. What does it mean? I slowly peel away each of the pages, there must be a hundred or more. Not a single word on any of them. Nothing. I toss the diary at the wall.

Why then do I suffer and weep?

Chapter 46

Eve

Edinburgh
22nd October

Nine per cent battery. I switch the phone off and rest my head against Artemis's rump. He nuzzles at my ear and it is real, a sensation I can understand, because I can feel it.

One of Mother-Not-Mother's favourite sayings was:

You don't deserve me.

When I was younger, I loved her for saying that. I imagined she felt like she was a burden, that my life was wholly consumed by her needs, to the exclusion of everything, and it preyed on her consciousness daily. Later, when I was in my late twenties, I began to see things a little bit differently.

Words are complicated things. They're like ingredients in a recipe and if only we tweak the recipe a little here, a little there, we can live quite contently by choosing one meaning over another, like choosing chocolate cake over lemon drizzle.

You don't deserve me.

By the time I'd reached my late twenties, I understood. What Mother was really saying was that she deserved better than me. I swallowed the chocolate cake whole and tried to do better and for another decade, until she died, I resisted tweaking the recipe.

Her death frightened me, and I wanted so badly to keep her soul close to me. But even if that could ever be possible, her soul must've been hollowed out and filled with poison a long time before I was born.

I am someone else's daughter. Whose daughter am I? Which daughter am I?

Madness & Ecstasy is a tale. A betrayal but just a tale, and Diana is a made-up hero.

Diana sets the wolves to Dionysus
He dies cursing his red, red heart
The wolves revert to the children they were
And peace, once again, resumes its navigational chart

'Now, let's be sensible,' I say to Argos, who is nudging his head into my armpit. He skitters away, I think, when I leap up and throw my arms in the air. 'I am your devoted Diana and I curse Dionysus. Together we will seek him out and restore peace to our earth.' I throw the gold-sequinned dress on over my clothes.

The dogs are leaping about my legs. They too have regained their verve.

'Behold my chariot of gold, my horses splendiferous. My wolves revived to their majestic selves. Be ready, my dutiful servants, for together we shall overcome.'

Shh. Shh. I do my best to quiet the dogs so I can listen. A door slammed shut. I'm convinced that's what I heard. There are footsteps above; definitely footsteps. I scramble to the top of the steps.

It must be Dionysus. Could it be Gilroy Flynn? Isn't this Gilroy's home? It must be, because Dionysus brought me here to meet him, or so he'd said.

I bang my fists on the door. Hope exists, even if you have no idea what to hope for. Detective Calmly has returned to look for me.

Bang, bang, bang.

The dogs bark. Yes, now they understand, the impossible sound vibrating all around me.

'That's it, that's it.' *Bang, bark, bang, bark.*

There's metal on metal. The bolt sliding, slamming into its latch. The door easing soundlessly open. The dogs push past me and, with my hand shading the blinding daylight from the hallway, I step out of the basement.

The dogs jump up and down, their great paws reaching Dionysus's shoulders, their woefully vengeful kisses making him smile. The fresh, clean air disturbs the dust in my throat; I bend over and try to spit the dust out.

Dionysus pats my back gently, a pat, a rub, a pat, a rub. 'You're okay now,' he says. 'Better, better.'

Hazy, watery eyes and nerves tingling, weakening my arms and legs, it's difficult to muster Diana's protective spirit. I don't want to. I am a wolf. So, instead, I let my head rest against Dionysus's shoulder when he pulls me into his arms.

'You're okay, now,' he says again. 'That dress suits you, madam.'

The hallway is ablaze with sunlight, filling me with a joyful freedom and it's as if I am renewed. As if I am beginning again. And I see hope wherever I look, in the beautiful intricacies of the chandelier, in the feel of the warm parquet under my feet, in the painted glass of the front door, in the warmth of Dionysus's hand resting on my hair.

No one has touched me like this. Gentle. Gentleman. Not hasty and lustful, the way Graham touched me, but kind and soothing, the way a mother should touch a daughter. In this moment, while my head rests and my mind is catching up with itself, I know for the first time that Mother-Not-Mother didn't want me. For the first time, because I have always known that she resisted my every attempt to touch her, but never acknowledged to myself, until now, that she too resisted touching me. I wrap my arms around myself and feel the gold satin against my skin and the goddess that I am becoming.

'It's okay, Eve. You will be okay now. We are going to put things right.'

He takes me by the arm and leads me into the kitchen. He hands me a glass of water and we stand together watching the dogs drink from a large bowl on the floor.

'Are you hungry?' he asks me.

'Did you mean to lock me in the basement?' I ask him. There's no sign of anyone else. Detective Calmly hasn't come.

He's silent, as if he's taking his time to choose the right words. Then, 'I can't allow you to be found, child. It is not safe for you here. You have brought ruin with you.'

I should be looking for an escape route. I should run from here as fast as I can. At least Diana knows why Dionysus slays the children. She refused his hand in marriage.

'Why?' I ask. 'What do you mean?' He walks past me, out of the kitchen, and I follow behind, the dogs leaping around our legs.

He's unlocking the door at the back of the hallway.

'Are all these questions really necessary?' he asks, pointing a finger at me, directing me to stay where I am.

The dogs bundle out of the door and into what looks like a back garden; a way out. I can't see if there's an exit out of the garden, Dionysus is blocking the way with his arm.

'I came back to rescue you as quickly as I could,' Dionysus tells me. 'It couldn't be helped, I'm afraid. But if it makes you feel better, I'm sorry.' He takes hold of my hand. 'I am, really, very sorry.'

His eyes are truthful and the way he's looking at me, his face sunken, his mouth resigned, makes me want to believe him.

Just like I wanted to believe I could rescue Mother-Not-Mother's soul and hold it close to me for the rest of my life. If I had, if I had that soul now, right here in my hands, it would poison me and turn my gold dress to blood.

I pull my hand away from him, raise my arm and, with the might of Diana's resolve, I dig my elbow into his chest bone. Instinctively, he twists away from me, bends into himself, and I run.

In the garden, I can't see a way out. Seconds are all I have. The hedges surrounding the garden are at least twice my size. I run to the far end of the lawn, grab hold of the spruce and pull myself up. Up. My foot slips. The dogs, barking, are leaping at the hedge, I can't tell if they're trying to come with me or trying to stop me.

Further up, the branches are less solid. With each foot up, I feel myself falling backwards. I take a chance and check my progress, only about halfway up.

'Eve,' I hear Dionysus say, softly.

Instead of ascending, I'm collapsing, deeper into the hedge.

What if I can burrow my way through? That must be possible. My hands are raw and bleeding, my face stings with each branch that clings to me, clawing at the gold dress to force me back.

'It's impossible, my dear. We must face our fate, which is all that can be done.' His voice calm, patient, and in my desperation I want to fall from here, into his protective arms.

Poisonous arms.

Keep pulling, keep tugging. I have a voice, I have a voice. 'Help. Help me.' In my head, this comes out as a scream, over and over, until all I hear is the vibration of my words and I'm not certain they can be heard by anyone.

A hand tugs at my ankle and pulls. I clutch the closest branch; keep my hand squeezed tight around it. My hair is caught in a branch too far away. With each tug of my ankle, the branch rips at my hair. My hand is sweaty and bleeding. Tears well up making it difficult to see.

There is barely any light through the path I was trying to forge in the hedge. A whole city of branches twisted tightly together, admirably supporting each other, fiercely determined to survive my attempts to split them apart. My grasp is weak in comparison.

Dionysus tugs. My hand loosens. My body gives way to gravity and all that is holding me is my hair until it parts, ripping itself from my scalp to cling to the branch while I fall backwards.

The ground is there to catch me, first my shoulder, my hip, ankle, and then my skull. The pain is a whole thing, something I can watch before me, a thing I can't yet recognise, as if it belongs to someone else.

Dionysus stands over me, a concerned look on his face. He kneels down to touch my forehead. Artemis rests his paw on my chest and licks my ear.

Chapter 47

DS Calmly

Glasgow
22nd October

Paula is busy poking about in Gilroy Flynn's office.

'I'll just go for a wander,' I say, leaving Paula to it.

I take myself off down the corridor. If Eve is here, someone will have seen her. The pansy girl didn't see her, or at least she said there's been nobody new hanging about.

I can hear a hoover and, when I turn left along the corridor, there's a middle-aged, or perhaps slightly older, woman furiously pushing a hoover over the worn, rust-coloured carpet. She sees me, switches off and barks at me.

'Can I help you?'

I show her my warrant card. 'I'm looking for a missing person,' I tell her.

'Aye, if you are, I can tell you right now, there's nobody here who's not meant to be.'

'She's a thirty-eight-year-old woman, brownish-reddish hair who goes by the name of Eve Park? Have you come across anyone that fits that description recently?'

'Nope, but it doesn't surprise me people are going missing. There's one hell of a rumpus going on around here, definitely. People getting fired, the boss getting beat up, even the old man has disappeared. I heard him and the boss arguing, and ken, that old man deserves to be treated better than that. I've known him most of my life, and he's never done nobody a bad turn.'

'Is that normally how it is?'

'Sometimes. Ken what, I think I might've seen that lass you're looking for. What you looking for her for, anyway? She didn't look a bad sort to me, in fact, I felt a bit sorry for her, truth be told. Aye, I think she said her name was Eve. She was stood outside the door early hours the other day. I wouldn't let her in, more than my job's worth.'

'When was this?'

'What? When I saw the lass? A few days ago I think it was.'

'Have you seen her since then?'

'Nah. Like I said, there's been mare bother than normal these past few days. The boss been kipping down in his office more than usual, no bothering to go home. When it's like that, I like to keep my head down, ken what ah mean?'

'What is it you do here?'

'What kind of detective are you? Can't you tell by my pinny? I'm the cleaner. My name's Annie Bingly, case you need it for your records like. Mostly it's just me cleaning, unless there a performance, and if they had their way it would just be me then tae. But I can't complain really. I get by fine, nowt else for it, eh.'

'Thank you, Annie, you've been a great help.'

'Aye, aye, nae bother.'

'You said there's been odd goings-on lately. Something about an argument?'

'Dare say the boss won't want me blabbing about his business.'

'The old man, you refer to?'

'Oh aye, old Mr McAllister. He's a gent, he really is. Wisnae fair for the boss tae sack him but, ken what, they're as thick as thieves that pair, I'm sure they'll work out their differences. I probably shouldn't have mentioned it. Can I get back to my cleaning now? I don't like falling behind.'

***

Back in Gilroy Flynn's office, I tell Paula what Annie said.

'So there's been a bust-up, has there? Wonder what that was about? But you have to admit, my theory is looking pretty good right now,' she says.

'You think Eve and Flynn are in cahoots?'

'That's it. Don't you?'

'Hmm. Let's keep an open mind.'

'How long are we going to wait? If my theory is correct, it could be that the reason Flynn hasn't turned up is because the pair of them have already absconded.'

'Let's just wait a bit longer. Flynn has a big production on the go, he'd need a good reason to up and walk out on that.'

I sit back, comfortably, on the sofa and pick up a copy of some theatre guide or other, with no real intentions of reading it. Paula sits herself on the armchair by the unlit fire.

Chapter 48

Eve

Edinburgh
22nd October

'You're awake then.'

Dionysus's voice is close to me. I refuse to open my eyes. I don't need to open my eyes to know that my wrists are tied to my legs because, if I move my hands, I can feel the pull of something, perhaps a rope, around my ankles. There is a strap across my chest. I am being driven. I know it's Dionysus's Ford Galaxy because I can smell the theatre, paint, wood, Dionysus's tobacco and his perfume, a woody, grassy smell that settles on my tongue.

I stay as still as I can, try not to hold my breath, try my best to breathe easily, as if sleeping. I study behind my eyelids and sense daylight has passed that, if I opened my eyes, the road ahead would be dark, lit only by the car's headlights.

The side of my face stings where it hit the ground when I fell from the hedge. I can grind my teeth, on the left side of my mouth, out of Dionysus's line of sight, and feel the dried blood and tears crack.

'Not far now,' Dionysus says.

How far is now? Not long enough to think. I can't imagine how far my thoughts have travelled, deserting me, my mind a black, empty space, useless.

I open my eyes. There is a dog lead wound tightly around my wrists and ankles.

'I'm sorry,' he says. His eyes are wide and sad, and he's about to say something else but changes his mind and turns back to face the road.

Outside is full of nothingness; no lights anywhere, no life carrying on as normal.

'Your life matters now, in a way you can never understand,' Dionysus tells me. 'You'll have to trust in that.'

Trust. To believe that someone is honest and means no harm. To expect, to hope, to have faith in something.

Dionysus is crying. A single tear slips from his cheekbone and lands on his seat belt.

'I don't trust you,' I tell him. I doubt that Dionysus means me no harm. I doubt we are on our way back to the theatre. 'You've tied me up.'

'You should never have come here,' he says.

I scream at him. 'Where? Where are we going?'

He growls. 'If you'd stayed away,' he mutters, shaking his head. 'She promised to keep you hidden.' His hands are gripping the steering wheel so tight his knuckles look like they're about to burst through his skin.

'Who are you?' I am part of a world where no one knows who anyone is. 'Do you know who I am?'

'I know who you are,' he says wearily.

We turn a bend sharply, and my head bangs off the window and, without being able to help it, tears well up, overspill and I try to wipe them away, but it's hopeless.

'Nearly there,' he says.

'Do you have dreams?'

He doesn't answer; he's sucking in air, like he can't breathe. He's sobbing.

I take my chance, he'll have to listen. 'I have dreams. I would like to know where they came from.'

He is quiet now, listening. 'Tell me,' he says.

I rest my head back and close my eyes. 'Where do dreams come from? Do you know? I think I do. I think they come from the people you meet.' I didn't have dreams of my own before Mother died. I turn to Dionysus. 'Mother had dreams for me. She dreamed all the time that I would love her enough. She liked to tell me about these dreams.'

Dionysus doesn't take his eyes from the road, but I'm certain he's interested in what I'm saying because he's leaned his head a little closer to me.

'She's dead?' he asks, but I don't want to talk to him about that.

'Graham had dreams for me too. You don't know Graham, he dreams about me and him and our family.'

'No amount of love would ever have been enough for your mother,' he tells me softly.

'She was Ariadne.'

'Yes.'

'She was beautiful.'

'Yes.'

'You knew Mother.'

'Yes. Yes, I did.'

'She's dead.'

Silence.

'I see,' he says.

I listen to the hum of the car and think about the word, contentment.

He pulls up and turns the engine off. 'You're not anything like her, are you?'

'Mother? No, I don't think I am anything like her.'

I shouldn't have said that. Now he might hate me because I'm not like her. Maybe he wanted me to be exactly like her.

'But I have her talent,' I say quickly. 'Better talent than her. And...' I wriggle in my seat so he can get a better view of me, 'I look better in a gold dress.'

'You know, she refused to wear that dress. I got it made especially for her, and she demanded I burn it. Of course, I didn't, nobody can afford to waste that amount of money on a petulant whim.'

'This is the best dress I have ever worn.'

'You may keep it, my dear.'

He makes to get out of the car. 'Aren't you going to untie me?'

Pausing, he takes hold of my hands. 'I'm afraid not.' He plants a kiss on my forehead. 'Forgive me.'

Dionysus opens his door.

'Wait. You're not going to leave me here, are you?'

He closes the door again and sits back in the driver's seat. 'You've given me no choice.'

'Please, please.'

He shakes his head and sighs. 'She was a poison in all of our lives. She did this.' He turns to look at me, his eyes pleading. 'I've spent all of my life righting her wrongs. I can't stop now. I have to bring an end to this thing.'

'I can be like her. I know I can,' I say quickly, anything for him to untie me and let me go.

'An impossible dream, Eve. Choose another one.'

I will not give him my dreams to steal away into the night. I turn my back to him and try with my tied wrists to open the door.

'It won't open,' he tells me.

He's lying. I keep trying, but even though I can pull the handle the door doesn't swing open.

'I disabled the mechanism.'

I keep trying. He's not getting to see me give in. I will fight. I will fight.

'Did she tell you, Eve, about your birth?'

'No. No, I don't know anything. Please let me go. I don't know anything.'

'I suppose you could be telling the truth.'

'I am. Now let me go, or I'll scream at the top of my voice and people will come.'

'There are no people, Eve.'

It's hard to tell where he's brought me with the absence of any lights outside.

'Are you going to hurt me? I don't know anything.'

'Your existence is enough to destroy him. As is hers.'

'Hers?'

My phone. I stretch my back and try not to show my relief, the phone against my thigh, it's still there, tucked away in the pocket of my jeans. Please let there be a signal. Even if he doesn't untie me, I should be able to wrestle my phone out and call Blythe, as soon as I get a chance.

'You are the chosen daughter of Ariadne. Picked out, the same way she may have chosen a rose. Or a gold dress.'

Dionysus climbs out of the car. He walks around and opens the passenger side door, drags me out. I'm grateful for the air that shoots into my lungs. All too quickly, he pushes me into the caravan, the one I've been sleeping in, must've been towed along with us, and he locks me in.

I will wait until I know for certain he is gone before I pull my phone out and call Blythe.

His footsteps tread gravel.

I am Diana, the goddess of all children.

The car door slams shut giving me a fright. His footsteps are on the gravel. His face at my window.

Dionysus flattens his hand against the window, tears falling down his face.

I don't know what to do so turn away.

I turn back to the window and Dionysus has gone. His footsteps disappear into emptiness. He could be hiding somewhere, watching me. Watching to see what I will do. Wait. Just a little bit longer. I hear the car skid on gravel and drive away. I try my best to pull hard at the window, it's too difficult with the lead tying me all up. The window doesn't budge.

A pop. A sizzle. Another pop. Melting rubber. I put my face up close to the window and see a tiny flicker of a light coming from below. Is it a torch?

No time. I reach for my phone.

A terrifying bang vibrates in my head. Something has exploded.

I glance down at my phone. The battery is dead.

Bang, a roar, then another, then another. What is it?

Fire. I smell fire.

I remember the fireworks at the end of *Madness & Ecstasy*, when the wolves are devoured and the children released. Dionysus falls to the ground, clutching Diana's spear that has pierced his red, red heart.

Chapter 49

DS Calmly

Glasgow
22nd October

The pansy girl returns bearing a tray with a teapot and three china cups in saucers.

'I just noticed Mr Flynn's car pull in the car park at the back. Saw him from the kitchen window, and I was making tea for myself anyways, so I thought I'd bring you in a tray. You'll have time to drink it while you chat with the boss. He should be with you in a couple of minutes.' She lays the tray down and skips back out again with a wave goodbye.

Gilroy Flynn is exactly what I'd expected him to be, if not more bumptious than I'd anticipated. He greets us with a flourish of his outstretched hand and welcoming introductions. I have to stop him mid flow; I'm not interested in the history of the theatre or the trials of funding and procurement.

'I'm sure you're very busy, Mr Flynn,' I say. I try to ignore the about-turn in his face, the way his mouth tightened and the way his eyes widened at the sudden interruption. 'We won't keep you. I just have one or two questions, and then we'll be on our way.'

'Of course,' Flynn says, grudgingly.

'Excellent,' I say. I wait for him to seat himself behind his desk. That's okay. If he's comfortable, he may be more eager to talk.

The tea is left untouched.

'Can you tell me what you know about the whereabouts of Eve Park?'

The side of his neck twitches, and he begins tapping his fingers on the blotter. I allow him the moment, sometimes it's best to stand back and watch what happens when presenting direct questions.

'I don't think I've come across that name,' he says.

I catch Paula glaring at him then turning her gaze on me. I'm guessing she's waiting on me pulling him up for the lie. Lies are not easy to spot, contrary to popular belief, but this was an easy one. Flynn nodded his head in the affirmative, when he spoke, as if desperately seeking to agree with himself; classic.

'You perhaps are more familiar with Maureen Park?'

'You may think I am a man with an abundance of friends, but musical theatre is my life, Detective. If you're not in my production, I don't know you.'

I present him with my most empathic smile. 'You, of course, know Ariadne Fairchild?'

'Ariadne?' he says, as if he's swallowed something disagreeable.

I note Paula holding her breath. She has sense enough to remain silent. Flynn's shifty eyes make me suspect he's going to lie about knowing Ariadne.

'Yes,' he says at last. 'Yes. Of course I know Ariadne. You've disappointed me, Detective. Why, might I ask, must you present me with a question that you clearly know the answer to? The world knows my association with Ariadne Fairchild, it's written in the history books. I take it she is alive and well, although, you must understand that I have neither seen nor corresponded with Ariadne for the past however many years.'

'Then you do know Maureen Park,' I say, before Flynn's hackles rise any further, 'Ariadne Fairchild's given name.'

'Oh,' Flynn picks up a pen and taps it on the desk. 'Is that her real name? I don't think I ever knew it, if I did, I've forgotten.'

'Eve Park is her daughter.'

This causes Flynn to drop his pen.

I continue, 'We are investigating Eve's last know whereabouts which appears to be this here theatre, Mr Flynn. She came, by all accounts, specifically to see your good self.'

'I had no idea Ariadne had a daughter. I'm sorry I can't be of more help, Detective. I can assure you, you won't find her in my theatre.'

'Do you own a burgundy Ford Galaxy?' Paula reels off the registration number. I catch a flicker of confusion cross his face but he quickly recovers himself.

'We use a vehicle, such as you describe, for maintenance purposes, scenery and the like. What has it to do with your investigation, may I ask?'

There's a rapid change in Flynn's demeanour, as if he's lost his place in the conversation. His relief that I'd moved on from the Parks was palpable, and he showed no fear when questioned about the Ford Galaxy, the suspected hit-and-run vehicle. Am I connecting the two deaths when there is no connection to be had? Possibly. But I'm not finished with Mr Gilroy Flynn quite yet.

'Who has access to the vehicle, Mr Flynn?'

'How am I supposed to know?' he says, reasserting himself. 'If something has happened with that car there will be hell to pay. I've not got time to deal with petty issues, I'm in the middle of producing the greatest musical of our generation. Someone else will have to deal with it. In fact, I don't even want to know what's happened, that's to say, if anything has happened.' He takes a breather, but he isn't finished. 'Please be aware, Detective, if this involves any of my cast, I can assure you that you will not find carrying out an investigation, at this time, advantageous, or indeed, permitted by me.'

I'm tiring of this bloke by the second.

'Do you have any idea of the location of the Ford Galaxy?' I ask.

Before Flynn has a chance to respond, the pansy girl, having come to retrieve the untouched tea tray, pipes up, 'Mr Murdo drove off in it the other day. I saw him. Must've been in a hurry because I waved to him from the window and he ignored me.'

'Er... that's our musical director,' Flynn tells us, 'Murdo McAllister.'

Flynn opens a green folder on his desk and pulls a bundle of documents from it. He begins leafing through the papers then stops to look up at me with a questioning eye, as if he's already dismissed me and is wondering why I'm still standing here.

'Was there a falling out between you and Mr McAllister?' I ask. I always find it best to move past whatever proves to be irksome.

'Gossip thrives in the theatre, Detective.' Flynn sighs heavily and leans back in his chair. 'A minor quibble,' he says. 'No murders on my stage,' he says in a half joking kind of way.

'Interesting you should talk about murder,' Paula says.

Good point. I wait to see Flynn's reaction. Paula explains the importance of examining the vehicle in question, in relation to the death of a man in Dunkeld. At this, Flynn shows no recognition or any signs of discomfort. Then she informs him, rather clinically I suppose, of the murder of Maureen Park, aka Ariadne Fairchild.

'Dead? Ariadne is dead?'

'That's correct,' Paula says, then remembers herself. 'I'm sorry for your loss.'

I take back the reins. 'We're trying to establish whether these deaths are linked, Mr Flynn.'

Flynn says nothing for a very long few minutes. Both Paula and I wait, neither of us willing to hamper the obnoxious git's thought processes.

Flynn barely moves. It's as if he's retreated into a world of his own making.

I do my gruff cough manoeuvre, but he's barely returned to the room.

He stands, rigid, and searches my face. 'Did I kill her?' he asks me.

PART THREE

Chapter 50

Gilroy

Until this moment, he'd not once considered his choice to be wrong.
He hadn't considered there to be a choice at all. Was that all Murdo's
doing? Has Murdo nurtured him so intently that the line between
right and wrong doesn't pertain to him, the great Gilroy Flynn?

He'd received a call this morning from Jackob. Of all things, it
was the last thing on his mind. How about that, admitting that. Jackob
wants to meet him and has chosen this exact spot. For what reason?
Jackob had quickly assured him that nothing untoward had happened,
that's something to be grateful for, at least. So here he is, leaving
Murdo to deal with the investors. That's not what's worrying him,
these types of meetings always enrage him, Murdo is much better at
mollycoddling than he.

Isn't a man made up of many things? He's so focussed on his
career to the extent that nothing else matters. Or so he's thought all
these years. Now he's back, it's as if he's about to do it all again, in
his head it's excruciating, but can he honestly say that's how he felt
at the time? He stares out across the Firth of Forth and wonders if he
would make that same choice today.

A man is made up of many things. It's The Taxidermist's line
from *Madness & Ecstasy*. The Taxidermist is trying to persuade
Dionysus against pursuing Diana. But Dionysus knows only of self-
entitlement. His is a god unworthy of the title. He could apply the
same logic to himself.

The moment his daughter left the security of his arms, had he
ceased to become a man and, instead, sealed his fate as an empty god?
A fraud?

He takes the path under the Forth Road Bridge to meet, once again, after so many years, with Jackob Winter. The water is calm, he leans against a low wall and stares out across it, wondering if what he's about to do will tear his life apart. He waits.

***

You lose your mother suddenly and feel as weak as her heart had apparently been. As a fifteen-year-old boy, you know the life you're about to embark upon will be merely a shadow of what it might have been with her in it.

You fall in love at the quickest opportunity. She is a goddess. Everything your mother was and more, so much more. You would die for Ariadne Fairchild. She shares your dreams, your hopes, your pedestal. She is golden, and when you touch her she fills you with promise. And you take that promise and you rise. You rise, and she's willingly there by your side. Until she's not.

The child changes everything. As it grows inside of her, you imagine holding the child to your breast, becoming your primitive self, stripped of the certainty of your future, for the first time in your life.

You look to Ariadne. You search her face for the woman you love only to discover her gone, replaced by a mutilated version of her.

Taking her place is a woman you don't recognise, a woman on the point of giving birth, a woman suffering from the fate of her twisted desires.

This, this pale shadow of his Ariadne, drowning in delusion, swallowed by such fierce envy of every woman and desire for any child other than her own beautiful daughter. He listens to her tormented screams, sees for himself her rejection of their daughter, the child she sinfully elects imperfect and untouchable.

She doesn't hear her child cry. She's isn't listening. She looks deep into the infant's eyes and sees something indescribable, something to hate, she screams, something to loathe, an innocent she intently rejects. Bring me my child. *My* child. She screams it all night long. In the morning, she takes me to where other babies sleep and points to this one, that one, another. Your child, your daughter isn't among these babies; that daughter lies in a cot in an empty room while her mother presses her face up to the nursery window and demands this child, that one, the other.

To a young man, besotted, this statement will mean something entirely different to the man you are today.

North Queensferry, 1981

Gilroy wraps the blanket tighter around his baby daughter. The daughter Ariadne has rejected, has declared repugnant, has scratched and clawed at tiny, wet cheeks and a fragile skull and has threatened with a fleecy, pink blanket.

Jackob Winter should be here by now. They had agreed an appropriate time, 2 a.m. It's now a quarter past. He tries not to let his mind run ahead.

Ariadne has not changed her mind, as he'd hoped she would. She'd handed over their child, and turned her back on them.

'You're late,' he says to Jackob Winter, coming towards him at a slow pace.

'I was watching you from the hotel window.' Jackob points to the building behind, the Albert Hotel. 'Part of me was begging for you to get back in that car of yours, take your daughter home, where she belongs.'

'You know I can't do that, man.'

Jackob shakes his head. 'What would your mother think, Gilroy?'

'I didn't come here to talk about her.'

'Gilroy, I need to make sure this is really what you want. This little thing is your child. Your daughter.'

Gilroy puts the child into Jackob's arms. 'She's yours now, Jackob. My mother would understand.'

'Even if you think that's true, how will you live with yourself?'

'That's not important. I know, with you, my daughter will have a good life. It has to be this way. Ariadne will not accept her.'

Gilroy allows himself one final stroke of his daughter's face.

'This little girl deserves better than that.'

It is over. His mother's Uncle Jackob will take good care of his child. Ariadne is gone. He will have to live with himself, knowing his daughter exists without him, but nothing will make him return to Ariadne's waiting arms.

He climbs back in his car and sits watching the sunrise over the River Forth. Time escapes him and he lets the day pass him by.

North Queensferry
11th October

'Gilroy.'

Lost in his thoughts, he hasn't heard Jackob come up behind him. 'She's not with you?'

'You thought I was bringing Nora? My apologies, I should've been clearer. Nora doesn't know I'm here. In fact, I have kept my end of the bargain and she knows me to be her biological father. That is why I called and asked to meet with you.'

'I see.' He returns to the low stone wall and rests against it. He wants a moment, just a moment. He hadn't thought it, hadn't formed the thought in his mind, but the tremor inside him, that hollow in his heart and the rock in the pit of his stomach has him yearning for the years he's lost. 'Can I see her?'

'Yes.' Jackob puts a hand on his shoulder. 'It is time.'

'When?' His head is clear. He will go with Jackob now if that's what Jackob wants.

'I see you are to be a big showman. It is keeping you busy?'

Madness and Ecstasy. He can't walk away, not now. Murdo has gone. He must see it through, but...

'Your mother would be proud of you.'

He shakes himself away from Jackob and turns to face the water. 'Would she?'

'Of course. You've nothing to worry about, Nora is a good daughter. She will come to you when the time is right. Wait for her, Gilroy.'

'Yes,' he says. 'I will wait.'

Chapter 51
DS Calmly

Edinburgh
22nd October

'If Murdo had found out, well, it was easier to argue with him, to get rid of him for a while, I don't know, I thought he suspected me of something, and I couldn't risk him finding out about Nora.'

Paula sits down in the chair opposite Flynn's office desk and leans towards the man. 'Tell us about that, Mr Flynn. You argued with Mr McAllister. What was the argument about?'

My phone vibrates in my pocket. I hand the phone to Dunbar.

'Mr Flynn,' I say. 'What didn't you want Murdo McAllister to find out?'

Paula gets up from her chair and motions for me to go to stand outside in the lobby. She gives me the update she's just received on the phone.

I return directly to Flynn. 'Mr Flynn. The Ford Galaxy has been spotted on the A82 road to Crianlarich. Any idea where Mr McAllister is going?'

Eve Park could very well be in that car.

The team are on it, Paula had informed me in the lobby. She'd said it with a grimace, and I caught her meaning well enough. When this is over we will both be in trouble. But Paula was right to call it in, and it's a stroke of luck that the vehicle in question is heading back to our patch, it will help smooth over any irate powers that be once this is all over.

Paula questions him about Eve but Flynn looks clueless.

'I don't know anyone called Eve or any reason why she would come here to find me.'

'What about McAllister?' I fire at him. 'Does he know her?'

265

'I've never heard him mention an Eve.'

I sit in the chair opposite him, lean across the desk and face the man. 'Who is Nora?'

He leaps from the chair and leans his arms on the filing cabinet behind his desk, his head in his hands. He's thinking. Deciding what he wants me to know and how much he can keep to himself.

I repeat, 'Who is Nora?'

He drops his arms swiftly to his side then grips the back of his chair.

Gilroy Flynn glares across the desk at me, but not angrily, as I'd expected, more childlike, desperate.

'Nora is my daughter,' he admits shyly.

The thought had been in my head that Gilroy could potentially have been Eve's father. Now there's another daughter in the mix.

'Where does Nora fit into all this?' I ask.

Gilroy Flynn returns to his seat. 'What do you mean by, all this, Detective?'

If only I knew. I'm wasting my time here. I should be out chasing the Ford Galaxy.

'Tell me, Detective, tell me what happened to Ariadne. I feel I really should like to know.' Flynn is pale, his eyes watery, his hands fidgety.

'After,' Paula says, rather more aggressively than I'd like. 'First. Tell us how you know Bruce Lawrence. And what reason you might have had for killing him.'

Flynn's head shoots up, and this time there are proper tears that spill over onto his face. He brushes them away.

'I did not kill him. I want that known.' He grasps Paula's wrist. 'I did not kill him. I don't even know who you are talking about.'

'Then who did?' she fires back.

'I don't know.'

'Do you think Eve could be in the Ford Galaxy that we're tracking? Who's driving it, do you know that?'

'I don't know.'

'Eve could be in danger. Do you want another murder on your hands?' Paula reels out.

'No.'

'Then help us.'

'Take a deep breath, Mr Flynn,' I interject. He takes three long, drawn-out breaths. Perfect.

'I need time to think,' he says. 'Just, just go away. Give me time. I need time.'

'We might not have time,' Paula says, gravely.

I think she's thinking along the same lines as me. Eve was here. Now, it seems, she's not. We know that vehicle was most probably used to kill Bruce Lawrence. If the person driving it also killed Maureen Park, it's safe to assume that Eve may be in danger. Particularly if it turns out she is travelling in the Galaxy.

Somehow, this all started with Lawrence. I don't want it to end with Eve.

'Come on, Mr Flynn. What is it that you're not telling us?'

This time, both my own and Paula's mobiles kick off. This is never good. I take the call. Listen. Hang up.

I look at both expectant faces and try to keep my tone official. 'There's been an explosion. A caravan. On the outskirts of Edinburgh. I'd say not too far from your home address, Mr Flynn. The remains of a body were found inside.'

Flynn screams out, 'Murdo? Is it Murdo's body?'

'I don't have any information of that kind, yet.' I slump on the arm of the leather couch. 'Now,' I fix my professional face, a penetrating gaze, right between Mr Flynn's eyes. Inside, I'm struggling, can feel my gut clenching. 'Start talking, Mr Flynn.'

Flynn opens a desk in his drawer and pulls out a leather-bound book. 'How did Ariadne die?' he asks.

'We can get to that later,' Paula says. 'Earlier today there was a Ford Galaxy parked outside your house. That car belongs to you, is this correct?'

'When? When did she die? At least tell me that, for heaven's sake.'

I get up from the edge of the couch and perch on the desk, to make sure I have Flynn's full attention. Some people respond better to gentle coaxing.

'What's on your mind, Gilroy?'

A long, painful whine escapes Flynn. 'No. No. No.'

I quickly hold my hand up to Paula. Wait.

Flynn begins sobbing uncontrollably. Paula and I are left staring at the man, neither of us quite sure how to proceed. I'd hoped my soft approach would've given us what we need to move on this. If something happens to Eve, because of my bumbling efforts, I'll never forgive myself.

'Nora,' Flynn blurts out. He leaps up and makes for the door, then has second thoughts and turns to face first me, then Paula. 'Nora,' he repeats. He skips back around his desk and lifts the book he'd brought from the drawer. He opens it. 'It's not here,' he says. He drops the book on the desk and throws open each of the other two drawers in turn, pulling everything out and throwing it on the floor. 'It's not here.'

'What?' Paula demands.

Flynn runs back to the door and yanks it open. 'Come with me, Detectives,' he says firmly. 'I'll tell you everything you need to know on the way.'

Chapter 52

DS Calmly

Towards Skye
22nd October

When I'm on a chase, I usually find it more advantageous if I know who I'm chasing and why. In this case, there's no time to check everything out. The three of us, myself, Gilroy Flynn and Paula, pile into the car, and Paula weaves us seamlessly through the Glasgow traffic, onto the Great Western Road and the A82.

There are three potential scenarios. The first: Eve is safe and well and wandering around Glasgow having a whale of a time. The second: Eve is in the Ford Galaxy we are chasing and, if she is, we don't as yet know why. Third: Eve is the body in the caravan. I want my money on the first scenario, but I've never been a betting man.

I turn to Flynn, crouched and panic-stricken in the back seat. 'Any joy?'

Flynn drops the phone on his lap and shakes his head. For the past fifteen minutes, I've had him call Murdo McAllister in the vain hope that we can dodge whatever it is that is about to unfold.

'At first it just rang out,' Flynn tells me. 'Now, I think he's switched the phone off, or it's out of charge.'

'I'm getting every sighting of the Ford Galaxy sent through to my phone.'

'In that case,' I say, 'there's nothing we can do until we catch up with him. He has at least a thirty-minute start on us. It would be helpful to know where we are heading. Paula is well-versed in these roads; she'll know all the shortcuts.'

Flynn leans forward from the back seat. 'Murdo has been at my book,' he says. 'Tucked inside the back cover is – was – a letter I once wrote to my daughter but never found the courage to send.'

'Your daughter?' Paula shouts from the driver's seat.

'Murdo must've taken it,' Flynn says. 'But how did he find out?' He looks at me with doleful eyes, like he's begging me for answers I don't have.

I ask him. 'Find out what?'

Flynn looks about to wither away into thin air. I snap back at him, repeat my question. 'What?'

'That I'd met with Jackob Winter when I was supposed to be meeting our investors.'

'Who is this?' Paula growls.

'He lives on the Isle of Skye,' he says.

All at once chaos flies in my face, like sharp edges, scratch after scratch.

Paula bangs the steering wheel. 'The exact location?'

'I'll have to get it from memory; Murdo has stolen my letter with the address. Why would he do that?' Flynn mumbles. 'It's a complicated business, something… Ale of Sleat? No. Aird. Aird of Sleat, that's it. A cottage there, a good… a…' Flynn pulls his knees up to his chest and wraps his arms around them. He's is visibly shivering.

***

The island of Skye, at least a four-hour drive, even with Paula's rather impressive speed. The Ford Galaxy, having a thirty-minute head start, is worrying me a great deal. There is a slight chance we can get to Nora Winter in time. I get on the phone to Fletcher Cunningham.

But what about Eve? I've received no update on that front. All we know is that a caravan that Flynn tells us belongs to Murdo McAllister was found burnt out with a body inside. I wish I could kid myself, but instinct is telling me it was Eve in that caravan. I've asked to be informed of any progress.

In the meantime, I want to be brought up to speed, and there's only one person who may have all the pieces. I twist around so that I can get a clear view of the man sniffling in the back seat.

'Gilroy. Talk to me.'

'I can't,' he says. He clasps his head in his hands. 'It must be a mistake. Murdo isn't a murderer. It mustn't be him driving the

Galaxy. It can't be Murdo. He would never do this to me.'

'Do what, exactly?'

A determined look flashes across Flynn's face, a sob catches in his throat. 'Kill Ariadne. He would never do that.'

'I think it's time for you to stop prevaricating and tell me what's going on.'

'A dead body,' Flynn utters. 'What reason? What reason would Murdo have to kill all these people?'

'Why don't you tell us, Mr Flynn? You know him better than anyone.'

Flynn turns his gaze away from me to look out of the window. Paula signals left at the roundabout, about to take the Oban road.

'Take the second exit and stay on the A82,' I tell her. 'It will be quicker, a straight route through the Trossachs.'

'People are dead because of me,' Flynn says.

I can't see his face, because he's looking out of the window.

He carries on, as if rambling through his thoughts. 'He shared my dream, but now I must wonder if it ever was my dream?'

'To be a musical theatre producer?' I ask.

'To be the greatest impresario of all time. Together, we were going to achieve that with the return of *Madness & Ecstasy*. It was to be the first production of my glittering new career.' This comes across as a sneer. Not his general self-promotional hype.

'No,' I say, as calmly as I can, which involves a great deal of swallowing back my frustration, 'you're not making sense.' I stretch my neck. This is definitely not my favoured interrogation style. It's difficult enough to get a person of interest in a murder enquiry to open up in the safe and relatively comfortable confines of the station. To have to do it here, like this, having to twist and turn just to see Flynn's face and to try to block out the noise of the car and the road so I can hear his incoherent mutterings is not something I hope to make a habit of. 'If I'm right and your friend, McAllister, is the perpetrator of three murders, are you telling me he did it to save your show? I find that difficult to digest as a motive, Flynn.'

Flynn shrugs but then he quickly holds his finger up to me. I take it as a warning not to speak, not sure how else I'm supposed to take it. I remain silent, give him the space. There's something that connects these three murders and Flynn knows what that something is. And I intend on knowing too, before we reach the scene of a fourth murder.

A few minutes pass then he speaks. 'You mustn't let him kill Nora.' He leans between the two front seats, taps Paula on the shoulder. 'Can't you drive any faster? You're a cop. Don't you people get trained in driving fast?'

I nudge Paula with my knee so she knows to let the comment go.

'You must listen to me,' Flynn says. Finally, I sense an urgency in his tone. 'Many years ago, thirty-eight to be precise, a child was born. At that time, there was no intention, either on my part or that of Ariadne's, to begin a family. Nevertheless, Ariadne gave birth to our daughter. For the first time, I learned that I was not good enough for Ariadne and, to my utter humiliation, that neither was our daughter.'

'I don't have the patience for a long story, Flynn,' I say.

His face is close to mine now, an expression of painful dejection and what looks like fear. More than that, his eyes are wide, his jaw clenched, his hand gripping my armrest.

'How long now?' Flynn asks. 'Do you have a single clue regarding Murdo's whereabouts?'

I hold up my phone and nod. I have an earpiece in and am listening to real-time updates on the Ford Galaxy's location.

'We're keeping track,' I tell him. 'I estimate he's half an hour ahead of us.'

'Ariadne was in hospital for five days after the birth of our daughter,' Flynn says. 'I was Judas Iscariot in *Jesus Christ Superstar*. I couldn't get away to visit her. She was alone for most of that time, and I dare say, to my shame, I didn't have thoughts of my daughter at the forefront of my mind.'

My phone rings out. 'I have to take this,' I tell Flynn. I listen, hang up. I clear my throat. 'There's yet to be a formal identification. But, a mobile phone was found among the debris of the burnt out caravan. It was in a decent enough state to power up and be analysed. The phone is registered to Blythe Burrell.'

We are all jolted forward due to Paula's foot hitting the brake. An involuntary reaction that she quickly rectifies without any damage to our persons, but enough damage to our nerves for us to fall back in our seats and take a moment to recover.

272

'I don't know anyone by the name of Blythe Burrell,' Flynn says. 'The Galaxy and caravan must've been stolen.'

I turn to face him. 'Blythe Burrell is Eve Park's next-door neighbour. She gave Eve the phone after her mother died.'

'Eve is Ariadne's daughter?'

I wait for him to digest this. There are various scenarios that could place Eve's phone in that car beside an unknown victim, but if I've learnt anything in this job it's that if there's something you don't want to happen, that is exactly what has happened.

'Flynn, Flynn, Flynn,' I bellow at him. 'Why would McAllister want to kill Ariadne's daughter?'

'I don't know.'

I thump my hand down hard on his which is still clutching my armrest. 'I don't believe you.'

'I didn't even know she had a daughter,' he wails.

'That's a lie for a start. You've just finished telling me about the daughter, your daughter, which Ariadne gave birth to.'

'The day before Ariadne was due to leave hospital, I went to visit my child for the first time. I held her in my arms and, I'm not ashamed to admit it, I cried. I can still feel the softness of her hair against my chin.'

'Get on with it Flynn,' I shout. 'You're contradicting yourself; a clear sign that you're lying. If I find that you lie to me from now on, I will make sure that your involvement in this comes at a high price.'

'My child wasn't given a name,' Flynn tells me. 'Ariadne placed the child in my arms and repeated her instructions which were for me to remove the child from her sight and make sure she was never to lay eyes on it again.'

'You took her to Jackob Winter.'

'That is correct.'

'Because Ariadne…?'

'She'd taken an instant dislike to the child. Such a dislike that, if I hadn't done what she wanted, I feared for my daughter's life.'

'You had no inclination to care for the child yourself?'

'I made no decision lightly, Detective. Ariadne was my life, after musical theatre, but her rejection of our child forced her into a new light. I felt it as a rejection of us, of everything we meant to each other. I was rising in my career, professed to be the… well, you know. Doesn't mean anything now, if that makes you feel any better?'

I'm really rather good at containing confrontational thoughts, and this very moment is what I could call, advanced training.

I pull away from him and stare out of the windscreen. Finally things are beginning to click into place, but it doesn't make me rest any easier.

Chapter 53

Nora

Skye
22nd October

Mhona has finally let me listen to Dad's tape. It took only a few words to tell me he was dying.

'It was my idea,' she says, handing me a glass of water. 'He was vexed about the whole thing. If you ask me, he'd carried the burden for all these years, it was all getting too much for him. The thing is, lovely, he didn't want you to know he was ill.'

The burden my dad carried was me. That's not how he put it on the tape, but in some ways it is how it is, he took me into his care when nobody else wanted me.

I look up from the tape I'm holding in my hands. I've listened to it, over and over again. Even I could see that listening to Dad's voice was hard for Mhona. I didn't care about that, I've lost Dad, nothing can be worse than that. Maybe she did feel something for him, but her feelings don't count. He was my dad. He was my dad.

'What was killing him?'

'He wanted to tell you to your face, my lovely, but, well. Ach, you know him better than me, I'm just saying, it's hard, you know. He loved you more than he minded life. More than life. He felt he was letting you down, stupid as it sounds. I told him; don't think I didn't tell him.'

I wait for her to continue, but Mhona disappears into a world of her own. It's still difficult for me to look at this woman and imagine her with Dad. To think she knew a part of him I never could.

She comes to sit with me on the sofa, puts her hand on my arm. 'I told him you'd want to know. He had a sickness, you know, the doctors weren't able to offer him a cure.'

She's going to tell me Dad stepped off a cliff because of some illness? She doesn't know him at all if she believes that. I pull my arm away and slam the glass of water down on the table in front of me.

'What was wrong with him?' I ask.

'His heart was getting awfy tired, lovely. That's all. But he wanted you to know the truth. He'd never have had the heart to tell you to your face.'

'And the tape was the next best thing.'

'That's right. I tried to get him to record on my phone but you know what he was like with modern technology.'

I start to ease myself off the couch. Mhona's hidden away the walking sticks until the doctor says it's fine for me to use them. But I want away from her and all her talk about my dad, and how it was fine to talk to her about his secrets but not to talk to me.

'Sit there,' Mhona says, holding her hand up. 'I've got something I think you need.'

Minutes later, Mhona returns and places a box of Dairy Milk on my lap. 'I'm not saying this will cheer you up, I'm just… Well, I wanted one myself. She rips off the wrapping, opens the box and we both take a chocolate. I sit back and hear the birds singing outside, the water lapping against the rocks and I try to make sense of my dad's intentions.

'When you turned up the other day, I wasn't expecting it see,' Mhona says. 'I'd thought I'd give it a few weeks, you know. Let you get used to the idea that your dad isn't around any more. I think your dad needed you to understand. I thought it would be hard for you in the beginning, harder still for you to hear your dad's story.'

A grassy breeze from the open door makes me desperate to be outside. 'Mhona, I want to go home.'

'You will, my lovely. You will, when you're moving about better. Listen, let's go for a wander around the island. There's nothing better than letting that feeling of the water surround you. I often stand up on the top hill and let the sea envelope me, it's like a comfort blanket. And it's going to make you feel so much better, I promise.'

***

It's blowy but strangely warm for October. Mhona pushes the wheelchair, stopping every now and then to tell me a story about this or that, an old legend or myth. Or about the family that grew up here, and how they ran a post office.

I don't know how she manages it, she might not be as old as my dad but she's a fair age herself. She's fit, right enough. Dad would've been impressed by that. I imagine them walking up here together and wonder what they talked about. If they talked about how to tell me that I've no biological links to my dad. Who cares about that now? He's dead. My dad is dead. And he spent his last moments being intimate with her and not me.

'Look down there.' Mhona turns my chair and points to the bottom of the hill. 'It's a cave,' she says. 'There are a few of them. We can explore them once you're back on your feet.' She goes on to tell of the myths related to the island.

I'm only half listening. I gaze at the cave entrance and wish my dad had trusted me enough with his secrets. I don't want to explore the caves. Not if I can't do it with him. Since I was a little girl, Dad made sure I was educated in what he liked to think of as his Skye. Always south, he rarely ventured north, unless he was in his taxi. That was for tourists mostly. People from the north have no need to visit the southern fringes of the island. Those of us in the south rarely venture far from home. Exploring any aspect of this part of the world without him feels like a betrayal. Even if he has kind of betrayed me, I have to believe he did it for the right reasons, reasons that meant something important to him.

'Who is that then?' Mhona puts the brakes on the chair and walks to the edge of the hill to get a clearer view of the small rowing boat making its way towards the island. 'Someone you know?' she asks.

Right away I think it must be William. Probably come to give me an update on the animals. But as the boat slips onto the shingle, I can tell it's not him. This man is older, much older, with a yellowish white beard and a woollen hat.

Mhona looks at me, but I just shrug my shoulders. 'Let's go see then, lovely. See what he's about. I don't like strangers turning up unannounced.'

Mhona parks me at the edge of the jetty and scrambles down

the shingle towards the scrunched up man. The wind is picking up, thwarting his efforts to step off the boat. He manages to plant his feet on dry land, straighten himself then he raises his oar.

'Hey,' I shout. He's raising his oar above his head as if he's going to strike Mhona. I wheel down to the edge of the shingle, but it's useless, my wheels sink and skid and my arms aren't strong enough to push across such uneven ground. I scream out to warn her, but my scream is stolen by the wind. Mhona is too busy minding her footing to realise what's about to happen. The oar batters down on Mhona's head. She doesn't raise her arms to protect herself, it's too sudden, she wasn't ready for him. She crumples on the water's edge.

Chapter 54
DS Calmly

Skye
22nd October

Paula nudges the car off the ferry, and we head along the road to Sleat at as fast a pace as the road will allow. It must have rained earlier and the ground is sludgy, slippery under the tyres and is slowing us down, doing nothing for my mood. Confirmation that it was Eve's body in the burnt out caravan has brought a sickening halt to conversation.

I find it curious that I have no feelings of homecoming. I'd expected to land on the island and reassert myself. I have the deputy chief super breathing down my neck on the phone, a whining civilian in tow illegally and a PC not afraid to admonish me for the mistakes I've made in this case.

Paula breaks the silence. 'I keep thinking if we'd…'

'Don't you dare give me that told you so lecture,' I snap at her. It makes me feel better to spit and snarl. 'You're not experienced enough to know how to run an investigation. There's plenty you can learn from this, but you're far from ready to know what should and shouldn't have been done, lady.'

'Lady, eh? You've never called me a lady before. Sir.'

'If we can't trust each other, then we're no use to each other, PC Dunbar,' I say. I'm in no mood. It matters not to me that I'm gruff and unbending. 'That's the cottage there, pull into the side.'

Before the car's stopped, I'm out, instructing them to remain where they are.

William Ghilista. He's the last fellow I'd expect to find disrupting my investigation. He's the island's shadow, often spotted but no one is ever quite sure of him.

'She's not at home,' he tells me.

'Where is she then?'

William is standing at the open door to the cottage. I try to push aside the investigation that captivated the entire island like nothing ever has or likely ever will. I've been distracted enough in this case by what now seems like a ludicrous idea that Eve and I had some kind of connection, something that connected she and I to my sister Jenny. See where that's got me.

William picks up an empty pail and makes to walk off, changes his mind and turns to face my direction.

'She's had her troubles recently. You lot were no help to her. If she sees you, it'll no help in her recovery.'

I take a step towards him. 'Just tell me where she is. I'd say trouble with the police is not in your best interests, Ghilista.'

He drops the pail. 'There's nothing you can do to me now, nothing that the police haven't done already. What's Nora done to have you looking for her?'

Nora. It can't be. Can't be the same women, she was dealing with her dad's suicide. I'm not even going to ask myself how many Nora's there are on this relatively tiny island. There's going to be one hell of a debrief back at the station.

'You helping her out here? Not like you to make friends, William.' I can see I've got his back up. I'm already on borrowed time.

'You'd do best to follow my lead, Lark, and not renew friendships around here. There's some who still blames you for what happened to Jenny.'

My hand at his neck, I push him up against the stone of the cottage wall. 'I should advise you to be very careful,' I tell him. A snarl snakes through me, my own spit lands on his shoulder. His breathing is curtailed, my fingers digging into his neck. He barely moves a muscle, his eyes fixed on my own, wide, watchful, his arms redundant at his sides. Jenny and William had been close as youngsters, but it's the underlying suspicion in his tone that riles me now.

'Nora Winter is in danger,' I spit at him.

I release him, shake out my stiff hand and turn away from him before I do any more damage to the pair of us.

'Like I told the other bloke came here threatening me. You'll find her on Pabay,' he tells me. 'What kind of danger?'

He asks the question, but I've already turned down the side of the cottage and am scrambling back into the car.

Chapter 55

Nora

Skye
22nd October

I open my eyes and know instantly I'm in a cave. Water is dripping on my neck from the rock above me. Moving my left shoulder is excruciating.

The shadow of my wheelchair, abandoned, is at the opening to the cave. The light coming in from the entrance doesn't reach as far as where I'm lying, but I can sense his presence, hear his ragged breath. And mixed with the wet stone and the salty air, I can smell him, damp tobacco and something citrusy, soap perhaps, or a light perfume.

I roll onto my back and push my feet against the mulchy earth, ignoring the shard of pain in my knee, and I'm able to sit up, lean against the cold cave wall. I have to support my left elbow and try not to move my shoulder, keep the pain to a minimum, so I can think.

He's sitting a few feet away, leaning against the cave wall; I can just make out the shadow of him. He pushed me down the hill. He pushed me down the hill and then dragged me in here. Have I been unconscious? Is he crying?

'Who the hell are you?' I ask him. How can I be sure he's going to let me go?

'I'm sorry this has all happened,' he murmurs. 'I didn't mean for any of it to happen.'

A sharp pain from my shoulder jolts me into action and I try to get up, but I've been winded, my arms and legs are useless.

He keeps talking as if he can't see me. 'I thought with the chap Lawrence out of the way that would be an end to it. I truly believed that to be so. But all my action has caused has been to bring me to you.'

I pick up a pebble and throw it at him. It grazes off him and disappears pointlessly into the dark. The light seeping into the cave has moved and I can see him a bit clearer now. He looks old, how did he manage to pull me out of my chair and this far into the cave?

He keeps talking, is he talking to me? Does he think I'm listening? He pulls his knees to him and wraps his arms around them.

'You look a lot like her,' he says.

Half of me wants to lie down and sleep. The rest of me wants to run. On my elbows, I ease myself forward, he's not watching me, he's lost somewhere in his own conversation.

I ease forward a tiny bit more, but this time my trainers scraping the gravel catch his attention.

I haven't got very far, have hardly moved at all. I feel about for a rock, because I'm not just going to sit here and let him kill me. He's watching me do it, but he doesn't seem to be in any hurry to stop me. My hand clasps onto a palm-sized rock. I feel along its wet edge and discover a sharp point. It's not very reassuring, it will have to do. I've never needed a phone, never bothered with one but I wish I had one now. I grip tight to the rock.

'Who are you?' I ask.

He laughs quietly to himself. He bends his head between his legs as if he's been hurt. 'Tá brón orm. Tá brón orm, mo cheann beag.'

He's speaking in Gaelic, the words Dad used to whisper to me when I was a child, if ever I was hurt, or if he thought he'd been too sharp with me, although he never was. I'm sorry. I'm sorry, my little one. Hearing Dad's words coming from this stranger makes my throat constrict.

'Don't say that. You have no right.' My hand grips the stone, the sharp edge cutting into the fleshy part of my palm. I tell him. 'My dad taught me that everyone deserves a second chance. This could be it, for both of us. A second chance for you. If you let me go, no one needs to know about this. People will come soon, there's not long. Let me go. Please.'

'We were close once, Jackob and I. But then I killed Gil's father and, even although Gil and his mother forgave me, Jackob couldn't. He hated me after that.'

'What?'

'It surprised me to find out Gil could lie to me. He hid you, all these years he hid you, and neither he nor Jackob gave their secret away.'

He draws himself away from the cave wall and comes to sit closer to me. I tuck the rock underneath me, away from his view.

'In one sense, I suppose, you must have rescued Jackob from despair; afforded him a way out of his unrelenting loneliness. For he was so very lonely in those days. It is heartening, you see. I paid no attention to his leaving us, I had other things on my mind, or should I say, Ariadne had other things to occupy my mind. I was happy to oblige, give her what she wanted just to get her out of Gilroy's life so I could keep my promise to his mother. Ariadne was a poison that would have killed him in the end.'

His thin lips grimace at me, his eyes darting from me to the scarf in his hands. From me to the scarf.

'How long was I unconscious for? You could've killed me then?' I ask him, playing for time.

'Oh, just a few seconds, I would say,' he says assuredly. 'I prayed it was over. But after I laid you down in here, I felt your pulse. You have a strong pulse. We are not always entitled to the things we pray for.'

I'm not going to get out of here alive. I've never thought about my own death before. The worse thing that could've happened to me has already happened. Or so I'd thought this morning and the days since Dad died.

But it's not true. I want to live. My life is worth something, at the very least, it's worth fighting for. I grip the stone and gather the fight up inside myself. I am ready for him.

I think of the minke whale, the way she throws back her head when she catches sight of me. As if she's closing the gap between us, drawing me in, so she can become a part of me, and I, a part of her.

She knows the sea is welcoming but doesn't care if I live or die. That's all on me.

Chapter 56
DS Calmly

'There has to be a damn boat, this is an island for Christ's sake.'

I send Paula to the nearby houses, the café, tell her to look anywhere she might find a thing that will take us from Broadford across to Pabay.

Meanwhile, I lock Flynn in the car and search the quayside. I struggle along the dirt path through nettles, seagrass and jagged bushes, as close to the water's edge, where there's likely to be a boat but am unlucky. I consider, for a crazy moment, the idea of swimming across. I'm a good swimmer, wouldn't be the first time I've swam in this water. In those days, I was fitter, stronger. In those days, I respected the strength and power the sea can teach us on land and, from where I'm standing, my body already hot and shivery, I'm analysing the distance between me and that island, Pabay, watching the sea rise and fall over itself, listening to its quiet counsel. I am not the man I used to be. I shout this aloud to the sea. It gives me its acknowledgement; a boat.

Dunbar calls out to me. She's manoeuvring an inflatable dinghy. 'We're in luck,' she says when I catch up with her at the quay. 'It belongs to the guy who owns the café. It's got an outboard motor.'

'Did you hear back from DS Cunningham? Any sign of backup?'

'Not yet, sir.'

I climb into the dinghy. 'You wait for them. Make sure Flynn stays where he is.'

Chapter 57

Nora

Skye
22nd October

He hasn't emerged from the back of the cave.

I thought he was about to strangle me but then he stood up and walked further into the cave. I can't see him.

Is he giving me a chance to get away?

I drag myself along the ground using my good shoulder and hip and pressing my back against the cave wall to give myself some purchase. Slow, too slow.

The drumming of my heartbeat in my ears is faster, and the sound of my own ragged breath echoing off the walls is like I'm calling him back, saying, come and kill me, come and kill me.

It's as if I'm lugging the weight of ten bodies. My body is unrecognisable to me. It is a thousand times heavier, fiercely resistant and utterly incapable of free movement. Inch by inch it resists. Cut by cut it screams inside my head; every graze, every smear of earth, the screams are thunderous but they're in my head. I'm too scared to scream out loud in case it brings him running to me to finish what he's started.

Inch by inch, until I catch a faint change in the air. I'm easing closer to the cave entrance. I open my mouth, gratefully gulping in the tiny speckles of air dancing within the light that's filtering into the cave. Nearly there.

I fall onto my front, use my hand, my chin, my elbow, hips, my good knee; anything that's going to get me closer to the wheelchair.

Just a few more centimetres. Reaching out, I can almost touch the chair. I take a deep breath, a deep, long breath for one final push.

I grasp the cold steel of the wheel, yank the chair to me and snap on the brake. Now all I have to do is, somehow, lift myself into it.

I'm okay. I'm okay. This is going to work.

I push the chair up against the wall to make it steady. I've no idea how I'm going to hoist myself up.

His voice. He's speaking to me. 'If only you knew how much I want to let you go.'

His footsteps coming toward me. He's close, behind me. Don't turn around. Pretend he's not here. Let him do what he wants, I can fight. I can fight back.

He keeps speaking, on and on. 'Ariadne's stolen child was a nobody. But you, you are Gilroy's daughter. Killing you means killing a part of him.'

I stop moving.

He's walking in front of me, pacing beside me. 'But I have no choice. I have no choice,' he says, over and over.

Don't listen. Don't pay attention. Keep moving. His footsteps, his voice, how close? Too close.

'If the world were to find out about you, he would be finished. Do you understand?'

Is he pleading with me? Pleading with *me*?

I'm trying, trying so hard to pull myself up, it's impossible. My arms don't have enough strength to lug my body up off the ground. It's not working. My body is incredibly heavy. I pull and tug, it's no use.

He drops down to his knees in front of me. 'I have to keep the promise I made to Gil's mother. Do you understand?'

'No, no, no, no,' finally I've found my voice. I scream, 'no, I don't understand.'

It's no use. I collapse on to the murky ground.

'This is useless,' I yell into the open cave. 'Help me. Help me.'

I curl up into the dust. Can't move my legs.

'Help me.'

His hand is on my hair.

'Rest,' he says. 'Rest now.'

He sits beside me.

I lay my head back. He's watching me, his eyes oddly tender.

'What's happening?' I ask him.

'I am keeping my promise, keeping her forgiveness.'

He unwraps the scarf that's been bound up in his fist.

'I was back there.' He points to the inside of the cave. 'Watching you. I should've finished it when you were unconscious. It would've been over then. I suppose a part of me is desperate to know you. Watching you like that, you couldn't see me, and I saw his spirit in you. I was watching you fight to save yourself, and you reminded me of Gil all those years ago when he still needed me. Really needed me.'

I punch his leg with my fist. 'Are you going to help me into this chair or are you just going to talk me to death?'

'Spunky.'

I kick him with my plastered foot.

He laughs, gently. 'Gilroy would be proud of you.'

'Gilroy?'

'Your father.'

'This has something to do with my biological father?'

'I want you to know about him, before... before this is over. It's important. You'll see why it makes sense.'

'Why what makes sense?'

'Why we're doing this.'

'We are not doing anything.' My clothes are soaking through to my skin. I'm sure the temperature has dropped and my insides are shivering. 'I'm not helping you to kill me. You're on your own with that.'

He takes in a tiny gasp, as if he's about to say something, but he says no more.

'My dad loved me. Even if he wasn't my dad, biologically, I am Jackob's daughter, and he is my dad. You're making a mistake if you think I want anything to do with my biological father.'

'Jackob was simply your guardian. Gilroy is your father. Gilroy will see his mother's dreams realised. The rest of us, well, we have to make sacrifices. I've sacrificed my life for her forgiveness. You must sacrifice your life for her dreams for her son.'

He winds the ends of the scarf around his hands. Climbs onto his knees and pulls the scarf tight.

'Wait. Tell me about him. About Gilroy. I want to know.'

'He is everything. That's all you really need to know. Gilroy is all there is. He is about to become the greatest man there ever was.'

'Does Gilroy know about me?'

'I had thought not. But then, I was under the misconception that Ariadne had had you adopted. I should have known better than to believe her.'

Somehow, I've managed to lose the rock I had in my hand. I feel about me, but there's nothing but gravel and mud. I close my eyes and hear Dad's words. I've always considered you to be my daughter. See the minke, searching for me, calling me. I'm not alone. I'm not alone.

'Nora. Nora.'

Someone is close, a man's voice, so close.

His hand is over my mouth, the scarf around my neck. He releases his hand from my mouth but, before I can scream, he pulls the scarf tight around my neck.

I hear her, my minke. Feel her pulse. She's calling for me, calling my name. Calling my name. I try with all my failing strength to tug at the scarf with my one good hand. I can't grip it. My hand flails in front of me. I close my eyes and listen to her calling me. Her sound is sweet, urgent, it's filling me up. A tear tickles my cheekbone. My arms fall limp to my side. She's lifting me, her long beating pulse coursing through me, begging me to go to her. She is releasing me. Together we will break the waves, skim the rocks, look out upon the world in wonder. Search for the broken and together we will heal. Them and us.

Chapter 58

DS Calmly & Nora

Skye
22nd October

I am now fully aware that I've magnificently cocked up this entire case. I'm no sooner back from a pointless visit to Skye, to find myself here again running back with my tail between my legs. I spoke to Nora Winter for Christ's sake. I gave her all that shite about acceptance and grief, and now what? Now her life is in my hands. It's true what they say about history repeating itself.

I delve into the cave, hardly aware of what is in front of me. My thoughts stubbornly drawn to the past, it's all trickery and I hesitate, acutely aware that the man I am is, by each second, being replaced by the man I was, if I could call myself a man then.

I hear feet scraping, muffled sounds coming from just inside the cave. It's difficult to see anything, and I almost trip over Nora's wheelchair. If nothing else, this suggests I'm on the right path. I quicken my pace; try to bring myself to the present. It's not easy.

It makes sense now, this mingling of the past and the present. Nothing can be clearer in my mind.

I failed to save Jenny. I failed to save Eve. This time I am not going to fail.

His eyes, I can see them glinting in the shadows, are fixed on me and I've lost the element of surprise. I reach for my phone, swipe it and face the torch right at him. He blinks, twists his glare from me downwards. He has Nora on the ground, his hands at her neck.

In an instant, defeat swipes at my legs and I almost crumble. Nora's body appears lifeless. I'm too late. I feed myself on the rage that overtakes my senses, and I toss the phone aside and throw myself at him.

My chin smacks against his skull. The momentum takes us both with it to the wall of the cave and his body goes limp beneath me. I try to catch my breath, the darkness is wavering in front of me, the urge to close my eyes is overwhelming, and my heart beats loud in my ears. I touch the trickle down my face, must have cracked my head against the cave wall.

The body beneath me twitches. Lowering my hand, it brushes against his beard, his hot breath on my palm. I raise myself and check for a pulse. Slow but steady. I've knocked him unconscious.

I crawl across to where I think she lies, feeling the damp ground, until I find her arm. I almost can't bring myself to a point where I want to find out that I've failed once again.

***

'Nora?'

It's the policeman who'd turned his back on me, turned his back on Dad. He helps me sit up and rest against the cave wall, then, guided by the torch on his phone, he leaves me to check on the man who tried to kill me.

'Mhona?' Her name comes out of my mouth like a gust of wind and returns to me in a faint echo.

'She'll be all right,' he tells me.

I long to be anywhere but here.

'And him?' I ask.

'You've no need to worry, Nora. He can't get you now.'

'I can't remember your name.' My chest is wheezy. Strangely, I feel no pain. My leg is quite content in its position, the temperature, the icy stillness from inside the cave, soothing against my face. I ask no more questions and let the wheeze abate.

'I'm sorry,' the policeman says and comes to sit by my side. 'I'm sorry I didn't really try to listen to you. I'm not convinced I would've made the connection even then, but I could've tried harder, I know.'

'Calmly. That's it. Detective Calmly. I was so very wrong, in the end, Detective Calmly.'

He says he'll sit with me until they come to take me back to the house, where they will interview me and I will have to give a statement.

'You know, my dad often said to me that it's alright to be wrong, as long as you're wrong for the right reasons. I know what he meant by that now.'

Detective Calmly positions himself in front of me and takes both of my hands in his. 'You did nothing wrong, Nora. You thought you were finding justice for your dad. Your dad's right in what he says. He taught you well.'

His hands are grimy and damp but there's comfort in them. 'I don't know about that, Detective. He was a man with a very big secret.'

'We all have secrets, Nora. But not all secrets are kept for the right reasons.'

It feels a strange thing for him to say. 'Are you talking about him?' I point to the unconscious man whose secret was me.

'Yes,' he says. But there was a tiny pulse in his hesitation that makes me wonder.

Chapter 59

Nora

Skye (3 months on)

The wind grabs at us fiercely but kindly, all the same, happy for us to sit here together on the edge of The Point, the lighthouse behind us and the guillemots diving. The donkeys are fed, the pigs are lazing about and we've left Bear to keep them company. Last we saw of Mhona, she was wrestling with Dad's old Aga, promising to deliver a 'right good roast' and boasting about her special recipe for rice pudding. Me and Dad, we never used that old cooker. Dad was a plain old sort, a pot of soup or tin of beans suited him. It suited me too. But I don't have the heart to spoil Mhona's attempts to mother me.

'Two fathers is one too many for any lass to make sense of,' she'd said. 'About time you had a bit of something different.'

Two dads. I would've settled for my dad, Jackob, still being here with me. They tell me he'd have died the instant he hit the ground. I hope that's true.

'The rain's not far off,' William says.

If the rain gets heavy, it'll be tricky to climb our way back to Camas Daraich and surer footing. As for the other 'father', the biological one, we've said a few words over the phone a couple of times. I believe him when he says he wants to put things right. I believe he wants to very much. I can't imagine how he can. That's why I can't see him. Not yet. He's asked to visit. Not yet.

'Here, take these.' William tries to hand me the binoculars.

'No, I don't need them. She'll come close enough.'

'I believe she will,' he says, patting my hand. 'I heard it, like. Mr Styles is back in the jail.'

'Aye.'

I got a letter from Raymond Styles, but I'm not ready to show it to anyone yet. It's a letter of apology, owning up to stealing from Dad, to running me over with his tractor, saying he's signing the Old School House over to me as it was rightly mine in the first place. I don't know what made him have a change of heart. Mhona reckons hearing about Dad's suicide would've hurt him, no matter what troubles they shared over money.

'William, do you think you'll ever settle in one place?'

'Maybe I will. One day.'

He'll have a use for the old school; when he's ready.

I see the minke. It's hard, sharing her with someone else. William hasn't seen her yet, and I'm not inclined to point her out to him.

'That man. Your dad, like. Will he be coming here?'

William is suspicious of strangers. I can hardly blame him. He'd said, after it happened, his wife must have been a stranger, even after four years of marriage. He told me his story the other night, while we were stabling the donkeys out of the storm. His wife had fallen asleep with the baby in her arms. She'd been smoking a secret cigarette. Her secret, William had said. The cigarette had fallen out of her hand and burned through the rug; through the entire cottage with mother and daughter inside.

'I don't know, William.' I do know that Gilroy Flynn is somewhere on the island. He has never left, never returned to Glasgow and his theatre dreams. Now his dreams are here, he tells me. Wherever I am.

When I talk on the phone with Gilroy Flynn, I am filled with regret. He owns my regret and must now live with it. Dad would say, a person dying for their sins is a person worth saving. Maybe that's true.

We have a few moments, just the minke and me. Maybe she feels the same and is signalling to me out of William's line of sight, just the tip of her tail visible. I know it's her.

My constant. My calm. My clarity.

Chapter 60

Graham

Perth (3 months on)

The puppy is a right handful. He hasn't got the sense that Bentley had. But he's a loyal little bugger and Graham is fair taken with him. Soon he'll be too heavy to lift.

'Not too heavy the now though, are you, wee man.'

'He's a proper scoundrel. Get him away from my feet, Graham.'

'Can you not see that's what I'm doing, woman. Hud yer weesht, Blythey.' He puts a finger to his mouth.

Graham lets the dog loose outside. He jumps at the sensation of the phone vibrating in his pocket. These days anything that makes a noise has to be carefully considered. He follows the dog along the newly laid path and well out of earshot of Tippermuir House.

'Aye, Lynn, we're all settled now.'

Lynn wants to come for a visit. Not right now he tells her. She's never wanted to visit before, never taken to Blythey. She was always good at seeing the bigger picture was Lynn and was happier when she thought she was saving Graham from Blythe, helping him set up a new life with a new family. Danger is she's got herself too involved. That's a worry right there, and he'll have to put his foot down.

'Not right yet,' he tells her. 'You know what Blythe is like. She needs time to get used to the idea.' It's only been three weeks since they all moved into Tippermuir together.

The dog snakes through the trees and bounds up to the front door of the lodge, scrapes to get in.

Shame, he hasn't brought the keys with him. Poor sod just wants to be home, in his own spot in the linen cupboard, doesn't like it up at the big house. But, like the rest of them will have to, he'll soon get used to his new home. Lynn's still harping on in his ear.

'Ah, come on, Johnny boy.' He'd had to name the dog himself as Blythe doesn't care and, well, Eve didn't get a chance. The name came to him when he was helping the movers ordered by Mr Flynn to pack up Eve's stuff. By the projector was the reel of the musical she'd tried to get them all to watch, the one that would show Detective Calmly how to save Maureen's soul. After that, Eve talked a lot about Surabaya Johnny from this musical, so he can't have been a bad character. 'Let's get back and see what they're both up to, eh?' He pulls at the dog's collar, picks up a stone and throws it. The dog scampers off. 'You're a simple mutt, aren't you,' Graham shouts after him.

'Lynn, I have to go. Give my best to Stuart. Yes. Yes. Speak soon. Promise. Soon. Soon.'

He tucks the phone back in his jeans' pocket. The dog begs at his ankles for another stone. He picks one up and throws it on the fresh, new lawn. The new landscaping makes Tippermuir look a bit spartan, a bit too big for its boots. Eve wouldn't like it without the tall weeds and impenetrable bushes that hemmed her and her mother in the old place. Blythe says it right when she says Eve always had her head on backwards. She went looking for something she already had, a family. If only she'd understood that.

He wanders back into the drawing room. Johnny is sitting back at Blythe's feet.

'He's awake then.'

He peers down at the tiny smile playing on his son's lips; his shiny eyes wide open, staring back at his daddy.

'Oh yes,' Blythe says smiling. He'd never have believed Blythe could smile like that, a smile that she has no control over because it comes from inside her. Must be kind of like his own perpetual wonder. His days are filled with moments to marvel at, included in that is his admiration of Blythe for gallantly receiving his son.

He sits opposite them, content to simply observe. It's a sight he likes to take his time over. No need for words. A sight like the source of falling water, with tastes of life and scents of energy. A sight that fills up all the empty spaces inside of him, giving him a strength he never could've imagined. This is the bigger picture.

In his silent conversations with Eve, when he's out in the woods with Johnny late at night, this is what he tells her. And if somewhere, she's listening, she'll be happy to know it.

Chapter 61

DS Calmly

Skye (3 months on)

Recreate the steps
different
identical
the rock beneath recalls,
with a whisper
too precious
our connection
our faults, our fears
echo the vast Cuillin
and lead the reluctant rover

Home.

I have brought myself here. So I tell myself.

Earlier this morning, before I set out along the Old Corry Road, heading for Beinn na Caillich, Fletcher Cunningham delighted in reminding me that fairies can spot a liar, so always be honest was the implication. It made me wonder how much he knows.

According to the weather forecast, there's to be barely a spot of rain. I've made good progress across the gentle slope to the Beinn; I've reached the boulder field without incident. I've managed to keep my pace steady, stopping here and there to breathe in the peaty air or right my footing in the boggy marsh. Now, passing over the last few hundred metres of boulders, I have to grapple not just with my feet, but it's necessary to use my hands also. It's not always possible to gauge of any one boulder whether it will hold my weight. The climb is steep and the boulders have a fancy for rolling unexpectedly. I

don't remember having been so hesitant the times I shared this climb
with Jenny. Cautious the pair of us may have been, but never without
courage. Climbing alone, as I am this day, I fear is something of a
different encounter. Or, it is possible that I am being blighted by the
monsters I have been unable to rid myself of since the day of our final
climb together.

***

It is a fine day for this time of year. Had there been a chance of snow,
I'd have thought twice about attempting this pilgrimage. I like calling
it a pilgrimage, my own crucifixion. I doubt I will be given the honour
of resurrection. My pilgrim's journey, I believe, is infinite.

I breathe easier and make better progress when the ground
under my feet allows for grass chasms between the boulders. Soon
enough, I'm able to haul myself up to the summit and am met with the
Cuillins. The red hills pronounce themselves proudly to me, but it is
the black ridge that sucks the air out of me and forces me to a seated
position with a rush of guilt and nausea. I recover quickly enough and
turn my back to the sight before me, in favour of the familiarity of the
welcoming cairn of the Norse princess, who, it is told, lies with her
beloved Norway forever in her gaze.

I consider going no further. Goddess or mortal, not one amongst
my descendants attended Skiach's school of heroes. Jenny, though,
she lived by the heart and professed to own the Firblog, a weapon
of magic powers made by the little people of the mountains. On our
climbs, she told me all her stories. On that day, she spoke of a cave of
gold, its location in the Cuillins unknown. He who finds the cave is
welcome to take his worth in gold and to return as often as he needs.
She told of a price a man must pay for greed. Each return to the cave
will create in the man a little evil, a little more evil and a little more
evil, until his final return when he loses his soul.

For Jenny, the magic of our climbs together was that, if only in
this place, we shared in our admiration for the earth beneath us; she
with her fantastical stories, and I with the wonder of her. Our walks,
scrambles and slips on the scree represented the opposite to our lives
at home, just as slippery but void of understanding.

Reluctantly, I turn to face the black ridge, knowing once I reach its first steep pull, I will have reached the end of my journey.

What is an end, if not a beginning? This question was asked of me, in her usual blunt manner, by PC Paula Dunbar. I had no desire to answer such a question, however, I had felt that, as some way of recompense for being the cause of her two-week suspension, I had to tell her at least a portion of my warped motivation in the Eve Park case. Eve's story is still front-page news, alongside a picture of the burnt out caravan. I know now that what clouded my judgement with Eve was my own guilt over Jenny. I don't speak of this with Paula, but there was something captivating in Eve's manner, something that drew me to her. I searched in Eve for answers. No, not answers. I think I was searching for absolution.

I, myself, am on indefinite leave until the assistant deputy chief constable decides what to do with me. But that's by the by. I feel as if I have let Paula down, and so I told her of my intentions to revisit my past and of my hopes that I can, in some small way, learn something that will encourage me to view my responsibility for the death of Eve in a healthier, less cumbersome light. I am aware that I share that responsibility with Murdo McAllister, currently residing in Saughton Prison awaiting sentencing.

McAllister confessed to the murder of Bruce Lawrence and Eve Park. He maintains that his crimes did not include the murder of Maureen Park. We, or I should say, the team since I was taken off the case, found no evidence pertaining to any known suspect. That included Graham and Blythe Burrell. Both had strong motives and, if I'd had my head about me, I would've acted on this information. Graham wanted the Park woman out of the way so she could no longer have a hold over Eve and they could set up home together with their son. Blythe wanted Tippermuir House and saw an opportunity, and she was the only one with access to the key to the front door. Neither motive proved to be substantial enough. Why would McAllister confess to two murders and not the third, it wouldn't make much difference to his sentence? Paula will make a good detective. She's had a change of heart about Eve Park. At Eve's funeral she appeared to be crying but swore vehemently she was not. The investigation of Maureen Park's murder remains open.

It is raining heavy drops the size of my fist. The rain is slanting towards me as if pushing me back and preventing me from entering the cave of gold. I continue down the slippery rock face, reach the scree and tumble most of my way to the exact point, the very foothold, as I remember it. The wind is beginning to roar as it did that day. My wrath is beginning to rise, as it did that day. The day I killed my sister.

Epilogue

Lark Calmly

The Black Ridge, Skye
Nov 2017

Her elbows are pummelling my ribs, her angry screams taking flight, drifting off into the dark clouds above us. I'm holding Jenny back. My arms are tight around her middle.

'We have to turn back. I warned you the weather was to take a turn.'

I'm hissing in her ear, trying to remain calm so she sees I'm serious. We are not hardened climbers. That's not to say we haven't climbed the Cuillins many times, but we have sense and we have an agreement.

'If one of us wants to turn back, we both turn back. Remember?'

'Why did you come anyway?' she screams in my face. 'Go back if you want.'

She tries to wriggle away from me and almost manages it; her puffa jacket is already drenched, difficult to keep a grip on. I release her and grasp hold of both her wrists instead. This only enrages her more. She kicks out at my legs. Keeping hold of her, I pull her down to the ground and face her towards the black ridge.

'Look.'

The squint rain is forcing much of the scree to slip, tiny rocks shifting position. The light breaking through the clouds glistens and bounces off the narrow ridgeway.

'Why risk it?'

For minutes, we sit huddled together, the wind bending and lashing around us. The scent of dusty, damp earth rising to greet us. I couldn't guess at how much of our lives have been spent together, listening close, asking the landscape for answers. Jenny has the fire of a volcano inside her.

'I'm not going back home. I can't live with her. I want away from here, Lark. Take me back to Perth with you.'

It's not the first time she's asked. At twenty-two, she acts as if she's already tired of living.

'Mum's getting on. You need to be patient with her.'

'Aye, and you'll leave tomorrow and forget about us.'

There's nothing stopping Jenny from setting out and leading a life of her own, out from under Mum's wearisome ways. There's no point repeating this to her, we've spent too long traversing in circles.

'Let's head back, Jenny. This isn't the place for talk.'

She catches me off guard. Up on her feet, she secures her backpack and marches towards the ridge.

Jenny can't come to live with me in Perth. It wouldn't work. We're close, but we're different. She wants life to deliver itself at her feet. She hasn't moved past her teenage expectations. It riles me. It riles me more than it does Mum. Mum continues to spoil her. That's another irritation. I need the miles distance between us; the sea that separates us.

I'm thinking all this and, although my eyes are fixed on Jenny's back as she begins the black ridge, I'm not really paying attention. It's only when the wind changes direction that the danger she's in awakens me.

I shout her name, and either she doesn't hear me or she's choosing to ignore me. I have no choice but to go after her. Instantly, I feel foolish. Born to the isle, we're supposed to know better. Anger stiffens my bones, making it all the more tricky underfoot. I stop shouting and conserve my energy.

She's walking too fast, reckless, her stupidity knows no limits. As hard as I try, I can't close the gap between us by being cautious. I quicken my pace.

My racing heart sinks when Jenny's foot slips and she tumbles. She manages to right herself, but it's given me an advantage over the distance between us. I reach her before she can get to her feet. I grab the hood of her jacket and pull her up.

She pushes me away. 'Get lost, Lark. I don't want you in my life any more.'

'Stop with the drama, Jenny. We're going home.'

She pushes me once again. 'Home is a place where you're supposed to be wanted,' she spits at me. 'I have no home.' This is her thing, one stupid argument with Mum and she believes she's been abandoned.

The wind pushes me one way. Jenny pushes me the other. Our dad died a year after she was born, and I think of all the love, all the opportunities Mum has made possible for her since.

'What kind of daughter are you?'

'The wrong one,' she spits back. 'Obviously.'

I hardly know what I'm doing. I lift my hand and strike her across the face.

The shock causes Jenny to lose her footing. She lands heavily on the edge of the ridge, cracking her head against a rock. Once again, she's slipping down the steep slope, stones and scree giving way under her semi-conscious body. Her eyes are wide, her gaze fixed somewhere off in the distance.

I throw myself down, one hand gripping the ridge, preventing me from going over the edge, the other reaching out for Jenny.

I catch hold of her in time, her soft hand in my own.

Two hands clasped, bound together with blood, sweat, grit. Slipping. Slipping. Slip, slip away, Jenny.

END

Acknowledgements

Some extraordinary people have helped me create this book.

I'd like to thank Spiffing Covers for helping me bring it all together and making it happen: James Willis, my shoulder to cry on and clarity of ideas genius. Andrea Billen who took my rough edits and helped me unscramble my messy brain. Stefan le Roy for designing a cover that excited me the moment I saw it.

That this book made it to the finishing line at all is thanks to such a great bunch of writers and I am truly grateful for their enduring support and cheer.

Alpha Writers, an amazing online group that I've been a member for many years, thanks for our three weekly 300 word challenges, support and love. I miss you.

My amazing critique group, Gillian Duff (https://gillianduff.com/), Michael Lynnes (https://www.michaellynes.com/) & Katrina Ritters. I can't imagine ever writing a book without your brilliant insight, knowledge and patience. Thank you, you amazing, crazy, beautiful bunch.

It takes my breath away when I think about how stuck I was a few years ago before I joined Sophie Hannah & the Dream Authors, how lucky I was to stumble across an invitation to join on twitter, this is true serendipity! I've grown from being a nervous writer alone to being part of a wonderful thriving and inspiring writing community. We're all growing. Thanks Sophie.

While I don't consider this book a police procedural, not even when DS Calmly showed up in the 2nd draft, I'm grateful to Graham

Bartlett and Kate Bendelow for their expert knowledge in all things crimey. Any and all mistakes are my own.

I firmly believe that writers need writers and all writers need editors and I'm grateful to Anne Hamilton for her careful and expert editing of early ideas for this book. Anne is a brilliant editor and writer and I feel lucky to have her in my corner.

I'd especially like to thank my two grown up and beautiful children. They've given their lives to teaching me what it means to be a mother and how easy it is to get parenting wrong. My children and their extended families are a part of who I am and I love them.

Nobody inspires me more than my eight year old granddaughter who charges through life in her own special non-verbal way. I could never be as magnificent as she; she holds my hand and fills me with awe.

I'd like to give a special nod to the writer's that I've worked with. In particular, Liz Webb (https://lizwebb.co.uk/ and Lisa Buchanan (https://www.thehighlandfeminist.com/). They believe I'm their mentor but I get as much learning and joy out of our sessions, if not more.

And thank you to nature, for showing me everything I didn't know about who I am as a writer and who I am as a human being.

Finally, I'd like to thank Mike, my long suffering husband, believer and trusty polar bear. Spotter of typos and corrector of grammar, timelines, and geographical realities – his input and support are immense. He has a red pen.

Visit my website
www.writewildbooks.com

Printed in Great Britain
by Amazon

36289339R00173